MUNICH WOLF

Rory Clements was born on the edge of England in Dover. After a career in national newspapers, he now writes full time in a quiet corner of Norfolk, where he lives with his wife, the artist Naomi Clements Wright. He won the CWA Ellis Peters Historical Award in 2010 for his second novel, *Revenger*, and the CWA Historical Dagger in 2018 for *Nucleus*. Three of his other novels – *Martyr*, *Prince* and *The Heretics* – have been shortlisted for awards.

To receive exclusive news about Rory's writing, join his Readers' Club at www.bit.ly/RoryClementsClub and to find out more go to www.roryclements.co.uk.

Also by Rory Clements

Martyr
Revenger
Prince
Traitor
The Heretics
The Queen's Man
Holy Spy
The Man in the Snow (ebook novella)
Corpus
Nucleus
Nemesis
Hitler's Secret
A Prince and a Spy
The Man in the Bunker
The English Führer

MUNICH WOLF

RORY CLEMENTS

ZAFFRE

First published in the UK in 2024 by
ZAFFRE
An imprint of Zaffre Publishing Group
A Bonnier Books UK Company
4th Floor, Victoria House, Bloomsbury Square, London, WC1B 4DA
Owned by Bonnier Books
Sveavägen 56, Stockholm, Sweden

A CIP catalogue record for this book is
available from the British Library.

Hardback ISBN: 978-1-80418-142-3
Trade paperback ISBN: 978-1-80418-143-0

Also available as an ebook and an audiobook

1 3 5 7 9 10 8 6 4 2

Typeset by IDSUK (Data Connection) Ltd
Printed and bound in Great Britain by Clays Ltd, Elcograf S.p.A.

Zaffre is an imprint of Zaffre Publishing Group
A Bonnier Books UK company
www.bonnierbooks.co.uk

For Max,
With love

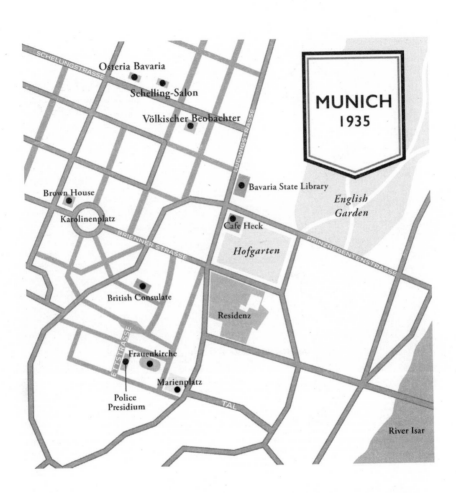

Osteria Bavaria

Schelling-Salon

Völkischer Beobachter

SCHELLINGSTRASSE

LUDWIGSTRASSE

Bavaria State Library

English
Garden

Brown House

Karolinenplatz

Cafe Heck

BRIENNER STRASSE

PRINZREGENTENSTRASSE

Hofgarten

British Consulate

Residenz

ETTLSTRASSE

Frauenkirche

Marienplatz

Police
Presidium

TAL

River Isar

MUNICH
1935

BAVARIA, GERMANY

● NUREMBERG

HESSELBERG

● GEROLFINGEN

MUNICH

DACHAU ●

LAKE STARNBERGERSEE

EBERSBERGER
FOREST

GARMISCH-PARTENKIRCHEN
●

CHAPTER 1

MUNICH, JUNE 1935

On the day they found the English girl's body, Sebastian Wolff was otherwise engaged.

His problems began at lunchtime in one of his favourite beer joints, the Tirolkeller, around the corner from police HQ in the old town. His girlfriend Hexie was supposed to be meeting him there because it was his thirty-fifth birthday and they were going to head off to a secluded beach in woodland on the far bank of Lake Starnberger. Complete privacy there. No need for swimsuits or modesty. He checked his wristwatch. One thirty and he was still alone.

So where was she?

Hoffmann must have kept her at the shop, which was pretty typical of him. The pompous, drunken shit thought he was a cut above the rest of the world. And what did he do that made him think so highly of himself? Fawn over the boss, hold his little Leica and take snaps all day, hoping at least one might be in focus. Hardly a job for a man, in Seb's book. A child can hold a box and press a button.

Across the echoing beer hall, half a dozen young men in leather shorts were becoming tiresome, baiting a little guy in spectacles and suit, telling him that Jews were not welcome and that he should fuck off back to Jewland, wherever that was. He was protesting that he wasn't Jewish, but that just fed their scorn and aggression.

They were clearly country lads in town for the day. Farm boys with several litres of Augustiner brew inside them. They were spoiling for a fight, their mocking voices drowning out the house zither player's vain efforts and everyone else's conversation.

Seb wasn't worried about the likelihood of a full-scale brawl. A year ago, in the weeks before the bloody events at Bad Wiessee and elsewhere, he would have expected it to kick off. But today? Not a chance. Nobody dared riot in Munich these days. Peace reigned in the utopia of Adolf's golden dawn and everyone was happy. Even the Brownshirts had put away their clubs and knuckle-dusters.

'You been stood up, Detective?'

He turned and smiled at the waitress, her ample bosom spilling out of her dirndl, her double armful of beer jugs perfectly balanced and spilling not a drop. 'Looks like it, Gudrun.'

'Silly girl, that Hexie. I'll have you any day.'

'Ah, you're out of my league.'

'Try me.'

He kissed her sweaty, rouge-free cheek. 'Another time, Gudrun. I'm going to see if I can meet Hexie halfway. If I miss her and she turns up here, tell her to wait and I'll be back in ten minutes, traffic permitting.'

'Don't go anywhere near Königsplatz, Seb. They've sealed it all off again for the big development. God knows what they're doing this time.'

'Thanks.'

'And get those youngsters to settle down before you go, will you?'

'For you, darling, almost anything.'

The inn's black cat snaked sinuously through his legs. He handed Gudrun the empty, which she somehow managed to balance among the full steins, then he reached down and stroked the beast, before wandering over to the farm boys. They were all in their fanciest shorts, probably chamois and handed down from father to son through the generations. Were they ever washed? Hundreds of years of sweat, piss and other secretions.

They turned their attention to him, their bleary eyes suspicious. As one, they pushed out their chests and eyed him up like prize-fighters, but he merely smiled. 'Keep it down, boys.'

One of them, the biggest, grimmest one, pushed his face into Seb's but he didn't back off.

'Who do you think you're talking to, Mister?'

Seb drew his service pistol and shoved the muzzle into the young man's ugly nose. The farm boy recoiled as though he'd actually been shot, which he hadn't, and his *gamsbart* hat flew off.

Seb gave them all another smile, took out his badge and flashed it at them.

'Another peep out of you lot and there's a nice cell waiting just around the corner in Ettstrasse.'

Suddenly they went quiet. The big lad bent down and picked up his hat.

You could hear the zither again. Such was the power of a badge denoting membership of the criminal police – the Kripo – or anything else vaguely official-looking in the third year of the Third Reich. With the big gangsters in charge of the country, the little villains had lost their confidence. A shame, though, thought Seb, the heaviest, loudest one could have done with a bloody nose and he would have been more than happy to oblige. Instead, he merely tapped his chest with the Walther. 'Enjoy the rest of your day, boys. Quietly.'

As Seb left, the little man they had been tormenting approached him. 'It's a lie what they were saying, I am not a Jew.'

He looked at the man coldly. He was a weasel. Seb said nothing and continued out into the open air where he took a deep breath. He was thirty-five, it was a fine June day and it felt good to be alive.

Looking both ways down the street, his eyes rested momentarily on the fruit and vegetable stall where the old one-legged veteran who had been trading there for as long as anyone could recall was doing steady business, selling new potatoes to a couple of grandmothers and a stubby little Brownshirt.

In the other direction, a group of tourists – American by the cut of their clothes – were staring up at the high bulb-topped towers of Munich's most famous church, the Frauenkirche. You could always tell the Americans; they were so well fed and so loud and they loved all the Nazi kitsch, eagerly buying up picture postcards of the Führer. They were here in Bavaria for 'health and culture', as advertised on the travel bureau posters and in the New York newspapers.

Gudrun was right. The traffic really did look heavy. Vehicles were crawling and the driver of an almost stationary brewery dray pulled by four weary horses was cracking his whip at the vans and cars and cursing them.

Seb's own pride and joy – a Lancia Augusta cabriolet – was parked outside the inn. Three years ago, the little beauty would likely have been stolen or smashed up by one of the SA gangs that roamed the city, but these days, following the death of their leader, Roehm, in Stadelheim jail after the Wiessee raid last June, the Brownshirts had been castrated like the dogs they were, and the streets were mostly safe.

The Lancia was painted red and Seb loved it almost as much as Hexie, though she thought he loved the car even more. Not that he had ever told Hexie that he loved her. Didn't want the fräulein getting ideas above her station. He left the car and set off at a brisk walk. Pointless trying to drive.

The cause of the snarl-up was Adolf's grand plan for Königsplatz, turning it into yet another oversized parade ground and shrine to Nazidom, as if there wasn't enough stamping and marching around the city in metal-heeled boots. On and off for months now, the building work had been having a knock-on effect throughout the city centre. Roads were dug up and two temples were being constructed to house the remains of the putsch martyrs of '23.

White-gloved traffic cops were causing even more havoc with their frantic arm-waving as they tried to divert vans and cars in directions they didn't want to go.

No matter. It was a pleasant day for a stroll and it was less than two kilometres to Heinrich Hoffmann's photographic studio in Schwabing.

He made his way to Lenbachplatz, then across to Barer Strasse and strode north by way of Karolinenplatz, which was teeming with builders' vehicles and SS guys. The road west, past the Brown House and on to Königsplatz, was completely cut off. There was noise and dust everywhere.

Hexie wasn't at the Hoffmann studio. The other girl, the one who was filling in for Evie Braun and whose name escaped Seb, told him she had had to dash to the Osteria Bavaria with a package of prints for Hoffmann. Seb thanked her and wandered off along Schellingstrasse.

A crowd had gathered on the pavements and across the road outside the restaurant. That could mean only one thing: word had got out that Adolf was driving down from his mountain retreat at Obersalzberg to lunch there.

Even as the thought struck him, the leader's cavalcade appeared; three large black Mercedes open-tops, bristling with SS and with Adolf himself in the rear of the middle car, sitting beside his chief bodyguard and adjutant, the enormous giraffe of a man Wilhelm Brückner.

Seb stopped and stared. The crowd began to scream and, as one, thrust their arms out in rigid salutes. Two young women – they couldn't have been out of their teen years – tore open their blouses and thrust their pert breasts in the direction of their hero. Two grinning SS men immediately placed themselves in front of the girls to protect their modesty and their leader's dignity.

If Hitler had seen the amateur strip show, he didn't give any indication, merely flapping his hand at his worshippers in a rather languid version of his celebrated salute. The cars pulled to a halt and the crowd was held back by a squad of heavily armed SS men.

As the car door opened, the familiar figure of Hexie Schuler emerged from the front entrance of the osteria and, seeing the new arrival, shrank back into the wall. Seb caught her eye and she grimaced at him as if to say, *what have I walked into?*

After alighting from the Mercedes with his dog on a short lead held in his left hand, Adolf spent half a minute flapping his pasty right mitt at the crowd – rather like a performing sea lion – then turned sharply and ducked into the doorway of his favourite Italian restaurant, dragging his handsome Alsatian behind him and brushing past Hexie as though she didn't exist.

Seb and Hexie had just embraced and she had just wished him a happy birthday when he felt his upper left arm being pulled and turned to find himself face to face with an expressionless man with thinning hair and pockmarked cheeks. He was about thirty and wore a grubby grey suit, soup-stained tie and battered fedora. Seb knew instantly that he was Bavarian Political Police – the sort of slimy drudge known in Berlin and other parts of Germany as Gestapo. He had seen him around the Police Presidium in Ettstrasse occasionally and he knew he wasn't part of the regular non-political criminal corps.

Nearby, the crowd was being urged to disperse by SS men, but they were still milling around as though hoping that Adolf might re-emerge any moment to take a bow and perhaps give an arm-flapping encore. The girls who had exposed themselves were buttoning up their blouses and flirting with the SS men who had shielded them from the leader's eyes. Something told Seb that the girls and the guys would be meeting up again later in the day to become better acquainted.

'I hate that place,' Hexie said, ignoring the political cop and nodding towards the Osteria Bavaria. 'The awful Englishwoman was there with Hoffmann. You know, the tall blonde one with fingers like Munich white sausage.'

'Her name's Mitford. She's always there.'

The man's grip was tightening and Seb turned on him, right arm up with fist clenched to do some damage to his unpleasant face. 'Yes?' he said irritably. 'Can I help you?'

'Bavarian Political Police. You didn't salute the Führer. Every-one else did, but not you.'

'Forgive me, I was distracted by the girls' tits.'

'What did you say?'

'You heard me, now take your hand off me.'

'You disgust me. You don't look like a filthy Jew, so what are you – a Bolshevik?'

'I said remove your hand.'

'You think you can talk to a BPP officer like that?'

'I will talk to you exactly how I please. Now go away and annoy someone else before I draw blood.'

'How dare you talk to me like that? You're a damned Red, yes? A dangerous element.'

'You'll soon discover how dangerous I am.'

'What is your name?'

Seb pulled out his badge. 'Wolff. You can see it there. Inspector Sebastian Wolff. Murder team, Police Presidium, Ettstrasse 2. Criminals think I'm a dangerous element, but not law-abiding citizens. Are we done now?'

'Ah, you're a cop, eh? I thought I'd seen you before. Well, that won't protect you. I'm taking you to BPP headquarters.' The man dropped a cigarette stub to the ground and stamped on it.

Hexie pushed herself between Seb and the little greasebag. 'This is ridiculous. Crawl back into your disgusting hole, you vile slug.'

Words that Seb couldn't have said better, but they didn't help. Herr BPP wasn't going to back down now, not confronted with an irate woman. That would be humiliating. 'Give me *your* name, too.'

'My name is none of your business. Just know this: I am employed by the Führer's best friend Heinrich Hoffmann and they are in the restaurant together at this very moment. If anything happens to me, you'll be rat food. *Capisce?*'

And that really annoyed Herr BPP. Which is how Sebastian Wolff ended up in the Dachau concentration camp. *Thanks, Hexie,* he thought as Herr BPP summoned the assistance of uniformed SS officers and pushed him into the back of a car. *You always did have a mouth on you.*

CHAPTER 2

No trial. No legal counsel. No phone call to his chief at police HQ or to his mother and his son at home. Merely an order from a senior member of the secret state police that he was to be despatched to Dachau to be held in protective custody pending inquiries, and he was on his way in a van heading north-west out of Munich with three other prisoners, one of them a professor at the technical university who told Seb he had been denounced for complaining about the sacking of a Jewish colleague. The others were a glum communist and a bright-eyed Jehovah's Witness. None of them guilty of any recognisable crimes, simply designated 'dangerous elements'.

At the camp, he was marched to the so-called shunt room where he was registered at great length, then relieved of his clothes and personal effects which amounted to no more than his wallet, ID and a few coins. His Walther PPK 7.65 police-issue pistol had already been removed at political police headquarters in Wittelsbach Palace.

He was made to stand naked for a full ten minutes as SS men wandered in and out of the room, occasionally glancing at him with varying degrees of disinterest. Then he was marched to the prisoner baths where he was disinfected and made to scrub himself before returning to the shunt room where he was handed an ill-fitting set of second-hand camp clothes which, he was informed, had previously been worn by a prisoner who had died while attempting to escape. Seb imagined they told all the newcomers that to focus their minds on staying away from the electrified wire.

Finally, he was handed a toothbrush, a small bar of soap, a tin cup and plate and was escorted to one of the barrack huts with its rows upon rows of wooden bunk beds, each of them three decks high with a complete absence of comfort. No mattress, just hard wood, a palliasse and a single blanket – bearable in June, but bitter in winter.

The block leader was a curious fellow named Rudolf Höss, an SS Death's Head NCO with the skull and crossbones badge on his cap. He had a ready smile and surface good humour, but Seb knew it was unreal. He was a good reader of faces, an important asset for a detective, and he didn't like him. It seemed to him the world might be a better place if Herr Höss were the prisoner here, not the guard.

Höss told Seb that if he kept out of trouble, his stay in the camp would be relatively painless, but that if he was slow in obeying orders, failed to keep clean, didn't do his work properly, stole food or cigarettes, he would be flogged. Or worse.

He looked at his new prisoner's notes, quickly spotted that it was his birthday and that he was a cop and admonished him for disloyalty to the Führer. He told Seb in a cold, indifferent manner that he was a stain on the force and needed to be re-educated. 'You come here as an enemy of the state. You will leave here as a good, dutiful German, or you will not leave here at all.'

If he behaved well and was considered rehabilitated, he would be freed in six months.

Seb didn't bother to respond. What was the point?

'And remember this,' Höss continued. 'You have no rights. You are a piece of shit and will be treated as such.'

The other inmates were marching back from their day's work. They were sullen and exhausted. Most of them seemed to have been broken by their imprisonment, their very souls sucked out through their dead eyes. None of them bothered to talk to Seb, which didn't worry him because he was in no mood to strike up a conversation.

Collecting their tin plates, they were marched to the kitchens. Supper was a piece of black bread with a cup of thin, unseasoned soup – cabbage, potato and a few scraps of gristle. He couldn't be bothered with it, but seeing Seb push the bowl to one side, the fellow next to him happily grabbed it and devoured it in seconds.

'Was that good?' Seb enquired.

'It's never good, but tomorrow you will eat it. I promise you.'

'Why are you here?'

'No one asks that. We are all here for the same reason. The pasty-faced man with the moustache.'

At evening roll call, block leader Höss was missing, but word of the newcomer's birthday had been passed on to his deputy, an even less appealing figure than his chief, and he made Seb step forward from the ranks.

'This man is the lowest of the low,' he informed the assembled inmates. 'He is – or was – a police officer in the Munich Criminal Police, but he has shown disrespect and disloyalty to the Führer, the very man who has provided him with employment and put food in his belly. Today is Inspector Wolff's birthday, however, so let us celebrate. No cake, I'm afraid, but we can offer him a night out to mark the big day and as a "welcome-to-Dachau" gesture.'

A night out. That was his idea of humour. A night out in Dachau meant standing to attention on the parade ground from dusk to dawn.

At least it was summer, so the hours of darkness were not only short, but warm and probably rain-free. Standing there as the night wore on, pain began to tear into his shoulders and lower back, but he had endured worse on night-time guard duties in the trenches, and he would get through this too. The problem was his bladder; by the early hours he desperately needed a piss.

As the sky began to lighten and reveille was called for the other prisoners, he began to think he could hold out. And then the sun nudged over the barbed wire and grey concrete wall at the eastern perimeter, beneath a guard tower, and he realised he had managed it. He had beaten the bastards.

It was a small victory and short-lived.

Even as he was congratulating himself, his tormentor reappeared. 'Well done, prisoner Wolff, you haven't collapsed.'

'No.'

'What did you say?'

'I said no, meaning I haven't collapsed.'

'Did I say you could talk? You talk only when it is demanded of you.'

'I understand.'

'There, you have done it again. Put your arms out at right angles to your torso.'

Seb obeyed the order.

'Now you will stay like that until noon. If you say another word or move in any way, it will be midnight. After that, the lash.' With a grin that exposed yellow-black teeth, the guard slapped both sides of Seb's face with his riding crop. Hard.

He didn't cry out but the battle was lost; he gave up on bladder control, and pissed himself.

It was impossible to protest. If he complained, the punishment would simply be intensified and extended and he would be there for many more hours. But he was mortified. His cheeks were red from the riding crop and from embarrassment. He hadn't pissed his pants since he was a small child. Now the warmth of the urine spread down his legs and he could smell it.

There was no wound on his body, no bruises or stripe, but the pain and humiliation were real enough for all that. And now he faced a new problem: thirst.

His mouth was parched, his throat raw.

And then, at eleven o'clock, block leader Höss arrived again.

Seb tightened his shoulders, kept his arms rigidly in place and his lips sealed.

Höss looked at him for a full minute, then sighed. 'Well, prisoner Wolff, you're free to go. Consider yourself fortunate to have avoided the bullwhip welcome.' He glanced down without comment at the dark urine patch on his coarse cotton uniform. 'Return your soap, toothbrush, utensils and camp uniform to the shunt room and collect your own clothes and effects.'

For a few moments, Seb did not react. This was another trick designed to heap more punishment down on his head.

'Move, Wolff. We don't have all day.'

Slowly, Seb lowered his aching arms. Höss handed him a piece of paper with official Dachau heading. It was a signed and stamped pass. 'Show this at the gate and you will be allowed out. You will find a car waiting for you. It seems you have friends in high places.'

Seb didn't thank him. More than anything he hoped never to see his rather bland, emotionless face again. He returned to the hut, which was empty. All the other inmates were out on a work detail. He glanced at the plain wooden bunk beds which he had avoided sleeping in. Gathering up his toothbrush, soap and eating utensils, he walked out across the parade ground, hoping never to see the camp again. His arms ached badly, as though he had been lifting weights all morning. It was an experience he had no wish to repeat.

This was a terrible place, he decided, designed to destroy, not rehabilitate.

The car waiting for him was yet another open-topped Mercedes, the type beloved of every senior Nazi in Munich. Two swastika flags mounted on short poles decorated the rear offside and nearside wings. It was driven by a uniformed chauffeur but Seb knew who it belonged to, of course. Uncle Christian, his mother's younger brother.

He nodded to the driver. 'Good day.'

'*Heil* Hitler.'

'Ah, yes, *Heil* Hitler to you too.' He waved his arm back at the driver, wincing from the pain occasioned from holding himself in an unnatural position for several hours. 'Drive me to my house in Ainmüllerstrasse if you would.'

'I have orders to take you to the Residenz. Councillor Weber wishes to see you.'

'Can't it wait? I could do with some coffee and a couple of hours' sleep.' He knew he was wasting his breath even as he spoke the words.

The driver shrugged his shoulders and pulled away. He threw the Mercedes into a U-turn and sped off at 100 kph straight towards the heart of Munich, ignoring traffic cops, cutting up other vehicles at crossroads, slewing past trams and buses with centimetres to spare. Seb closed his eyes, deciding he had no desire to witness his own death hurtling at him in the shape of a ten-tonne truck.

When they came to the gridlocked traffic close to the old town, the driver simply pressed his hand on the horn and kept it there until the hapless occupants of the other cars saw that this was an official Nazi vehicle and pulled aside to let him through as though he were an ambulance driver racing towards hospital. Big, black, open-topped Mercedes had that effect on people in the Third Reich, especially when decorated with the hooked cross flag.

The driver did, however, slow down as they passed the Feld-herrnhalle, taking great care to thrust out his right arm like a stallion's pizzle in salute to Hitler's friends who had died there in the ill-fated putsch of 1923. Seb did likewise, not wishing to return to Dachau in a hurry, for this salute was mandatory and was policed by a permanent guard of SS men. Anyone failing to honour the fallen heroes of the Third Reich would be in serious trouble. Old ladies on bicycles wobbled and swerved as they removed their grip on the handlebars to make their obeisance; others simply took detours to avoid paying tribute to the Nazis.

The driver bore left and stopped on Max-Joseph-Platz. 'Here we are, Inspector Wolff,' he said without turning in his seat to address his passenger. 'You are to make yourself known at the main entrance and then you will be escorted to the Black Hall and wait there for Councillor Weber.' He looked at the little clock on the dashboard. 'You are to be there in five minutes, no more, so get a move on.'

More orders. Seb rather fancied that his driver might be happier as a block leader in Dachau concentration camp than working as his uncle's chauffeur. He had that way about him and he clearly loved his uniform. Getting out of the car, Seb did not thank him, or even say farewell. He merely left the rear door wide open so that he would have to shift his overfed arse from his comfortable seat to close it.

The Residenz was a remarkable place, one of the royal palaces of the Wittelsbach family, kings of Bavaria until the monarchy was abolished at the end of the Great War. With its vast maze of rooms – one hundred and thirty of them – and its ten splendid courtyards, you could easily get lost. Seb certainly would have without one of his uncle's secretaries as guide.

Upstairs in the Black Hall – not really black, but a little dark perhaps beneath the richly painted trompe l'oeil ceiling – he was ushered across the marble floor to an antique chair at the base of one of the windows and told to sit and await the master. The sun was streaming down on his neck as he gazed at the portraits of long-forgotten princelings and his eyes grew heavy.

Another assistant appeared. 'Councillor Weber is delayed. He has asked me to offer you refreshment.'

'Breakfast would work for me.'

'It's more like lunchtime, sir.'

'Then lunch, with coffee.'

'I have some liver dumpling soup.'

'I'm sure that would be excellent. Also perhaps some bread and cheese.'

'Very good, sir.'

Five minutes later the food arrived on a tray and the servant set up a little trestle table for his guest. The soup was delicious, the bread was fresh and the cheese was an Italian blue. There was even butter and a small plate of pickles and he ate it all hungrily and felt a great deal better. It was wonderful, the best meal he'd had in days, but he had had a night without sleep and the food made him even drowsier. Now he really needed a siesta and quickly leant back in the chair and fell asleep.

He had no idea how long he was out, but Uncle Christian woke him with a prod in the belly with the leather riding crop he habitually carried. 'Wake up, boy.' He had always called his nephew that, never his name.

'Sorry,' Seb muttered. 'I didn't get any sleep.'

'Well, you shouldn't have got yourself sent to Dachau, you fool. Are you trying to embarrass me? Humiliate your saintly mother?'

'Thank you for getting me out.'

'For myself, I wouldn't lift a finger to help you. I did it for my sister.'

Christian Weber was large and ill-favoured and smelt as though he had bathed in a sea of eau de cologne. He was probably the richest and most corrupt man in Munich. And the most despised. Everyone called him The Pig, though never to his face.

He had started life poor, shovelling shit for a racehorse trainer, but luck was on his side because he was with Hitler at the very beginning; they had beaten people up together, plotted and campaigned together, and they were still friends. Few men could laugh with the Führer and even make jokes at his expense these days, but Christian Weber was one of them.

Thanks to a mixture of graft, intimidation and guile he now ran the city council and owned half of Munich, including most of the transport system, a huge number of properties, including hotels, the brothels, the racecourse out at Riem, and a profitable portion of the tourist industry. He had also somehow contrived to set up his home in a sizeable corner of the Residenz, which was just about big enough to accommodate his layers of excess fat.

Not just any part of the old palace – he had chosen the richest, most comfortable and heavily ornamented quarters, using the Elector's bedroom with its embroidered silk walls and its extraordinary old bedstead as the place to bring his chosen girls each night. How none of them suffocated under his 160 kilos was a mystery to Seb. He didn't envy them, but guessed that The Pig probably tipped well.

Now here he was, bulging out of his new SS-Oberführer's uniform, his whiskery, rather Prussian moustache twitching as he eyed up his nephew like a cat with a songbird at its mercy.

'Well, I shouldn't have been there,' Seb protested. 'It was all a ridiculous misunderstanding. The BPP guy was just throwing his weight around. One of Heydrich's new recruits getting one over the Kripo.'

'You're just lucky that fool Deubel is in charge at Dachau. Soft as blancmange. I'm told it's like a holiday resort there. Anyway, why don't you join the party, boy – move over to the political police yourself? You've got friends there, haven't you? I've discussed you with the coming man, Reinhard Heydrich, and he assures me you would be welcome to apply. He's bringing a new sense of comradeship to the operation and is fighting hard to get pay increased.'

'It's not for me. I'm a straightforward detective.'

'But you could do me a lot of good there and life would be a lot easier for you. I'd find you a luxurious place to live. How about a comfortable house in Bogenhausen? You could marry that girl of yours, give her babies, get her in the kitchen. She's a good girl – she came to me when you were arrested by that BPP man. That's how I discovered you were in Dachau. If she wasn't yours, I'd have her for myself. So marry her, start a family together, join the party – you'd make your Uncle Christian a proud man.'

Seb didn't bother to remind his uncle that he already had a family – a seventeen-year-old son. 'I'll give it some thought. Once again, thank you. I really need to get home now and have a few hours' sleep.'

His exhaustion was all too obvious. He yawned and, without asking permission, Weber pushed some sort of tablet into his mouth, then clamped it shut with his meaty palm. 'Swallow that. It'll keep you awake.' He couldn't spit it out, so he gulped it down.

'What is it?' he said when his choking fit had subsided.

'Magic pills from America. They keep you up and fucking all night.' Weber shook his porcine head and a little smile spread across his snout. 'I have to say there's another reason you've been released. If it was just me, I'd have left you to the tender mercies of the Dachau guards for a week, to concentrate your mind. But it seems you're needed on a murder case.'

Was he supposed to be happy about this news? 'I'm not the only detective at Ettstrasse 2.'

'Apparently you're highly regarded, though, and the case is important. Adolf himself is taking an interest.'

'And does he know that I have recently been in Dachau?'

'Well, I have no intention of telling him. Anyway, you should feel honoured to have been chosen for this task.'

He thought for only two seconds, then shook his head. 'Not me. I don't want it.' Seb didn't need to sip the bitter wine to know the chalice was poisoned. Even Dachau might be a safer place than working on a case where failure would incur the wrath of Herr Hitler. 'Ettstrasse isn't short of good operators. They can get someone else.' A party member, perhaps; someone who had mastered the art of the Hitler salute.

'Well, well, boy, and there was me thinking you detectives all fought to get the best cases. I thought you would be pleased to test yourself on such a high-profile murder.'

'If the Führer is interested, it will invariably involve politics. This could be a rabbit hole, and who knows where that will lead?'

The Pig grinned. 'I'm afraid the decision has already been made. The case is yours. It seems you've got the best clear-up rate in the corps and, perhaps more importantly, you're the only one at Ettstrasse who speaks good English. Don't let me down on this, boy. I've had to call in favours to get you out of Dachau.'

CHAPTER 3

Half an hour later Sebastian Wolff was in an office on the first floor of the Brown House on Brienner Strasse, just to the east of Königsplatz. The window was wide open to allow in the warm summer air, but it also allowed the peace to be shattered by the incessant noise of heavy machinery and pneumatic drills digging up perfectly decent lawns and paving stones to make way for Adolf's great parade ground.

The Brown House, an imposing hundred-year-old mansion, had become Nazi headquarters when the party outgrew its earlier premises. Adolf kept an office here for the times when he was not at the Chancellery in Berlin or at his mountain retreat at Obersalzberg. It was where the party was run and, Seb had to concede, they did it very efficiently.

The pill, whatever it was, had already kicked in and he was a great deal more awake and alert than he had been. A group of three men awaited him. He recognised two of them, though the only one of that pair that he actually knew was his boss, Deputy Police President Thomas Ruff.

He had always liked Ruff without exactly respecting him as a policeman. In fact, he had never been sure why the man had become a cop in the first place, because he simply wasn't made for the job. He had a nervous disposition and his jitters had become a great deal worse following the death of his own chief, Munich Police President August Schneidhuber, during the so-called Night of the Long Knives a year earlier when Hitler and his black-clad SS boys disposed of the leadership of the Brownshirts and anyone else they considered disloyal. And so Ruff didn't sleep well at nights. With reason – for if Schneidhuber could be liquidated, so could he. And anxiety was not a good quality in a senior police officer.

The other recognisable figure was another of Hitler's old chums, the well-connected and urbane foreign press chief Ernst Hanfstaengl, known to one and all as Putzi. With an American mother, he had spent many years in the States, had studied at Harvard and had no shortage of money thanks to the family's art publishing business and their art shop.

He was extremely tall at almost two metres, dressed well and had a reputation for schmoozing and bamboozling reporters from all over the world, protecting Hitler's reputation and smoothing over the little bumps in the road when the Nazis quietly or not so quietly disposed of political enemies.

The third one wore a dark pinstripe suit and even before he opened his mouth Seb guessed he was English. Munich was full of upper-class English men and women these days, and they had a certain superior air about them that irritated the hell out of the Nazis. He doubted that this man would be an exception to that general rule.

Both Ruff and Hanfstaengl heiled Seb and he returned the greeting. The fact was he hadn't voted for Adolf or his party in the elections two years earlier, so he wasn't quite sure why he should use their salute, but the events of the past twenty-four hours had brought him to the conclusion that it really wasn't worth arguing the toss. Sometimes in life you just had to go with the flow, and there were more important concerns than the holding up of an arm. It was just a friendly greeting, he reasoned. Wasn't it?

Anyway, it wouldn't last. Germany liked changing governments so there was every possibility this new regime would be consigned to the dustbin of history sooner rather than later. And then they'd all stop saying *Heil Hitler* and go back to *Guten Tag* and *Grüss Gott*. God, surely, would have to trump a mere mortal.

Police boss Ruff introduced him to the other two. 'This is Herr Hanfstaengl, Inspector. He is foreign press chief in Berlin and has flown here today for this important meeting.'

Seb bowed his head dutifully and shook his hand. Of course, he knew of Hanfstaengl, one of the greatest stars in the National Socialist firmament. But, more recently, he had also heard rumours that Hanfstaengl had fallen foul of Hitler and that his job was hanging by a thread. Perhaps his life, too. Nothing firm, just whispers. It was hinted that he had spoken approvingly in public of the Night of the Long Knives murders, proclaiming that such drastic action was essential for the survival of Hitler's revolution. But privately he had not been so certain of the action and was under the influence of friends in America who were appalled. Worse than that, word of his misgivings had seeped back to the man who had ordered the killings: Adolf Hitler. A man who did not take kindly to being challenged or contradicted.

So Putzi Hanfstaengl would probably be going the same way as SA chief Ernst Roehm and the other victims sooner or later. When you fly too close to the sun, you will get burnt.

In the meantime, while he was still alive and in post, it made sense to defer to him.

'And this is Mr Gainer, the British consul-general in Munich,' Hanfstaengl said in English, indicating the pinstriped one, a kindly looking, rather reserved man with smooth, healthy features and intelligent, civilised eyes. Seb guessed his age at mid-forties, but he could have been five years out either way.

'Pleased to meet you, sir,' he said, also in English.

'How do you do, Inspector,' Gainer said, extending his hand to the detective. Seb took it in the English way, with a firm handshake and their eyes met. Seb knew that such things mattered a great deal to the English. Weak handshake, no character. No eye contact, no honesty. Gainer gave him the hint of a nod in return, but he looked grave.

'I am well, thank you,' Seb replied. It was the courteous thing to say. English people always said they were well, even when close to death.

'I am told you are fluent in English. As a matter of interest, how did you learn my language, Herr Wolff?'

'I worked on a British freighter, sir.'

'Indeed. And how did that come about, may I ask?'

Was this really the time to be discussing his own history? Gainer was waiting for a reply, so Seb seemed to have no option but to plunge in head first. 'Well, during the worst of the great inflation in 1923 I couldn't feed my young child so I walked from Munich to Hamburg and from there I was able to find employment aboard the *Eastern Star* out of Tilbury. I worked on the ship for four years, sending money and food parcels home to my mother, who was caring for my boy. I picked up the language quite quickly.'

'Were you well treated by your British crewmates?'

Seb was surprised by the question but managed to answer it diplomatically. 'For the most part, yes. Of course, there were those who wouldn't talk to me at first given that they had lost family and friends in the war. Probably some who wanted to throw me overboard. But I believe I won most of them around and showed that I was just a human being like them, and that we, too, had suffered great losses.'

In fact he had been given a hard time by almost everyone except the skipper, who was an unprejudiced good-natured man. The rest of the crew resented the fact that he had been given work at all. He was called Hun or Boche or Jerry. No one called him Wolff or Sebastian or Seb. He had stuck it out because he had to, so that Jurgen and his mother could eat. In the end he had been accepted, grudgingly, because he did not shirk and did not react to the taunts. And there were even those who, almost affectionately, began to call him Wolfie.

'Well, good for you. Do you know why you are here?'

'I am told I have been assigned a murder case and that my language skills, such as they are, are needed. I know nothing more as yet.'

'Then I will let Deputy Police President Ruff explain what has happened.' Gainer nodded to Wolff's boss. 'Feel free to speak German, Herr Ruff. I am quite at ease with your language.'

'Thank you.' He returned the nod then brought his nervous attention to bear on Seb. 'In short, Inspector, the matter is this: a young Englishwoman was found dead yesterday in the Herzogpark, just across the river from the English garden. She had been murdered.'

For a moment, Seb wondered whether they might be referring to Hitler's friend with the fat white sausage fingers, the Rhine maiden Miss Unity Mitford, the one who had been lunching with the Führer at the Osteria Bavaria yesterday.

The girl had certainly made enemies during her stay in Munich. The League of German girls hated her because she wore lipstick and smoked, and most senior party members loathed her because she had easy access to Adolf when they didn't.

Her death would undoubtedly be an event with seismic repercussions.

Hanfstaengl took up the story in English with a strong American accent. 'Her name was the Honourable Miss Rosie Palmer.'

Ah, so not the Mitford girl, well that was something of a relief.

'Her mother is a lady-in-waiting to Queen Mary, the consort of King George V. Do you know what a lady-in-waiting is, Wolff?'

'No, sir.'

'She is an attendant in the British royal palaces, but far more than a mere servant. She is a close friend and companion of the queen consort and is an aristocrat in her own right, widow of a viscount. The royal family are said to be devastated by the terrible news and wish very much to know how such a thing could have happened. It is a bad look for the Third Reich. And so the murderer must be discovered without delay. A day or two at the very most. The Führer will expect regular bulletins regarding progress.'

Had he considered this case a poisoned chalice? It was suicide. Seb groaned inside. *Why not just give me the arsenic and kill me now, Herr Hanfstaengl?* He did not show his feelings. 'How did the young woman die?' he asked.

'The body is with the pathology department at the university. I believe there were extensive injuries but some uncertainty about the actual cause of death,' Ruff said. 'I suggest you go and talk to them in the first instance and then take it from there. You will need to speak to her English and German friends to determine her movements. They shouldn't be difficult to find. And she was lodging at Karolinenplatz in the home of Herr Regensdorf, who will give you all the help you need.'

Seb nodded. Of course, he knew the great name of Walter Regensdorf and he had passed his palatial house on many occasions. As had everyone else in this city.

'You are to conduct this case at speed but also with discretion. The Führer does not want the whole Munich police corps swarming over the city causing panic. In particular, he does not want our young English and American guests to be made to feel uncomfortable or scared or treated with anything but the utmost courtesy. Very little will be made of the story in our own papers, but we won't be able to keep it out of the foreign press, and I personally will liaise with them. If approached by a foreign reporter, you will say nothing but refer them to my office. You will not even acknowledge your name or that you are in any way associated with the case. Is that understood?'

'Yes, Herr Hanfstaengl.'

'Good. And you should know that I am deeply shocked that such an event should have happened so close to my own home in Herzogpark. Now, one or more members of Miss Palmer's family will fly into Oberwiesenfeld tomorrow afternoon, probably her brother, Viscount Braybury. They will be staying at the Vier Jahreszeiten Hotel. They will certainly want to meet you so you will be expected to deal with them and keep them informed. I will introduce you as soon as it is convenient. Oh, and you will not be working alone on this, but given your language skills and your seniority, you will be expected to take the lead.'

Seb nodded. He had no option but to accept the case.

'And please keep me informed, too,' Gainer added. 'My door at the consulate in Prannerstrasse will always be open to you, Inspector.'

'Thank you, sir. I will do my utmost to solve this case to your satisfaction.'

Hanfstaengl, a big man with an easy-to-like way, allowed himself a half-smile. 'In the meantime I will be staying in Munich until this matter is brought to a satisfactory conclusion. You can contact me at any time of day or night on my home number at Pienzenauerstrasse 52, or here at the Brown House. This room is my private office. If I am not here one of my secretaries will get a message to me. It is essential that I hear from you at regular intervals. The importance of this affair cannot be overstated. Clearly you should feel honoured that you have been entrusted with such a matter. The Führer's gratitude for a successful outcome will be boundless.'

'Yes, sir.'

'And I reiterate – be prepared for intrusion by the international press. They will be all over this story. Keep them at arm's length, but be polite. It is important that the world knows that the Third Reich is a safe haven for the young people of the world.'

'Of course.'

'There is one other thing, a matter of utmost delicacy which cannot be repeated beyond these four walls,' Hanfstaengl continued, his eyes drifting towards the Englishman. 'The Führer wishes very much to be friends with the English, whom he greatly admires. Negotiations concerning a proposed naval agreement between our two countries are at a critical stage. It is Herr Hitler's fondest desire that this will bring warm and lasting friendship between Berlin and London. It would be a great tragedy for both our nations if this case were to impinge on that fine ambition in any way.'

Seb nodded again. Beads of sweat dampened his collar.

'Do you wish to add anything, Mr Gainer?' Hanfstaengl said.

'No, no, I'm sure that I echo everything you have said.'

Seb's eyes now met those of the British consul whose subtly raised eyebrows seemed to tell a story of their own. Perhaps he was less interested in the propaganda aspect of the murder and more with the human emotions of horror and grief. In which case, Seb could only agree with him.

'Now then,' Thomas Ruff said. 'I want you to get down to work immediately. Your assistant will be a junior officer from the political police whom I have not met, but I am informed is very sharp and will be extremely helpful. Proceed to Ettstrasse and he will be awaiting your arrival. His name is Sergeant Winter.'

This was a demand too far. 'Could I not choose my own man from among my Kripo colleagues – a man with investigative experience?'

'Your point is well made, Wolff, but this decision was taken at a higher level. I'm sure you will understand why the political office might have certain concerns regarding your assignment to this case.'

Because they put me in that damned concentration camp, thought Seb, and they're furious that I have been released and are not about to let me off the hook. And who might the 'higher level' person be, the one who took the decision? Given the Führer's personal interest in this case, two names came to mind: Heydrich or Himmler. Both had their fingers in the political police pie and neither was a man to be denied.

As he was leaving, Ruff took him aside and handed him a sheet of paper with the details ascertained about the girl – the place where the body was discovered and the name and address of the man who found it. He was also given back his Walther PPK. 'The political boys weren't keen to return it, but I insisted,' Ruff said. 'And by the way, Wolff, you should note that I could not have effected your release without the intervention of your uncle. You owe him a drink.'

Seb was pretty sure The Pig could afford his own booze.

CHAPTER 4

If there had been any way of getting out of Munich and away from Germany, Seb would have taken it. But he couldn't leave, couldn't run, not with his mother to care for and a son to be raised to manhood. Anyway, where would he go? Back to sea, perhaps?

As he entered the Police Presidium, a vast complex of buildings which included its own prison, he had an uncomfortable feeling that everyone was avoiding meeting his eyes, but staring at him with pity when his back was turned. Perhaps he was imagining it. Perhaps it was the after-effects of the pill Uncle Christian had shoved down his throat. It had kept him awake for the meeting at the Brown House, but now he was ready to collapse and his mind was wandering. It was not a good state to be in.

Sergeant Hans Winter was waiting in Seb's office on the second floor, sitting at his desk as though it were his own. Seb's heart sank; it was the pockmarked BPP swine who had lifted him off the street outside the Osteria Bavaria and effected his confinement in Dachau. He hadn't given Seb his name at the time; political officers didn't have to. Their warrant badge was enough. Secrecy and anonymity were all important in a secret police force.

Winter instantly jumped to his feet, clicked heels, arm straight out. 'Heil Hitler.'

'Heil Hitler.' Seb managed a cursory imitation of the salute.

'Inspector Wolff, it seems you are a fortunate man.'

'Really?'

'Yes, you have somehow inveigled your way out of the Dachau KZ and you have gained me as your partner. Remarkably good fortune for you, I would say.'

'You are not my partner, Sergeant Winter. I am your superior officer and you will take orders from me.'

Winter looked nonplussed, his rough, stoat-like features travelling through a series of contortions as though trying to compute what Seb had said. At last he came to a conclusion: 'Be careful, Wolff, you're not out of the fire yet. The BPP has authority over all other police departments – and I will be watching you.'

'Just obey orders, do your work and we'll get along fine. You might even learn something, Winter. And in future, you will address me as Herr Wolff, or Inspector Wolff.' He smiled at the grubby man. 'Now pick up your disgusting hat, we're going to inspect the corpse. We'll go in my car – it's just around the corner.'

He didn't give Winter time to argue or complain, simply marched out of the office, down the stone staircase, out into the main entrance yard, through the wrought-iron gates and then strode around the corner to the beer cellar, outside which his red Lancia was safely parked.

'How do you afford a car like this, Wolff?'

'*Herr* Wolff. And none of your business, but if you must know it is because I am careful with my money.'

The girl's body lay pale, naked and horribly defiled on a slab in the mortuary of the university hospital. The pathologist, Professor Lindner, nodded to Wolff. They had met many times before on other cases and had mutual respect, but perhaps not friendship. Seb rather doubted that Lindner had time for friends; he sometimes seemed to be less interested in the quick than the dead.

'You took your time getting here, Herr Wolff.'

'I was detained elsewhere.'

'Yes, I think I heard something about that. And what's this specimen?' Lindner jutted his lean chin towards the BPP officer at Seb's side.

'This is Sergeant Winter. He has been assigned to help me.' He stressed the word *help* as though the very concept that this man could be of any use was preposterous.

Lindner's eyes bore deep into the political policeman as he might peer into the entrails of a cadaver. 'Are you all right, Winter? You don't look well.'

Seb looked sideways. Winter was shivering and did, indeed, look as though he were about to vomit or faint, or both.

The BPP man suddenly lurched and his hand went to his mouth. But he couldn't keep his lunch in and it sprayed through his fingers onto the floor.

The pathologist grimaced. 'Get him out of here, Wolff.'

'Of course.' He took Winter by the arm and pulled him from the lab, then made him sit on a chair in an adjoining room. 'Wait here,' he said.

Winter nodded. The blood had drained from his face and he looked as if he were about to puke again.

'Have you never seen a body before?'

'No,' he said quietly and then lurched again, but this time managed to keep the remaining contents of his stomach inside him.

'What did you do in the war?'

'I wasn't in the war.'

'Ah yes, I suppose you are a bit too young. Anyway, stay here. I'll be back soon.' Still, he was surprised to discover that anyone in the secret police was squeamish given their penchant for playing football with the heads of those they deemed enemies of the state.

A mortuary assistant was finishing mopping up the sick. 'Who's your weak-stomached friend, Wolff?' Lindner asked. 'He seems about as useful as ice skates in the Sahara.'

'He's political police and I've been lumbered with him. God alone knows how such an unimpressive man was ever promoted to sergeant.'

'Perhaps he has good connections.' Lindner raised an eyebrow. 'You certainly do, don't you, Inspector?'

'Was that supposed to be an insult, Professor?'

Lindner laughed. 'Merely an observation. Anyway, why, if I may ask, would one of Himmler's rodents be working on a murder case? This is one for you Kripo boys, isn't it?'

'There's a political element to the case.'

'Really? Should I be worried?'

'This girl,' he said nodding towards the cadaver, 'was an aristocrat with links to the British royal family, and our beloved Führer is taking a keen interest. I rather think Sergeant Winter's role is to keep an eye on me rather than do any serious detective work.'

'We'd better get it right then, hadn't we? Come on, let me give you a tour around the deceased. You will see that I have not opened up the chest cavity yet, because I wanted you to be able to examine the external cuts and markings before they were disturbed. You will note that the throat has been slashed with a single stroke and, given the spray of blood, that is almost certainly the cause of death, but there are at least thirty other lesions, mostly quite shallow and so not fatal, all done with a sharp knife, postmortem. Perhaps a surgical scalpel.'

'Or a butcher's blade?'

'Possibly.'

'Was there sexual interference?'

'There were superficial wounds there, yes. But no semen. Which doesn't mean she hadn't been penetrated, of course.'

Seb examined the body closely. She had long fair hair, a slender frame and fine athletic legs. Her breasts, which were not large, had been desecrated by cuts. He had already been told that she was twenty years old. There must have been an enormous loss of blood from the throat because much of it was evident, but something else, too, on other parts of the torso. A brighter red than the dark, coagulated blood. 'Is that lipstick on her belly and breasts?'

'I rather think so,' Lindner said. 'At first it seemed haphazard, but then I wondered if it was some sort of script. Perhaps it means something to someone, but not to me, I'm afraid.'

Seb scrutinised the markings more closely. 'Nor me,' he said at last. 'A series of horizontal and vertical lines and the occasional curve and swirl. They look rather childlike. No, not childlike – hurried. Or frenzied even. I think we need the body photographed.'

'I'm ahead of you on that. I've ordered two copies of the prints and one set will be couriered to you at Ettstrasse.'

'Thank you. And the cuts? Do you think there could be some sort of pattern to those as well as the lipstick?'

The pathologist shrugged. 'Who knows? That might become clearer when the body is washed. I will have more photographs taken when she's clean and before opening her up.'

'Thank you, Professor. By the way, was she a virgin?'

'No. Oh, and I believe your men have the rather nice Persian rug in which she was wrapped when her body was found. Quite an expensive item, I imagine. It's plain that she was murdered elsewhere and then dumped. She was naked and I am told her clothes were nowhere in the vicinity.'

'Do you have a time of death?'

'My best estimate is the evening before last, probably just before or shortly after midnight. But there's a fair margin for error. We don't know whether the body was kept indoors, whether it was wrapped up the whole time. Such things can affect body heat retention. The remains were found at one o'clock yesterday after-noon. It was actually quite well concealed, down by the water on the far side of the river. A fisherman found it.'

'I've got his name.'

'Well, I can't imagine you'll get much from him. I believe he saw the carpet and thought he could sell it. Rather horrified when he discovered its contents. And that's about all. I believe she was identified some hours later when someone called the police to report her missing.'

They both turned at the creak of the door. Winter had returned and was standing there looking at them.

'Get out,' Lindner said. 'I don't want you in here.'

'I'm sorry, Professor. It won't happen again.'

'Damned right it won't, because you won't be in here. This is my department and I say who is allowed entry.'

'I have to see the corpse.'

Winter moved forward. It was clear to Seb that the man was making a huge effort to hold his digestive system together. 'You don't have to do this, Winter. I've got all the information we need so far. We'll know more when the professor has carried out his autopsy.'

'What are those marks?'

'We'll talk about that later. Come on, let's leave Herr Professor Lindner to his work. Photographs will be sent to us and we can examine those.'

'No. I've seen marks like that before. That's Jew writing.'

'Don't be ridiculous.'

'What do they call it – Hebrew? That's what it is.'

Lindner summoned his two assistants. 'Get this man out of here, now.'

Outside in the warmer air on Ludwigstrasse, Winter was vainly trying to brush down the creases of his suit where he had been manhandled by the two mortuary men. 'That's Jew marking, I tell you. When we know what it says, we'll know the name of the dog who killed her.'

'It's one avenue we'll pursue, but in the meantime we'll keep an open mind.'

'We have to get a Jew expert to look at her. She's been murdered by a Jew in one of their foul blood rituals.'

It occurred to Seb that Winter had spent too much time reading the anti-Semitic rants in *Der Stürmer*. 'As I said, we'll explore every avenue. But right now, Sergeant, I am going home for supper and a long sleep – sleep of which I was deprived last night by your malign actions. I will see you at Ettstrasse at eight in the morning and we shall then visit the place where the body was found.'

'We should go there now. There is no time to waste.'

'No, Winter. This investigation will be done methodically and with rigour – and that works better with a clear head after a refreshing sleep. You know as well as I do that we can't afford to make mistakes or jump to conclusions in this matter. If we get it wrong, both our heads will roll.'

He climbed into the Lancia and left Winter on the pavement to find his own way home, or wherever he wanted to go. Probably to see his masters at Wittelsbach Palace to report on the shockingly disrespectful behaviour of Inspector Sebastian Wolff and Professor Lindner.

CHAPTER 5

Angela Wolff threw her arms around her son and hugged him to her breast. 'Sebastian, Sebastian, where have you been?'

'Oh, you know, Mutti. I had a late night, that's all. Slept at the office.'

'There is a telephone in the hall now, so why didn't you call me at least? You were with that tart Hexie, weren't you?'

'No, Mutti, I wasn't with Hexie and she's not a tart.'

His mother looked at him with sceptical eyes. As always, she was dressed in black. Seb had never known her to wear anything else, for she had dressed that way ever since her husband died of tuberculosis in 1904; Seb had no memories of him, only the bleak photograph on the mantelpiece in the parlour: a stiff man with a severe moustache. But perhaps the picture didn't do him justice, perhaps that wasn't the way he was.

'She's got you wrapped around her sly little finger. Hexie – it means witch. Why doesn't she have a Christian name?'

'She does, it's Herta. But Hexie's what everyone calls her and it's the name she likes, so let's leave it at that. And she's not sly and nor does she wrap me around her finger. Now, where's Jurgen?'

Even as he asked the question he knew the answer. His son was where he was every evening, out with his Hitler Youth troop, of course. He was seventeen years old and he should be studying in preparation for university, but instead he spent his time marching along country lanes doing military training, learning racial theory, testing sporting prowess and sitting around campfires singing approved songs such as 'I had a Comrade' or the 'Horst Wessel Lied'. Oh, and more recently, doing his best to re-educate the recalcitrant peasants who preferred the traditional blue and white colours of Bavaria for their flagpoles to the new black and red of the swastika. Seb had heard numerous reports of Hitler Youth tearing down traditional maypoles and an equal number of reports of villagers tearing down swastikas. Truth be told, he rather sided with the old-fashioned peasants.

Seb, by contrast to his well-schooled son, had educated himself. He had joined the Bavarian police in the lowest ranks of the uniformed force, the Schutzpolizei, commonly called the Schupo. To rise from the ranks to become a plain-clothes detective with the title 'inspector', he had had to present himself smartly, had had to study and pass exams and prove his intellect.

He wanted a simpler faster route through the world for his son; a university education and, hopefully, a doctorate. The boy had the brain, but he was in danger of throwing it all away, wasting these precious years on the Hitler Youth.

If he thought it would do any good, Seb would give him a piece of his mind. But he had tried that before, on several occasions, and it was all just hot air. He couldn't get through to him.

'Well, I'll make you supper,' Angela Wolff said. 'You look exhausted. Last night's food was wasted.'

'Some soup would be fine.' She always had a pot of soup made from leftovers.

'I have some veal. I will make you schnitzel with spätzle.'

'You really don't need to, Mutti. I have to get to sleep early.'

'First you eat. No son of mine goes to bed hungry.'

'Thank you then.'

They lived in a spacious though rather dark apartment on Ainmüllerstrasse in Schwabing, a northern area of the city, sometimes thought of as the artists' quarter, but more generally known for its reasonably priced housing. There was a kitchen with a range, a sink and a big table and a walk-in larder. Also, a small parlour with a new wireless set – a large, impressive Telefunken machine – that was turned on for an hour each day, between six and seven in the evening, but no more. Anyone who happened to be at home at the time was expected to sit and listen to the latest broadcast from Herr Goebbels's ministry and, usually, some splendid music by one of the great German composers, played by one of the great German orchestras. Or perhaps some lieder.

There were three bedrooms: one for Jurgen, the largest one for Seb and the warmest, cosiest one for his mother. It was an old building, almost certainly eighteenth century. Certainly not luxurious, but comfortable enough – cool in summer and warm in winter. Just the way you want it. Seb had fought against his mother's desire for heavy, dark furniture, the sort of status symbol she had longed for in her impoverished childhood out in the countryside, but he had lost the argument. And so the parlour, in particular, with its oversized mahogany chest and comfortless wooden chairs, was faintly oppressive.

As he tucked into the supper, accompanied by a half-litre glass of beer, the door opened and Jurgen entered. He was a lean and muscular lad, towering at least six centimetres over his father, who was himself tall at one metre eighty-four. The boy's hair was fair and cut short, his bearing was athletic and he did look extraordinarily handsome in his uniform: dark shorts, long grey socks, buckled belt, shirt with armband and loosely knotted tie, and his most prized possession, the Hitler Youth dagger with its inscription *Blood and Honour*.

He was – and Seb hated to admit it – the ideal specimen of Aryan manhood. *Slender of body, swift as the greyhound, tough as leather and hard as Krupp steel.* Just as Herr Hitler wanted every German youth to be.

It was obvious to anyone who knew the family that he got his god-like looks, his bearing and his complexion from his mother, Ulrike Brandt, now far away in Berlin doing whatever it was that she did these days. The only element of the young man that he might have inherited from his father was his quick brain. At least, that was what Seb liked to think.

The boy gave a sharp Heil Hitler salute and snapped a respectful bow of the head to his grandmother, who returned the salute with a smile. Seb said, 'Good evening to you, Jurgen. Just in time for supper,' but was ignored.

Jurgen was deliberately looking away from him. He took a seat at the table opposite his father while his grandmother returned to the hob to prepare his food. The boy's face was grim and hard.

'What have you been up to this evening?' Seb asked in what he hoped was a cheery, good-humoured tone. 'Lovely day for marching.'

'You can never say a decent word about the Hitler Youth, can you?'

'Did I say something wrong?'

'You just mock us.'

'God in heaven, what's brought this on?'

'You think we just march and sing songs. You've no idea, have you? They teach us to sail, to ride motorbikes, to fire rifles, to hunt, build shelters, play war games and much else besides. When did you ever teach me anything?'

'I'm sorry then. What do you want me to teach you?'

'Damn it, that's not what I want to talk about. Why don't you tell me what *you've* been up to. Where were you last night, Father?'

'I slept in the office.'

'Really? You even lie to your own son.'

Word travelled like wildfire in Munich. He hadn't wanted to worry his mother with the events of last night, but the news was obviously out and Jurgen had heard about it. 'It was all a stupid misunderstanding,' he said.

'My father in Dachau concentration camp! How do you think that went down with the troop? Was I supposed to defend you? I was humiliated. They all laughed and sneered at me – and not just behind my back. To my face! They even asked if I was a Jew.'

'Well, now you can tell them the truth, can't you? It was all a mistake. The proof is in front of you – I am here, not in Dachau.'

'What is this?' Angela Wolff demanded. 'What are you two men talking about?' She had returned with a plate of bread and was hovering over Jurgen.

Seb sighed with exasperation. 'It's nothing, Mutti.'

'I thought you mentioned Dachau. My old friend Hannah Fischer from Polsingen has moved there. Did I tell you, Sebastian? She loves the town and has invited me over for lunch. I thought I might take the bus out there next week.'

Jurgen slammed the palm of his hand down hard on the table. 'If you don't tell her, I will. You have brought shame on this family! You have tarnished our reputation.'

Seb had had enough. This was not a conversation to be continued while he was so tired. He would say things about the Nazis that would probably drive an even deeper wedge between him and his son. He put down his knife and fork on his plate, rose from the table and gave a little bow to his mother. 'Thank you, Mutti, that was delicious. Now I must go to bed for I had little sleep last night and I must be up early.'

'So you just walk away?' Jurgen shouted. 'I despise you – you're a traitor.'

Seb stopped and turned. This was too much. He was about to say, *I fought for this country, Jurgen. I risked my life and I watched my friends die. Is that treason?* But he couldn't bring himself to do it. All he could say was, 'I have never betrayed my country.'

'You called the Führer a murderer. *That* is treason.'

'He ordered the deaths of Ernst Roehm and hundreds of others. He had them shot in cold blood, without trial or any semblance of legal process. The fact that Roehm was a despicable human being does not excuse the action. And as a murder detective, I think I know what constitutes murder.'

'Roehm was a traitor. He was plotting against Hitler. They all were. They had to be put down like swine.'

'So what will you do? Denounce me?'

'I should do. Maybe I will. I know what you think of the Führer so, yes, I have more than enough dirt on you.'

Seb gritted his teeth. He was about to spit vitriol back at his son, but instead managed to hold his tongue. 'Goodnight, Jurgen. We will talk when we've both calmed down.'

He was sure he would go straight to sleep, but instead he twisted and turned in his narrow bed. His body seemed to itch everywhere and his shoulders still ached. Most of all he could not stop thinking about Jurgen. How could a son speak to a father like that? Had he raised him badly – been too soft, too slow to use the back of his hand when he stepped out of line? The Englishmen he had met aboard ship and in British ports had acquainted him with one of their time-honoured aphorisms – *spare the rod and spoil the child.* Perhaps there was some truth in that.

Or perhaps the problem simply stemmed from those four years when he was away at sea and the boy had no male presence in his life.

But none of that really made any sense. He knew that other people struggled to come to terms with the new ideology and that some young people had indeed denounced their parents, teachers and priests. One old man he knew had ended up in Dachau concentration camp for three months for a careless joke at the expense of Hitler, spoken in front of his granddaughter, a member of the League of German Girls.

This conflict within the home was not so unusual. Somehow the National Socialist machine had gained a more powerful hold on Germany's children than their own parents.

The NS claws went deep, and didn't let go.

And then there was something else that rankled. He, Seb, had been the one who had had to undergo the rigours of the concentration camp, and yet his son had made no enquiries about his welfare; he just assumed the worst – that he was some kind of traitor.

Perhaps he just had to accept that he had lost the boy.

Seb woke later than he intended, seven thirty, which left little time to get to the Police Presidium for his 8 a.m. meeting with Winter. Jurgen didn't have school on a Sunday, but he had already gone out, probably to the local Hitler Youth hut – the *heim* as they liked to call it – so at least he didn't have to endure an early morning confrontation. It would come later, of course, couldn't be avoided forever. God in heaven, he couldn't be the only man in Germany who felt constantly hemmed in, both at work and at home.

He had been to Jurgen's *heim* once and was appalled. It was just an old youth club place, but it had been turned into a temple to Hitler. Pictures of the Führer and all the top men – especially Hitler Youth leader Baldur von Schirach – adorned the walls. There were ceiling-to-floor swastika pennants and a dangerous array of armaments – old swords, daggers, even Great War rifles and pistols.

But the most alarming things of all were the quotes from Hitler, painted in large letters on any available space, like Holy Writ: Anti-Jew, anti-Communist, anti-French, pure German above all.

Seb kissed his mother goodbye and could see she was upset.

'It's all right, Mutti. We'll be fine.'

'Please don't fight. I can't bear it.'

He kissed her again. 'I know. It's his age.'

'You were like that, Sebastian. Nothing I could say made any difference when you were seventeen. You couldn't wait to go off to the war, couldn't wait to get a girl. All that stuff with Ulrike's pregnancy. I aged twenty years overnight.'

He gripped her gnarled working-woman's hands in his. Then hugged her tight before leaving without another word. In the hall-way, he was about to take the steps down, but instead he stopped beside the telephone and made a quick call to the Hoffmann studio. Hexie answered.

'Seb, what's going on? I heard that ghastly little BPP worm had you sent to the KZ and so I went to Weber. I hope I did the right thing. It's all the talk.'

'Fuss about nothing, but thank you for your help. I'm out and back at work. I've got a busy day, so perhaps we can meet up this evening.'

'The Schelling-Salon at eight? I still have a birthday present waiting for you.'

He was pretty sure he knew what it would be. 'I'll do my best,' he said. But he wasn't overly hopeful. He had a case to solve, and it had to be done with thoroughness and speed.

CHAPTER 6

'Been waiting long, Sergeant Winter?'

'Of course I have, Wolff. You were supposed to be here half an hour ago.'

'*Herr* Wolff. You will address me with proper respect or I will have you on a charge for insubordination. And what's happened to the Hitler salute this morning?'

Winter's face betrayed his bemusement and indignation. He was supposed to be the one doing the threatening. He was the one who had the power to have Wolff despatched to Dachau. Or, at least, he had had that power. Things had somehow turned on their head and the new situation was confusing for the secret policeman. Unable to explain these feelings, he clicked his heels, threw out his right arm and said the two magic words.

'That's better. Now, let's head for the river.'

'I have already been to the spot where the body was found. I went there yesterday evening after we parted.'

'And what did you find?'

'Grass. Leaves. Mud. What do you expect?'

'Who knows? That's where murder team training comes in. Well, I haven't been to the spot, so you can accompany me there now. It's a fine day, let's walk.'

Without another word, Seb led the way out of police HQ, heading north and then eastwards along Prinzregentenstrasse across the old Luitpold Bridge over the Isar river and turned north into the picturesque but rather discreet woods.

Sunlight filtered through the ancient trees, all in their summer green finery, hugging the bank between the river and Maria-Theresia-Strasse, one of the loveliest residential streets in the city. Putzi Hanfstaengl had had a house built here as had the writer Thomas Mann in the old days before he became a nonperson and fled for his life to Switzerland.

Seb stopped and consulted the map he had been given. It had been carefully drawn by the first officers on the scene and passed on to him by Thomas Ruff. It looked like they must be close.

'It's just down there, Herr Wolff, to the left,' Winter said.

'Thank you, Sergeant.' That was an improvement. Winter had said something useful and had addressed him correctly.

They sidestepped their way down the bank, which fell away steeply down a muddy incline to the water's edge, where roots tangled driftwood and other detritus.

'Right, Winter, get down on your hands and knees and examine the area with extreme care. I shall do the same. We will be looking for anything that could possibly be a clue.'

'Such as what, Inspector? I have already looked here.'

'And what did you find?'

'I told you. Leaves and mud.'

'Then you didn't look very hard.' Seb took out a clean handkerchief from his jacket pocket, bent down and used it to pick up a cigarette packet, carefully. 'Was this here when you examined the area.'

'Perhaps. I don't know. And if it was, so what? It's a cigarette packet not a clue.'

'Well, maybe it belonged to the killer, or the victim. Maybe there are fingerprints to be recovered. Maybe the killer is known for using this brand of cigarette.'

Winter shrugged irritably. 'I suppose it's possible. In which case why would the killer have left it here? Anyone could have dropped it.'

'Or it could have fallen out of the killer's pocket. Take nothing for granted.' He removed a brown paper bag from his other pocket and deposited the carton in it.

For a few moments he wondered why he was bothering to explain such basic and obvious procedures to Winter. The man wasn't there to investigate a murder, merely to report back to his political bosses at the Wittelsbach Palace.

Trying to teach Winter anything was clearly a hopeless task. And yet Seb couldn't resist the challenge; it was his nature to inform and enlighten. He had trained up several detectives in the past few years and had been satisfied with the results of his endeavours.

'Did you look for footprints?'

'There was nothing. Lots of scuffed dust from the uniformed police who were here first and the stretcher bearers who carried the corpse away.'

They spent the next half-hour on their knees, scrabbling through the dry earth and vegetation.

'What about this?' Winter said, holding up a tube about the size of a slim half-smoked cigar. 'Lipstick by the look of it.'

'You're getting your own fingerprints on it.' Dear God, the man was a lost cause. The BPP was welcome to him. Seb took the lipstick in his handkerchief and examined it. It was almost empty but what remained was bright red, not unlike the lipstick on the body of Rosie Palmer. There were no identifying marks on the object for either owner or maker.

'Well done, Winter, that's a good find. It could be important.'

'You really think so?'

'It's possible. Come on, we've seen enough here. I want to talk to the people she lodged with.'

'You know who that is, I take it?'

Yes, he knew. And going there was not a comfortable prospect. The well-connected Miss Palmer had been living with Walter Regensdorf, the wealthy industrialist and early sponsor of one Adolf Hitler back in the mid-twenties. He and his wife Maria had introduced the would-be Führer to other rich and powerful industrialists and had taught him how to feel at home with the upper classes. They were Nazis to the core.

'Do you not think we should ask for an appointment?'

'No, Winter, this is a murder case. We just go and knock on their door. I am sure we will be expected. They must want to find the killer of their guest as much as we do.'

The Regensdorfs lived on Karolinenplatz in an enormous square mansion house – a five-storey palatial monolith named Villa Saphir, that dominated the circular crossroads of Brienner Strasse, Barer Strasse and Max-Joseph-Strasse. The house lacked beauty but impressed by its sheer power-exuding size, right at the heart of Nazidom.

It was close to the Brown House and various other important party and Reich buildings, and within a hundred metres of political police headquarters in Wittelsbach Palace. Towering over the centre of the square was an obelisk dedicated to the Bavarian soldiers who died in the Napoleonic Wars.

Karolinenplatz was, perhaps, the most sought-after address in Munich, even allowing for the present dust and noise and traffic chaos around nearby Königsplatz.

Seb imagined he would be expected to go to a side or rear entrance where tradesmen might make their deliveries to the grand household, but he walked straight up the stone steps to the front door and pulled the bell-chain.

The door was answered by a liveried serving man who looked at Seb and then the ill-dressed Winter with disdain.

'No beggars.' He was about to close the heavy door.

Seb flashed his badge. 'We're Kripo, regarding the murder of Miss Rosie Palmer.'

The servant stopped in his tracks. 'Ah, yes, indeed. Please wait here, gentlemen.' He clicked his heels, gave the Hitler salute, then closed the door on them before they had a chance to return the courtesy.

Maria Regensdorf should have been the height of elegance, given her place at the forefront of Munich society. Yet here in her mid-forties her glum face was a veritable potato. She was dressed in expensive Bavarian *tracht* – a dark green knee-length skirt and jacket with deer-horn buttons – and yet she managed to look vaguely unkempt. Untold wealth did nothing for her appearance. Perhaps, thought Seb, she just felt comfortable in herself with no necessity to put on a show for the world, which suited him just fine.

Seb had seen her picture in the papers several times, for she was a doyenne of the opera and arts in Munich and even further afield, but in the flesh, she was *hausfrau* writ large. That said, she retained vestiges of the attractive young woman she once was.

'You must be Herr Wolff,' she said. 'My good friend Putzi Hanf-staengl has told me all about you. In fact he spoke very highly of your skills as a detective.'

'You are very kind, Frau Regensdorf.'

'Oh, and he said you were fluent in English, which may be very important in getting to the bottom of this dreadful tragedy. Such a lovely girl, Rosie. I can't believe anyone would wish her harm. She had become like a daughter to me these past few months. You might know that my husband and her late father were good friends at school in England.'

'I believe I heard as much, yes.'

She turned to Winter as though only just registering his presence. 'And who is this? Is he your assistant?'

'He is, madam. This is Sergeant Winter.'

'Well, you had both better come in. Herr Regensdorf is on the telephone presently, but he shouldn't keep you waiting long.'

They stepped inside the magnificent hallway and were directed towards a side room. 'You should be all right in here. It's our little library. My husband so likes his books.'

'Actually, I was hoping I might have a few words with you, too, Frau Regensdorf. I am very keen to get the names of her friends and any thoughts you might have about the murderer and his or her motive.'

'Really? I'm sure my husband can fill you in about all that.'

'But when did you last see her? Did she go out with friends? I need to understand her last movements.'

'You know, much as we loved Rosie, she was merely lodging here. She came and went as she pleased. She was a young woman not a girl.'

'I understand, of course. But was there a moment when you realised she was missing – that she hadn't come back here?'

Maria Regensdorf sighed. 'You don't seem to be hearing me, Herr Wolff. I told you – she did as she pleased. She sometimes ate with us, but not always because she had a life of her own. We didn't keep checks on her. That was the arrangement we agreed with her family.'

This was not going to be easy. 'Would I be permitted to talk with your servants?'

'Another question for my husband, I think. He is the master of the house.'

'I believe you have a daughter of your own. Is she here?'

'My stepdaughter is married and living in Ingolstadt. Rosie Palmer was staying in her old room.'

'Might we have a look at the room?'

'Dear me, you are asking rather a lot. This is a private home, you know.'

'Of course, madam, and we will ensure that we leave everything as it is. But this is a murder inquiry.'

'At the risk of repeating myself endlessly, all I can say is that you can talk to my husband about that. Also, if he says I should talk to you, then of course I will comply. But that is his decision. In the meantime, I shall leave you here. Please, do make yourself comfortable.'

Without another word, she wafted from the room and closed the door behind her.

Winter stood in awe of his surroundings. The little eyes in his rat face became almost wide as he turned and looked at the exquisite panelling and the shelves with thousands of books.

Seb was irritated. He rather thought he would acquire more information from Maria Regensdorf than her husband. She, surely, would have had more to do with the English girl and her education on a day-to-day basis, especially as she had described her as becoming like a daughter.

Idly, he examined the books. All Goethe's works were here, of course, bound in leather and very probably first editions. Shakespeare, too, and all the greats of European literature, from the Greeks and Romans to Cervantes and Zola. Everything was in alphabetical order and so he looked under H and was not surprised by what he found. Hitler's *Mein Kampf* was there, but no Heinrich Heine. Then his gaze went to M and R, just out of interest. No Thomas Mann; no Remarque. Even in this house they had been consigned to the Nazis' bonfire of history.

There were other German works, though, much of it rather obscure. Histories of the Nordic peoples and gods, particularly the works of Guido von List and Helena Blavatsky and Nietzsche. *Völkisch* tracts that stressed the closeness of the Germanic peoples to the land and the hunger for a German religion distinct from Christianity, along with other tracts that stressed the superhuman nature of the pure-bred German. He supposed it made sense that Regensdorf would be a man of such racial sensibilities given his closeness to Adolf and his ideology.

The library door swung open and the liveried serving man appeared. 'Herr Regensdorf will see you gentlemen now. If you would follow me, please.'

They were taken along a wood-lined corridor to the great man's study, a room that seemed to contain as many books as his library, as well as a large desk and a window with an expansive view over the tree-lined square.

Walter Regensdorf was scribbling something on a pad of paper with a fountain pen. With an expansive gesture, he dashed off a signature, folded the paper and slid it into an envelope. Only then did he look up.

'Ah, Herr Wolff and Herr Winter, is it? Do sit down both of you.'

'Thank you, sir,' Seb said. 'I am Inspector Wolff.'

'Well I'm very pleased to meet you both, though the circumstances are extremely unhappy. In truth, I am devastated by the death of my late friend's lovely and delightful daughter.'

Two chairs had been placed in front of his desk. Seb took the one on the right.

Walter Regensdorf was at least ten years older than his wife and wore the tweeds and brogues of an English gentleman, which was not surprising for one who had spent their tender years at an exclusive boarding school in the English Midlands. He was almost certainly in his mid-fifties and had evidently lived well, given the thickening of his cheeks and the smooth, untroubled sheen of his large forehead and bald pate. With his Lenin beard, he had an aura of power and had most certainly been a sportsman in his younger days; perhaps he still was, reflected Seb.

'And you should know,' Regensdorf continued, 'that I have just got off the telephone to the Führer. He is as deeply saddened as we are and demands that the killer be brought to book and despatched without delay. This matter must be dealt with at speed and there must be no errors. Herr Wolff, perhaps you can tell me exactly how you intend to proceed.'

'Well, first of all, sir, I need to talk to the occupants of this house, including the servants. I need to know all about Miss Palmer's movements in the days and hours before she was murdered. Who did she meet? Where did she go? I have told Frau Regensdorf that I would like to inspect the young lady's room. Also I would like the names and addresses of her tutors and her friends.'

'Of course, of course. I will put you in the capable hands of my secretary, Frau Huber, and she will assist you with all of that.'

'And for yourself, sir, do you have any suspicions of anyone in Miss Palmer's circle?'

'Good Lord, no. If I had, the suspect would be under lock and key by now.'

'Do you know of any boyfriends she had? Were there men in her life?'

'I suppose there must have been. She was an attractive girl.'

'When did you last see her, sir?'

'Well, that would have been the evening before last, about nine o'clock. I chanced upon her in the hallway. She was all dressed up and she told me she was going out with her English friends and that they would most likely join up with some young SS officers. I wished her a pleasant evening and carried on into my library. I didn't see her again. It was only the following day at breakfast when my wife and I realised that neither of us had seen her that we spoke with the servants and it became obvious she was missing. Frau Huber telephoned the police on our behalf.'

'I would like the names of these friends she was to meet and, if possible, the SS officers you mentioned.'

'I couldn't say with certainty because I didn't interrogate her, but I wouldn't be surprised if one of them was the Mitford girl – Unity Mitford, daughter of Lord Redesdale. I was introduced to him last year when he visited Munich, but I couldn't tell you much about the family. All I know is that young Unity has enchanted the Führer with her beauty and delightful conversation. He enjoys her company greatly and she was a close friend of Rosie.'

'Do you have an address for Miss Mitford?'

'Well, at the time I met her father I believe she was lodging with Baroness Laroche in Koniginstrasse. Certainly the baroness will be able to help you further. Yes, that might be your best course of action, Wolff. Talk to the Mitford girl. She should be able to give you a list of Miss Palmer's acquaintances.'

CHAPTER 7

The bedroom was immaculate and Seb quickly realised that it had already been cleaned and tidied by the Regensdorfs' domestic staff. It was a large, airy space, furnished at expense with a double bed, a goose-down duvet, modern dressing table and chest of drawers, heavy drapes pulled back to reveal large windows with sweeping views of the lawned garden and the city beyond. Nothing but the very best.

Frau Huber, secretary to Regensdorf, was with them, standing watch by the door.

'You can go if you wish,' Seb said.

'The master asked me to remain with you at all times, Detective Inspector.'

Of course he did, thought Seb. We are the lower orders and he wants to make sure we don't steal anything. He examined the dressing table and found a hairbrush, a comb and a silver tray with kirby grips and some sort of hand cream. There was makeup, too, including eyeliner and powder, foundation, scent and various other cosmetics. No sign of any lipstick, but she would probably have carried that in her handbag when she went out.

An exquisite inlaid wooden box, about twenty centimetres by fifteen, stood on the table in front of the mirror. It appeared to be of Far Eastern origin. Seb removed a penknife from his pocket and prised the box open without making contact with his fingers. It was a jewellery box with rings, necklaces and brooches. Good gold and some fine gemstones. No paste, he judged.

Seb turned to the tall, slender secretary. 'Have any of Miss Palmer's effects been removed, Frau Huber?'

'Not to my knowledge, sir.'

He moved away from the dressing table towards a wardrobe. From the corner of his eye he saw Winter about to pick up something on a bedside table. 'Touch nothing, Sergeant.'

Winter's hand recoiled.

'Anyway, what are you looking at?'

'It is a book, Herr Wolff. I believe it is on the list of the banned.'

'What is it?'

'I cannot understand the title, but the author's name is given as Sigmund Freud. A notorious Jew.'

Seb wandered across and saw that the book was *The Interpretation of Dreams* in English translation. 'Yes,' he said. 'I suppose you're right. It was probably one of those on the bonfire. But Miss Palmer was English and they have different laws in England, so perhaps it was permissible for a foreigner to import it.'

'She must have smuggled it through the border.'

'Would you like me to have it removed and disposed of?' Frau Huber asked.

'No. Her family will be arriving within the next few hours. It is up to them to have her belongings returned to England. And you, Sergeant Winter, make a note of it.'

'If she had a Jewish book, perhaps she had a Jew acquaintance here in Munich. Find the Jew, find the killer.'

Seb ignored his absurd line of reasoning and delved into the wardrobe. It was full of fashionable dresses, certainly more than the average woman might own in a lifetime. Miss Palmer had not been deprived of luxury in her short stay on Earth.

He addressed the secretary again. 'These dresses . . .'

'They are all Miss Palmer's. She had them sent here when she arrived last August. A dozen pieces of luggage, I recall.'

'When did you last see her?'

'The day before yesterday, at breakfast outside on the terrace. I was fetching coffee for the master and I saw her there reading an English newspaper. I bade her good morning and she returned the greeting. That was all.'

'Did you not see her again during the day?'

'No, sir. I believe she went out for German or painting lessons. By the time she returned my shift had finished for it was my half-day, so I didn't see her.'

'Who killed her, Frau Huber? Who did this terrible thing?'

The secretary wore a plain black dress with a modest collar. She wore no makeup and had a serious aspect with short hair, without looking severe. Probably excellent at her job. In another life, she might have been a mother superior in a convent, but she was not unattractive.

The woman's brow creased. 'If I knew I would tell you, of course. But I don't have any idea. I am as shocked and horrified as everyone else.'

'No idea at all? No clue? What are the servants saying? You must hear the gossip. Everyone has some theory in a case like this, however far-fetched.'

'No, sir.'

Was there hesitation there? Was Frau Huber keeping something back? 'Then answer me one thing: do the servants believe the killer was German or foreign?'

The secretary looked uncomfortable.

'Well?'

'I shouldn't speak ill of the dead, Inspector, but there had been a bit of gossip about Miss Palmer even before her death. She ran with a fast crowd. I have been told that at times she did not arrive home until morning. I can't find a delicate way to phrase this, but I must say that there are those in this house who were not exactly surprised when they heard she had been killed.'

'By whom then?'

'One of the men she saw.'

Winter had been looking around in the background, examining pictures, dresses, the handbasin, the towels. Now he stepped forward. 'You mean they thought she had it coming?' he said.

Frau Huber flinched at the words. 'Well, not exactly that. No one deserves such a fate.'

'You all considered her a whore and worthless?'

'Please, I didn't say that,' the secretary protested. 'I was simply making the point that it was thought she might be taking risks.'

'Perhaps we should take you all down to the Wittelsbach Palace, see what you know.'

Seb had had enough. 'There won't be any need for that.' He wanted to remove Winter from the interrogation. 'Did you ever see her wearing lipstick, Frau Huber?'

'Oh yes, sir. Always. It marked her out as un-German. A German woman does not decorate herself.'

'Then why is there no lipstick on her dressing table?'

'I'm afraid I don't know. I have never had cause to be in this room before.'

'And Herr Regensdorf informs me that it was you who informed the police that she was missing.'

'Yes, sir, as he requested.'

'And there is nothing more that you wish to tell me?'

'No, sir.'

Seb wanted to talk with everyone in the Regensdorf house, but that would take too much time and would have to wait. First, he needed to speak with the victim's friends, for they would know her movements better than anyone.

The house on Koniginstrasse was delightfully close to the west side of the English Garden. It was not a large property, certainly not grand in any way. But like so many members of the old Bavarian nobility, Baroness Laroche lived in reduced circumstances, having lost almost all of her inherited fortune in the great inflation.

To make ends meet she took in young English boys and girls while they socialised and learnt the German language and various other skills such as a musical instrument or singing. They were keen to come to Germany for the exchange rate was extremely favourable.

She was just one of several such aristocrats making a living from their upper-class cousins and old acquaintances in wealthy England and America. They were expected to arrange lessons in art and music and ensure a modicum of discipline.

For the young people themselves, it was one long social whirl: skiing at Garmisch-Partenkirchen – a convenient train ride away; picnicking, swimming and sailing on the many beautiful lakes of southern Bavaria; tennis afternoons; lots of tea parties, nights at the opera and theatre, dancing, drinking; and – perhaps most of all – adventures in love, however fleeting. They had regular allowances from their families back home and they had smart little cars. It was a sort of finishing school for the offspring of the English and American upper classes, but mostly English. In 1930s Europe, Munich was *the* place to go, the culmination of the grand tour.

Seb pulled up outside Koniginstrasse 121, the baroness's house, which was rendered in a light ochre. For a few moments, he simply looked up at the building with its three storeys of regimented windows, then turned to Winter. 'Come on.'

'I'm told you speak English, Inspector.'

'Yes.'

'Why would you learn an enemy language?'

'I didn't know they were the enemy. I thought the war was over.'

'How can they not be our enemy? If you are not pure-bred German, then you are of a lower order. *Deutschland uber alles . . .*'

'And yet the Führer wishes to be friends with them, which is why this case is so important to him.'

Winter had evidently not thought this paradox through, for his eyes blinked and his brow creased. Seb gave him a long look. He almost felt sorry for the man. 'Enough of this, let's go and meet the baroness. Just keep your mouth shut unless I ask you to speak.'

'You cannot talk to me like that, Herr Wolff! If you insult me, you insult the political police.'

Seb ignored him and strode up to the door, which was answered almost immediately by a plump grey-haired woman in a dress that must once have been chic and had clearly been let out several times in the intervening years.

He saluted her then immediately showed his badge. 'I am Detective Inspector Wolff. Could we speak to Baroness Laroche?'

'You *are* speaking to her, young man. How may I help you?'

'Ah, good day, my lady, and Heil Hitler.' He gave her a half-hearted salute, which she returned with a similar lack of enthusiasm. 'We are looking for a young English lady named Unity Mitford and I was informed that she lodged here.'

'Indeed she did, but she has now moved out. You will find her either at the girls' student hostel – Haus Gertrud on Kaulbachstrasse – or staying with her friend Erna Hanfstaengl.'

'Herr Hanfstaengl's sister?'

'Indeed. I'm not sure if Erna resides at Uffing or Solln these days but I believe I have at least one of her telephone numbers if you'd care to wait a moment while I fetch my book.' She raised her index finger and smiled. 'Actually, you might do well to try the student hostel first – it's just around the corner.'

'Thank you.'

'May I ask what this is about?'

'I'm afraid I can't say.'

'Would it involve the terrible tragedy of Rosie Palmer?'

'Did you know her?'

'Of course. A delightful child. Prettiest English girl I ever saw.'

'Might we step inside? Would you be prepared to tell us what you know about the young lady?'

'Yes, of course. We'll have coffee in the garden and you can fire questions at me to your heart's content.'

They sat at a circular wrought-iron table with a wide umbrella, the sort they have at the best outdoor cafes. A maid had been despatched by the baroness to fetch a pot of coffee and three cups.

Winter rose almost immediately. 'Might I be permitted to use your toilet, Baroness?'

'It is in the hall where we just came in. I'm sure you can find it.'

He snapped a salute, then bowed and disappeared into the house.

'Is your young friend quite all right, Herr Wolff?'

'He is new.'

'Ah, well, good luck with him. He's rather unprepossessing, isn't he? His nose was dribbling and he looked as if he probably smells.'

Seb smiled. He didn't know this woman and so he was not going to reveal his personal feelings about Hans Winter or any other topic to her. 'You said you were acquainted with Miss Rosie Palmer. How did you meet?'

'Well, Unity Mitford lived here until last October. When Miss Palmer arrived in Germany in the summer, Unity considered it her duty to introduce her to Munich society, for they were of a similar class and knew people in common, though I'm not sure they had met before. Unity can clarify that for you. Anyway, they got on well and she brought Miss Palmer here several times and I thought she was charming. We hit it off immediately and she used to visit me even after Unity moved out.'

'Tell me more about Miss Palmer, if you would. I believe she was very popular with the local men.'

'Of course she was. How could such a pretty girl not attract a large following? They were like bees around honey. But it was all quite innocent, I think.'

'Any men in particular?'

'Oh dear, Herr Wolff, I really couldn't say. But all the English girls love the SS boys. They look so dashing in their uniforms, don't you think?'

'So you didn't see her with any particular men?'

'You know, I really don't think I did. None that stood out and certainly none that I recognised. I must sound an awful snob to you, Inspector, but quite honestly these handsome SS lads all look rather alike to me. So many of them are tall, fair-haired with strong chins. If I heard any of their names, I'm afraid they didn't register.'

Winter reappeared. It occurred to Seb that he looked rather pleased with himself in his greasy way. What exactly had he been doing indoors? He was followed shortly by the young maid, carrying a tray with real coffee, cream, sugar and cups.

'Do you recall any conversations with Miss Palmer when she visited?' Seb asked the baroness. 'Did she have any fears? Did any of the men make her feel uncomfortable?'

'Oh I'm sure not. These young girls know how to look after themselves, and the SS boys wouldn't allow any harm to come to them.'

'Well, harm came to Rosie Palmer.'

The baroness stiffened. 'That's very cheap, Inspector.'

'Forgive me.' The problem was he was receiving decidedly mixed messages about the Honourable Miss Rosie Palmer. The servants at the Regensdorfs' house apparently saw her as little more than a painted whore, while this woman thought of her as a rather giddy innocent playing kiss-chase with equally virtuous members of the SS. The only actual evidence available was Professor Lindner's assertion that she was not a virgin. But that did not make her a harlot.

'Now that I think about it, the only time I ever saw her with anyone other than Unity and their young friends was when Otto Raspe dropped her off here. I saw him out of the window and waved to him. He waved back and then drove away.'

'Otto Raspe the writer?'

'Is there another Otto Raspe?'

'Do you know why he was dropping her off?'

'Well, I didn't really give it much thought, but I suppose he must be a friend of Walter and Maria Regensdorf. Perhaps he was driving in this direction and offered Rosie a lift. That's all I can think of. I was surprised he didn't stop and say hello.'

Otto Raspe. Now that was a name he hadn't expected to encounter. Raspe, formerly a colonel in the Bavarian military before and during the Great War, was now a columnist for the *Völkischer Beobachter* and *Der Stürmer*. His speciality was the Völkisch movement – harking back to the primitive warrior culture of the Germanic peoples – and it was said he had been a member of the Thule Society whose members had included such leading Nazi lights as Rudolf Hess, Alfred Rosenberg and Hitler's mentor Dietrich Eckhart. It had always been an organisation of the upper and middle classes, the well-to-do and the academic. They had formed the creed that lay at the core of Nazism – and indeed used a sort of round-edged swastika as their emblem.

But it had been quiet and hidden in recent years, its influence downplayed, perhaps because Hitler didn't want anyone else to take credit for his own policies and convictions.

'So you know Colonel Raspe, Baroness?'

'Oh, we're old acquaintances from times past. I haven't seen much of him recently probably because our fortunes went in different directions. He has carved out his career as an esteemed columnist while I am reduced to taking in paying guests.'

'My lady, you live in a delightful house.'

'Well, it's all I have left, isn't it. Anyway, Raspe's not really my type, truth be told. Always going on about blood and soil and Teutonic mythology. Very Wagnerian. I suppose you'd call him a bit intense and I prefer a helping of laughter and witty repartee in my male acquaintances.'

CHAPTER 8

'What was that about going to the toilet, Winter? What were you up to in the house because I'm damned certain you weren't having a piss?'

They were in the car outside Koniginstrasse 121, having finished their coffee and bidden farewell to Baroness Laroche. Seb had given her a number to call if she had any other thoughts on Rosie Palmer or recollections that might offer clues. He also made it clear to her that there was to be no gossip about the crime; she was to say nothing to anyone, especially not to foreign reporters, who might seek her out.

Now Winter was grinning, revealing uneven teeth. 'I went to the kitchen where the maid was preparing coffee. Pretty young girl, didn't you think? Keen member of the BDM.'

'And why would you do that? What possible relevance could there be in a servant being a member of the League of German Girls? You do what I tell you, Winter, nothing more.'

'I wanted to know about the baroness. She's one to watch, that one. The maid has her doubts, believes she's a monarchist. Apparently she is always going on about the time she was presented at the Imperial palace in Vienna and met the Emperor Franz Josef. I'll be interested to know what Herr Meisinger has to say on the matter.'

Seb had encountered SS captain Josef Meisinger in the hours before he was consigned to Dachau. Meisinger was a career sadist and a persecutor of homosexuals. One of the less pleasant men in the Bavarian Political Police. He had goaded Seb, demanding information about his sexual proclivities, and encouraged Winter in his so-called interrogation (which amounted to an hour of flinging unsubstantiated accusations of treachery). Seb had soaked it up, but it was all extremely tedious. 'He's your immediate chief, I take it.'

'The very best. It is an honour to serve him. I'm sure you will meet him again in the not-too-distant future.'

Seb knew exactly what Winter was saying: *When this is all over, we will come for you, Wolff. You are free because you speak good English and know how to conduct a murder inquiry and because you are nephew to city boss Christian Weber. But those things will not protect you for long, and then we will get you. You think you have friends in high places, but mine tower over them. Do you think you or Weber or Thomas Ruff can withstand the power of Josef Meisinger or Gestapo director Reinhard Heydrich? Or me?*

He knew, too, that truth and facts meant nothing to these people, for he had seen them in action. Winter had embellished their confrontation outside the Osteria Bavaria. 'I heard him insulting the Führer,' he'd told Meisinger. 'He said things I cannot repeat, intimations of impropriety by Herr Hitler.' He had also said that Seb threatened him and that a lesser man would have feared for his life.

And there would be other lies if necessary. It was their way and people were right to fear them, because there was no appeal and no redress for injustice in the Third Reich. The words block leader Höss said at Dachau remained firmly in his memory: *You have no rights. You are a piece of shit and will be treated as such.*

The only hope was that this malign regime would implode, collapse in on itself, and sooner rather than later. It was a forlorn hope, but it was the only hope.

'And this maid you interviewed, this keen young Nazi girl, what did she say that will help our investigation?'

Winter's grin disappeared and his face resumed its customary blank bewilderment. 'I told you, she cast doubt on the loyalty of Baroness Laroche.'

'Which helps us how?'

The political policeman was squirming, lost for words.

'Forget it,' Seb said. 'From now on, stand at my side and keep your nasty little mouth shut and we'll get on just fine. Let's go.'

As Seb engaged reverse gear, Winter's eyes widened. 'There was something else I wanted to discuss.'

'Yes?' Seb didn't bother to camouflage his lack of interest.

'Something that has been nagging at me since we were at the mortuary with Professor Lindner. You mentioned my lack of war service. Were you saying that those who have seen war are somehow superior to those who haven't?'

'Not at all. It merely explained why the sight of mortality distressed you. I'm sure you'll get used to dealing with blood and body parts in the BPP.'

'What are you suggesting?'

'I think you know.'

'The BPP treats people with courtesy and kindness. Herr Heydrich insists it be so. He wishes the Gestapo and the BPP to win the respect of the German people.'

'I'm sure the German people will be delighted to hear it.'

'You are mocking me now, Herr Wolff, and by extension you are mocking Reinhard Heydrich. But you must realise that one day the tables will be turned.'

'And you must realise that your pathetic attempts at intimidation mean nothing to me, Winter. Let me remind you, this investigation is being carried out on the specific orders of the Führer and I am your senior officer.'

'Of course, Herr Inspector Wolff. I understand entirely. But please carry on, about the war. I would very much like to hear of your experiences.'

'Did you ever read Remarque? *All Quiet on the Western Front?*'

'You know that's not allowed.'

'But it wasn't always so. Maybe you can't read, or perhaps you read it before 1933 in the days when it was readily available and even lauded.'

Winter shifted uncomfortably in his seat.

'You can tell me, Sergeant – it'll be our secret. I won't rat on you.'

'You disgust me, Wolff.'

'*Herr* Wolff, and I'll take that as a yes, in which case you know what the war was like, for Remarque was there and was badly wounded fighting for Germany and he told the truth.'

'He is a traitor. A pacifist. A defeatist. Our youth should be reading Beumbelburg for an accurate description of comradeship in war.'

'Then I must be wrong, so I'm sure you'll put my words in your report to Meisinger and Heydrich. That should get me locked up, eh?'

'Were you in the infantry, Herr Wolff?'

'It's no business of yours but, yes, I was in the front line.'

'And did you kill anyone?'

What a question! 'If I did, it would not be something I would ever mention, let alone boast about. We did what we had to do, that's all. Many of us did not come home. Many friends of mine. And I pray we never have to do such things again.'

Had he killed someone? Of course he had. He was a machine-gunner; how could he not have killed? In one single day in the last weeks of the war, he slaughtered and wounded countless British soldiers, perhaps hundreds. They just kept coming, wave after wave, and he just kept cutting them down. The gun ran so hot that steam scorched off it as bucket after bucket of water was poured over it in a vain attempt to cool it. And there were other days, too. Other slaughters.

Kill or be killed. In late 1918, he was eighteen years old and already a father. A father and a mass killer. But these were matters for his own haunted nights, not for discussion with Hans Winter or anyone else.

The Haus Gertrud hostel was only five minutes' drive south of the baroness's house. It occurred to Seb that it was well past lunchtime, but perhaps meals were not permitted while working on this case. So far he had no clues and no suspect. He still had no idea where she had gone – or with whom – when she left the Regensdorfs' house on the night of her death. So how could such a puzzle be resolved in a day or two?

He parked the Lancia directly outside the house of the old apartment block that now housed the student hostel. The victim's friend, Unity Mitford, was not there. She had a room in the building, but she was out and no one knew where she had gone.

'Probably with darling Adolf, sipping tea and eating cake with pink icing,' a young Englishwoman said, collapsing in giggles as she spoke. 'Anyway, why do you want the bloody Valkyrie?'

Seb was doing the talking while Winter skulked at his side, clearly unable to comprehend a word of the conversation because it was conducted in English. The BPP man looked very unhappy.

There was every chance the other young women in this hostel, not just Unity, had known the victim and so they had to be approached. They were in the large and rather messy common room on the ground floor. One young woman was at a table with a pile of texts, writing in an exercise book. Another pair were playing cards, Skat by the look of it. Seb had broken into their game.

'Because she was said to be a friend of Miss Rosie Palmer,' Seb replied. 'Anyway, why do you call her that – Valkyrie?'

'Because she looks like one and because it's her middle name.' The English girl gasped. 'Oh gosh, you're investigating the awful murder!'

Suddenly all eyes in the room were on the two police officers.

'Did you know Miss Palmer?' Seb asked.

'I met her, but we weren't friends. She and Unity were almost inseparable though. They went everywhere together when she wasn't with the Führer. Actually, she introduced Rosie to him in the Cafe Heck. Rosie was glowing that day.'

Could it be true that she had met Hitler? That was all Seb needed. As if this investigation wasn't difficult enough as it was. Why hadn't Hanfstaengl and Ruff mentioned it? Perhaps they didn't know.

'Can I have *your* name, please, miss?'

'Me? Why would you want my name?'

'Regular police procedure. We need to talk with everyone who knew Miss Palmer.'

'Goodall. Clarice Goodall.'

He turned to her card partner, who seemed rather less forth-coming. 'And you, miss?'

'Becky Waverley-Jones.'

'And you're evidently both English?'

They nodded. 'We all are,' Clarice said. 'All of us here at Haus Gertrud. Actually, there was an American girl a short while back, but she's gone home now.' Her voice lowered. 'She was Jewish, so it was all getting a bit awkward with Bobo.'

'Bobo? What's that?'

'Oh, that's Unity Mitford's family nickname. I'm not sure she likes us using it, but all the more reason to do so. Valkyrie, Bobo, Unity – all the same person. Actually, we don't really have too much to do with her. She doesn't like us very much because we're not signed-up Nazis. And we all think she looks ridiculous when she goes out in those black shirts and black gauntlets she some-times wears. Only trying to shock people, of course. But she has a mean streak and she's a frightful bully. She was really hideous to Ruth – that was the American Jewish girl. I do believe that if it were in her power, she would have had her locked up in that concentration camp. In fact I think she'd put all of us in there if she could.'

'I presume she'll be back this evening, Miss Goodall?'

'Who knows? She doesn't always come home. And she has her SS man in her room here sometimes. Bobo's a naughty girl – a very naughty Nazi.' She grinned.

'Do you have a name for the SS man?'

'Fritz.'

'Just Fritz?'

'I'm not sure. Manning or something similar. No, Mannheim. That's it – Fritz Mannheim. Bobo says he's a junior adjutant in the Hitler bodyguard, but who knows? I'm never quite certain whether to believe a word she says.'

'Can you tell me a bit about him?' Seb was still addressing Clarice, but he had one surreptitious eye on Winter and he had noticed him react to the name Fritz Mannheim. The name meant something to him.

'Well, unusually for one of the SS Übermenschen, he wears glasses,' Clarice said. 'But despite that, he's quite handsome and about the same height as Bobo. You probably know that she's about six feet tall. I'm not sure what that is in metres, I'm afraid.'

'When did you last see Herr Mannheim?'

'A few days ago.'

'Thank you, Miss Goodall. I may well be back.' He turned to Winter and reverted to German. 'I think we're done here, Sergeant.'

On the way out, they were waylaid by the other girl from the room, the studious one with the pile of books on her table. She was tiny, with a blonde bob and intelligent eyes.

'Can I help you, miss?'

She replied to him in perfect German. 'I heard your conversation with Clarice. You know you shouldn't listen to a word she says. Bobo's really very sweet and some of the other girls are jealous of her.'

'Why jealous?'

'Tea and cakes with the Führer!' She switched to English. 'Who wouldn't just die for such an experience? As for Fritz Mannheim, I don't believe for a moment that there's anything untoward going on between them. Bobo really isn't like that.'

'What is your name?'

'Frances de Pole.'

'And are you German or English?'

'Both. My father's English, my mother's German and I have French ancestry. A bit of a mongrel, you might say. I knew Rosie . . .'

'You heard she was dead?'

'Of course. The rumour is she was murdered. Who killed her?'

'I'm afraid I can't answer your questions except to say that we are investigating the circumstances surrounding the incident. She died the day before yesterday. It's thought it might have been around midnight, but that's not certain. Did you see her that evening?'

'No, which surprised me a little. We were at the Hofbräuhaus and we were sure she'd turn up with Bobo.'

'We? You and who else?'

'Three girlfriends and half a dozen SS boys.'

'Did Unity Mitford come?'

Frances de Pole shook her head. 'She probably had another engagement – opera with Adolf, perhaps. She sees so much of him, I can almost believe they'll get married. That's what people are saying, that she wants to snare her very own dictator. Isn't that mad? I'm pretty sure Bobo would have him like a shot if he asked her. Her room is a shrine to him. Mind you, she's also a very jealous person.'

'Go on.'

'Well, she hates it that anyone else knows any of the big names in Munich. She glares at me whenever I mention Maria Regensdorf, for instance. Bobo wants all the Nazi glamour and kudos for herself.'

'So you know the Regensdorfs?'

'Well, yes. My mama is German and is a distant cousin of Maria. It was hoped at one stage that I might lodge with them in Karolinenplatz, but Rosie got in before me. They only wanted the one student, you see.'

'You mentioned Miss Mitford's room. I would like to see it.'

'Well, I'm sure that's not allowed but we could take a little peek, I suppose. It's right next to mine.'

They went up two floors with Winter trailing in their wake. He had no idea what was going on and Seb had no intention of telling him.

Unity Mitford's room was a small temple dedicated to the Führer. There were three pictures: one large one on the wall and two smaller ones in frames on the bedside table and the little dressing table. The picture on the wall was positioned between two ceiling-to-floor swastika pennants.

The room was rather cramped with a suitcase on top of the narrow wardrobe and a bed that was obviously used as a sofa in the daytime. It all stank of some overpowering floral scent that contrasted alarmingly with the adornments, which included a cage on the sideboard with a rodent inside.

'That's Ratular,' Frances de Pole said with a smile. 'She has a pet snake, too, but I don't know where it is so perhaps it's died.

I really hope so because I don't want the horrible thing sliding into my bed in the middle of the night.'

'Well, I suppose she'll have to be back sometime soon to feed Ratular.'

'Oh, I am sure she will.'

Seb gave the young woman his Ettstrasse number. 'Get her to call me when she arrives, if you would.'

'Of course.' Frances began to laugh. 'Do you know, I really think her feelings for Adolf are like some sort of religious devotion. She's got a bad case of love, I'm afraid, and the object of her affection *isn't* Fritz Mannheim. If you must know, I rather think Fritz had more of an eye for Rosie. And vice versa. She was an awful lot more sexy than Bobo.'

'No one else in Rosie's life?'

'Adam Rock, I suppose. The most handsome and self-satisfied of the public schoolboys presently here in Munich. So pleased with himself and critical of others that he's actually rather dull.'

'Was there a romantic attachment between them?'

'Rosie and Adam Rock? No, I'm sure he'd have been far too busy admiring himself in the mirror or cruising along in his big flashy car to be gazing at her. But they did spend quite a lot of time together.'

'Do you know where he lives?'

'Oh somewhere over the river. Altbogenhausen, I think. He has a very good allowance.'

Interesting, thought Seb. Altbogenhausen was one of the most exclusive and expensive parts of Munich. It also just happened to be a short distance from the place where Rosie's corpse was found.

'And you, Inspector, what do you do in your spare time?'

'In what way?'

'I mean, wouldn't you like to ask a girl out for drinkies or dinner . . . and perhaps a little nightcap later?'

'I'm flattered by the suggestion, Miss de Pole, but I'm afraid I've got a girlfriend.'

'And your point is?'

CHAPTER 9

Seb wasn't usually given to panic. After fighting on the Western Front and somehow surviving, he made a conscious decision that he would never surrender to fear again. You either lived or you died, and when shells were raining down by the thousand, you really didn't have much say in the matter. Death was random. Courage or cunning wouldn't save you, and nor would fear.

But this impossible case was something else. The investigation was going nowhere. They hadn't even found Rosie Palmer's best friend and the only clue – if it could be described as such – was the presence of unidentified markings on the corpse.

Perhaps he should go along to the Führer's apartment at No 16 Prinzregentenplatz, knock on the door and ask if he could speak to Herr Hitler. 'Oh, hello, boss, I'm looking for a friend of yours, the Honourable Miss Unity Mitford, often known as Bobo. Sorry to interrupt your tea and cakes, but we were hoping she might help us find her friend's killer. Is she here?' Not funny. In the Third Reich, men could be locked up or shot merely for *thinking* such heresy.

'What now, Herr Wolff?' Winter said. 'I take it that as the most celebrated murder detective in Munich you have a plan.'

'Do you know Fritz Mannheim?'

He hesitated, then nodded. 'Yes, I do.'

'Where is he based?'

'Karlstrasse 10. SS central office.'

'Of course. Well, it's on our way. What luck. Perhaps we should go and talk to him?'

'Why would he speak to you?'

'Because he is a friend of Unity Mitford and he is an adjutant in the Leibstandardte-SS Adolf Hitler. And as you know, the Führer wishes this case to be cleared up expeditiously. Surely Mannheim would be delighted to offer all the help he can.'

'Very well. We can see if he's there.'

'I've had another thought. You go alone and talk to him, Winter. It's a simple enough task. All you need to do is ask him if he has any idea where we might find his friend Miss Unity Mitford – also whether he ever met the deceased and, if so, if he has any theories and whether he saw her on the night she died. Meanwhile, I can go and make my report to Herr Hanfstaengl.'

'My orders are to stay with you.'

'And my orders are to clear up a murder case, and you are my assistant. I have decided that we will make the best use of our time by going our separate ways for a couple of hours. So just do as I say, and make yourself useful. Who knows, I might make a homicide cop out of you yet. We will meet at Ettstrasse at eight tomorrow morning.'

'I think we should meet before then.'

'No, we're better going our own ways for a while, widening the search. If you find out anything, leave a message for me – either at the presidium or on my home number, which you have. If I'm not there, ask to speak to my mother, Frau Wolff, and she will take a message for me.'

Seb brought the car to halt, leant over and opened passenger door. Reluctantly, Sergeant Winter slid out. Seb threw up his arm. 'Heil Hitler, Sergeant Winter.'

It wasn't on his way, but before going to Putzi Hanfstaengl's office in the Brown House, he had another plan. He wanted to speak alone with the British consul-general.

Donald Gainer was easy to find. He was in his office at the superb building that housed His Majesty's outpost on Prannerstrasse, not far from police headquarters in the old part of town. The consul-general's secretary showed Seb straight through into his office on the first floor.

'Good afternoon, Inspector Wolff. How are your inquiries proceeding?'

'Not as fast as I would wish, sir. I am having trouble working out the movements of Miss Palmer in the hours before her death. My understanding is that she would be meeting up with some other young people at the Hofbräuhaus but she never arrived. I have to be honest with you, sir, I am struggling to make progress.'

'I'm sorry to hear that. Tell me, Herr Wolff, am I correct in thinking that you are not yourself a paid-up Nazi?'

The question floored Seb. At first he didn't reply.

'I only ask because of the difficult diplomatic connotations of this case. Such things must be putting you under a great deal of pressure.'

Seb tried to phrase his response carefully. 'If you mean that I have not yet been accepted as a party member, then that is true.'

'Then you have applied to join?'

'That is not something I can discuss. But you must understand that there is a long waiting list and new membership has been suspended these past few months.' He had to steer this conversation back to the questions he needed answered. 'I am here because I was hoping you might have information regarding the English community in Munich. In particular, I wish to speak to Miss Mitford, for it was said she was Miss Palmer's best friend here. She above all might know of Miss Palmer's movements.'

Gainer sighed and indicated Seb to sit down on a sofa by the large window. 'Would you like some coffee, Inspector Wolff? I certainly would.'

'Thank you, that's most kind.'

Gainer pressed a button on his desk and his secretary appeared within moments. 'Coffee for two, please, Joan.' He turned to Seb. 'Milk? Cream?'

'Black, please. No sugar.'

'Likewise.'

After the secretary had gone, Gainer smiled at his guest. 'You seem like a reasonable fellow, Wolff. As a non-party member, I imagine you're not Gestapo.'

'These are very personal questions, sir, but you are correct – I am a regular criminal detective. Anyway, there are no Gestapo in Munich.'

'Ah yes, you call them the Bavarian Political Police here. Well, I suppose that will change in due course. Everything is becoming centralised in the new Germany. The point is, can we talk openly?'

Once again, Seb wasn't sure how to respond. What was Gainer suggesting?

'I'm sorry, that was rather clumsy of me,' the consul-general continued. 'I'm not suggesting that you say anything indiscreet. I merely wanted to discuss the way things are in Munich in 1935 without reference to politics.'

'That is fine by me, sir.'

'Good, good. The thing is, my job has become a bit of a trial lately with all these young British people arriving here. Particularly the girls. They're let loose from parental and school control and they go wild. Damn it, there have never been so many complaints of drunkenness, brawling, insulting Nazi officials and all the usual stolen purses, lost passports and unhappy landladies. And on top of that I've had to deal with the fallout from two pregnancies in the first six months of this year alone.'

'As you say, sir, a bit of a trial.' A trial he could easily identify with, having been the wild youth himself at the time of Jurgen's conception. A picture of Ulrike flashed across his mind as it did every day and many nights. God, she was beautiful. He hadn't seen her in sixteen years since Jurgen was a baby, but he could imagine that she would still be as stunning as the day he met her in that bar in Schwabing.

'Has a young man called Adam Rock ever crossed your path, sir? I'm told he knew Rosie quite well.'

'Yes, I've met Adam. He brought a letter from his father asking me to look out for the boy when he arrived last year. Shropshire people, I seem to recall, father's a rather successful lawyer and was keen that his son should soak up German culture. Since then I've heard nothing so I have assumed all has been going well for the young man.'

'Would you have an address for him?'

'Of course. I'll look it up for you before you go.' He sighed heavily. 'You know, Wolff, the fact is I rather feared something ghastly like this might happen one day.'

Once again Seb was almost lost for words. 'Something like what, sir? You don't mean you thought one of the young English girls would get killed?'

'That was my terror, yes. I had a horrible premonition that something awful might occur. I suppose it goes with the territory of being a consul – prepare for the worst so that you can advise your nationals and protect them. It seems I failed on that score.'

'I really don't see how you can blame yourself, sir. The only culprit is the murderer. Do you have any thoughts on that score, any suspicions?'

'I'm afraid not. It's this city that scares me, Inspector Wolff. Munich is the most wonderful town, my favourite in all of Europe, and the National Socialists have brought peace to the streets. And yet . . . and yet below the surface I sense a terrible undertow of violence. Do you not feel it?'

'I won't say a word against my city or my country, Mr Gainer.'

'No, of course you won't. My country right or wrong, as an American once said. What I mean is, it's all this pagan stuff. Munich has some of the most beautiful churches in the world and a fine history of Christendom, but the pagans are winning, and their ways are not ways of kindness and love. I sometimes fear that Germany is in the process of renouncing two thousand years of Christian civilisation. Am I alone in this? Do the ordinary German people not feel it?'

This was all too much for Seb. He was well aware that this room might be bugged by Heydrich's crew. He would have to report this meeting to the Wittelsbach Palace or be damned for not doing so.

Why, in the name of God, was Gainer talking to him like this? Was it because they were conversing in English? Did he perhaps believe that his experience of the English had made him think like them? Gainer might not understand, but this was dangerous. Seb had to regain focus.

'I'm under immense pressure to solve this crime, Mr Gainer, so any thoughts you might have could be invaluable. That's why

I have come here. You obviously know Miss Mitford, for it seems everyone does. She has gained a little bit of fame for herself both here in Germany and in England, I believe. If I could only get to her, this might be cleared up in a moment.'

'Well, I know she spends a great deal of time with the Führer and she does come here from time to time. But not in the past few days – so that's not much help. No, I really don't have a clue where she might be. But I am hoping that you and I will get together again tomorrow because Rosie's brother has arrived and there is to be another meeting at the Brown House, ten o'clock. Perhaps Putzi Hanfstaengl has already told you. Anyway, with luck, Unity Mitford will have turned up before then.'

'We must hope so.'

'And I am truly sorry if I have embarrassed you, Inspector Wolff. But you see I am trying to understand the new Germany, so it is always helpful to talk with the less-political Germans. The people in the middle, if you like.'

Seb nodded. He would very much like to be able to talk to this man honestly, for he recognised a kindred spirit when he met one. But he couldn't speak openly. No one could in Munich in 1935, not even at home in their own kitchen, with their own son.

He downed his coffee and took his leave of the British consul-general. It had been an interesting conversation, particularly being told about the difficulties he faced with the wild antics of the young Britons. And at least he had the address for this boy Adam Rock in Altbogenhausen. But apart from that, Seb wasn't sure that he was any the wiser.

He decided against calling in at the Brown House because it now seemed he would be going there in the morning anyway. Instead, he stopped for some more coffee and some much needed cake at the Hofgarten Cafe. His peace was quickly disturbed as a young man came and sat opposite him at the small round table.

'Good afternoon, Detective Inspector.'

'Did I invite you to join me here, Pope?'

Ernie Pope shrugged. 'It's a free country . . . isn't it?'

Was that supposed to be a joke? Of course it was. Seb merely smiled.

Pope was an American reporter who wrote for London newspapers. He had arrived from Berlin earlier in the year and had quickly made his presence felt. 'A little bird told me you were investigating a rather important case, Detective.'

'A little bird, eh? A crow? A vulture? What sort of bird – does it have a name?'

'No names, Seb. You know me better than that. I always protect my sources.'

Seb cut a slice of his apple cake and slipped it into his mouth. Ernie Pope was onto the story, but the order had been clear: stay away from the foreign press. The thing about Ernie Pope, though, was that he had good contacts in all sections of Munich society and he could be useful.

'I have an idea what you're after, Ernie, but it's more than my life's worth to help you on this one. Maybe you could help me, though. I'm looking for the girl with fat fingers.'

'What would I get in return?'

'Something down the line. A favour owed. Just not this case.'

'But this is the big one. This is the one I want – the one my London and New York editors are screaming for.'

'Do you want to put me in Dachau?'

Ernie grinned. He was a tall, slender guy with an easy manner. 'My little bird told me you'd already been there. Now what was that all about?'

'Oh, a simple misunderstanding. Nothing newsworthy.'

'Well, I'm glad you're out, Seb. I've taken the sanitised press tour of the place and I wouldn't wish a spell there on anyone. Can I buy you another coffee?'

'That's a kind offer, Ernie, but I've got to get back to Ettstrasse.'

'OK, I'll keep my eyes and ears peeled for Bobo.'

Back at the Police Presidium, Seb changed his mind again and put a call through to Hanfstaengl's office, merely to say that he had nothing to report but that investigations were proceeding as planned and he anticipated news soon. It was a lie, but he knew that Hanfstaengl would rather have a lie to report onwards than nothing at all. He also told him that he had got the message about the meeting in the morning.

He then called in to see his chief, Deputy President Thomas Ruff, who was agitated, pacing his office like a wound-up tom in a cage.

'You're getting nowhere and I'm getting it in the neck, Wolff.'

'I'm sorry to hear that, sir.'

'Calls every half-hour from every direction, all demanding updates. Have we caught the killer yet? If not, why not? Heydrich, Himmler, Hanfstaengl, Hitler's office – they're all demanding answers yesterday. Get on with it, they say. Have you got the right man on the case? they say. God in heaven, Wolff, we'll both be in Dachau or worse if you don't clear this up soon. Where are we?'

'Looking for the dead girl's best friend, Miss Unity Mitford. We have to know Miss Palmer's movements in the last hours of her life and Mitford is our best hope.'

'Unity Mitford. Why have I heard of her?'

'She's become friendly with the Führer.'

'God in heaven, and now she's missing, you say.' The blood drained from Ruff's face. 'You don't think ... you don't think she's been killed too?'

Seb shook his head. 'No, I have no reason to think that. Now if you'll excuse me, sir, I have a couple of phone calls to make.'

'Yes, yes, get on with it, Wolff. Don't waste a minute.' He tossed across a brown envelope. 'These are for you – pictures of the deceased. I also had a call from Herr Professor Lindner; no evidence of internal injuries or toxic substances. Cause of death was blood loss through severance of the carotid and jugular.'

Picking up the envelope, Seb nodded, dispensed with the Hitler salute and returned to his desk, where he put a call through to the Solln home of Hanfstaengl's sister Erna using the number the baroness had given him. No, was the brusque response, Miss Mitford was not there though some of her belongings were. No one had any idea where she might be at present. And no, she was certainly not at their home in Uffing. No one was there at the moment save the housekeeper.

He slid the photographs from the envelope. Three of them – one showing the body unopened the way he had seen it in the mortuary, another with the blood cleaned off, showing the cuts and lipstick marks more clearly and the third with the chest opened up revealing the internal organs.

For a few moments, he simply gazed upon the images of the dead flesh with utter desolation and wondered why he even did this job. The way he had talked to Winter he probably gave the impression that he was used to death and mutilation, that the war had made him so callous and indifferent to mortality that it had all become meaningless and had no effect on him.

That was the opposite of the truth. The fact that he was not squeamish did not mean he was not profoundly affected by what he saw.

Once again he reminded himself of why this work mattered so much to him: because he had seen so many innocent lives cut down, indeed had killed so many himself. This was a vain attempt at atonement, some small way to bring justice to the innocents and perhaps redeem himself, if only in part.

He gazed at the cuts on the body, the horizontals and the verticals, the spiral of lipstick on the abdomen clearer now, though smudged, still livid even though the pictures were monochrome. Did these obscene marks mean anything or were they merely the random slashings and scribblings of a diseased mind? Winter had said instantly that they were Hebrew script. Well, that had to be checked, of course, but Seb was far from convinced. The truth was, he had no idea and he didn't really think that Winter had either. But he knew someone who might.

He pushed the pictures back into the envelope and stepped out into the warm air of a late afternoon in June.

It was not a long walk to the Bavarian State Library on Ludwigstrasse, an institution that had been collecting great and not so great volumes of work for over three hundred and fifty years. It was now, perhaps, the most important research facility in Germany and a magnet for remarkable minds, so long as they were of the required racial background. A sign over the front entrance told Jews that they weren't welcome.

As a self-taught man, Seb had always loved coming here to discover the wonders of a world that he had not encountered in his fractured childhood and teen years when he failed his exams and went to war rather than university. Today, he merely wanted to visit an old friend, Caius Klammer.

He found him in his remote and modest office, deep in the heart of the building. He was poring over a book. Klammer looked up, peering over his half-moon spectacles. 'Seb?'

'*Grüss Gott*, Caius. Are you well?'

'Oh, you know, trying to survive. Like everyone else. And you? How is my favourite autodidact?'

'Not so bad – and before I met you I didn't even know that word.'

'Still reading avidly?'

'Of course, but these days one must be careful to read only the correct books.'

Klammer allowed himself a nervous smile. He was a small pale man, mid-fifties, with narrow shoulders and a permanently worried expression. His whole life had been books.

'What are you perusing today, Caius? It looks old.'

'Very old, but newly acquired by us. It's a sort of ledger – a fourteenth-century book of accounts from one of the Hanseatic League outposts. Sounds dull, but it's remarkable what you can learn from such things. Anyway, what brings you here, Seb?'

'I have a favour to ask. How is your stomach? I have some rather unpleasant photographs of a murder victim for you to look at. There are strange markings.'

'For you, Seb, I will take the risk.'

He handed over two of the pictures, not the one showing the opened-up chest; there would have been no point to that. 'The thicker marks are made with lipstick, the others are cuts. What I need to know is whether they are telling us something.'

Klammer smoothed out the large-scale pictures on his table and examined them carefully. He reached for a magnifying glass and took some time looking at each of the marks individually Then he sat back in his chair, grimaced and closed his eyes.

'Well?'

'I'm sorry, but there's nothing obvious. Could I have a little more time?'

'Hebrew possibly?'

'Definitely not. I know Hebrew as well as any rabbi, and this is not Hebrew. I'm not even sure it's a regular script – just the manifestation of rage you mentioned.'

'All right, Caius. Keep the pictures until tomorrow, but keep them safe because I'll need them back.'

'I heard that a girl was found dead in the English Garden, not more than a few hundred metres from this office. Is that her in the pictures?'

Seb nodded. 'I'm afraid so. Actually, it was on the far bank of the river in Herzogpark. An English girl name Rosie Palmer, and it's very sensitive with political connotations. So say nothing to anyone. Don't show these pictures around.'

'Are you trying to scare me? Because you're succeeding.'

'Just being honest. Look, I've come to you because you're almost certainly the best man on rare and obsolete languages and scripts in Munich, perhaps in the whole of Germany, so if you don't know, then I'm pretty sure no one else will either. Understood?'

'Of course.'

'And you be careful, Caius. It's a dangerous world out there for people of your persuasion.'

'My persuasion?'

'Just take care.'

CHAPTER 10

The Schelling-Salon taproom and restaurant on Schellingstrasse was crowded and noisy, but Seb saw Hexie straightaway. She was at the bar beyond the billiard tables with a half-litre of her favourite wheat beer in her hand. She waved to him and gave him her beautiful smile as he wove his way through the throng of early evening drinkers.

'Seb, my darling, you look as though you need a beer very badly.'

'I was just diving in to say hello. Life is a bit frantic.'

'And look who's here.'

His eyes drifted past her and there was the enormous shape of his best friend in the whole world. His schoolfriend, his war comrade. The one man he could trust above all others. Suddenly, if only momentarily, the day looked brighter. 'Max! Max Haas, what are you doing in Munich?'

'Drinking, of course. What else would I be doing in the city of beer?'

'Seriously, Max. It must be five hundred kilometres from Dortmund. Have you come home?'

'No, no, I'm committed to Dortmund. The good wife insists because her family is there – and you know how she rules me. Actually, I'm here because two Bolsheviks needed a lift to Dachau and I, of course, obliged, because I'm an obliging sort of fellow. If you must know, I volunteered so I could stay overnight and see you and your beautiful girl.'

'Well, this calls for drinks, but I can't stay long.'

'Already ordered for you, my friend.'

'And what, pray, had your two commies done to warrant a relaxing holiday in Dachau?'

Max laughed out loud. 'Since when did a Gestapo officer need an excuse to put a Red in a concentration camp? If you must know, they had plans to rob a bank, but we nipped that in the bud. Funny how they want to redistribute wealth, but only if it's distributed to them.'

Seb was puzzled. 'But bank robbery is not a political crime. Why were they not simply put in jail?'

'The idiot jury found them not guilty. Perhaps not idiotic – perhaps the jury were Reds, too. Plenty of them in Dortmund.'

Seb raised an eyebrow.

'Come on, Seb. You know what juries are like. These guys were armed and guilty as hell – no one would want them back on the streets.'

In all their years together, first as neighbours and schoolmates in Munich and later in the same unit on the Western Front, Seb and Max had never had an argument. But that didn't mean Seb was happy when his friend accepted a post as an officer in the Dortmund Gestapo bureau. His feelings were conflicted, and so he avoided thinking about it. Nor would he say anything, because it was Max's choice. Anyway, perhaps he could use his influence to civilise those around him; Max might never walk away from a fight but unprovoked brutality was not in his nature.

Seb turned his attention back to Hexie and put an arm around her shoulders and accepted a kiss. 'Is that it then?' he said when their mouths parted. 'Is that all I get for my birthday, a beery kiss?'

'Your present would have appeared as if by magic on the banks of the Starnbergersee, but you insisted on irritating that BPP snake. No matter, I've still got it, tucked away about my person. You can unwrap it in my bedroom later.'

She really was a remarkably sexy girl. The British seamen aboard the *Eastern Star* would have called her Sexy Hexie, had they known her. Perhaps *girl* was the wrong word since she was now in her twenty-eighth year. She deserved the honour of being called a woman. If a *fräulein* wasn't married by that age, it was only fit and proper to do her the honour of addressing her as *frau*.

What made Hexie different in Seb's eyes was that he liked her company as well as her body. He liked waking up with her, not just taking her to bed. Perhaps Uncle Christian was right – perhaps he should marry Frau Hexie Schuler. Her short summer skirts and dresses, her long tanned legs, her soft rounded breasts, all ripe for childbearing. Seb doubted she'd wait long if he dithered.

He raised an eyebrow. 'Sounds good. I can hardly wait to see my surprise. For the moment, though, I'll join you both in a beer.'

A litre stein had already been drawn for him, along with glasses of schnapps for all three of them. For the next hour, they drank beer and schnapps, ate sausages and pickled cabbage, shared jokes and gossip, much of it in whispers about Hexie's colleague Evie Braun and her affair with Adolf.

'You really think they're shagging?' Max asked, astonished.

'I can't imagine it, but who knows? What do you think?'

'I don't know. No word of this woman has even reached Dortmund. How old is she?'

'Twenty-three.'

'And you say she tried to kill herself?'

Hexie put a finger to her lips. 'Ssh, that really is top secret. Henriette von Schirach – the boss's daughter – told me. We'll all be shot if it gets out.'

'How?'

'How what?'

'How did she try to kill herself. Gun or rope?'

'Overdose of sleeping tablets, just a couple of weeks ago. Twenty-four Phanodorm to be precise. Poor thing. Such a nice girl – I really like her – but she's awfully dim. Not a political bone in her body. God, though, Max, please don't mention a word about this. I'm really not supposed to know. No one is.'

'What do you think she sees in him?'

Hexie gave him a look of derision. 'Do you really know nothing about women, Max? How on earth did you ever end up married?'

This large, untidy drinking hole was like a non-political oasis in one of the most political parts of Munich. The Osteria Bavaria, Herr Hitler's favourite restaurant, was here on Schellingstrasse, just a few doors down, so was the vast frontage of the *Völkischer Beobachter*, official news sheet of the Nazi Party. The Hoffmann photo studio owned by the Führer's lap dog, Heinrich Hoffmann – and where Hexie worked – was a few doors away. And not far to the south, the whole National Socialist apparatus – the Brown

House, the building site known as the Führerbau and all the offices of party and state.

But no one cared about any of that in the Schelling-Salon. Yes, the SS guys and the Nazi high-ups sometimes came in here for a drink, but so did the artists and writers. Here the talk was about art, theatre, literature. Goose-stepping hordes were figures of fun and tongues were loose; sometimes dangerously so.

And yet still the bar survived and no one was quite sure how.

A band started playing and people danced. Seb had drunk a litre of beer and three or four glasses of schnapps, but he was cold sober. This should have been the best birthday celebration ever; Hexie was here and so was Max, but he, Seb, was elsewhere. In a white laboratory, on the banks of the river, in the Brown House, on the parade ground at Dachau, in deep trouble.

'Did Hexie tell you I had a night in the luxurious Hotel Dachau, courtesy of the Bavarian Political Police, Max?' He had to raise his voice above the din.

Max nodded. He was tall and broad. A lumbering bear. He liked his bratwurst, he liked his pork knuckle. He could eat a double helping of *kaiserschmarrn* pancakes with extra sugar at one sitting. 'She told me.'

'I bet she didn't tell you that the BPP sergeant who was responsible for booking me in has now been allocated as my investigating partner. His name's Winter, and he's well named because he's a cold bastard.'

'Winter? Not Hans Winter by any chance?'

'The very same. But why would you know his name?'

'Because he was in the Gestapo in Dortmund. And then he got transferred here.'

'Really? Why?'

'I've no idea, Seb. They just said family reasons, but it was all a bit sudden. He's a slimy swine. Licks the arses of the chiefs and reviles the rest. No one likes him.'

'He's quite young and inexperienced to have made sergeant.'

'Young and inexperienced are kind words. I would restrict myself to one: useless.'

'Well, I'm stuck with him and he's not going to rest until he's had me thrown me back in Dachau or put a bullet in my head in Perlacher Forest.'

At midnight, Seb said he was going home. He had to be up early and he'd need a clear head in the morning.

'So, not tonight then, Seb?' Hexie adopted a pout. 'You've had your way with me and now you're casting me away like yesterday's milk.'

Their eyes met and they were smiling. 'I'll make it up to you. I promise.' He held her tight, then turned to Max and they wrapped their arms around each other. 'I wish I could spend more time with you, Max, but this is serious. To be honest, I shouldn't have been here this evening.'

'I understand. Of course, I've no idea what you're investigating, but I can tell it's a tough one.'

When he arrived home, far later than planned, he noted the open-topped Mercedes on the street outside the front door. No one in Ainmüllerstrasse owned a black Mercedes.

A uniformed SS officer was in the front seat. In the back seat, her eyes straight ahead and unblinking, sat Unity 'Bobo' Mitford.

CHAPTER 11

Unity Mitford turned and gazed at Seb as though he were some sort of insect to be either examined under a microscope or squashed.

And then her right arm shot out. 'Heil Hitler,' she said, a great deal too loudly.

Seb thrust out his own arm. 'Heil Hitler,' he said, with what he hoped sounded like conviction.

'Are you Inspector Wolff?' she said in halting but serviceable German.

'I am. And you are Miss Unity Mitford, I believe?'

'I heard you were looking for me, Herr Inspector.'

'Indeed, miss. Perhaps we could talk.'

'Get in the car and we'll go for a little drive.'

Seb wanted sleep. He also had to speak with this dull-eyed woman, but preferably at his office at Ettstrasse, not in the back of a car driven by an SS officer, going on a mystery tour of Munich. What option did he have, though? In the circumstances, she held the whip hand. He needed her evidence and he could not afford to have her disappear.

Opening the car, he climbed in beside her and noticed that she wasn't wearing her famous black shirt, but a white blouse and a lightweight powder-blue cardigan. Nor was she wearing her gauntlets.

'I take it you know what I want to talk about, Miss Mitford?' he said in English.

'I'd rather speak German, Herr Wolff. And yes, I know perfectly well what you wish to talk about – the murder of Rosie Palmer.'

'She was a very good friend of yours, I believe.'

'Yes, she was the very best of friends and she was beautiful and her death is a terrible outrage. And we all know who to blame, don't we?'

'Do we? I'm afraid my investigations have not got as far as I would have liked, which is why I was so keen to talk to you. The last time she was seen was about nine o'clock in the evening the day before last, in the hall of the Regensdorfs' house at Karolinen-platz. It was thought possible – likely even – that she was going out to meet you.'

She leant over and tapped the SS man's shoulder. He had shiny, neatly combed dark hair and even in this low light his uniform appeared immaculate. 'Drive on, Fritz. You know where to go.'

Was that Fritz Mannheim at the wheel, the one said to be Unity's boyfriend? Yes, of course it was, because he was wearing spectacles as Seb had been informed by the English girl Clarice Goodall at the student hotel. As she had pointed out, very few of the SS supermen wore glasses. Seb supposed that Sergeant Winter must have located him and passed on the message.

Mannheim engaged gear and set off northwards into the suburbs of Munich.

'Rosie was going to meet me at the Schneider,' Unity said. 'We were going to have a quick *leberknödel*, then join some other friends at the Hofbräuhaus, but Rosie didn't show up.'

'You didn't go on to the Hofbräuhaus?'

'No, I met some storms and they took me to their secret club next to the House of Artists on Lenbachplatz. What was it called, Fritz?'

'Valhalla.'

'It was wild. Anyway, I never saw Rosie. Clearly, she must have been abducted and murdered somewhere between Karolinenplatz and the Schneider on Tal, which is no more than a twenty-minute walk across the old town. Perhaps she was forced into a car.'

The Mercedes drew to a halt on an anonymous street in the northern part of the suburb of Schwabing, no more than a kilo-metre from Seb's home on Ainmüllerstrasse.

'Here we are,' Unity said. She indicated an apartment block. 'If he's at home, your killer is in there, on the third floor. His name is Karl Friedlander. You can arrest him right now – you and Fritz together. Hopefully, he'll resist arrest and you can shoot him.'

This was ridiculous. How could she possibly know the identity of the killer? And who exactly was Karl Friedlander? 'You'd better tell me a bit more, Miss Mitford. Who is this man and what makes you think he is the murderer?'

'He's a dirty Jew, and I don't *think* he's the murderer, I *know* he is.'

'I take it you are personally acquainted with this man?'

'Unfortunately yes, Herr Wolff, though I wish neither I nor Rosie had ever set eyes on the worm. Just the thought of him makes my flesh crawl.'

'Tell me, clearly, what makes you think he killed your friend?'

'Because he was besotted with her and she spurned him. He murdered her out of revenge. If he couldn't have her, then no one could.'

'But Miss Palmer was not meeting him on the night of her death, she was supposed to be meeting you.'

'He was obviously lying in wait for her when she left the house. He's as devious as a serpent. They all are.'

'They?'

'Jews.'

This conversation was pointless, but at least he had found Unity Mitford and if she had an idea of the potential culprit and the motive behind the killing – however tenuous the evidence – then it had to be investigated.

'Very well,' he said. 'You have not given me a lot to go on, but let's go and talk to him. If I think there is any reason to do so, I will take him back to the Police Presidium for questioning. Yes?'

She nodded her blonde Aryan head. 'We'll all go and catch the beast. Come on, Fritz. And I mean it – if he tries to escape, shoot him.'

The front door to the block was unlocked. They walked up the stairs to the third floor. There was no sound in the building, no sign of life. Seb realised that it must be well after midnight and it was a working day tomorrow. Most of Munich was asleep.

He raised his fist to rap his knuckles on the door and hesitated, reluctant to wake people on what might be no more than a whim.

Unity pushed him in the back. 'Go on, do it.'

He knocked. Nothing. Unity stepped past him and knocked harder and longer. Seb hadn't noticed that she had a pistol, a small 6.35 mm Walther customised with a nickel finish and mother-of-pearl. She had pulled it from her purse and was holding it by the barrel as she banged the butt against the solid wood, like a harsh drumbeat.

At last they heard sounds from within and then a woman's voice. 'Who is it?'

'Criminal police. Open up.'

'What do you want with us?'

'Open the door.'

Unity took hold of the door handle and tried to turn it, but it was locked.

They heard the sound of the key being turned, then the door opened. A woman in her fifties, with iron-grey tangled hair and an old dressing gown wrapped around her tiny frame, was standing there. Behind her were two men. One of them was a little older and taller than the woman and looked like the stereotype of a university science professor. Seb reasoned that he must be the husband. At his side was a good-looking young man in his early twenties with curly dark hair. He was wearing striped pyjamas and was trembling. The older pair's son, without a doubt.

Seb stepped into the room, leaving the SS officer and Unity outside. He looked at the young man. 'Are you Karl Friedlander?'

'Yes.' He nodded slowly.

'Do you know why we are here?'

'Maybe . . . I don't know . . . I'm not sure.'

'It's regarding the death of someone you know. Do you have any idea who that might be?'

'Rosie.' He lowered his eyes. His voice was choked and it seemed to Seb that he would burst into tears. 'Rosie Palmer. My beautiful Rosie. My heart is broken.'

'Did you kill her?'

He looked up. The horror in his eyes was palpable. 'Kill Rosie? Of course I didn't. Why would you think such a thing?' His gaze drifted beyond Seb to Unity and something like realisation seemed to enter his soul. 'Surely you didn't suggest such a thing, Miss Mitford?'

'Didn't I?'

'But why? You know I love her.'

'People like you are not capable of love.' She was inside the room now, walking around, examining paintings on the walls as if it was a gallery or shop, running her palms over expensive pieces of furniture. She stopped in front of a painting that Seb recognised as a Kandinsky.

'Degenerate art,' she said. 'Why am I not surprised? And how did you afford a flat like this? Who did you cheat and defraud?' She held up her hand and rubbed her fingers together like a grotesque cartoon Jew from *Der Stürmer*.

It suddenly occurred to Seb that this inquiry could not take place here, in front of the young man's bewildered parents and in the presence of Unity and her SS boyfriend. This had to be put on a regular police footing. He raised his hand. 'I think we should continue this conversation at the Police Presidium. Would you please accompany us, Herr Friedlander?'

'Am I under arrest?'

'No, but I am led to believe that you were known to the deceased and that you might have knowledge of her movements, and so I would ask you to cooperate.'

'And if I refuse?'

'I really don't think that would be wise. Much better to come in with us and answer a few questions, don't you think? If you're honest and cooperative, you should be home again in no time.'

The young man's parents hadn't said a word since Seb entered their home. They simply stood there in their sad dressing gowns, their shoulders slumped, their faces down, their bewildered terror evident. Everyone knew what a late-night or early-morning police call meant, and it was never good, especially if you were Jewish or homosexual or any of the other proscribed groups of people.

'I don't know. I need sleep . . . can I not come in the morning?'

'Herr Friedlander, reluctance to assist the police with their inquiries is never a good look. Come, sir, let us deal with this matter expeditiously.'

Friedlander's whole body was stiff and taut, but he acceded with a nod. 'Do I have to wear handcuffs?'

'No, sir, indeed not. You are coming with us voluntarily to answer a few questions, nothing more.'

Unity moved to Seb's side, her face hard and cold like a statue in marble. 'I say handcuff the swine – he'll run given half a chance. They are all the same these people.'

'I'm the officer in charge here, Miss Mitford, and my judgement is that handcuffs are not necessary. You're not going to run, are you, Herr Friedlander?'

'No.'

'Good. Then let's go.' He turned to the SS man who had remained a quiet, intimidating presence in the background. 'Perhaps you would be so good as to drive us.'

'Of course, Inspector.'

'And you could drop off Miss Mitford at her lodgings on the way. I believe they are quite close by.'

CHAPTER 12

It was not easy to persuade Unity Mitford that her presence at the Presidium really was not required but, with Fritz Mannheim's help, he eventually managed to get her out of the car and into the student hostel, still protesting angrily that she should sit in on the interrogation. Her last trump card was to threaten to call Adolf, but then Fritz Mannheim stepped in with a shake of the head.

'No, Bobo, the inspector is right. This must all be done by the book.'

She glared at Mannheim for a few seconds, then climbed out of the car, slammed the door and strode into the hostel.

The three men drove on south towards Ettstrasse in silence, Mannheim at the wheel, Seb and Friedlander in the rear.

The Presidium was operating on a skeleton staff in the early hours. Before taking his farewell of Fritz Mannheim at the front desk, he found himself wondering about the SS man's part in all this. He had barely said a word in their time together and so Seb was left in the dark as to how he had become involved. Had he approached Unity to tell her Seb was looking for her, or was it the other way around? Had Unity asked for his assistance?

Without ceremony, Seb put Friedlander in a small waiting room under the night desk's watchful eye, so that he could take Mannheim aside and talk to him in private.

'Can I ask you, Officer, how you came to be involved? Did Sergeant Winter contact you? He is my detective assistant on this case.'

'There was a message left for me at Karlstrasse with your name and subject matter. I had already heard of the murder and I knew that it was a matter of grave urgency. As I knew the whereabouts of Miss Mitford, I took it upon myself to bring her to you. She and I had been to Chiemsee with others for much of the day and returned home late.'

'And you knew my address?'

Mannheim smiled and pushed his glasses up his nose. 'That was not difficult to find.'

'Well, I must thank you for your prompt attention to the matter. By the way, I believe you knew Miss Palmer?'

'I had met her a few times. She was a very pretty, charming girl, but I never had any sort of one-to-one conversation with her. She was just there, one of the English crowd.' He chuckled. 'They adore us.' He brushed his uniform with his palm. 'Especially this.'

'So there was nothing between you, no suggestion of romance?'

'Who have you been listening to, Inspector?'

He had been listening to the girl at the student hostel, Frances de Pole. She had hinted at an attraction between Mannheim and Rosie, but he didn't refer to it. 'No one,' he said. 'But as you say, she was a beautiful young woman, and you are a handsome young man.'

'Oh, I'm just another SS officer, but thank you.'

'I might need to talk with you again.'

'By all means. If I'm not at Karlstrasse, they'll always know where to find me. If I'm on duty, I will be with the Führer's guard, so may not be available to you.'

'Of course.' They saluted each other and Mannheim disappeared into the night. Watching him go, Seb got the distinct impression that his real mission with Unity Mitford was not as a lover but as her minder. His main task? To keep an eye on the Führer's new friend and make a note of all her movements, her friends and everything she said. And then to report back – whether to Hitler or Himmler was another matter.

Seb took Friedlander up to his office. He noticed that the young man was still extremely tense and tried to put him at his ease. 'I'm afraid I can't offer you coffee, but perhaps you'd like a glass of water?'

'No thank you. I just want to get this over with and go home to my bed.'

'Indeed. I understand perfectly. So tell me exactly what you know about this murder?'

'I know nothing about it. I am completely innocent.'

'But you clearly know it happened.'

'Yes, I was told by a friend that an English girl had been found dead in Herzogpark, somewhere in the woods, and that murder was suspected. I enquired further and discovered to my horror that it was Rosie – Miss Palmer.'

'Well, you can give me the name of this friend in due course, but first tell me about your relationship with Rosie Palmer. When did you last see her?'

'Four days ago, at a party.'

'What sort of party?'

'Just an ordinary party. Thirty or forty people – dancing, drinking, socialising. Mostly English and American – I am not always welcome at parties where the guests are German. My race, you understand.'

Yes, Seb understood. 'Again, I may want details of this party and the names of all people there. But back to Rosie Palmer. How did you come to know her?'

He smiled for the first time, a sad smile. 'Three years ago, I was at Cambridge University in England, Peterhouse, studying natural sciences. I had a very good friend, Tobias Russell, who invited me to a grand house party at his home in Northamptonshire one weekend. I felt a bit out of my depth. You have seen my parents' apartment, so you know that while we are not poor, we are certainly not endowed with extreme wealth. My father is an academic, a physicist like me. Anyway, Rosie was among the guests at the house party and she was kind to me, not at all snobbish or prejudiced. I suppose you could say that we hit it off.'

'What do you mean, hit it off?'

'I mean we liked each other's company very much – we were attracted to each other romantically. She is – was – very beautiful.'

'Did you become lovers?'

Friedlander began to shake again. 'In what sense?'

'Did you have sexual intercourse?'

'Surely you can't ask such a question?'

'I can ask whatever questions I like. A young woman lies in the mortuary at the LMU and I have to discover who killed her and why. Well?'

'If you insist, then . . . no. She was a virgin. I wanted to marry her intact.'

Seb knew he was lying, whether to protect the dead girl's reputation or his own, he wasn't sure. 'Then this was not a sexual relationship between you?'

'It would have been had we been able to marry.'

'Did you *ask* her to marry you?'

'Of course, but she said she was too young, only seventeen, and so we had to wait. It became increasingly difficult to see her in England because she lived in Warwickshire and our paths didn't cross. With Tobias's help we managed to meet secretly for a few happy days now and then, but they were all too short. And so we wrote to each other constantly. When I finished my degree in 1933, I returned to Munich. Rosie came out last year to learn German. It was against her family's wishes. Her mother and brother, Viscount Braybury, wanted her to do the coming-out thing. Do you understand about that? It is a custom among the English upper classes.'

'I believe I have heard about it. They call them debs, yes?'

'Debutantes. They are introduced to the King and have lavish balls. The aim is to find a husband from among the young men of their class. But Rosie refused to participate and came here instead, much to my delight.'

'And you took up where you left off?'

'I wish it had been that simple.'

'Please explain.'

'Well, you know, all the English and American girls spend a lot of time in the company of young SS officers, and I am not welcome there.'

'That sounds as if you were no longer in any sort of relationship. Tell me, Herr Friedlander, what do you do for a living? I take it you are no longer a student?'

'No I'm not a student and I find myself unable to work, so I live off my parents' savings. But I did see Rosie, despite the difficulties. I knew a lot of the English people because I spoke the language, and occasionally she was able to invite me to dinner or a nightclub with them when Miss Mitford and the SS were not involved. I was still in love with her and I felt sure we would be together in time. But I understood that things were not easy for her.'

'Where were you the night before last?'

Friedlander seemed to be thinking.

'I was at home, with my parents.'

'That took a while to work out.'

'I had been out during the day. I got back in the early evening. I was making sure I told you correctly.'

'Were you out working?'

He laughed humourlessly. 'I told you, I do not work. Nor does my father, who was sacked from his post at the Technical University for the crime of being a Jew. I came back from England with my Cambridge degree having been offered a place at BMW in aircraft design and engineering. I had already decided academia was not for me. I was supposed to start in the autumn of 1933, but it was cancelled. I am sure you can guess why.'

'I'm sorry to hear that.'

Friedlander shrugged. 'I should have stayed in England. Not so easy to get there now.'

'Be careful what you say to me, Herr Friedlander. I am a law officer.'

'Of course, but you are not—'

Seb broke in. 'Don't presume to know what I am or am not. Disloyalty to the Third Reich comes at a price. Now then, you say you were in all evening. Specifically, between nine o'clock and midnight, where were you?'

'I told you, at home. Even before that. From six o'clock.'

'In which room?'

'The sitting room, the dining room, the kitchen, the bathroom, my bedroom.'

'And you didn't go out?'

'No.'

'Your parents were with you the whole time?'

'Yes.'

'Even in the bathroom and your bedroom?'

'No, not there.'

'So they weren't with you the whole time?'

'I suppose not, but they would have seen me if I had gone out.'

'What time did you all go to bed?'

'My parents always retire at nine thirty.'

Seb raised an eyebrow. 'You can see where I am having a problem here?'

'I'm trying to be honest. I was at home all evening and all night, as were my parents. That does not mean we were all in the same room at the same time.'

'You must also know that parents are not seen as the most credible of alibis. What mother or father would not swear to God on behalf of their child?'

'There's nothing I can do about that.'

'All right, let's try another question. You mentioned that you and Miss Palmer exchanged letters. I would like to see them.'

'But they are private!'

'No, I'm afraid they are not. If I were to offer you one piece of advice, I would say that you would do well to make things as easy as possible for yourself by cooperating with us. As a Kripo inspector, I will see all the evidence I wish. Do you understand?'

'I still think—'

'No, sir, you are not in a position to think. You will merely provide any evidence required of you. These letters, were they written in English or German?'

'Always English.'

'And tell me – do you speak or write Hebrew?'

'No, I have never learnt. I speak German, English, a little French and some Yiddish, but not much. I couldn't read one word in Hebrew, or write it.'

'One more thing, and then we'll call it a night: why do you think Miss Mitford is accusing you of being the murderer?'

'That's easy. Because she is a terrible human being. She hates me for no other reason than I am Jewish. I truly believe that if she were given the chance, she would pull the guillotine lever and laugh hysterically as my head fell.'

CHAPTER 13

Seb accompanied Friedlander home in a taxi and told him that he might be required for more questioning. For a while, he had considered having him locked up in one of the Presidium cells, but eventually thought better of it. He seemed to be the only suspect on the horizon, but there wasn't a speck of evidence against him.

After dropping Friedlander off, he took the taxi home to Ainmüllerstrasse and was surprised to find a wrapped package on the kitchen table in front of his chair. It had an accompanying card saying 'Why not read this before judging us, old man? Happy birthday, Jurgen'.

Carefully removing the brown paper wrapping so that it could be reused he found himself laughing at the contents: a brand new copy of *Mein Kampf,* the infamous tract written by one Adolf Hitler during his spell in Landsberg Prison following his attempt at violent revolution in 1923.

His own son putting royalties into the bank account of Hitler! Though it had sold in the millions and made the Führer a rich man, Seb had never had any inclination to read it, but perhaps he owed it to his son. If it was meant as a peace offering, then it had to be welcome.

He scribbled the words 'Thank you, I will' on the card and left it at Jurgen's space on the table. He considered adding 'and unlike certain others, I won't burn it' but thought better of it.

Bed beckoned. It was late and the day had been long. He set the alarm, crawled between the sheets and fell asleep almost instantly.

He woke five hours later surprisingly refreshed, had a quick breakfast of bread and cheese and coffee – all provided by his mother who bustled around him, happy to have her son back in the daily routine – then drove to Ettstrasse. Winter had arrived just before him.

After exchanging salutes, Sergeant Winter went on the offensive. 'Where is he?'

'Who?'

'Karl Friedlander. The killer. Which cell?'

'Probably still asleep at home. It was a late night.'

'You mean you have let him loose without charge?'

'With what should I have charged him, Sergeant? I would require some evidence to charge a man with murder.'

'But I know that you have the word of Miss Mitford. I caught up with Fritz Mannheim this morning and he told me everything. And the Jew clearly had the motive. I told you those markings were Jew script.'

'Motive alone is not enough – and show me the proof that the markings were Hebrew, if you can. Anyway, Friedlander has an alibi. So our hunt goes on.'

'Why was he not slung in the cells? He is a Jew – the corpse was defiled with Jewish markings. Fräulein Mitford has given you the motive. What more do you need?'

'Are you stupid, Winter? Or is this just an act? In the Kripo, we uphold the law of the land, and that means making arrests when we have reason to believe we have the guilty person. In this case, we have no evidence against Herr Friedlander. Perhaps the BPP does things differently, simply ignoring the concept of justice.'

'And so you resort to insulting me again, and you slander the BPP. In doing so you defame Heydrich and Himmler and, indeed, the Führer himself. You will pay a heavy price for this, Inspector Wolff.'

It didn't seem worth continuing this verbal combat, so Seb simply ignored his outburst. 'I am going to Friedlander now to talk to his parents to ensure his alibi is confirmed. Also I would like a few more words with Miss Mitford. I leave it up to you whether you accompany me, or follow some other lead.'

'There are no other leads. And I have been told again that I must accompany you at all times until this matter is completed to everyone's satisfaction. And that means conviction and execution, nothing less.'

'Then let's go.'

Seb tucked his Walther PPK in the shoulder holster nestling against his shirt. The phone rang and he picked it up.

'Hello. Criminal Inspector Wolff.'

'Heil Hitler, Wolff.'

Seb recognised the voice immediately. It bore a strong hint of American. 'Heil Hitler, Herr Hanfstaengl.'

'Could you be at the Brown House in twenty minutes, please? The Honourable Mr Edward Palmer, Viscount Braybury, will be here and I am told he would very much like to meet you. He is brother to the late Miss Rosie Palmer.'

Of course. The meeting. It had slipped Seb's mind. And what was he supposed to tell this poor Englishman? Your sister's killer is still at large and we are bereft of clues. 'Yes, of course, sir, I shall be there.'

He replaced the phone.

'What did Hanfstaengl want?'

'The dead girl's brother is over from England. I am to meet him.'

'Then I will come too.'

Seb looked at the unimpressive Sergeant Hans Winter with dismay. He was not a good advertisement for the Third Reich. 'Come on then, but we'll be speaking English.'

'You can translate for me.'

Outside the main entrance of the Brown House, a pair of uniformed SS men stood to attention, rifles clasped diagonally across their rigid torsos. Inside, the atmosphere in Hanfstaengl's office was sombre. Consul-general Donald Gainer was there, standing beside a young Englishman, who was introduced as Viscount Braybury, Captain Edward Palmer.

Everyone shook hands, except Winter who tried in vain to force the Hitler salute into the proceedings. Hanfstaengl turned on him and whispered harshly in his ear. 'Mr Palmer is an honoured guest from England, you ignorant dolt, and as such cannot be expected to use the new greeting.'

'But it is required.'

'All that is required, young man, is that you leave the room and wait outside. Your presence is not helpful here.'

Winter gave Hanfstaengl a deadly look, then turned it on Seb. 'I have been ordered to stay with Inspector Wolff for the duration of this inquiry, Herr Hanfstaengl. Orders direct from the offices of both SS-Reichsführer Himmler and SS-Obergruppenführer Heydrich.'

The names cast a chill over the room. Winter had clearly included their titles as weapons. Hanfstaengl's face tightened and he glared at the political policeman. 'Do you speak English?'

'No.'

'Well then you won't understand a word we are saying.' He turned back to the young Englishman with a grave look and changed languages. 'Forgive me, Captain Palmer. A slight confusion.'

Edward Palmer was a product of his class. What the seamen with whom Seb once sailed would have called a solid six-foot toff. He was lean and powerful and had a languid air. In normal times, his demeanour would probably be considered affable and good-humoured, today it was serious, but somehow lacking the appropriate melancholy. Even at this time of emotional devastation when other men would be weeping for the loss of a beloved sister, his face betrayed nothing. So this was the famous stiff upper lip. To Seb, it was a denial of humanity and he didn't like it.

The Englishman met Seb's eyes and their mutual gaze held. 'And I understand that you are leading the investigation, Inspector Wolff.'

'Yes, sir.' He clicked his heels and gave a respectful bow of the head. An officer was an officer, whatever his nationality. And having served in the Bavarian army, it was second nature for Seb to defer to the officer class.

'And what do you know so far?'

How much to tell this young man, whose age he estimated at the mid to late twenties? 'Miss Palmer – your sister – was found dead in woods on the banks of the River Isar the day before last. She had been stabbed to death, her body wrapped in a rug.'

'Stabbed? I heard that her throat had been cut.'

'Forgive me, that is correct. I was trying to lessen the horror.'

'I'm not a child. I want the truth. Unvarnished.'

Seb bowed again. 'Professor Lindner at the LMU laboratory puts the time of death at about midnight the evening before she was found. The last known sighting of her was by her Munich host, Herr Walter Regensdorf, in the hallway of his house at Karolinenplatz. It was around nine o'clock in the evening and she was about to go out. After that, nothing. Which leaves a missing three hours before her death. I have been attempting to fill in that time. The best I have come up with so far is evidence from her good friend Miss Unity Mitford that they were planning to meet at the Schneider Bräuhaus in the city centre, then go on to the Hofbräuhaus to join some other friends. Your sister didn't turn up at the Schneider and Miss Mitford ran into some other acquaintances and went to a club on Lenbachplatz. I'm afraid that is all I know so far.'

The young Englishman was stiff and gaunt. 'In the past hour, I have seen the body following the autopsy, also photographs before she was cleaned up and cut open. There were many cuts and curious markings. The picture obviously does not show the colour but I'm told these were red lipstick.'

Seb nodded. 'Indeed, sir. And that is a major part of our inquiry. It is possible the marks mean something, but as yet we have not been able to ascertain what. I am, however, in touch with an expert at the Bavarian State Library, who is a student of many scripts, both ancient and modern. He is examining photographs of your sister's body and I am hopeful he will report back to me today.'

'So what you're saying, Herr Wolff, is that you've got precisely nowhere. No suspects, nothing.'

The words stung because they were true. Seb felt the eyes of the men in the room boring into him. He knew that Hanfstaengl was suffering, too, for his neck was also on the line.

Winter broke the echoing silence, speaking urgently to Seb in German. 'Have you told him about Friedlander? I didn't hear you speak his name. You have to tell him about the Jew.'

Edward Palmer turned towards Winter. 'What did you say?' He was speaking German.

Seb felt a surge of panic. He had deliberately avoided mentioning Friedlander. 'Just something Miss Mitford said. Your sister had a friend called Karl Friedlander and Miss Mitford had suspicions about him.'

'Good God, man, I know who Friedlander is. Are you saying he's here in Munich?'

'Yes, sir, but I have interviewed him and there is no evidence to link him to your sister's death.'

'I met the ghastly man in England. Hung around my sister like a bad smell. None of us could understand why she had anything to do with the fellow.' He took a step towards Winter and switched to fluent German. 'And you say Friedlander is a suspect?'

'Miss Mitford states that he is the killer, sir.'

'Well, where is he? Has he been charged?'

Seb moved between Palmer and Winter. 'I'm sorry but I really don't want there to be any misunderstanding. Karl Friedlander has been accused of nothing. There is no evidence that he has harmed Miss Palmer. Quite the opposite, I am pretty sure he was deeply in love with her and is devastated by her death.'

Palmer snorted. 'Love? You don't know what you're talking about, Inspector. He's taken you for a fool.'

'I really don't think so, sir.'

Hanfstaengl and Gainer were speechless witnesses to the conversation. At last Hanfstaengl cleared his throat. 'I think the best thing to do is to bring this Friedlander man back into custody for harder questioning, don't you, Inspector? Check his alibi. His fingerprints, his movements. Clear the air once and for all.'

Seb could do nothing. 'Of course, Herr Hanfstaengl, if that is what you wish.'

'It is. Go and pick him up now.'

'Because if you don't, Wolff,' the dead girl's brother said, his cultured voice now brittle and savage. 'I will kill the filthy Jew myself.'

CHAPTER 14

Seb had been surprised, shocked even, by the Englishman's brutal eruption. More than that, he was disturbed by the discovery that Rosie Palmer's friendship – relationship? – with Karl Friedlander had engendered such strong feelings in her family. Friedlander had not made this clear.

Did the family's hostility amount to anti-Semitic bigotry or was there something else about Friedlander? Had Seb completely misjudged his character? He had to accept the possibility. The interview had been conducted late at night and he had had a few drinks. Well, Friedlander certainly had more questions to answer.

As Seb drove northwards into Schwabing, no words passed between him and Winter, but he could sense the other man's self-satisfied smirk and had a powerful desire to smack it from his face.

They pulled up outside the apartment block. Both got out of the car, entered the building and walked side by side up the stairway.

There was no answer to their knock. They hammered harder. Still nothing. Seb tried the handle, but it was locked.

Without waiting for Seb's say-so, Winter hurled himself at the door, shoulder first. He howled in pain but the door was well built and didn't give a centimetre. The noise, however, roused the Fried-landers' immediate neighbour in the next apartment. She was a woman with grey hair and stern features. She wore a ragged floral dress and kitchen apron and stood with arms crossed, staring at them with a sour expression.

'We are looking for Herr Friedlander,' Seb said. 'The young one, Karl Friedlander.'

'I guessed you might be. What are you – cops or debt collectors?'
'Police.'

'Well you're too late. He's gone. They all have, first thing this morning. All three of them. Struggled downstairs with their suitcases and went off down the street, looking around them like thieves.'

'Do you know where they went?'

'I asked them that. Holiday, they said. That's a laugh. They've skipped out of the country like the rats they are. Good riddance to them.'

'You didn't get on?'

'Think about it, Officer. You know what they are, don't you?'

'Damn it,' Seb said.

'They've done a runner.' Winter was rubbing his shoulder.

The Friedlanders – Karl, his mother Miriam and father Benjamin – never stood a chance of making it. They were picked up by uniformed police when their train stopped at Freiburg, but they wouldn't have got across the border anyway, because they didn't have the exit visas necessary to leave Germany, nor entry visas for Switzerland and only Karl had a passport.

Within three hours they were back at the Police Presidium in Munich. The parents were slung into separate cells to await inter-rogation and their son was taken into a chilly cellar room with a table and three chairs to be grilled by Seb and Winter.

Seb led the questioning. 'What were you trying to do, Fried-lander? Are you insane? Have you fallen out of love with the Fatherland?'

'I was scared. So were Mother and Father. Please, sir, won't you let them go – they have nothing to do with any of this.'

'Any of what?'

'These suspicions that you have. They were just afraid – afraid for me. I am their only child.'

'They have questions to answer, as do you, Herr Friedlander. Attempting to leave the country does not help to make you look innocent. Nor will your parents serve you well as alibis after this. Perhaps you could tell me more about the evening when Miss Palmer was killed. Where exactly were you?'

'I told you, Inspector Wolff, I was at home.'

'You'll need to do better than that.'

'But what else can I say if it is the truth? I promise you, I have done nothing wrong. I have committed no crime. I have lost the love of my life.' His eyes were wide with terror and horror, flicking between Seb and Winter.

'Let's go back a bit,' Seb said. 'Tell me more about your time in England. Why does Miss Palmer's brother dislike you so much?'

'Edward? Why are you mentioning him? Is he here, in Munich?'

Winter entered the fray, banging his fist on the table. 'Just answer the question, you murdering bastard. Captain Palmer hates you and you clearly know why. He hates you because he knows what you are. Did you do something to his sister in England?'

Friedlander was shaking. His mouth was moving but no words were forthcoming.

Winter rose to his feet. 'Answer me! You dishonoured the poor girl.' He lunged forward and hit Friedlander in the face with a piledriver punch, making him recoil, throwing him and the chair backwards to the floor. The young man scrabbled about, dazed yet instinctively trying to get to his feet and back away from his assailant. Winter was about to hit him again, punching downwards, but Seb grabbed his arm and held it back.

'Enough, Sergeant, that's enough.'

'We should kill him now. Save the executioner a job.'

Seb helped Friedlander back onto the chair. He was bleeding from the nose, his eyes were bloodshot and he was groggy. 'Are you all right, Herr Friedlander?'

He nodded. 'Yes, I think so.'

Seb handed him his handkerchief, which was clean having been left out for him by his mother, as she did every morning. 'Here, wipe your nose.' The only thing on the table was a glass of water. Seb pushed it towards Friedlander. 'Take a sip and settle down.' He looked towards Winter and made a downward motion with the flat of his hand. *Sit, Winter, calm yourself.*

'Now then, Friedlander, tell me more about England and your time there. Something happened between you and the Palmers. What exactly passed between you? Did you have sex with Miss Palmer?'

'Yes, we made love.'

'You raped her,' Winter said. 'A girl like that would never consent to sleep with vermin like you.'

Seb really wished Winter was elsewhere; he was not making this any easier. And yet perhaps there was some curious benefit to his presence. He was confusing and discomfiting Friedlander.

'Do you recall what you said to me last night, Friedlander? You said you had not had sexual intercourse with Miss Palmer, that you both wanted her to be a virgin when eventually you married. And yet now you say you made love. Were you lying before – or now?'

'I loved her with all my heart and she loved me. We kissed. We caressed. Is that not making love?'

'And yet she wasn't a virgin.'

The words hung heavy in the cool air.

Friedlander was shaking. He was a good-looking young man with dark, softly curling hair. Maybe not athletic like the young woman's brother, but he had smooth skin and a pleasing figure and face. It was quite conceivable to Seb that Rosie Palmer or any other young woman could find him attractive. Yet not now, perhaps. Now he looked broken.

'Well?'

'I . . . you confuse me . . . I don't know what you mean . . .'

'I mean the pathologist has testified that Rosie Palmer was not a virgin. She had experienced sexual intercourse in her life, but probably not in the course of the attack, for there was no semen.'

'Is this true?'

'So it wasn't you?'

Tears were rolling down the man's cheeks. It was no longer his life that hung in the balance, but everything he believed in and stood for, or so it seemed to Seb. Love. Fidelity. Trust. All gone.

Either that or he was a more accomplished liar and fraud than Seb would have credited.

'So let us go back to your time in England. You wooed Miss Palmer and she responded to your approaches. Let us put the subject of sex to one side for the moment and merely say that you romanced the girl and told her you loved her and she led you to believe that she loved you back and would keep herself pure for you. Is that how it was?'

'Yes.' His voice was choked.

'But her family disapproved?'

He nodded. 'I was the wrong class, the wrong race, the wrong religion. But Rosie didn't care about such things. Her family forbade her to see me, but they couldn't keep us apart. And then her brother came for me. He was with a friend, another young soldier from his regiment. They came to my rooms in Cambridge with clubs and beat me senseless. I still have the marks if you'd care to look.'

'That won't be necessary at the moment.'

'I was in hospital for a week.'

'And so you took revenge by killing the person they loved?'

'No, of course not. I didn't even report Edward Palmer or his friend to the police, for that would have hurt Rosie – and I would never have done anything to harm her.'

'Strange that her family allowed her to come to Munich when you were here.'

Friedlander shook his head. Blood dripped from his nose and mingled with his tears. He held the handkerchief to his face again. 'They didn't know I was here. Rosie begged her family to allow her to come to Munich because this was where some of her friends came. She didn't tell them that I would be here.'

There was a sharp rap at the door, which immediately opened and a uniformed officer entered. 'Forgive me for interrupting, Inspector. You are wanted urgently by Herr Ruff.'

'Stay here, Sergeant Winter.'

'No, sir, I'll come with you.'

It wasn't worth arguing with the man. Seb nodded to the uniformed officer. 'Perhaps you would watch the room while we're gone, Officer.'

'Yes, sir.'

Deputy Police President Thomas Ruff was in his large and rather ornate office up on the fifth floor of the presidium. He was pacing, but stopped as the door opened. Seeing that Seb was accompanied by his political shadow, Ruff instantly went through the Heil Hitler rigmarole with them.

'Please sit down,' he said at last. 'There has been an important development.'

Seb took a seat in front of Ruff's oversized desk. Everything was too big here. A large window gave out on to Ettstrasse, filling the eyeline with the monumental eastern flank of the church of St Michael's.

'A witness has come forward, a maidservant who knows Karl Friedlander by sight. She was travelling home on the tram on the night of Miss Palmer's death – about nine thirty – and saw Friedlander at the southern end of Ludwigstrasse, walking hurriedly in the same direction. As she watched, he turned right just before the Wittelsbach Palace.'

'I knew it,' Winter said. 'I knew he was lying. That puts him right in the vicinity of Villa Saphir, the Regensdorf house on Karolinenplatz.'

'Not so fast,' Seb said. 'Who is this maid? How does she know Friedlander? And why has she come forward?'

'Her name is Marlene Popp. You will be able to interview her in due course and all your questions will be answered to your satisfaction. But for the moment, we have a more pressing matter: Friedlander must be charged with murder without delay so that I can convey the news to the Führer. So go now, Inspector Wolff, and formalise the charge.'

'Would it not be worth waiting an hour or two until after I have spoken to Fräulein Popp? How does she even know that Friedlander is a potential suspect?'

'All in good time. This is an international incident and there is not a moment to lose.' Ruff stepped forward and shook Seb by the hand. 'And may I be the first to congratulate you, Inspector, for bringing this case to such a satisfactory and speedy conclusion.'

'But what exactly have I done?'

'Oh, you realised that Miss Mitford was the key to the case. She pointed you in the direction of Friedlander and he has condemned himself by his own actions. This new witness is the final nail in his coffin. Well done, Wolff. And you, Sergeant Winter. Well done both of you.'

CHAPTER 15

Seb went and found Hexie and they got drunk together in the Schelling-Salon and then staggered down the road, arm in arm, to the House of Artists club on Lenbachplatz. It was that kind of night. A night when nothing really seemed to matter anymore. A night when you threw the law out of the window and got a pat on the back for your trouble.

He heiled everyone he passed and they heiled him back, and he and Hexie doubled over in laughter. It was a dangerous game; Munich was not short of people willing to denounce you for showing disrespect to the Führer. But Seb and Hexie didn't care, or maybe they were simply too far gone to realise what they were doing.

The House of Artists was alive with music, dancing and drinking within its glittering, voluminous halls. But that was only the visible areas. In nooks and corners, there was love play, salacious gossip and political whispering. Who was in, who was out? Seb hated the place for it had become the playground of the Nazi high command in the city of the movement's birth. Dance hall, bordello, the place to see the stars of stage and politics, and be seen. But tonight, perversely, he wanted to be here, to convince his beer-addled brain that he was on the right side of the struggle, that he wasn't simply deluding himself that he was solid and the rest were irrevocably corrupt.

Uncle Christian was holding court at a private table near the bar. He was surrounded by half-dressed young dancing girls and actresses from the theatre on Gartnerplatz, all drinking vintage champagne and brandy cocktails at his expense. He kept a tab here but it was doubtful whether he ever bothered to settle up. Who was going to challenge him?

Weber's hand frequently strayed to a breast or a thigh and no one seemed to care a jot. The girls knew what to expect. If they didn't like it, they simply stayed away. But if you were ambitious or hungry, this was the place to be. Christian Weber came here most evenings, to choose the lucky ones who would share his kingly bed in the Residenz that night.

He caught Seb's eye across the throng and waved him over. 'Come here, boy, come here. I've heard the good news. You've caught the stinking bastard.'

'Have I, Uncle?'

'Of course you have, and you're the hero of the Munich police. You have no idea quite what you've achieved, do you, boy. Tomorrow, Germany and Britain will sign a naval agreement which is entirely in our interests. We can build up our glorious submarine fleet again! And you have ensured that there will be no glitches over something as unfortunate as a murder. I think Adolf wants to give you a gold party badge, but you know what that means?'

'I'd have to join the party.'

Weber laughed and his porcine barrel of flesh shook like a minor earthquake. 'Tell him, Hexie Schuler, you tell him. Make an honest man of my sister's boy. Get him in the party and marry him. With my help he'll have a fine office in the Wittelsbach Palace in next to no time.'

'Oh, I don't think he's ever going to marry me, Herr Weber. Anyway, perhaps I don't want to marry him.'

Weber roared with laughter again. 'The girl's got spirit, boy. Take her. I'll pay for the wedding. It'll be the event of the year. The great detective wins the fair maiden Hexie. And your saintly mother will believe she's died and gone to heaven.'

Seb merely nodded and smiled. 'We'll see. By the way, Uncle, I know you pulled strings on my behalf to get me out of Dachau – so once again, thank you.'

'Yes, you owe me a favour.'

'You know, of course, that there are many more innocent people incarcerated up there. People who merely think differently, or have been denounced by unfriendly neighbours.'

Weber waved the suggestion away. 'Nonsense, boy. National Socialism believes in justice for all. Only the degenerates, asocials and criminals are locked away. But be careful, boy, there are men in the BPP who seem to have taken against you. You have power-ful enemies, so it may be out of my control next time.'

'So I gather.'

Weber clapped him on the back. 'But for the moment your star is in the ascendancy, and with Adolf's goodwill on your side, the likes of Meisinger or that worm Winter can't touch you. I still say you'd do well to join the political corps. Heydrich would love you. He's always on the lookout for good men.'

Seb shrugged. What could he say? They had been over this ground before and it was a futile conversation. The point was he was coming to the conclusion that he had to leave the police altogether. The tightrope he was trying to walk was just too inse-cure and he couldn't always rely on Uncle Christian's services as a safety net. Not that he wanted anything from him anyway. A small part of him died every time Weber used his corrupt influ-ence to help him or the family.

So he'd have to quit the force, but what would he do? What was he good for? One thing was certain, he couldn't leave Munich. At a pinch, Hexie might go with him, be willing to start again in another city or even abroad, but his mother and Jurgen wouldn't hear of it.

But that was a matter to be considered tomorrow when he was halfway sober.

Uncle Christian lost interest in him and buried his face in the ample cleavage of a dark-haired singer from the opera.

'Shall we?' Seb took Hexie's hand and moved away towards the dancing. A swing band was playing the sort of American music forbidden to ordinary Germans as a decadent influence. Seb and Hexie did a couple of frantic turns and then he spotted Unity Mitford and Viscount Braybury across the crowded hall.

He gave them a casual wave, but they affected not to recognise him, or perhaps they really didn't. People of their class did not notice the rank and file.

They were among a group of half a dozen and seemed to be laughing and celebrating, which was strange for a girl who had lost her best friend and a man who had lost his sister. And then

Seb spotted that one of the others in their group was Otto Raspe, the celebrated writer of all things *Völkisch*. Baroness Laroche had mentioned that he had dropped off Rosie Palmer at her house. So perhaps he was linked in some way to Munich's fashionable English scene.

He would have liked to talk with Raspe, in case he had any clues to Rosie's fate. But that was all yesterday's news now. Friedlander was banged up in the Presidium cells. He would be tried within days, found guilty and sentenced to death by guillotine. From the court, he would be taken to Stadelheim Prison, and within a short time, his head would be severed. And that would be that. Only his parents would mourn, probably from the confines of a concentration camp or prison.

Raspe was a good-looking man with greying sideburns and the air of a much-decorated soldier, which he had been. Was it in the army during the war that he had become obsessed with the ancient Norse gods and the concept of blood and soil and other esoteric beliefs? Many had come back from the conflict bitterly angry, blaming the Jews for their defeat and demanding that the land be returned to those with unsullied German blood. The fact that a great many German Jews had fought and died for their country – and even won the Iron Cross – seemed irrelevant.

In Raspe's world, racial hygiene, eugenics and German mythology trumped all. It was what he wrote about every week in his columns. Pseudo-scientific claptrap that might drive a man to slit his wrists out of boredom and which Seb could not bear to read.

Hexie snorted. 'I hate that man.'

'Which man?'

'Raspe. Colonel Otto Raspe. He brings his photos to us to be developed and asks me to go for a drink with him. When I point out to him that he's a married man, he just shrugs. He used to try it on with Evie until he realised Hitler was interested in her too.'

'He's a good-looking man. I'm surprised you didn't go for that drink.'

'I can't explain it, but I don't like him. And then there are his pictures. They always come back from the darkroom in a sealed envelope.'

'Because?'

'Who knows? I never get to see them and the darkroom guys won't even give us a hint. Naked girls, I suppose. Anyway, I need to pee.'

As she wandered off to the ladies' room, Seb felt a tap on his shoulder and turned around. It was the tall, slim figure of Ernie Pope, the American newsman. 'So you found Bobo without my help, Seb.'

'She found me.'

'And now you've solved the crime. Did she help you with that?'

'Ernie, I really can't talk about it. I'm as drunk as a farmer when the crop's all in and if I say anything I'll regret it.'

'You can listen, though, can't you?'

'I can do that.'

'So let me tell you what I know then, and there's plenty of it because Putzi Hanfstaengl is as proud as punch and giving the story out to anyone who'll listen. The killer is a guy named Karl Friedlander. He knew the victim and had been harassing her. He killed her in a fit of jealous rage. If he couldn't have the girl, no one else would either. He had an alibi but it was blown apart. And the murder involved some sort of Jewish blood ritual. How does that all sound?'

'Believe what you want, Ernie.'

'Are you suggesting you *don't* believe it?'

Seb shrugged. What could he do?

'I know, you can't talk to me. But I have to say, Seb, it all looks very convenient. Maybe a bit too convenient, eh? All sewn up nicely so as not to detract attention from the naval negotiations.'

'Leave it, Ernie, you're overthinking it. You've got your story.' Or perhaps he, Seb, was doing the overthinking. Without warning, the devil in him reared his injudicious horns again. 'OK, I'll tell you one thing: this all goes back to England. Rosie and Friedlander met when he was at Cambridge.' Reporters protected their sources, didn't they? Or maybe they didn't. He paused. 'No, forget I said that. I'm really not allowed to talk to you.'

'I'd offer you a drink but I guess you've already overdone it a little bit.'

'I'll take a cognac. Large one. You're on expenses, aren't you?'

'Naturally.'

'And my friend Hexie will have champagne.'

Pope clicked his fingers and the barman took his order.

Seb looked over towards Unity Mitford and Rosie's brother again and a thought struck him. 'Actually, you could do me a little favour, Ernie.'

'Name it.'

'Get one of your newshounds back in England to see what they can find out about Friedlander and Rosie Palmer. They met three years ago, introduced at a house party in Northamptonshire by a college friend of Karl's named Tobias Russell. The way Friedlander tells the story, he and the girl hit it off big time but her family went crazy. Edward Palmer gave Friedlander a going-over.'

'You shouldn't be telling me this.'

'Are you going to blab?'

'No, I won't blab, Seb. But you know there are many eyes in this room and they can see that you're talking to me. So smile and laugh as though I just told you a joke and then we'll go our separate ways. If I discover anything of interest in the next couple of days, I'll find you.'

'Thank you.'

Hexie was back at his side. 'What was that about?'

He shrugged. 'Oh, you know. Just passing the time of day.'

'You've been shooting your mouth off to that American reporter, haven't you?'

He shrugged again.

'And you accuse me of having a big mouth. Come on, let's go back to my place. I want you inside me, Seb, more than I've ever wanted you before.'

Seb didn't get away so easily. They were at the door on their way out when Viscount Braybury stopped him. 'Inspector Wolff?' He said the name as a question as if he wasn't quite sure he'd got the right man.

'Good evening, Captain Palmer.' Is that what he liked to be called, or did he perhaps prefer 'My lord'? That had not been a question that was widely discussed below decks on the *Eastern Star* or in the seamen's inns at Tilbury Docks.

'I wanted to thank you, that's all. This has been a painful time for my family. I'm glad it's all over. He's always been a bad lot, that Friedlander. We thought we'd nipped it in the bud, but he had some sort of diabolical hold over her. If only we had put two and two together we could have stopped her coming here. But she wanted it so much and it was the place all her friends spoke about. The thing is, we didn't know, you see, we didn't know he was in Munich.'

What to say to the man? Did he really believe Friedlander was the killer, or was his power of reasoning overruled by his anti-Semitism? Seb simply smiled blandly. 'We have to wait for the trial, don't we.'

'That's a formality, surely.'

'We'll see.'

'I'm not stupid, Inspector. I know you have doubts. That's your job as a policeman. So do you think we could meet tomorrow morning? I fly home in the afternoon and I just wanted to give you some more perspective on the way things were between Rosie and Friedlander. You probably think this is all to do with the man's race and religion, but actually there is a great deal more. It might help your case when it comes to court.'

'Very well. Where do you want to meet?'

'Won't you come to the Four Seasons – the Vier Jahreszeiten? I have a suite there. We'll have coffee downstairs. Eleven o'clock, yes?'

'I'll be there.'

'Goodnight to you, Inspector.' He smiled at Hexie. 'And you, Frau Wolff.'

'Frau Wolff, Seb, he called me Frau Wolff. Do we look like a married couple?'

'What does a married couple look like, Hexie?'

'I'm asking you.'

'I think he was being polite in the way Englishmen do. Giving you the benefit of the doubt.'

She laughed and guided him down the stairs from the House of Artists. 'It is very easy to make you uncomfortable, Herr Wolff.'

An hour later, after making love to Hexie in her narrow single bed, he dreamt of Ulrike. How could he still dream of a woman he hadn't seen in sixteen years? He found it both comforting and disturbing. At least, he thought, it was better than the other dream, the machine-gun dream in which he waded thigh-high through a swamp of blood to the drumbeat of bullets smacking into flesh.

Ulrike. His first love. Jurgen's mother. They met in 1917, two weeks before he went away to the war. They kissed that first night and saw each other every day thereafter before he and Max Haas and their schoolfriends marched away for military training.

Ulrike Brandt was beautiful and wild in equal measure. They were the same age, both seventeen, but he was a virgin when they met whereas she had long since become a woman in every sense of the word.

She was forthright and unashamed. 'Have you ever had sexual intercourse?' she demanded on the second night they met.

Sexual intercourse? He had never heard such words from the mouth of a girl, only from other boys, whispered with giggles in their times alone, smoking illicit cigarettes and speaking of forbidden mysteries.

He didn't know what to say to her, so he merely shook his head, unable to meet her blue eyes, knowing all too well that he was blushing horribly.

'I cannot allow you to die a virgin,' she said.

How could he die a virgin? The Holy Mother was a virgin. Girls were virgins, surely, not boys. Anyway, he wasn't going to die.

She took his hand and led him out from the bar into the warm late summer evening and they crossed into the English Garden, where she found a deserted copse and laid him down in the grass and leaves and taught him love.

After that, nothing could have stopped him. They were together all the time. Seb didn't bother with school anymore, and nor did Ulrike. They toured the countryside around Munich by bicycle and train and made love by lakes and in the mountains. Always outdoors because they had nowhere else to go. When he wasn't with her, he was thinking about her. Just the very thought of her tender, slender body aroused him.

Before Ulrike, he had been looking forward to going to the front line, desperate to prove his courage and his worth as a man. It had seemed he was about to embark on the adventure of a lifetime. Now he couldn't bear to leave her.

On their last night together they made love in the warm, teeming rain, their bodies sliding, slipping on the grass and against each other's flesh. He had never felt so alive and he knew that he was in love and that life would never be better than this.

He didn't see her again until New Year 1918, when she was six months gone. He already knew about her pregnancy because she had written to him.

His mother had written to him, too, and her letter was angry and unpleasant because Ulrike was staying in his room, having been kicked out by her own unforgiving father, a railwayman, when he discovered she was expecting. She had just turned up on Mutti's doorstep with a small holdall of her few belongings and had blurted out her story, begging to be allowed to stay for she had nowhere else to go. Mutti could not deny her, for she was carrying her grandchild, but she resented the intrusion and she was unhappy about the implications for Seb and the family's reputation.

'How could you do this to us, Sebastian?' Mutti wrote. 'Have you no shame? This girl, this Ulrike Brandt, she is a fallen woman. Nor will she do anything around the apartment. No cleaning, no washing. She won't even come to mass with me. Anyway, how would I explain her to the other churchgoers?'

What could Seb do? He had other problems to contend with: the little matter of slaughtering enemy soldiers by the score and staying alive.

And when he finally got some leave and arrived home, Ulrike's swelling belly and breasts enchanted him like never before. For the first time they were able to share a bed and make love every night and every morning, barely sleeping. Mutti must have heard them, for her room was only a wall away, though she said nothing, merely glared at them in the morning.

Sexually, they were still as one, but in other ways the relationship of the young lovers had changed. He was a man now, still only seventeen in years, but hardened in body and mind by war. Disturbed, too. The sound of a car backfiring outside in the street could send him ducking for cover. His temper had become shorter. Little things irritated him. When Herr Altmaier in the next apartment explained what the German army should be doing to break the French and British lines, he threatened to hit the man and told him he knew nothing and that people who had never been to war should keep their fat mouths shut.

Ulrike had changed, too. She rowed with Mutti or sulked and it became clear that she was beginning to hate the idea of having a baby. She wanted to live, to dance, to travel. She snapped at Seb when he took his mother's side.

Returning to the front was like a release from the tension of home. He felt deeply conflicted. He was no longer certain he was in love. He could hardly bear the company of either Ulrike or his mother. He wanted the company of Max and the others, his dwindling band of brothers.

The next time he saw Ulrike the war was in its death throes, almost all his friends had been killed and Jurgen was a healthy, gurgling baby. Ulrike was not the best of mothers. She would leave Jurgen with Frau Wolff and go out into the night with no explanation and no attempt at excuses.

Those were dark days for everyone. There was hunger and there was mourning. Every household in the country had lost a brother, a father, a son, a friend. And as if that was not enough, people were dying of the influenza, children included. Munich was in the grip of political upheaval. Revolution was in the air from both the Left and the Right. Defeat hung like a poison cloud. Laughter and simple pleasures were rare commodities.

Ulrike was still eighteen. She hated politics and she hated being confined in an apartment with a disapproving middle-aged woman and a demanding baby. She wanted to live.

By the following summer, she had gone. Simply went out one day alone and did not return. She sent Seb a letter from Berlin, apologising. She said Jurgen would be better off without her and asked that no one try to contact her. There was no return address on the letter, so Seb had not been able to reply, and going to Berlin to find her seemed a pointless exercise and far too expensive anyway. Mutti, though, was happy. 'Now we can bring the boy up properly, Seb,' she said. 'He will accompany us to church and I will be a mother to him.'

So why, after all this time, did he still dream about Ulrike Brandt? It made no sense to him. Hexie was ten times the woman she was, and now in the morning, she turned to him in her single bed in her small room in the lodging house she called home and hugged him close. He was soaked in sweat.

'What is it, my sweet?' she whispered, stroking his hair. 'The guns and bombs again?'

'Yes,' he said, his mind elsewhere. 'The guns and bombs.' It was a kind lie. No woman wanted to be told that her man was dreaming of someone else.

CHAPTER 16

When Seb arrived at the Presidium in the morning, he was surprised to find Hans Winter there in his office, smoking a cigarette.

'Good morning, Sergeant. I thought our partnership was successfully concluded.'

'Heil Hitler, Inspector.'

'Oh yes, Heil Hitler. Anyway, our time together is done, isn't it? Seems your idea that the markings on the corpse were part of some diabolical Jewish ritual was correct after all. What a clever guy you are.'

'You sound sceptical, Herr Wolff.'

'Do I? Why would that be, do you think?'

'Anyway, I am here to advise you that I have been assigned to the murder team on a permanent deployment, as your partner. Herr Meisinger has recognised my skills as a detective and has decided they are best employed here. I trust you will be very happy with this new arrangement.'

That was it, then. His drunken decision to quit the force had been the right one after all. At breakfast, drinking coffee with Hexie, he had begun to have doubts. This new development had cleared them away.

But first he had a couple of jobs to do: most importantly, he wanted to know more about this maidservant who had seen Friedlander and destroyed his already weak alibi.

'Well, Winter, I am delighted for you. Congratulations and may you solve many more murders.'

The BPP man smirked. 'And may you enjoy your undeserved moment of glory, Herr Wolff. For it will not last long.' He stubbed his cigarette in the ashtray. 'I look forward to putting out my smokes on your face. I am told it is very satisfying.'

Seb climbed the steps to the fifth floor. The secretary rose from her desk. 'I will see if Herr Ruff can speak with you.' Half a minute later she emerged from his office. 'He has an important meeting coming up, but he can give you one minute, no more.'

'That will be enough.'

As always, Ruff looked uneasy. It was his natural state but this morning, perhaps, he had more cause than usual for his discomfort.

'How can I help you, Wolff?'

'I need the name and address of this new witness, the maidservant who identified Karl Friedlander.'

'I'll have my secretary give you the details. Why do wish to know?'

Wasn't that obvious? 'Well, sir, I am the lead officer in this case and as such I will be required by the prosecution to help them prepare the case against Friedlander and give evidence at the trial. This maidservant's testimony will be crucial.'

'Of course, of course. Is that all?'

No, it wasn't. He was about to tell the chief of his decision to resign, but something stopped him. There was unfinished business and for that he needed to keep his badge. More than that, there was the indignation at having Hans Winter foisted on him. They knew he wasn't a Nazi and they wanted him to quit, to remove him from the protection of the police. Or, if not that, then discover some secret to condemn him. Well, that was as good a reason as any to stay. Sod Winter, sod Meisinger, sod all of them. 'Yes, Herr Ruff,' he said with a brief, respectful bow of the head. 'That is all.'

'Good. And once again, well done. You are a credit to the force.'

Guerrilla tactics were needed to avoid Winter and the ghastly prospect of him attaching himself to Seb, so he made his way down the back staircase from the fifth floor and exited the Presidium without signing out.

The maid's name was Marlene Popp, but she was known as Lena, and her address was towards Stadelheim in the less desirable area of Perlach, south-east of the city centre. Seb checked his watch. He would go to her later. First he had to meet Rosie Palmer's brother, though he doubted what value it could be.

Viscount Braybury was already in the cafe bar at the Vier Jahreszeiten, sipping coffee with Unity Mitford who immediately sprang up with an exaggerated heil and an arm thrust that might have put out the eye of a passing waitress had the poor young woman not swerved out of its upwards trajectory.

Seb returned the greeting in kind, then took Braybury's hand. 'Coffee, Inspector?'

'Thank you, yes.'

Braybury snapped his fingers and ordered another pot in good German, then turned back to Seb. 'English or German today?'

'English would be fine.'

'Well, what I wanted to talk about was our experience of the vile Friedlander when he was in England. You will doubtless have heard stories from him, a suggestion that he was somehow a victim of class discrimination or anti-Semitism, but nothing could be further from the truth. In short, *he* was the problem: he was a leech who attached himself to my sister and attempted to suck out her lifeblood.'

'He said you and one of your comrades gave him a beating.'

'Of course we did. So would you have if some creep was hounding and harassing your sister. Do you have a sister, Wolff?'

He shook his head.

'But you have loved ones, so I'm sure you know what I mean. There's only one thing these sort of people understand, and that's a damned good thrashing.'

'In what way did he harass your sister, Captain? It would be useful if you could give me detailed instances.'

'He wouldn't leave her alone. Wrote to her constantly, even turned up at her school and had to be escorted off the premises.'

'Do you have dates for these incidents?'

'Off the top of my head, no.'

'And the letters he wrote?'

'Burnt with the autumn leaves. I did it myself. They were disgusting.'

'In what way?'

'In the way he tried to inveigle his way into her affections. Promising kisses and what have you. Simply ghastly stuff.'

'Any details you have would be an asset. Perhaps you could write your recollections down and sign an affidavit which I could produce in court. Friedlander is our only suspect to date and there are inconsistencies in his story, but actual evidence is thin on the ground.'

'But he's been charged.'

'Yes, that is so. But he hasn't been tried and we want the case to be watertight before it is presented. Also, I wanted to ask you whether you had heard of a couple of other men who might have had an interest in your sister. One is English, Adam Rock. Does that name mean anything?'

'Of course it does. We were at school together. Chap talks politics all the time and has a very high opinion of himself, fancies he'll be prime minister one day, and who knows, one day he might be. He's good-looking in an Ancient Greek sort of way, but too caught up in himself to be much of a dreamboat for a young filly like my sis. She wanted dancing, romance and pleasure. But he's probably husband material for someone who fancies herself as a Westminster hostess one day. Why, is he here, too?'

Unity joined the conversation. 'He's staying with a good family in Altbogenhausen. Takes his German studies awfully seriously and is a great admirer of the Führer. He may be dull to you, Edward, but he's sound. One of us. I'm sure he wouldn't hurt a fly, Inspector.'

Seb made a mental note to seek him out.

'Anyway,' Unity continued, 'we know who the killer was. The despicable Friedlander. He was like a rash. Whenever I was with darling Rosie – and she was my best friend apart from you know who – he somehow always turned up. We'd be enjoying a quiet meal or a drink somewhere and suddenly there he was, ingratiating himself with her.'

'Did she object to this, tell him to clear off?'

'Rosie was far too well mannered. She treated him with kindness, which only encouraged the frightful man. But I saw the darkness beneath the smile, the evil worms slithering through his veins. I was terrified something bad would happen – and it did. He intimidated her into acquiescence, and then he killed her because he was a subhuman beast and because he couldn't have her.' For a moment, there was almost passion in her flat voice.

'Miss Mitford, you keep saying this to me, but it would really help our case in court if you could provide some solid facts. Or even better, some other witness to this intimidation.'

It puzzled him how such a bland, expressionless face could carry such a powerful element of cruelty, but in Unity Mitford's case it did. For some reason he could not have explained, Seb had a vision of her walking past a starving child and kicking it.

'I don't understand,' she said, the voice flat again. 'I have given you the name of the killer and his motive and now you have other evidence – the Jew marks on the body, the lie of the alibi, his attempt to flee – what more could you possibly need?'

'Will you stand up in court and testify?'

'Of course I will. Anything to have that man put down like the sick dog he is. You know, Inspector, your colleague does not share your doubts about the strength of the case.'

A cold chill ran down Seb's neck. 'My colleague?'

'Sergeant Winter. He is certain of Friedlander's guilt. It was he who identified the devilish cuts on the body as Jewish markings, I believe. That will be enough for any court.'

'When did you speak to Herr Winter, Miss Mitford?'

'Do you not talk to each other?'

'We have maximised our efforts by going separate ways.'

'Oh well, it was my good friend Fritz Mannheim who brought us together. And it was then that I realised what must have happened, which is when we came to you, for Winter said you were the lead detective and had to make the arrest.'

Seb was about to enquire whether Mannheim might have had an interest in Rosie Palmer, but thought better of it. 'Thank you, Miss Mitford. Perhaps we could arrange a time for you to come to the Police Presidium on Ettstrasse so that you can make your statement.' For all the good it would do. Unity, or 'Bobo', was a tainted witness and her testimony was nothing but malign speculation with no value whatsoever.

The court would love her.

He finished his coffee and took his leave of them. His meeting with Captain Edward Palmer, Viscount Braybury, had produced little of concrete value, but it had spiked his interest in two men: SS junior adjutant Fritz Mannheim and the English student Adam Rock.

Marlene 'Lena' Popp wasn't at home, but her mother was. Their small apartment was poor even by the standards of the other slum dwellings in the vicinity. Grease coated the walls of the tiny kitchen and the smell of boiling cabbage was overpowering.

'She's at work, Inspector. We need the money, like everyone else.'

'Of course. And perhaps you could tell me where she works?'

'At Baroness Laroche's house, of course. But you know that the other detective has already talked to her and made a full note of her testimony, surely?'

The other detective. Seb groaned inwardly. It was the reptile Winter again. Lena Popp was obviously the maid he had way-laid in the kitchen while Seb was talking with the baroness. An unpleasant thought immediately came to mind. It might not have taken many marks from Winter's wallet to persuade Fraulein Popp that she had seen Friedlander conveniently close to Karolinenplatz and the house of the Regensdorfs where Rosie Palmer had lodged.

Bribery. Was that possible? The poverty of these surroundings was obvious enough. A few extra coins in Lena Popp's purse could make all the difference. God, but this case was beginning to stink like a barrel-load of long dead fish.

CHAPTER 17

When he returned to the Presidium, Winter was still there, still smoking. The ashtray in Seb's office was overflowing with ash and butts.

'I wondered where you had got to, Inspector.'

'Matters to attend to. And get out of my chair.'

Winter ignored the order. 'You'll be pleased to know that the court case is being expedited. It will be dealt with in the next day or two.' He smacked the edge of his hand down on the desk, like the fall of a guillotine blade. 'Good news, eh?'

'We don't have all the statements yet. Now move your scrawny arse or I'll move it for you.'

Slowly, reluctantly, Winter accepted that he would be no match for Seb in a physical contest and rose from the chair. 'Statements?' he said, snorting with derision. 'A minor technicality, I think? Easily completed by the end of today. Anyway, Ruff wants you upstairs.'

That was surprising. Earlier in the day, he had seemed in a hurry to rid himself of Seb, as though his very presence was an embarrassment, which it should have been, given the potential injustice in which they were both complicit.

Ruff's secretary sent him straight through into the police chief's office.

'Sit down, Wolff. Perhaps a coffee?'

'Thank you, Herr Ruff,' he said, taking a seat opposite the deputy president of police. 'But no to the coffee.'

'Well, the Palmer case is complete, so I have another task for you.'

'There's still work to do, sir. The witnesses have not made their statements, and I need to interview Friedlander again to put the new evidence of the maidservant to him.' There were also others he wished to talk to; more of the dead girl's friends, particularly Mannheim and Rock.

'Pass that on to one of the other men in the murder team. We have another killing on our hands and I want you to take it on.'

'Is there a connection to the present case.'

'Good God, no. We don't even have an identification yet. A man killed in a back alley last night as he emerged from a rather disreputable club.' He lowered his voice and leant forward as though it were somehow a sin to even mention what followed. 'Paragraph 175.'

'Ah.' Paragraph 175 of the criminal code outlawed homosexual acts.

'Killed with a bullet to the head and then mutilated . . . down there.' He dipped his eyes towards his trousers.

'Where is he now?'

'With Lindner at the LMU. The professor is expecting you.'

'Should I not finish off what I'm doing? There are people I need to speak to. I haven't even heard the evidence of the maidservant yet.'

'No, this takes precedence. Oh, and you're still to work with Sergeant Winter. Orders from above, I'm afraid.'

'So I gather. I don't think they'll rest until I'm back in Dachau.'

'Come, come, Wolff, don't take that attitude. There's no danger to you after your fine work. You have the Führer on your side and there can be no greater insurance than that. Just smile and take things easy and Winter will be no trouble. He's not so bad is he?'

'Isn't he?'

'You just got off on the wrong foot. A misunderstanding, that's all. You might even make a detective of the man and then I'm sure he'll move on to other things and bother you no more.'

Seb just smiled. He was more likely to kill Winter first, but probably best not to say such things here. Who knew which walls and phones harboured BPP microphones these days? And there was another thing: if anyone thought that he was just going to let the Rosie Palmer case rest with his misgivings unresolved, they didn't know him very well.

As Seb rose from the chair and prepared to depart, Ruff leant forward and shook his hand. 'You're a good man, Wolff. I'll be putting your name forward as captain of detectives before too long.'

Seb wasn't fooled. Ruff knew very well that he had played little or no part in the arraignment of Friedlander, but this was about high-level diplomacy. It suited the purposes of the party's high command to have a heroic police figure to present to the British. Seb was that figure.

'God in heaven, Wolff,' Lindner said by way of greeting, his eyes straying towards Winter, 'what possessed you to bring this creature with you again?'

'He's promised he won't vomit.'

If Winter felt uncomfortable about being discussed in derogatory terms he didn't show it, just did his habitual salute and slunk at Seb's side like a whipped dog.

'So, Professor, what do we have?'

Lindner pulled back the sheet covering the corpse. Seb went cold with horror. The head was badly damaged by a bullet wound, which had exited through the right cheek, but the thin-shouldered little body was instantly recognisable as that of Caius Klammer, his friend from the Bavarian State Library. He had intended calling on him today to find out whether he had made any progress in identifying the marks on Rosie Palmer's body.

Involuntarily, Seb's eyes strayed lower, down below the abdomen. Klammer's penis and testicles had been removed, leaving a large red gash. 'Dear God.'

'Before you ask, the severed parts are in a dish over there.' He inclined his chin towards a shelf. 'I believe the killing took place close to an illicit club frequented by 175s, which might go some way to explaining the mutilation. The officer who brought the body here mentioned that neighbours had complained about the place and it was due to be raided and closed down. Perhaps one of the outraged neighbours took matters into their own hands.'

'I know the man,' Seb said. 'His name is Caius Klammer and he is – was – a librarian and expert in ancient scripts at the State Library. He had a remarkable mind.'

Seb wanted to avert his eyes, and yet he still gazed upon the sad remains. The pathetic, skinny body, pale and weak through years of long days and nights working in dusty archives. The whiteness of the flesh was a shocking contrast to the dark red blotch where once his genitals had resided.

Winter snorted. 'Why exactly are we bothering with this case? We know what he was, so just roll the corpse into an unmarked grave and let him rot.'

'He was a human being, Winter. If this investigation offends you, feel free to go and I will deal with it myself.'

'Perhaps you met this friend of yours at the filthy club he frequented, Herr Wolff? Perhaps you, too, have 175 tendencies? I could easily arrange for you to join your warm brothers in Dachau.'

Seb very much wanted to hit Winter, to pummel him to the floor and then trample on his head to stop his mouth. Instead he turned away, his whole body rigid with rage, and addressed Lindner. 'Are there any other clues on the body, Professor? Anything to help our inquiry?'

'All I can tell you is that the shot to the head was fired at close range and the bullet was 7.65 calibre, and the mutilation was carried out with a very sharp knife, for the cut was clean and done post-mortem, which is something of a mercy. Nothing else. No sign of recent sexual activity although I can say that the man had been sodomised over the years.'

'Well, there's a surprise,' Winter said.

Seb felt sick to his stomach, yet he was also thinking fast and lucidly, his mind careering like a Bugatti around the Nürburgring. Was this an attack on poor Caius because he was a homosexual, or because he had discovered something?

What the hell had Seb done in asking the innocuous and gentle little librarian for help?

Half an hour later, they had made their way to the Bavarian State Library and had informed the administration office about the death. Klammer's demise was met with shock and sadness; he had clearly been esteemed for his knowledge, even if not held in high affection. Too many secrets in his life for that.

They discovered Klammer's home address from the library's records, but there was no information regarding next of kin.

Looking at his workspace they found no personal possessions, nothing to give any indication of the man he was or his life outside the library.

Seb did this with Winter at his side because he was unable to shake him off.

Finally, they left. Summer rain was in the air and a wind was whipping up. Caius Klammer's apartment was in the north-west of the city past the Nymphenburg Palace, part of the industrial heartland of Munich. The body had been discovered a couple of kilometres away close to an abandoned warehouse that had served as the illicit club he had attended.

The scene of the murder was a dark, dead-end street near the Dachau road on which Seb had travelled not many hours before. First, they looked at the spot where he had died. Tracks of his blood were being washed away by a light drizzle. They learnt nothing.

They examined the warehouse which had served as the premises of the illicit club. No one was around. Uniformed police had raided the place after the discovery of the corpse in the alley, but none of the men had been caught. They were well practised at making for the exits whenever there was a raid on one of the temporary clubs they set up, all designed to avoid the attentions of the law.

Seb and Winter spent the next three hours going door-to-door among the working-class tenements overlooking the murder. No one had seen or heard anything, or so they said.

'If it puts the warm brothers off coming here, then that's no bad thing,' said one old man. Others spoke in similar tones. There was no sympathy for the victim.

No one admitted to being the concerned citizen who called the police anonymously to alert them to the murder. This dead-end street really was a dead end.

'So,' Seb said at last as they walked back to the car. 'We're getting nowhere fast. Let's see what his home throws up.'

Winter wouldn't keep his mouth shut as Seb drove his Lancia through the city streets. He sounded off at the homosexuals, the

Jews, the communists, the Catholics, the French, the British until Seb had had enough and found a way to change the subject.

'Tell me, Sergeant,' he said. 'Your accent suggests to me that you are not Munich born and raised. You are a northerner, are you not? But which part exactly?'

'That's my business.'

'Come, come. We're friends aren't we? I'd like to know a bit more about you.'

'I'm not your friend.'

'Correct me if I'm wrong, but I would place you in the Ruhr – perhaps the province of Westphalia. Would that be close?'

Winter shrugged.

'What of the great industrial city of Dortmund? Yes, Dortmund. I have a friend there and I would definitely put you down as a Dortmund man. So you moved from one beer town to another, eh? What happened, you drink Dortmund dry?'

Winter was shrinking in his seat. It was obvious that he really didn't like this line of questioning. Max Haas had been right, there was something strange and unspoken about his move from the Dortmund Gestapo to the Munich Political Police.

'My questions seem to be making you uncomfortable, Sergeant. Perhaps you have something to hide.'

'Of course not.'

'A fine city, Dortmund. But you prefer Munich. Well, that's understandable.'

'I haven't said I come from Dortmund. My origins are my business. Anyway, what are you getting at Wolff?'

'Herr Wolff. What am I getting? Well, you have asked me about my war service, so why don't you tell me about your background. Dortmund, eh? Is your family still there? Are you a married man? Do you have children? Perhaps we have friends in common.'

'My family is not your concern, or anything else about me. I am a professional policeman doing a job, that is all.'

'Does that mean we can't share a beer after work and have a few laughs together?'

'It means exactly that. I have absolutely no desire to drink beer with you, let alone laugh.'

'No, I can see that. I don't imagine you laugh much.'

'There is nothing remotely amusing about you, Herr Wolff. You may think yourself clever, but I always know when you are mocking me and my BPP badge, and I make a note. One day you will pay your dues.'

'In the meantime, here we are.' He pulled up at the kerb in front of a pleasant block of flats in a leafy street. 'The home of the late Caius Klammer, who was a decent man. And you can make a note of that, too, Sergeant.'

Klammer's home was on the ground floor, next door to the land-lady who let them in.

She was a young mother with two small children around her skirts and she was genuinely shocked as Seb flashed his badge and gave her the news of the murder.

The woman put her hand to her mouth, her eyes wide with horror. 'This is terrible news. He was such a lovely man.'

'He was a 175,' Winter said. 'Whoever killed him did the world a favour.'

Seb pushed him away. 'You speak when I tell you to, Winter.' He turned back to the woman. 'Excuse my partner, he is new to the job and is not over-endowed with brains. Please ignore him.' He put his arm around her shoulder to lead her towards her tenant's door. 'Now, perhaps we could go into the apart-ment and you can tell us all you know about Herr Klammer. Did he have family?'

She opened the door onto his living space. Seb had expected it to be spotlessly tidy, like his office at the library, but this was anything but. Books and papers were scattered across the floor. Drawers were open and, in his bedroom, blankets and sheets were crumpled and tossed into a corner of the room. The mattress was half-on half-off the bed.

'Someone has been here,' the landlady said. 'Caius was such a tidy man, such a good tenant. He always kept his rooms so well.'

Indeed, it was clear to Seb that this was not Klammer's work. Someone had been here and had been looking for something. 'Did you not hear anything? An intruder?'

She hesitated then shook her head.

'Are you sure, dear lady?'

'I don't know. I sleep at the back of the house and these walls are thick, but I thought I heard something late last night, but then I was too scared to go and look and decided I must have been mistaken.'

'And the front door?'

'It was locked as usual this morning.'

'Herr Klammer had his own key?'

'Of course, yes.'

Seb nodded grimly. What were the odds the murderer had removed his victim's keys from his pocket after killing him? Klammer's wallet, fountain pen and a few coins were with his body at the LMU, but Seb did not recall seeing any keys.

'Do you have any idea what the intruder might have been looking for?'

'Only books. His whole life was books.'

Seb spent the next hour collecting up Klammer's scattered belongings while Winter sat in an armchair and looked on. Seb was happy with that; he didn't want any assistance from the man. Meanwhile the landlady, who gave her name as Frau Kulmann, brought them ersatz coffee.

'Did you know he was a 175?' Winter demanded of her with unwarranted aggression.

'I had no idea.'

'For if you did – if at any time he brought men back here at night – then it would have been your duty to report it to the authorities. You understand that?'

'Of course, but there was nothing like that.'

Seb paid little heed to the conversation. He was looking for three things and found only one of them: several letters from a woman in Vienna who began every missive with the words 'Dear Brother' and ended each with 'your loving sister, Ingrid.' So he had some family. Seb would make the difficult telephone call to Ingrid when he returned to the office.

The other two things were not there. Most notable by their absence were the photographs of Rosie Palmer that he had taken away in an attempt to decipher the lesions and lipstick markings on the body. The other thing Seb had hoped to find was some clue to the nature of the markings if, indeed, they had any meaning at all. But there was nothing.

CHAPTER 18

Seb stared at the phone in his office for a full five minutes before picking it up and making the call he dreaded, to Caius Klammer's widowed sister Ingrid Grosse in Vienna. It was sad and painful. She was shattered by the news and could barely speak.

'But who would want to harm him, Herr Wolff? He had never hurt a soul.' She was trying to speak through heart-wrenching sobs.

'There will always be bad people in the world. We are trying to find a motive, but it seems senseless. Perhaps robbery.' He wasn't going to tell this poor woman any of the obscene facts involved in this atrocity.

'What happens now, Inspector Wolff?'

'We can talk later about funeral plans,' Seb said. 'You could perhaps come to Munich or perhaps you might wish to have the body removed to another place for burial? Just let me know and I will help you with the arrangements. And, of course, I will keep you informed regarding the progress of our investigations.'

'Thank you, sir, thank you.'

'And you might like to know that I was a friend of your brother. He was a great help and mentor when I was trying to make up for my lack of education a few years ago. A wonderful man.'

'Yes, he was. He always came to us in Vienna at Christmas to celebrate the Lord's birth with my children and me. I am a widow, you see. Christmas was the last time I saw him, six months ago, but we always felt close in our hearts.'

'And no other relatives?'

'A few distant cousins that's all. But we're not in touch.'

'What of his friends here in Munich?'

'He never spoke of his friends. I suppose he must have had some, but I have no names. As you know, he was a quiet man and kept himself to himself.'

'Well, if any thoughts come to you, Frau Grosse, please call me. Without knowing more about your brother, this is going to be a difficult case to solve. We have no witnesses and no clear motive.'

'You think it is possible he knew the killer?'

'It is always a starting point in a police investigation.'

Putting down the phone, he closed his eyes and took a few deep breaths. Winter was not in the room with him. Seb dialled again, this time to the LMU and got put through to Professor Lindner.

'Do you have copies of the photographs of Rosie Palmer showing the marks?'

'Your lot took all the evidence, Wolff, and the body has gone for burial. I believe it is being flown back to England.'

'My lot?'

'Police. They wanted everything filed away for use in court.'

'Did these officers give you a name? Not Sergeant Winter by any chance?'

'No, not him. A couple of BPP heavies, I think. Anyway, I'll ask my secretary and get back to you.'

'How do you suggest we proceed, Sergeant Winter?'

'What do you mean?'

'I mean the murder of Caius Klammer. Where do we start? We have few enough clues. I wondered if perhaps you might have some idea.'

'Round up some 175s, get them to talk.'

'Why would a 175 kill another 175? Surely it is more likely to be someone who resents them? I thought it was interesting that the bullet was a 7.65 mm. That could be a Walther PPK, of course – standard police issue.'

'You think a cop shot him? That would be commendable, perhaps, but unlikely.'

Seb choked back his renewed desire to crush Winter's windpipe and smiled instead. 'So, back to my first question. How do you suggest we proceed?'

'You're the great murder detective, Herr Wolff, so you lead and I'll follow.'

'We should talk again to his colleagues at the library. Someone must know something. Why don't you do that while I make a few phone calls, talk to people who might know more than we do about the underworld in which Herr Klammer moved.'

'You're trying to brush me off again.'

'I'm trying to make some use of you.'

Seb found Lena Popp at Baroness Laroche's house in Konigin-strasse. The baroness listened in silence as he explained why he wished to speak to her.

'Well,' she said at last. 'She'll be upstairs changing the bedding, so make yourself at home, Inspector. See what she has to say for herself.'

'Just one thing. To be certain, she would have seen Rosie Palmer here at your house?'

'I suppose she would have. Yes, of course, most certainly. As I told you, Rosie came here often. I liked her very much and we got on very well despite the difference in our ages.'

'And Karl Friedlander, would she have seen him?'

'You know, at the risk of repeating myself, these SS boys are all cut from same cloth.'

'Friedlander is not SS, he is a Jew and his looks are not Nordic Aryan. He has dark, curly hair. A very handsome young man.'

A light came on in the baroness's eyes. 'Of course, yes, when you put it like that, yes, indeed, I did meet him. Just the once. A lovely young man. He and Rosie seemed very close. Laughing and chatting a lot. I recall that Unity seemed put out, a bit miffed. You know she takes all this anti-Semitism stuff rather seriously, and it did seem to me that the young man – Karl, did you say? – was probably Jewish.'

'Yes, he's Jewish. And he has been accused of killing Rosie. Lena Popp is giving evidence that she saw him in the vicinity of her lodgings.'

'I'm shocked, Herr Wolff, truly I am. He appeared to be a rather gentle soul.'

'Well, your maidservant's testimony against him is likely to be crucial. So I repeat, would she have seen him here in the weeks before Rosie's death? Would she have known him by sight?'

'It's possible. Why don't you ask her yourself? I'll call her down.'

*

Lena Popp was small with a sweet, open face. But she was visibly nervous, which was no surprise to Seb. She stood upright, her shoulders taut, her hands twisting together in front of her crisp white apron.

'Heil Hitler, Fräulein Popp.'

'Heil Hitler, sir.'

'I am Inspector Wolff from the murder team at the Munich Police Presidium in Ettstrasse. Have you heard of it?'

'Yes, sir.'

'I believe you met my colleague, Sergeant Winter?'

'Yes, sir.' The girl's gaze moved between Seb and the baroness, who stood to one side of the parlour, her arms folded across her ample figure, watching with interest.

'And you told him something about a young man named Karl Friedlander. Is that correct?'

'Yes, sir.'

'How do you know Herr Friedlander?'

'I . . . I don't know him, but I have seen him here.'

'When was that?'

'Maybe last autumn?'

'You don't sound sure.'

'It was a while ago, but I remember him.'

'Then perhaps you can describe him to me.'

'He . . . he looked Jewish.'

'Jews come in all shapes and sizes. Some are fair-haired, some dark, some tall, some short – and everything in between. Perhaps you could manage a more detailed and precise description.'

She was blinking rapidly now. Seb guessed her age at no more than eighteen; hardly older than his own son. And she was becoming flustered. She didn't expand on her statement.

'Well, Fräulein Popp?'

'I suppose he was dark-haired. A big nose.'

'That doesn't sound like Herr Friedlander.'

'Maybe not such a big nose. I don't know. You're confusing me.'

'But you would recognise him?'

'I . . . yes, I would recognise him.'

'You know, of course, that lying to a court of law is a serious offence. Those who do not speak the complete truth to a judge could end up in prison themselves. Now tell me, did you ever have occasion to talk to Herr Friedlander?'

Her pert face creased and twitched. She no longer looked remotely sweet. 'Do you think I am lying then? I know what I saw. It was him, the Jew, the murderer. I saw him from the tram on my way home.' Her soft, light voice was sharp, both defensive and accusing. 'You are just twisting my words.'

'In what way?'

'You are doubting that I saw the man, and yet I did – and he will pay the price for his foul deed.'

'How did you discover that Herr Friedlander was under investigation?'

She shrugged. 'Word gets around.'

'But who specifically?'

'I don't know. I was in the Löwenbräukeller at Stiglmairplatz, waitressing because we need the extra money. I do shifts some nights. People were talking, that's all. It might not be in the papers, but everyone's talking about the English girl being killed. Someone mentioned that a Jew called Friedlander had been arrested. That's when I remembered seeing him, the swine.'

'And then what did you do?'

'Called you lot, didn't I? Sergeant Winter took the call.'

'And you're certain of what you saw?'

'Of course.'

'You realise your testimony could cost that young man his life?'

'Good. He deserves everything he gets for what he did to English Rosie. Lovely girl, she was.'

Karl Friedlander didn't move, did not even raise his eyes when Seb entered cell number 40 on the fourth floor of the police prison at the Presidium. The room was narrow – six metres by two – and a foul smell emanated from the water closet. There was no bed, just a low pallet with a black sack stuffed with straw. No mattress or pillow. The only light came from a tiny window, close to the ceiling and out of reach. Friedlander sat hunched up on the pallet, his head hanging.

'Stand up.'

The prisoner leapt to his feet.

'Get used to obeying orders, instantly. This is bad for you, Herr Friedlander – don't make it worse.'

'No, sir.'

'Have you been told of the new evidence against you?'

He nodded. 'Yes, but it's a lie.'

'That's as maybe. What matters is what the court believes. Do you remember this maid, this witness?'

'No, I didn't notice her. But then I only had eyes for Rosie.'

'Have you got a lawyer?'

'My father has used a lawyer in the past, but he is a Jew like us and he has had the sense to leave the country.'

'Do you have money to pay a lawyer?'

'That depends on the price.'

'I'll see whether one can be found.' Preferably Aryan, he thought. The court might not even accept a Jewish lawyer.

'Thank you, sir.'

'No promises, though. In the meantime, answer questions honestly and openly. Silence will be taken as evidence that you are hiding something and you will be presumed guilty.'

'Do you believe I am innocent, Inspector?'

'I collect evidence. Guilt or innocence is for a court of law to decide, not me.'

'And my parents, what of them? I have been told nothing.'

He didn't want to be the conveyor of bad news, but he had to be honest. 'They are in custody and if you are convicted, they will almost certainly be accused of harbouring a criminal and helping you try to evade justice. But it is possible that your mother will be treated leniently and allowed to go free.'

'But not my father?'

'We must hope for the best. For him – and for you, Herr Friedlander. This is out of my hands now.'

CHAPTER 19

'Anything, Sergeant?'

'Still nothing. None of the library guys want to even admit knowing him. All they will say is that he kept to himself and didn't socialise so they didn't really know him. None would admit to being his friend.'

Seb wasn't surprised. Caius Klammer had led a secret life and let few people in because it was safer that way. It always had been. Paragraph 175 of the criminal code preceded the ascent to power of Hitler and his party. Germany had never looked kindly on homosexuals.

'Well, I'm calling it a night. We'll meet up again at eight tomorrow morning and take it from there.'

'I know what you're up to, Wolff.'

'*Herr* Wolff . . .'

First stop was the Residenz. He had called ahead to Uncle Christian's secretary and after a two-minute pause was informed that Councillor Weber would indeed afford his nephew a short audience if he cared to call in within the next half-hour. After that, the councillor would be at the opera.

Once again, they met in the Black Hall. 'What is it now, boy? Haven't I done enough for you already?'

'I have a favour to ask, but this isn't for me. It's for the accused man, Friedlander, and for Germany and, by extension, for us.'

'Get to the point. *The Merry Widow* awaits and I do not intend to miss her.'

'He needs a lawyer, a good lawyer.'

'Have you taken leave of your senses? Why would you care if the Jew has a lawyer or not?'

'For the British. I know them from my time aboard the *Eastern Star* and they will not believe justice has been done for the dead girl unless the trial is held to their standards. And that means Friedlander must be properly represented. If not, then this could very easily come back to haunt Germany.'

'So?'

'Well, guess who will be blamed? I will be, and so will you.'

Weber clasped his hands around his enormous belly and blinked while he thought. Seb could almost see the cunning cogs turning in his brain. Uncle Christian had rarely done anything that did not bring him benefit. Finally, he nodded.

'You're right, boy. My lawyer, Brühne, will be with the killer in his cell first thing in the morning.'

'Thank you, Uncle. Enjoy the opera.'

He would have liked to meet up with Hexie but she was seeing her mother, so instead he drove home, where he found Mutti in a state of distress.

'I tried calling you, Seb, but no one knew where you were.'

'I'm sorry, what's the matter?'

'It's Jurgen – I don't know what's happening.'

'What do you mean? Where is he?'

'He's gone. Oh, Sebastian, he came home limping, his face all bruised and bloody, collected a few things from his room and then hugged me and kissed me and told me not to worry – and just went.'

This wasn't making sense. His mother was walking back and forth across the kitchen as if she didn't know where to put herself.

'You mean he's left home?'

'It's that Silke, I know it is. I looked out of the window and she was there waiting for him. Then they went off together towards Leopoldstrasse. In that direction anyway.'

'Mutti, please sit down. Now tell me, what time was this?'

'Just before seven. It all happened so fast I didn't know what he was doing.'

'And his face was battered?'

'He looked in such a state. I wanted to clean the blood from his face and have a look to see if he was badly injured, but he wouldn't let me. He just said it was nothing, a scratch.'

'And Silke? You mean Silke Stutz from his elementary school years?' Seb recalled the girl from way back. She and Jurgen had played together as children and were close in age. He hadn't seen her recently, but he imagined that she must have developed into a fine-looking young woman. Well, of course, Jurgen was going to chase after someone like that. One day you look at someone you've known all your life and suddenly you see them in a new light.

'I think they've been stepping out together for a few weeks now. You just don't notice these things, Sebastian, you're so busy. But to me it's like you and Ulrike all over again and it breaks my heart.'

Seb put an arm around his mother's shoulders and she sank her head against him.

'Come, Mutti, don't fret. He's a boy, a young man, and he's got in a fight, that's all. It's a commonplace thing. Probably over the girl. Do you know where she lives?' Even as he asked the question, he was pretty sure he remembered her living nearby. In fact just a couple of streets away in Wilhelmstrasse, but he didn't know the number. He was sure he could get it with a quick call to the late desk at the Presidium.

'No. Oh, Sebastian, everything seems to be going wrong. Just everything. You and that Hexie, now Jurgen and this girl.'

'Nothing's going wrong, Mutti, it's just life. But tell me about Jurgen: do you think he hurt himself in an accident, or was it a fight?'

'He was in a fight, Sebastian, I'm sure about that. I don't know what to make of it all. He didn't even have his supper. Have I upset him?'

'I'll go around there. Don't worry, we'll sort it out. He's just fed up with me, that's all. It's nothing to blame yourself for.'

She squeezed her son's hands. 'I know you think I am a foolish old woman, but I know things and I have seen things in my life. I saw Bismarck once, did I ever tell you that? And I saw the bullets flying when Hitler tried his revolution in 1923. Did I tell you that?'

He smiled, and squeezed her hands back. *Yes, Mutti,* he thought but didn't say, *you have told me those things countless times.*

Leaving the apartment, he called the Presidium from the phone in the hallway and they soon found the address for Dr Helmut

Stutz in Wilhelmstrasse. Now Seb recalled, the girl's father was a physician.

It would only have been a few minutes' walk, but he climbed in the Lancia without really thinking. Two turns later, he screeched to a halt outside the Stutz house, jumped out of the car and knocked at the door. It was quickly answered by Frau Stutz and he nodded to her. They had only ever known each other to say good morning or good afternoon at the school gate and that was years ago.

She smiled, but there was concern too. 'Ah, Herr Wolff, you've come about Jurgen.'

'So he's here?'

'He's been in a fight at the Hitler Youth and he's very upset. My husband is just cleaning up his cuts and checking his leg. Just two or three stitches in his head, I think. No bad damage done fortunately. Would you like to come in?'

Seb accepted the invitation with thanks. Looking at Frau Stultz, he remembered her daughter, because they had always appeared similar in appearance. She was a woman in her early forties, filled out from eating well and adding a few years, but still good looking. There was both intelligence and kindness in her face.

'A glass of schnapps, perhaps, Herr Wolff?'

'Thank you, but no.'

'This must all be terribly upsetting for you, and I have to say I really do sympathise, as does my husband.' She lowered her voice. 'Silke is in the League of German Girls and takes it terribly seriously. We don't really mind – why would we? – except that her school work suffers. Oh, and she has this silly idea that it is her duty to start having babies for the greater good of Germany.' Frau Stutz raised a weary eyebrow. 'Well, she knows perfectly well that I'm not having that until she's got her medical degree at the very least, and preferably a marriage certificate in her drawer.'

Seb nodded. 'I understand. You must know that Jurgen is at the gymnasium and, of course, I want him to go to university, perhaps study law – or even medicine – but he doesn't have much inclination for schoolwork at the moment. Sport and outdoor activities are everything and his brain atrophies.'

'Oh, he's still clever though. It's the comradeship, that's what Helmut says. Young people of that age just want to be together, to be on the same side.'

Seb didn't need to be told that. He remembered all too well the comradeship as he and Max and the others marched off to war. And then, in the trenches as Ulrike faded into the background of his thinking, it was that friendship and loyalty of men and boys that kept them all going through the terror and the hell. Comradeship, unto death itself.

'And now you have the other problem, it must be awful for you.'

Seb assumed that Jurgen had told the family about the night he spent in Dachau. He trotted out his new mantra. 'It was a misunderstanding, nothing more. Is that what caused this fight he's been in?'

She smiled sadly. 'I do think that's it, yes. The way I understand it, there's another lad vying with Jurgen to be senior troop leader. These past couple of days he's been saying things about you and Jurgen lashed out at him.'

Seb could well imagine what insults had been thrown. Much the same sort of insults that Jurgen himself had been throwing around the house whenever anyone upset him. *Traitor, Bolshevik, Jew lover.* Well, Seb only considered the first of those three an actual insult. He had nothing against Jews and a man or woman's politics should be their own concern. But that was not a discussion to get into with Frau Stutz.

The question that immediately raised itself in Seb's mind was whether Jurgen had been protecting himself, or defending his father's honour. Probably the former, but the latter would have been gratifying.

'Anyway, let's go through and see them. Silke has begged us to let him stay here tonight. We really don't mind either way, but if it helps you take the heat out of the situation, then it's fine by us. They wouldn't be sharing a room, of course.'

'Let me talk to him first.'

'Very well. I'll show you through.'

It dawned on him suddenly that this was a bad idea. There really was too much heat, too much rancour. It wouldn't be fair to have a full-scale row in the home of this decent family. Even worse, an argument now could only make matters worse between father and son in the long term. One or both of them would say things that couldn't be unsaid. 'On second thoughts, perhaps I won't talk to him now. If he could just stay here tonight as you offered? Would you please tell him I came by.'

'Of course.'

'Perhaps you would tell him that I think we should talk tomorrow when we both feel a bit calmer. I know that in his mind this is all my fault.'

'Oh, I'm sure he doesn't really think that.'

'I'm afraid he does – and so I'll go now.'

'Are you sure?'

'Yes, and my thanks to you and your husband for looking after him. I can tell he is in the very best of hands. Jurgen and I may have disagreements, but he means everything to me.'

She smiled again and this time there was hope and warmth in the expression. 'I'll be sure to tell him that. And please don't worry, Herr Wolff. We'll take care of your son. He might have a bit of a headache but if you give me a telephone number one of us will call to let you know how he is. The important thing is that he's a good lad, and I can tell that you're a fine man.'

CHAPTER 20

How could he sleep? The rift with Jurgen was ugly. The boy was seventeen and Seb knew that age all too well. It was an age when decisions were made that could affect a man's whole life. An age when parents and their children broke apart, sometimes irrevocably. As far as Seb knew, Ulrike had never spoken to her parents again after they threw her out for getting pregnant.

That was too high a price to pay.

Calling in at home, he reassured his mother that Jurgen was fine, and then ate a quick supper, more to comfort her than because he was hungry. 'I have to go out now, Mutti. Don't wait up for me.'

It was still daylight, a good time to get out into the city, talk to people and try to make some headway. A time when Sergeant Hans Winter was not at his side. He had no doubt that Caius Klammer had been murdered because someone feared he knew something; that the killer of Rosie Palmer wanted to silence him before he could pass on the significance of the markings on her body. Nor did he have much doubt that Karl Friedlander was innocent.

The air had cleared of rain and the evening sky was bright and blue. The days were long and the summer heat was coming through. Of course the days were long. It was almost the solstice.

With the top of the Lancia down, he drove over the river to Alt-bogenhausen with the breeze in his hair. It should have felt good to be alive, but too much was crowding in on him. Too many unanswered questions, too much tragedy.

The house was large and more like a traditional Bavarian village house than a town dwelling. Its walls were rendered and had been daubed with paintings of rural scenes. There was a balcony with window boxes overflowing with geraniums and it was well positioned in an enviable tree-lined street. He knocked at the door with no idea what to expect. A young woman in her twenties answered. She wore a dirndl and no makeup and might have been mistaken for a servant, but Seb had a feeling this was the lady of the house.

He gave her the salute, which she returned in kind, then showed her his badge. 'I am Inspector Wolff, Kripo. I was given to believe that a young Englishman named Adam Rock lodges at this address.'

'Adam? Yes, he is out at present. But why did you want him, Inspector?'

'Just tying up loose ends in a case involving a young English-woman. It seems he knew her and might be able to provide some information.'

'Do you mean the murder of Miss Palmer?'

'Ah, you have heard of the case?'

'Of course. I had met the poor girl.'

'May I ask your name, madam?'

'I am Frau Raspe. Heidi Raspe.'

Raspe. It was not a common name. Seb found himself computing the possibilities. 'Are you, perhaps, Colonel Raspe's daughter?'

'I am his wife.'

She was at least thirty years his junior. 'Forgive me, Frau Raspe.'

She smiled. 'You are not the first to make that error.'

So this was the wife of Otto Raspe, the writer of all things *Völkisch*. And she had known Rosie. 'Perhaps you would be willing to answer a few questions about your knowledge of Miss Palmer?'

'But I thought the matter was all settled. The killer has been found and is due in court. Is that not correct?'

'A man has been charged, but he intends to plead not guilty, so it is necessary to make the case as strong as possible. It is my duty to firm up every detail for a successful prosecution.'

'Well, I can't tell you much and my husband isn't here. He would, of course, need to give me permission to talk to you.'

There was no way to argue with irrational subservience. It seemed to be all over Munich these days. No makeup, no smok-ing, no talking without permission of your father or husband. Not all women, thank God. The idea of Hexie ever taking orders from a man was laughable in the extreme.

'Then do you have any idea where Adam Rock is this evening?'

'Why, he's at his German class. With Frau Baum. Do you know of her?'

'Gretchen Baum? Indeed, I do, madam. And I thank you.'

He was halfway over the bridge when he noticed the motorbike in his rear-view mirror. It was nothing special, he didn't even register the marque, but it was the heavy, hunched shoulders, the darkened goggles and the thick leather jacket of the rider that he noted, for he had seen the man earlier – on the way to Altbogenhausen. He seemed too big for the machine.

It was definitely the same man.

Having crossed the bridge, Seb slowed and pulled to a halt at the side of the road close to the military museum. He waited. The motorbike carried on past, not slowing. The rider, however, could not resist looking back before carrying on his way, turning left on to Ludwigstrasse.

Seb immediately followed him. As expected, the rider had stopped and was waiting, to follow him either to left or right. The Lancia slowed and ranged alongside the motorcyclist. Seb got out and approached the man, who was lifting the bike onto its stand and dismounting.

'Can I help you?' Seb said.

'What do you mean?'

'I saw you following me and imagined you must want something.'

'I'm not following you. I am just parked here, minding my own business.'

He was undoubtedly too big for his motorbike. Bigger and brawnier than Seb. His eyes were still covered by his round smoked-glass goggles, giving him an other-worldly look. Like a mole, perhaps, though that might be an unkindness to moles. The corners of his mouth were set down in a fixed scowl.

'Who do you work for? Do you have identification?'

'Mind your own business.'

'It is my business. I am a criminal inspector with the Munich police. If you like, I will take you to the Presidium for a little questioning. The choice is yours.'

'I shit on you, Wolff.'

The man was reaching into his coat pocket, but Seb was faster. He slammed his fist into the rider's face, then hit him again as he was reeling backwards onto the kerb. The big man's hand was out of his pocket now, clasping an automatic pistol, but the blows had loosened his grip and the gun fell away into the drainage channel.

Seb knelt over him. 'Pull a gun, would you? Now, you really are coming to Ettstrasse with me.' He hit him again, this time in the belly, just below the ribcage and the man gasped with shock and pain as the air was knocked from his lungs.

Reaching across, he picked up the man's pistol, slipped the safety lever off and pointed it between his eyes. 'Now get up, slowly. A false move and I'll splatter your brains across the road.'

'You're making a bad mistake, Wolff.'

'Up.'

'Damn it, Wolff, I'm BPP.'

Why was Seb not surprised? Clearly, the political boys wouldn't be able to keep tabs on him simply by glueing Winter to his side during the regular working day. And there was something else. If Caius Klammer had been killed because of his connection to him, how would their enemies have even known about the link. Someone other than Winter must have been reporting back on Seb's movements, but to whom and why? Why would anyone in the political police want to protect a murderer, if that was what was happening?

He had been watched and shadowed ever since his exit from Dachau. And whoever was behind it was either part of the BPP or protected by it.

'Show me your badge.'

The big motorcyclist wiped his sleeve across his blood-streaked face, then put his hand in his jacket pocket.

'Slowly, carefully.'

'I've only got the one gun.'

'Walther PPK 7.65, like mine. The bullet that killed Caius Klammer was 7.65.'

'Who?'

'Never mind.'

'Shit, Wolff, I think you've broken my nose.'

'I can do worse if you tempt me.'

He showed the card. The man was BPP all right, but that was all it said.

'What's your name?'

'You're really going to pay for this, Wolff. Do you realise that?'

Seb hit him again hard, knocking him back and almost unconscious. Blood was seeping from his grim mouth and he was groaning, his head lolling. Behind him, on the paving, there was a large, fresh dog turd. Seb dropped the BPP man's service pistol into the stinking mess and pressed it down with a twig. Then he kicked the motorbike over for good measure.

'That should give you something to put in your report.'

CHAPTER 21

Gretchen Baum lived in a large ground-floor apartment in Schwabing, close to the house of Baroness Laroche and the student hostel. It was convenient, because that was the area where most of the English and Americans stayed, and they were the ones who would pay for language lessons.

'I don't know why you didn't come here sooner, Detective,' she said, smoothing down her skirt. 'I know everyone in the English student community.'

'You're right – a bad mistake on my part.' He had been close to Gretchen Baum for many years, since childhood. She had been betrothed to a schoolfriend named Johann Frick, who caught a lethal bullet in the belly in the last week of the war. Seb had promised Johann that he would always keep an eye out for the girl; they had all made that promise about their girls, all the friends. Gretchen had never found anyone to replace Johann and Seb felt ashamed today that he hadn't been to see her in a while.

Not that she needed looking after. She was a free spirit and more than capable of looking after herself.

'So why do you come to me now when you already have the killer locked up?'

'Oh, just making sure. I wanted to speak to a young man named Adam Rock. I believe he's here with you this evening.'

'He was, but he's gone off with Unity. The Löwenbräu, I believe.'

'Tell me about him, Gretchen. Is he a good student?'

'Yes, he is. The best. A very quick learner. He loves all things German, which I admire in any man. But I don't like him. The way he looks at me, as though he's searching for something, some secret that even I don't know about.'

From what Seb had already heard it occurred to him that perhaps the young man was looking for his own reflection in Gretchen's eye. 'When you say all things German, what exactly are you referring to? The beer, the local costumes, the music, our architecture?'

'All those and more. Mostly, I mean the stupid *Völkisch* movement. Perhaps he has been influenced by his host, who knows?'

'You are referring to Colonel Otto Raspe, of course.'

'Well, he is the king and emperor of all things *Völkisch*, isn't
he? Blood and soil and ancient German mythology. All that
Thule stuff. All nonsense. Mind you, Adam Rock fits the bill
for that – he looks like one of those muscular Aryan statues
by Thorak or Breker. Carved out of rock, perhaps.' Gretchen
laughed at her own little joke. When she smiled, her face lit up
and her eyes shone.

What was Thule? Where did the word come from? He had
heard that it was the name of some mythical Aryan island in the
far north, somewhere like Iceland. But that sounded like nothing more than a fairy tale, a word the Brothers Grimm might
have conjured up. 'Some people take it seriously, Gretchen. Some
important people. So try not to laugh too loud.'

'Will you arrest me then?'

'I would do, of course, but I'm too busy right now. By the way,
how well do you know Unity?'

'That's a tough question. Talk to half a dozen people and you'll
get six assessments of her character. Some love her, some admire
her, some loathe her, some think her utterly brainless. I reserve
judgement. But she does work hard at her German and can stay in
a conversation pretty well when she's with himself at the Osteria
Bavaria. Not in the same league as Adam Rock, though. He's not
only very Aryan, but very smart, too.'

'Thank you, Gretchen. I suppose I had better crawl off into the
night to see if I can find her and Mr Rock before they move on to
another bar.'

'My pleasure as always, Detective. And give my love to Hexie.'

'I will.'

'Oh, and by the way, I met the killer once or twice.'

Seb's ears pricked up. 'Friedlander?'

'The very same.'

'You call him the killer. Does that mean you believe him guilty?'

'Well, don't you? Isn't that why you've charged him?'

'Some people at Ettstrasse aren't so sure.' He was talking about himself, of course, and knowing Gretchen, she would probably understand that.

'Really? Actually, I wasn't the slightest bit surprised that he was charged. He was an utter pain and more than a bit creepy. Used to hang around in the street in front of my door whenever Rosie was here for her lessons. Like a puppy waiting for its master. I threatened to call the police on him once and then he skulked away. But he was back a few days later. Pathetic piece of work.'

'Why didn't you mention this before?'

'I didn't think it was relevant. Hardly compelling evidence of murderous intent, is it?'

He found Unity and the young man named Adam Rock at the Löwenbräukeller, among a group of young men and women, all sitting at a large table. Well, Seb assumed it was Rock from the description given to him by Gretchen Baum.

On the way here, he recalled that this was the beerhouse where the maidservant Lena Popp had said she was doing a waitressing shift when she heard about Friedlander being taken in for questioning. Seb's detective brain tended to spot such coincidences.

Seb did not go straight up to Rock because he rather suspected the reaction to his arrival from Unity would not be positive. Instead he went to the bar and bought himself a beer and watched them from a distance.

Fritz Mannheim was with the group and, not for the first time, it occurred to Seb that the SS officer was probably there with orders to keep an eye on Hitler's blonde friend.

Next to him, he recognised one of the girls from the student hostel: Frances de Pole, the one who had shown Unity's room to Seb and suggested they might like to go out for a drink or two. She had been the one who first mentioned Adam Rock.

Another young man and woman were with them. Both English from the cut of their clothes and general demeanour.

Most interesting, though, was the one he took to be Rock. He was built like a straight-backed boxer with carved features and short fair hair, shaved close at the sides, and he wore German clothes, including a lightweight linen jacket in traditional Bavarian style with cut-away collar and horn buttons.

The bar-room was as busy as ever. The air was sweet with the stink of beer, smoke and sweat. An accordionist was playing for a group of six *schuhplattler* dancers in leather shorts, with much slapping of thighs and shoes.

At Unity's table, the girls all wore bright red lipstick and Seb couldn't help noticing some fumbling under the table. Frances de Pole had her hand in the lap of the unnamed Englishman and he was obviously becoming aroused.

Seb took deep draughts of his beer and continued to watch, hoping not to be noticed. There was a lot of talking and laughing. Unity stood up and thrust out her arm and her friends all did the same. They had become a centre of attention, other drinkers turning away from the dancing to watch them. A few men among their German audience saluted them back, whether with irony or sincerity was uncertain.

The unnamed Englishman's hand was now on the thigh of Frances de Pole, pushing up her skirt, exploring. This was what the consul-general had been talking about; inhibitions cast off in the heady climate of a foreign city and with an excess of alcohol. This was what Donald Gainer had to deal with on a week-by-week basis, desperately trying to get young English boys and girls out of trouble.

Seb ordered another half-litre of beer and a plate of sausage and fried potatoes. As he was waiting for it to arrive he saw the one he assumed to be Adam Rock stand up from the table and walk in his direction with the gait of an athlete.

He was going to the toilets. Seb looked back at the table. No one was taking any notice of Adam Rock's progress. They were all guffawing at something Mannheim said.

Seb waited a few moments, then followed Rock into the toilets. He was standing in front of the long metal urinal, undoing his fly. Seb held back and let him commence pissing, then said, 'Adam Rock?'

The young man's head swerved around to see who was addressing him and his urine splashed on the tiled floor. 'What?'

'I'm Detective Inspector Wolff of the criminal police, murder team.' He was speaking in English and already had his badge out. 'I was keen to meet you because I understand you knew Rosie Palmer quite well.'

'Ah yes, Wolff, I've heard of you. Bobo and Frances both mentioned your name. You've got your man, haven't you? Now can I finish pissing?'

'Be my guest.'

Rock pissed like a horse while Seb moved back and waited by the door. When the Englishman had finished, he turned around, buttoning his fly. 'Now, how can I help you, Wolff?'

'I believe you and Rosie Palmer might have been quite close. Perhaps you were involved romantically.'

'That's a bit direct, don't you think? Anyway, what if I was? Is romance a crime in Munich?'

'Did you see her on the evening she died?'

'No, or I would have mentioned it to the police. Is that it?' He was standing in front of the small, mottled mirror, using his fingers to comb back his oil-slicked hair and reshaping his blond eyebrows.

'Perhaps we could talk some more tomorrow. I don't wish to keep you away from your friends.'

'I don't think we have anything more to talk about.'

'Let me be the judge of that.'

Rock strode towards the door back into the main part of the house and affected a deliberately insincere smile. 'That's your lot, Wolff. And in future I suggest you avoid approaching people while they're pissing or you'll get yourself a reputation. And you know what happens to 175s in the Third Reich.'

CHAPTER 22

Arriving home, he was exhausted. He had finished off the beer-house food at gut-inflaming speed and downed the rest of his beer, all the time aware that he was being looked at and laughed at by the group at the table. The words 'arrogant' and 'unpleasant' came to mind when he thought of Adam Rock. Nor could he get the Englishman's final remark out of his mind: *you know what happens to 175s in the Third Reich.* Was he referring to anyone in particular? One name came to mind: Caius Klammer. Or was he speaking in general terms?

The phone in the corridor outside his front door was ringing. Without thinking he unhooked it. 'Yes?'

'Can I speak to Sebastian Wolff?'

'That's me. Who are you?' It was a man's voice – Bavarian accent – but one he didn't recognise.

'You don't need to know my name. I was a friend of Caius Klammer, that's all I'm going to tell you.'

A friend of Caius. The man who wasn't supposed to have any friends.

Seb didn't like unidentified callers. 'I'd really like your name, sir. Perhaps we could meet?'

'I don't think that's a good idea, do you, given what happened to our mutual friend?'

'Can you at least tell me how you knew Herr Klammer. Perhaps you worked together . . . or shared an interest?'

'Please, Detective, just keep your peace for a few moments and listen to what I have to say. I won't be calling again, so this will be the last time we talk.'

'Go ahead.'

'It concerns the photograph of the dead girl that you showed to Caius. He came to the conclusion that the markings were runes – ancient Germanic symbols.'

Runes. Seb had heard of such things, of course, but he knew nothing about them.

'Can you tell me more?'

'A little.'

'If Caius said these symbols were runes, what did they symbolise? Did Caius have any theories?'

'He told me that these things are almost impossible to decipher at the best of times because they were used in a variety of languages, throughout northern Germany, Scandinavia and England over hundreds of years. He told me that they might represent either letters or sounds or, more broadly, whole words or concepts. There was one mark on the body – a sort of side-on M or W (𝌆) – which he said was generally accepted as meaning "sun" in the oldest of the known runic systems and is known as the sowilo. In other forms it can apparently look like the flashes on the SS collars.'

This again meant nothing to Seb. 'And why exactly did he mention all this to you?'

'Because I was his friend and he was worried about the implications of markings which might be seen as *Völkisch*, given the history of National Socialism. He believed that you were his friend, too, which is why I am calling you.'

The *Völkisch* movement: the folk mythology of Germany as espoused by such as Otto Raspe and other members of the Thule Society. Bringing together the German *völk* – folk – as the super-race. And everyone knew where the Thule Society led – straight to the door of the nascent Nazi Party in the early 1920s. Men like Hess and Rosenberg and other mentors of Adolf Hitler. If anyone knew about runes, they would be found there, at the very heart of Thule.

The voice on the phone continued. 'Caius needed to talk to someone because he feared he had stumbled onto something dangerous. Rightly so, as it now turns out.'

Seb was silent for a moment. What was he to do with this information? It would surely help if he could meet the man behind this disembodied voice. 'Sir,' he said quietly, suddenly aware that this was a public telephone that anyone in the apartment block could use. Anyone could walk past or shelter in the shadows of doorways and listen in. 'Could we not find a way to meet that would not compromise you?'

The voice did not reply to the entreaty. 'He said one other thing. He said our ancestors – the ones who used runes – had strange, barbaric rituals. They made blood sacrifices – *geblōts*, as he called them. That's all. Do with it what you will, Herr Wolff.'

A click. The phone was dead.

His mother was still awake, still fretting about Jurgen. 'Everything's fine, Mutti,' Seb said. 'Silke Stutz's parents are good people and they are looking after him. He got in a brawl at the Hitler Youth and he has been fighting with me and he needed to get away, that's all. He'll be back when he's sorted himself out.'

'And who's going to look after the baby?'

He found himself laughing. 'There is not going to be any baby,' he said, though his mind wasn't laughing, was telling him that it was a ridiculously bold statement to make given his own history.

'I can smell the sin after he has been with that Silke, just as I can smell the sin when you have been with that Hexie.'

'We're all sinners, Mutti, that's why we go to confession.'

'And when did you last go?'

It was a fair question. The last time he went to confession was December 1918, when he sought absolution for all his killings. The priest didn't even seem to be listening but eventually gave him a dozen Hail Marys as penance. Probably bored by the guilt of all the young killers back from the war. He didn't bother to tell his mother any of this.

'And will Jurgen be home in the morning?'

'Perhaps. He's seventeen, Mutti. My influence – what little influence I ever had – died years ago. He's probably old enough to fight for Germany, so what can I say?'

'You should have taught him to learn from your mistakes, not copy them.'

'As my mistakes go, I'd say he was one of the better ones. Don't you agree? Anyway, I'm not sure he would thank us for calling him a mistake.'

'Well, of course, he's a beautiful boy, but you shouldn't have had him so young.'

Seb shrugged with a smile. Nor, he thought, should my friends have died so young, nor should I have been slaughtering Englishmen so young. Or at any age for that matter.

He hugged his mother and she melted into his strong arms, as always. Of course she was overprotective of her son and grandson; she had brought them both up alone and they were all she had. One day, he thought, he must ask her about his father because he knew nothing of the man, just the austere shades of grey that made up his photographic image in the parlour.

'Goodnight, Mutti.'

In bed, he should have been worrying about Jurgen and what could be done about their relationship and the boy's other problems, but instead he could think of nothing but the anonymous phone call. The word '*geblōt*' kept running through his mind as he tried to sleep.

It was not a word that he had ever encountered before, but the idea of human sacrifice was a concept he had read about in boys' adventure stories when he was eleven or twelve. Tales of Norsemen with their axes and longships and blood rituals. But in this case? A bit far-fetched, surely, even for the likes of the Thule Society.

And the marks on the body? They were so haphazard, so frenzied that he could not imagine them as runes. He and Professor Lindner had immediately dismissed the suggestion that they were Hebrew script, so why should runes be any more feasible?

It was not going to be an easy confrontation, but there was one person he would have to talk to. Otto Raspe had to be the expert on such matters.

In the morning, he could not avoid Winter.

'You're in trouble, Inspector Wolff,' the BPP man said after going through the Hitler salute palaver. 'Big trouble.'

Seb had no doubt what the trouble was. His shadow – the pork knuckle on the motorbike – must have complained about being clobbered. Hardly surprising, he supposed. And the pistol in the dog turd must have been the final straw. A bloody nose for a miserable failure of a political police shadow could be filed away under *serve the swine right*. Lack of respect for state property, now that really was a crime.

'And there was me thinking I was the hero of the hour.'

'Were you? Then you were deluded. Your hour's just about up. Oh, and you'll never guess who I saw last night.'

'Surprise me.'

'That girl you were with outside the Osteria Bavaria when I arrested you. What was her name, Hexie Schuler, wasn't it?'

'Well seeing her must have made your evening, Winter, because she's a very beautiful young woman.'

'Indeed she is – and you and I are not the only ones who think so. She was having a high old time with some handsome fellow in the bar. All over her, he was, and she didn't seem to mind at all.'

Seb gave the sergeant a hard look. Was the bastard lying or had he really seen Hexie? She had told him she was visiting her mother. Before the conversation could go any further, Ruff's secretary arrived and told Seb he was wanted on the fifth floor by the deputy president of police. That suited him fine, because he also wanted the meeting.

Ruff had tried to compose his nerves, but he still looked on edge, pacing behind his desk. He turned sharply when Seb entered the huge office.

'You'll know what this is about, Wolff?'

'Good day and Heil Hitler to you, too, sir.'

'Ah yes, of course, Heil Hitler.' He raised his right hand as though swatting a fly.

'I imagine it has something to do with my contretemps with a guy on a motorbike who followed me and then drew a gun on me.'

'God in heaven, what were you thinking? You beat up a BPP man and damaged official property.'

'The stinking pistol.'

'And the motorbike. You will be billed for repairs, which is the least of our problems. You are most definitely not popular with the senior BPP men at the Wittelsbach Palace and it reflects on me. In fact I have had Josef Meisinger on the line this morning demanding you be despatched back to Dachau with immediate effect. Luckily for you, he doesn't have the power to do that and he knows it, given your excellent work on the Rosie Palmer case. Heydrich and Himmler are not getting involved while you still enjoy the Führer's grace, but that may not last forever the way you're carrying on. This is really your last warning, Wolff. So be careful. Be very, very careful.'

'Is that it, sir?'

'No, I want to know how you are progressing with the other case. We can't have people shot dead on the streets of Munich.'

'Quite so, it's not 1923 or 1934 anymore, is it, sir?'

'What did you say?'

'I said my sentiments entirely, Herr Ruff. The dead man's name was Caius Klammer. He was a quiet, inoffensive librarian and he was a friend of mine.'

'Really? Good God.'

'So this is personal.'

'Well, who did it?'

'Who knows? Perhaps the same man or men who killed Rosie Palmer. I'm still not sure how many were involved in her death.'

Ruff's brow knitted and he stopped pacing. 'Are you mad? Are you seriously trying to link the two cases?'

'Without a doubt. Herr Klammer was an expert in rare scripts. He was investigating the meaning of the markings on the girl's body on my behalf.'

Ruff's muscles went rigid. 'Was he the one who discovered that the symbols were Hebrew?'

'Well no, he said the opposite. It was only Sergeant Winter who suggested that they might be Hebrew and he, as we both know, is an ignorant bag of slime.'

'Be careful, you're getting into dangerous territory, Wolff. The nature of the markings is part of the prosecution. They were Hebrew. That is the official line, and there will be no contradicting that. You will ignore whatever this man Klammer said to you.'

'He said nothing to me, because he was shot dead before we could talk. But last night I had an anonymous call from a man who said he was a friend of Caius, who had told him the markings were most likely runes – ancient German symbols. Very *Völkisch*, you might think.'

Ruff slammed his fist on the table. 'Who told you this nonsense?'

'I wish I knew, but I don't. I repeat, the caller was anonymous.'

'And you took this call seriously?'

'Why wouldn't I?'

'Because you're a professional. Because it's insanity. You can't listen to some unnamed troublemaker, some Bolshie with an axe to grind. No word of this leaves this room. You never mention it to anyone, do you understand, Wolff?'

'I think the body should be re-examined by an expert in runes.'

'Well that most certainly won't happen. The corpse left Germany for England on a plane with the brother, yesterday afternoon.' He swept his left arm, flat, palm down, from right to left in a decisive arc. 'This case is closed, finished, done.'

'What about the photographs?'

'Missing. I thought you might know something about that.'

Seb ignored the implied accusation. 'So you want me to withhold evidence when I testify?'

'You won't be testifying. The case is being heard tomorrow morning, and Friedlander has indicated that he will be pleading guilty. The charge will be read, he will make his plea and the whole thing will be over in ten minutes flat. He killed the girl and he'll face the ultimate penalty for his heinous act. So get your head out of the sand and get used to the idea, Wolff. Now get out of my sight.'

CHAPTER 23

Ernie Pope was leaning against the side wall of the Jesuit church smoking a cigarette when Seb emerged into the fresh air of Ettstrasse. His jacket was slung over his shoulder and his tie was loose. Bells were chiming the quarter hour. The reporter nodded almost imperceptibly and then turned away, walking south in the direction of Neuhauser Strasse. Seb followed him at a distance, and when Pope ducked into a cafe, he did likewise.

'Sorry to be so bloody obvious, Seb,' the American said. 'But I wanted to see you and wasn't sure the best way to get in touch.'

They ordered coffees. Seb no longer cared about being seen with a foreign journalist, even though the stricture against it had been severe. He knew his police career was up anyway. There was no way of getting back on track after this morning's meeting with Thomas Ruff. He'd simply had enough and if he wasn't dismissed from the service he'd quit anyway. Either he was there to investigate crime and uphold the law, or there was nothing for him in the police.

'And I'm sorry, too, Ernie – sorry that I won't be much help to you. I'm off the case and the matter is closed anyway. Friedlander is going to plead guilty tomorrow and he'll get the death penalty. No witnesses called, no evidence required. One whisk of the guillotine blade and that's that.'

'He's pleading guilty? Are you serious?'

'Yes.'

The coffee came and they sipped. It was hot, too hot.

'Anyway, you wanted to see me about something, Ernie.'

'I'm not sure it matters now. I thought the guy was innocent, and I rather suspected that you did, too. I even get the feeling that the consul-general, Don Gainer, has his doubts, though he's too diplomatic to say anything.'

'The problem is you can't very well argue with a guilty plea. And he has an expensive lawyer, too – I saw to it myself. But tell me anyway, what have you discovered?'

'Oh, no silver bullet, I'm afraid. It's just that one of the Fleet Street rags I work for went in search of Tobias Russell – Friedlander's friend from Cambridge, the one you said took him to the house party where he met Rosie Palmer. They found him and talked to him and he spoke glowingly of his pal. Said he was the kindest, most wonderful young man he had ever met. The very thought of him killing Rosie – or anyone else for that matter – was preposterous. And he said he would happily come to Munich to say as much.'

'That's not going to help now.'

'He also said that Rosie's move to Munich was carefully planned by the two of them. Rosie went to great lengths to make her family believe that Karl Friedlander was a native of Berlin and, anyway, was migrating to New York after graduating. Friedlander was not the main reason she came here – he was the *only* reason. Before she came there were many letters between them, with Tobias as the conduit. Karl Friedlander and Rosie Palmer were deeply in love. There can be no doubt.'

Seb found himself wanting to tell Ernie about the markings on the body, but despite his anger he held back. Ruff had been clear that no word of the runes must be uttered outside his office. And if he, Seb, told the reporter what he knew, he would be for it, because there could be no other source for the information. He had to remember that Ernie, despite their friendship, was a journalist first and foremost – and a journalist's loyalty was always to his newspaper. Seb understood that.

'You don't think . . .' Pope began and didn't bother to finish the question.

'What?' Seb lowered his voice to a whisper. 'That he's been tortured into a guilty plea? No, I'm certain not. Intimidated, perhaps, threatened even, but no physical torture. The presidium isn't Wittelsbach Palace.' He drew a short breath and held it, then breathed out. 'Please, Ernie, forget I said that.'

'Of course. I didn't hear a thing, Seb. Silent as the grave, as always. Wouldn't dream of accusing the political police of using torture in their basement cells.'

'There are other things, things I would love to tell you, but I simply can't.'

'You don't seem like the type to scare easily, Seb.'

'It's not me I'm worried about.'

He met up with Hexie at the Schelling-Salon in her lunch break. His initial inclination was not to mention the snide remarks of Hans Winter, but he quickly realised that if he didn't address the matter it would simply prey on his mind.

'I heard some salacious gossip this morning,' he said as they tucked into beers and soup at a small side table.

'Do tell, Seb, I love gossip.'

'About you,' he said. 'The reptilian sergeant said he saw you in the arms of another man last night.'

Hexie laughed. 'And did you believe him?'

'What do you think?'

She pursed her lips. 'Oh, I don't know. I expect he made you wonder, otherwise you wouldn't have mentioned it.'

'He said you were in a bar and a man was all over you. I think those were his words.'

'Well, he was right on both counts. I was in a bar – Ratzinger's. I was there with my mother for a quiet glass of cherry schnapps and this hulking Brownshirt took a shine to me. Kept offering me drinks and wouldn't take no for an answer. And then he got really unpleasant and started pawing me.'

'I'm sorry to hear that.'

'Oh, Seb, it's the way of the world. What could I do? I would have kicked him in the balls or stabbed my fingers in his eyes, but then he might have lashed out and my mother would have been caught in the thick of it. I couldn't do that to her. When he went off for a piss, we just upped and left. It ruined the evening, to be honest. And yes, I spotted the little slug who put you in Dachau. He was with a couple of other slugs. They looked like BPP and they were smirking at me and my predicament.'

'I would very much like to do something unpleasant to Sergeant Winter.'

'Can I watch?'

'You're a bad girl, Hexie Schuler.'

'That's why you love me, isn't it?'

'And that's a loaded question.'

He had met her three years earlier during a straightforward investigation into a death in an apartment near Goetheplatz. An old man had been found hanging from a beam and it was assumed to be suicide but it had to be looked into anyway.

Hexie lived in the next apartment and Seb had interviewed her about the old man. She had liked him and sometimes cooked for him, but she hadn't been surprised that he would take his own life, because he had never got over the death of his wife; he often told her how he longed to join her.

There was a spark between Seb and Hexie straightaway. Nor was it just her slender body, her ridiculously long legs and wondrous breasts that attracted him. He liked her company, her laughter, her outrageous gossiping about everyone at work, her irreverent sense of fun and the joy she took from food, from dancing, from alcohol and from love-making. Hexie the hedonist.

Soon after they took up, she got the job on the counter at Heinrich Hoffmann's photographic studio. Now that was the best place in the world for a girl who adored gossip. She loved it there, liked Evie Braun and Henriette von Schirach – even got on with Henriette's father Heinrich Hoffmann, Adolf's best friend.

It was a bright, modern office, one of the most pleasant places in Munich, a good place to hang out with friends and do a little light office work. Hoffmann was becoming ridiculously rich through his monopoly on photographs of Adolf, and liked to decorate his studio with pretty girls, which is why Hexie and Evie fitted the bill so well. It didn't much matter whether they actually did any work or not.

She heard all the gossip from Henriette because Henriette knew *everything*. Not only did her father travel everywhere with Hitler, but her husband, Baldur von Schirach, was right at the heart of the party as leader of the Hitler Youth. No one knew more than

Henriette about the petty jealousies, the affairs and the intrigue involving the men and women surrounding the Führer.

And so perhaps he should marry Hexie. Do the decent thing. He was confident she'd have him, but she wouldn't wait forever, because she wanted children. She had made that obvious enough these past three years. And, yes, she would make a fine mother. One day soon, he'd do it. Ask the question. Perhaps.

He finished his soup and pushed the bowl away. He was still thinking about her confrontation at the bar last night and the fact that Sergeant Winter and his friends were present, watching her. 'Interesting that they were there, though, the BPP men,' he said. 'You don't think Winter was following you, do you?'

'It hadn't occurred to me. Why?'

'Because the BPP have been following me. For all I know, they're here now. They're not going to rest until I'm back where they want me, and we both know where that is. It's just possible they might try to get at me through you. I don't think Winter remembers you fondly after the names you called him outside the osteria.'

'Probably not. But don't worry, Seb, I'm a big girl. I can look after myself.'

He shrugged. 'You're probably right.' Yet even as he uttered the words, it occurred to him that the Bavarian Political Police might just be the least of his worries. He had to keep these matters separate in his mind: the two murders on one side, his run-in with the political police on the other.

'Oh, and Evie Braun called in to say hello this morning,' Hexie said. 'She's changed, you know. Used to be such fun – now, well, she's taking herself very seriously. I got the feeling she was expecting us to curtsy to her.'

'Maybe you should. She might be Frau Hitler one day.'

'A very pregnant Henriette von Schirach was there with her toddler. She had a big grin on her face and whispered in my ear that Evie very much wanted to kill the Mitford girl.'

'You hear extemely dangerous gossip, Hexie.'

'Henriette is *so* indiscreet and Evie is *so* emotional all the time that you can almost read what's going on in her face. Oh and Henriette said that Hitler actually tried it on with *her* once, when she was seventeen. He wasn't at all happy when she said a polite no to his advances.'

'As I said, very dangerous.'

Back at his office, there was no Sergeant Winter, which was a blessing, but there was a crate of bottled beer on the floor with a note from Putzi Hanfstaengl, the international press chief, thanking him for his work on the Rosie Palmer inquiry.

On his desk, there was an envelope which he immediately opened. An invitation card slid out. Printed in gothic script it was decorated with Uncle Christian Weber's smart new official insignia – his address at the royal palace along with an elegant line drawing of the building topped with a red swastika. Below this was a heading: NIGHT OF THE PAGANS. The card was inviting him and Hexie to a solstice party the next day and, scrawled in Uncle Christian's almost childlike writing, was a note apologising for not having invited him sooner. Weber insisted it was going to be the event of the season and Seb and his girl simply must attend. There would be dancing all night and marvellous entertainment, all at one of his newly acquired properties on a lake to the south of the city.

Seb was astounded. Uncle Christian had never invited him to anything in his life.

A secretary knocked at the door so he signalled her to enter.

'A Frau Stutz telephoned and asked you to call her.' She handed him a slip of paper with the woman's telephone number. He called immediately and Silke's mother picked up straightaway, as though she had been waiting by the phone.

'Thank you for calling, Herr Wolff.'

'What has happened? Is Jurgen all right?'

'I'm afraid he and Silke have disappeared. They left for school this morning, but it was only later that I found a note in my daughter's room. It simply said that they had gone and that we should not look for them. She said she would call in due course to let us know where they were and that all was well.'

Just left. Like the boy's mother sixteen years ago.

'I'm sorry, Frau Stutz. I think this is my son's doing.' It was all he could think of to say.

'Oh, Silke has a mind of her own, Inspector. She may be impulsive, but she's not stupid. I'm sure they will be all right. I'll let you know as soon as I hear anything. All I can tell you is that I did notice that she had taken her BDM uniform, and I think that Jurgen might have had his Hitler Youth outfit. I'm not really sure what that means, though.'

He took the crate of beer out into the main room and offered the beer bottles around to everyone who was there, then walked out of his office, perhaps for the last time.

CHAPTER 24

In all his years, Seb had never felt this impotent. Even in the worst days of the war, he had a gun and an enemy to fire at. But now he felt helpless. He no longer had any say over his son's life, he had not a single clue to the murderer of his friend Caius Klammer and he was powerless to prevent the execution of a young man who was surely innocent, despite his confession of guilt.

He wanted to see Friedlander again to ask him why he was changing his plea, but when he attempted to visit him in the cells at the Police Presidium he was informed that the prisoner had been moved to the main Stadelheim prison in Perlach on the south-eastern outskirts of Munich.

It was a move that made no sense to him. The trial would be at the Palace of Justice in the centre of the city, so why move him further away? He put a call through to Stadelheim and asked about paying a visit to the accused man, but his call was transferred to the governor who insisted that the only visitor Friedlander was allowed before tomorrow's trial was his lawyer, Herr Brühne.

'Why is that?'

'Orders from above, Inspector.'

'From who exactly?'

'From above. Good day, Inspector.' The phone call ended abruptly.

He made one more phone call, to the home of Otto Raspe in Altbogenhausen. The writer's wife Heidi answered the call. 'Ah, Inspector Wolff,' she said after Seb introduced himself. 'Do you want Adam Rock?'

'Actually, I was hoping to speak to your husband.'

'He's at work. You'll almost certainly find him at the *Völkischer Beobachter* offices.'

'Thank you, Frau Raspe.'

The weather was fine. He climbed into the Lancia and drove north to Schellingstrasse for the second time that day. What was it about this pleasant but otherwise unremarkable street that attracted Hitler: his favourite restaurant, his friend's photographic studio, his newspaper, his former party HQ?

Seb parked outside the newspaper office and introduced himself at reception. A call was put through and a minute later he was told that Colonel Raspe would be happy to talk to him, and he was shown up to his office.

The *Beobachter* was like any newspaper office anywhere in the world. The floor was littered with ash and cigarette butts, desks were piled high with paper and old newspapers from around Germany and the rest of the world. Smoke and noise filled the air. Men – almost exclusively men – hammered away at typewriters or scrawled in notebooks while holding telephones wedged between their shoulders and ears. There was a lot of shouting. Smell and noise, a little like a police department but even more so.

Many newspapers took political stances, but this one didn't even pretend to be independent. It belonged to Hitler and was an unashamed mouthpiece for the Nazi Party. Nothing went in it that hadn't been approved politically.

Otto Raspe, as a star columnist, had a room to himself, close to the editor's office on the far side of the main open-plan area. Seb was fully expecting to dislike him, given Hexie's antipathy. Her instinct was usually sound on such matters.

Three secretaries, all in smart dark skirts and crisp white blouses, were stationed outside his office. One of them immediately stood up and saluted Seb, which he returned in kind. She then welcomed him and knocked on Raspe's closed door.

'Come in.'

She nodded to Seb and opened the door to allow him to step past her into the office, then retreated, closing the door after her. Raspe immediately stood up and came around to greet him.

Seb was about to raise his arm in the Hitler salute, but Raspe merely reached out to shake his hand. 'Inspector Wolff, it's a real pleasure to meet you.'

'Colonel Raspe, thank you for agreeing to see me.'

'Dear fellow, it's my honour. I have heard great things about you. Munich's finest detective, I'm told, and you have certainly proved yourself these past few days. I hear, too, that you did good work in the Army Group Rupprecht in the war. Sixteenth Bavarian Reserve Infantry like our dear Führer, wasn't it? Machine-gunner on the Western Front, eh, shooting Tommies and Yankees? Iron Cross First Class?'

'Yes, sir.' How did Raspe know all that? It wasn't something Seb went around telling people.

'Good man. One of us, a true Bavarian and a true German. Worst day of my life when we capitulated. The cowardly swine in Berlin let us all down in November 1918. And don't even get me started on Versailles and the damned French.'

Raspe was a good-looking man, very much the soldier with his erect carriage, his polished shoes, fine clothes and his salt-and-pepper hair. He actually had a look of Bavarian royalty about him, not dissimilar to the handsome Crown Prince Rupprecht himself. Probably about fifty years of age, but he could have passed for ten years younger. The only untoward marks on his otherwise immaculate person were the fingertips of his right hand, which were black with ink where his pen must have leaked.

'Now then, coffee? Something stronger?'

'A coffee would be very welcome.' Anything to give him as long as possible in this man's company.

He stepped to the door, opened it and ordered a pot of coffee. As he turned back, he smiled. 'And how can I help you, Herr Wolff?'

'It's a long shot, sir, but I didn't know where else to turn. The thing is I was hoping to tap into your expertise of all things *Völkisch*. With your background in the Thule Society and the scholarly things you research and write for the *Beobachter*, it seemed to me you probably know as much if not more about the subject than anyone in Bavaria, perhaps the whole of Germany.'

'You flatter me, young man. But, anyway, what in particular do you want to know?'

'I was wondering whether you have any knowledge of runes – runic script.'

Raspe laughed. 'Does anyone really know them? They are perhaps the greatest mystery of our glorious past. What messages might our ancestors have been trying to leave us? What universal secrets might they reveal? They are things of beauty from antiquity, but they are abstruse. A man could study them for a lifetime and be none the wiser. And yet, their very darkness inspires us.'

Seb smiled. 'You are clearly a man of great learning, sir, which is why I have come to you. I know from your marvellous articles that you have an abiding interest in such things.'

'Flattery, more flattery. Really Wolff, you do lay it on a bit thick.'

The coffee arrived and the conversation paused until the secretary had poured two cups and departed.

'And yes,' Raspe continued, 'of course I'll help you in any way I can with what little I know, for I always wish to enlighten men of true German blood. But perhaps you'd give me a clue as to what exactly you want to discover, and why? Is this personal or a police matter?'

'It's a police matter. I'm afraid I'm not at liberty to discuss the details at the moment.'

'Nothing to do with the murder of my dear young friend Miss Palmer, I take it.'

And so they came to it, as Seb had known they would. This visit to this man was an act of foolhardy desperation, taken because he could think of nowhere else to turn. He didn't even know what he was hoping to find out. Colonel Otto Raspe was not his friend and never would be. But he was a last hope.

'Did you know her, sir? I confess I did wonder when I saw you with her brother and Miss Mitford at the House of Artists.'

'Of course, you were there, weren't you? Bobo pointed you out to me and said what good work you had done in following her lead and arresting the man. I should have come over and introduced myself and offered you my congratulations there and then, but it was a busy, hectic evening. As for Miss Palmer, yes, I knew her very well. A beautiful, charming young woman. Her death is an absolute tragedy for her family and friends, and I look forward to that young man losing his own life for his heinous deed.'

Seb nodded gravely. 'A wish many of us share, sir. Do you think I might confide in you?'

'Of course. An officer never betrays a confidence.'

'When you asked whether my interest in runes was personal or police work, it's actually a bit of both. And it does indeed involve the murder of the English girl.'

'Really? How extraordinary.'

'You see, this is probably not known to you – unless, of course, Lord Braybury mentioned it – but there were markings on the body. Cuts in strange shapes and red marks made with what looked like lipstick.'

Raspe was sipping his coffee hot. He looked puzzled. 'He did mention the markings, but he said they were believed to be Hebrew script.'

'That was never proved and I now believe it's possible they were runes. That doesn't mean the accused man is innocent because, of course, he has admitted his guilt. But it occurred to me that perhaps he had an accomplice. Professor Lindner, who carried out the post-mortem said he doubted the murder was carried out at the place where she was found, so her body must have been transported some distance. It can be no easy matter for someone to carry a body down through the Herzogpark woods to the water's edge.'

'So you think there was a second killer, eh? Well, that certainly is an intriguing theory. What does your chief of police say?'

'I won't speak ill of Deputy President of Police Ruff, but he has been under intense pressure over this case and now that one killer has been found, he simply wants the matter closed. You might think that is quite understandable given the political implications of a crime involving the British nobility and international diplomacy.'

'Yes, yes, I see that. And your theory is not implausible. Look, do you have a record of these markings – a photograph, for instance? I might know someone who could take a look.'

'There are photographs. I'll bring one.' There were no photographs; they had disappeared. Or had they? What about the original plates, they must be somewhere. 'Tomorrow, perhaps.'

'Thank you. I'm sure they will be painful to look at, but if there is a second culprit, he must be found, so I would be happy to help in that.'

Seb nodded with a smile, then drank his coffee. He wanted to see Raspe's face as he looked at the pictures of Rosie Palmer's mutilated corpse. Who knew? Perhaps he had seen it before.

There was little more to say. Otto Raspe thanked Seb for coming and confiding in him. He said they should meet for a drink one day. Perhaps the inspector had heard that the Thule Society had been re-formed in recent years despite some opposition within the party? In fact, said Raspe, it had never really gone away despite suggestions that it had disbanded in the early 1920s. 'Do you have an interest in the history of the German race, Wolff?'

'Indeed I do,' Seb lied.

'Well, you might like to consider joining; we could do with new blood. Not something you should mention to your superiors in the police, though, eh?'

'No, sir.'

'You see we have been rather overshadowed by the Nazi Party itself in recent years and there are those who resent us, even though we laid the ideological foundations of the movement and support it with every fibre of our being. What many don't realise is that Thule goes beyond politics, to the very depths of the Aryan spirit and soul.'

He was about to climb into the car, when he had a thought. It was just possible that the autopsy photographs had been developed at the Hoffmann studio, just over the road, no more than a hundred metres from the *Beobachter* offices.

Hexie could look them up. But he didn't want her to get in trouble, so perhaps he could ask the other girl at the counter, the new one. It would be an innocent enough question. He'd show his police badge and explain his enquiry. No need to mention that the prints had disappeared in sinister circumstances.

He stepped out into the road. He didn't see the black saloon car pull out and accelerate straight at him until the last second. Time slowed down and in that final fraction he knew he could not get out of the way, that the car was coming at him deliberately, and that he was about to die.

CHAPTER 25

All he felt was the strangely muted impact and he was sprawling in the road. He was aware of the weight of his body against the implacable weight of the stone, as though he should be sinking, going down, folding into the earth from which he came, but the solidity of the road was holding him back. And then he was aware of something else: he was alive.

His mouth tasted of blood and he couldn't move, but he was almost certain that he wasn't dead. Perhaps he was dying, but it didn't seem the way he had imagined it in the long hours of anticipating imminent death as shells and mortars pounded the trenches. He was face down, his eyes open but seeing only darkness. He tried to shift himself and he heard a voice, distant and weird, yet somehow familiar.

'Can you move?' it said.

'I think so,' he mumbled, still face to the ground, the blood seeping through his teeth.

'Then get up. Quickly.' The voice's hands were under his arms, hoisting him roughly.

Seb was on his elbows now. He twisted his head towards the voice.

Winter. Sergeant Hans Winter.

'What happened?' Seb asked, though he was pretty sure he knew the answer.

'I just saved your life, Wolff, that's what happened. I pushed you out of the way of a speeding car. Someone wants you dead.'

Seb was on his hands and knees, forcing himself up. He felt shaky but strong enough and stood. He spat blood and ran his tongue along his teeth. All still there. 'I thought *you* wanted me dead, Winter.'

'No, I want you in Dachau, where you belong. I'm not a murderer, I uphold the law.'

Seb dusted the gravel from his trousers and his jacket, then wiped his sleeve across his face. The cut was inside his mouth, with nothing more than a graze or scrape on his cheek.

'Well, thank you, Winter. Whatever your intentions, you did me a good turn.'

'You're a mess. What were you doing at the *Beobachter*?'

'Talking to someone.'

'You're still working on the Friedlander case, aren't you? You won't let it go.'

'Like you, Winter, my sole aim is to uphold the law. Anyway, what are *you* doing here?'

'Following you. We work together, if you recall.'

'Of course we do. How could I forget? Who was in the car?'

'I didn't see. I was too busy saving you. But if you want the answer, just ask yourself this: who wants you dead?'

The answer to that was obvious: whoever killed Rosie Palmer.

'And I have a message for you,' Winter continued. 'Hanfstaengl demands your presence at the Brown House.' He looked at his watch. 'In ten minutes.'

Seb nodded and realised his head was throbbing. Strange how the fall hadn't hurt while it was happening, but now he could feel it. He fished out his handkerchief and dabbed at the blood on his lip. So then, a quick drive down to the Brown House to see Putzi Hanfstaengl. Fair enough; he wasn't going to go to Hoffmann's studio anyway, not with Winter in tow.

He dusted himself down again and combed his fingers through his hair. Ironic that Winter should comment on his unkempt appearance, he thought, given the state of his own greasy attire. Seb climbed into the Lancia and opened the passenger door. 'Coming?'

'I have my own transport.' He indicated a small black car on the other side of the road. 'I'll follow you.'

'What's going on, Wolff? I have heard disturbing reports about you.'

Putzi Hanfstaengl had refused entry to Winter and was speaking with Seb alone. His face was twitching, his hooded eyes darker than ever.

'I'm sorry, Herr Hanfstaengl, I don't think I know what you mean.'

'I mean the affair of Rosie Palmer's murder is closed. The final act will be played out tomorrow and then a date will be set for the execution. And yet it seems you are still inclined to investigate the crime, as though a man's confession is not enough for you.'

'May I ask who told you this, sir?'

'Never mind who told me – is it true or not?'

'I believe there are loose ends, yes.'

'Such as?'

'The marks on the body. They have not been fully explained. The possibility of an accomplice. And the motive.'

Hanfstaengl, a tall man, rose to his full height, then clenched his fists and shook them. 'The motive is clear, as explained by Miss Mitford. Friedlander couldn't have the girl so he wasn't going to allow anyone else to have her. Call it what you will – a crime of passion or just plain old-fashioned brute savagery, but I see no reason to doubt that the killer has been caught.'

'What if there were two of them? What if the marks were not Hebrew script? What if the maidservant Lena Popp was lying?'

'God in heaven, Wolff, there are a lot of damned *what ifs* there. Here's another one: what if I tell you that you are in grave danger of enraging the Führer. He wanted this matter settled and you have settled it. Don't scratch at the wound, man. Talking of which, what's happened to your mouth? There's blood on your lip.'

'I nearly got run down a few minutes ago.'

Seb knew that Putzi Hanfstaengl was one of Hitler's oldest friends, going right back to the days of the attempted overthrow of the Munich government in Hitler's famous Putsch of 1923. Hanfstaengl and his sister Erna had tried in vain to protect him from arrest. It was even said that there was a love affair between Hitler and Erna. Certainly the Hanfstaengls had done all they could to introduce the would-be dictator to the upper classes in Munich – people like the Regensdorfs, the Bechsteins and the Bruckmanns. People who could raise money for the cause and give Hitler a veneer of respectability.

Now, though, Hanfstaengl did not sound like a close friend, he did not sound like a man who could charm the Führer with his piano playing. He sounded, rather, like a nervous underling – a servant petrified that his master would turn on him and cast him out into the wilderness or worse. And so there was no point in trying to reason with him, because it wouldn't work.

If there were any doubts about the guilt of Karl Friedlander, Hanfstaengl didn't want to know about them.

'Then you'd better be more careful crossing the road, hadn't you, Wolff. In fact you had better be more careful about other things, too. Get a grip on yourself, man. Your boss Ruff tells me he has given you another murder case to solve. Deal with that.'

'Yes, sir, of course.'

Hanfstaengl took a deep breath and at last the twitch disappeared. He forced a smile onto his broad face. 'Good man.'

'Thank you for the beer, sir. It is very much appreciated.'

'Oh, a very small gesture. And Councillor Weber tells me you've been invited to his big show tomorrow night. He tells me it's going to be very risqué and very pagan. You are coming, aren't you? And you'll bring a girl, yes? I'm told you have a delightful and very beautiful lady. My wife Helene will be thrilled to meet you both. A much better use of your time than chasing your tail like a dog.'

Seb smiled back. Yes, it would be interesting to meet Helene Hanfstaengl, yet another woman who was said to have won the heart of Hitler with her beauty, though there was no suggestion that anything had ever occurred between them. 'I'm very much looking forward to it Herr Hanfstaengl, but I haven't asked the girl yet.'

He lowered his voice to a conspiratorial whisper. 'Just don't bring your awful Gestapo shadow with you, eh?'

'He's Bavarian Political Police, sir.'

'Same damned thing.'

It had been a long day. Tomorrow promised to be longer. He wasn't going to be called to give evidence in the trial of Karl Friedlander, but he was going to be there anyway. Perhaps the young Jew wouldn't plead guilty, and what then? It was an interesting possibility.

And as for Jurgen and Silke, all he and her family could do was wait and hope. Silke sounded a reasonably sensible girl so the chances were she would call soon.

Tonight, though, he needed to lose Winter and somehow discover whether Hoffmann's studio had processed the anatomy pictures. Then he wanted to put his mind to the matter of Caius Klammer's murder. Yes, of course, the two cases had to be linked, but that fact alone didn't help much.

Not long ago he hadn't been sure he would ever enter the Police Presidium in Ettstrasse again, but everything had changed since then. Someone had tried to kill him, and he needed to keep possession of his police badge to find out who.

From his office, he called Hexie and agreed to meet her at the Schelling-Salon. It was too late to ask the new counter girl about the anatomy pictures, but hopefully Hexie would know whether Hoffmann dealt with such things.

He arrived a few minutes before her and she seemed uncharacteristically quiet.

'Is everything all right?'

'I don't know. There was a whisper of cutbacks. I don't want to lose my job.'

'You'd get another one easily.'

'But I like it there. It's easy-going. We have a few laughs.'

'And you hear everything.'

'Exactly.'

'How about a schnapps with your beer?'

'How well you know me, Detective.'

With her fears for her job it did not seem an opportune moment to bring up the question of photographic plates. Perhaps later in the evening. For the time being she needed cheering up, and no one liked a party more than Hexie Schuler.

'We're going out tomorrow night. Out of town to The Pig's lakeside palace. He's putting on some huge show and we're invited. It'll be champagne and dancing until dawn knowing him.'

'Are you asking me or telling me?'

'Asking, of course.'

'Then I'd be delighted to accompany you.'

'We'll drive out there and stay until dawn. We can sneak off from the party for some of the swimming we missed on my birthday. Don't bring a costume.'

CHAPTER 26

For such a high-profile case, Seb had expected the courtroom in the Palace of Justice to be packed, but the attendance was quite sparse.

Rosie Palmer's English friends were there – Unity, of course, Adam Rock, Frances de Pole – and a dozen others from the Haus Gertrud student hostel and elsewhere. Also Unity's SS shadow Fritz Mannheim. But Rosie's brother had gone home, so there were none of the dead girl's relatives. Nor did there seem to be any of the accused's family, certainly not his mother or father.

Seb assumed they were still under lock and key in the Presidium cells.

But there were reporters, both German and foreign.

The trial, such as it was, was brief and to the point. Friedlander was brought in. He had been allowed to wear his own clothes – a smart suit and tie – and his hair had been brushed and combed, but he looked a lost and beaten man. His good looks had vanished. His lawyer, Herr Brühne, the one hired by Uncle Christian, caught Seb's eye and smiled at him as though everything would be all right.

The prosecutor read out the charge and the judge asked Friedlander for a plea. He looked towards his counsel, who nodded, then said, 'Guilty, your honour.' The prosecutor spent five minutes outlining the gory details of the murder.

The judge spoke of an unspeakable crime which shamed Germany in the eyes of the world and warranted nothing but the full force of the law. He then pronounced sentence. Execution by guillotine within the confines of Stadelheim prison.

The court was silent. Seb gazed around and all he saw was the satisfied smirk on the face of Unity Mitford.

Karl Friedlander's expression did not change, but tears flowed down his cheeks.

It was all over. With brutal efficiency, a man's life was declared over. The prisoner was led away.

Outside the court, Seb breathed deeply of the fresh air. He felt dirty and complicit in something dreadful simply by witnessing the trial. By not standing up and demanding a rethink.

'They don't hang about, do they? Straight to the point.'

He turned. It was Ernie Pope. He had been with the other journalists on the reporters' benches in the court.

'Short and not very sweet, Ernie.'

'How long until he gets the chop?'

'Well, it's Friday, so probably not until Monday at the earliest. Difficult to know these days – so many of the old rules have gone out the window. How do you think this will this play out in England?'

Pope shrugged. 'Difficult. I know Donald Gainer doesn't feel good about it, which is why he didn't turn up this morning. But the problem is the guilty plea. Who can argue with it? The ghastly reality is that no more will be said and there will be no repercussions for Anglo-German relations.'

'I still don't understand why he changed his plea. The evidence wasn't overwhelming. Even if he is, indeed, guilty, he must have had a shout at getting off.'

'Hmm.'

'What is it, Ernie?'

'Well, just between you and me, I heard a little whisper from one of my BPP buddies about that. It seems Friedlander had a lawyer who told him that if he pleaded not guilty and was convicted, his parents would be incarcerated as accessories on account of the alibi they gave him and attempting to flee the country with him. But he could do a deal for them. If he pleaded guilty, they would be immediately freed without charge. And so the lawyer fixed it all. Seems to me the poor guy has sacrificed himself for his mum and dad.'

Seb felt physically sick.

It was a perfect afternoon for a ride in an open-topped car through the Bavarian countryside. The wind whipped their hair. High summer, the solstice, a day of endless light and hope. Seb had a beautiful girl at his side, but his thoughts were in a cold cell in Stadelheim where a young man awaited death.

'Talk to me, Seb. This isn't your fault, you know.'

'It doesn't feel good, accepting praise – promotion even – for an innocent man's death.'

'Assuming he *is* innocent.'

He gave her a sideways look, his eyebrow raised as if to say, *you know better than that, Hexie Schuler.*

'To hell with it, Seb, there's nothing you can do now. The gangsters may be in charge, but we've got to stay alive. So let's just try to enjoy tonight. Get drunk as hussars and think of nothing else but pleasure. You've earnt it. When did you last have a day off?'

He couldn't remember. Two weeks ago, maybe three. It didn't matter.

'Anyway,' she continued, 'what is this great event? What does The Pig have in store for us?'

'It's called the Night of the Pagans and it's not just us. If I know my uncle there'll be hundreds of guests and performers – every actress, whore and dancer in Munich plus many more shipped in. Every palm he wants to grease will be there, every old comrade from the Putsch, everyone who's considered anyone in Munich society or in the world of horse-racing. Anyone who can grease his palm or do him a favour. It will be a madhouse.'

'Good.'

'Uncle Christian might be the most corrupt, ugly, sleazy, pork knuckle in Munich, but he knows how to throw a party.'

Christian Weber's grand villa had a vast lawn that swept down to the edge of the lake. Fifteen years earlier, it had been the country home of an aristocratic industrialist. But in the twenties, his fortune had been swept away by the hyper-inflation tidal wave and the place had been left to go to ruin. It remained empty and neglected until Weber snapped it up and restored it with his newly grafted riches.

The setting was perfect. To the south, across the still waters of one of Bavaria's smaller but most beautiful lakes, the eyeline was graced with an extraordinary backdrop: green meadows, dark forests and then the great wall of the Alps, still snow-sprinkled in places even in June. Behind them to the north, the lush flatlands leading to Munich and beyond.

Plaster-cast statues of nymphs and satyrs decorated the enormous lawn. There were two performing stages, one on either side. To the left, an orchestra was playing airs from the operas, to the right – just far enough away to not disrupt the music – a comedian had gathered a large crowd, who were roaring with laughter.

Dozens of livery-clad men and women carried drinks around. Overhead, a squadron of light aircraft swooped and turned in an intricate aerobatics display. On the water, small motorboats and dinghies were available for anyone who desired a gentle cruise or paddle. A detachment of uniformed Hitler Youth lads about the same age as Jurgen was there to help with mooring and unmooring and, if required, do the rowing.

Seb's thoughts turned to Jurgen, and Hexie immediately sensed his fears. She clutched his hand. 'He's a bright boy. Let him be, and don't worry too much. He's not going off to war.' Seb nodded. She was right; no one would be hurling shells or bullets across no-man's-land at him.

Outside the main area there were stalls for target shooting, for archery, for gorging on exotic foods and drink, for fortune-telling (strictly illegal in the Nazi world, but no one was taking note of such restrictions this evening).

'Where do we start?' Hexie asked, overwhelmed by the sheer scale of what she was witnessing.

'A drink or two, I think. Champagne?'

'Is it the proper French stuff?'

'Always with Uncle. No Sekt here.'

'Then yes please, Sebastian Wolff.'

As they sauntered down the lawn, they were surrounded by a great crowd of people in a variety of attire – dozens of SS officers in their dazzling black uniforms tailored by Hugo Boss, international wheelers and dealers and their wives in couture from

London, Paris and New York, many young students who flocked to fashionable Munich but couldn't quite access the funds for such expensive clothing.

One little grouping in particular caught Seb's eye: the socialite Helene Bechstein from the piano manufacturing family; Walter and Maria Regensdorf who had taken Rosie Palmer into their home; their near neighbours Hugo and Elsa Bruckmann of the immense publishing empire; the Hanfstaengl clan – Putzi, his wife Helene and sister Erna; and the ubiquitous Otto Raspe and his wife Heidi. The very heart of Munich society, a sort of cabal who between them had used their wealth and influence to lift Hitler from beerhouse rabble-rouser to the dizzy realms of a dictator with unlimited power. Did they hope that he would return the favour? They might be disappointed.

Raspe spotted Seb and waved. He gave a half-hearted Hitler salute and little bow in return.

'God, I hate that creep,' Hexie said.

'Yes, you've mentioned that before. And he seems such a charming, good-looking fellow.'

'He probably hasn't put his hand on your tit and squeezed.'

'You didn't mention that.'

'Well, now you know.'

'In fact, I didn't think him at all charming. Handsome, perhaps, urbane and sophisticated even, but utterly untrustworthy. I really don't know what it is about the man I despise, except perhaps that he is part of the loathsome Thule Society.'

She frowned at him. 'Keep your voice down, Seb. You may not have noticed, but there are Nazis here.'

'You're right. But it's difficult to keep calm after this morning's courtroom farce. Actually, farce is too soft a word. It was and is a crime against humanity. And a tragedy. Anyway, let's go and see if the comedian can cheer us up.'

The comic was clearly enjoying himself. 'Just booked myself a nice little holiday,' he said. 'Place called Dachau. Have you heard of it? Lovely spot just north of Munich. Every comfort you could want. Cosy rooms. Hot and cold running bullets.' He grinned and was rewarded with a tinkling of nervous laughter.

'It's all right,' he continued. 'We're safe here. Our host SS-Oberführer Weber says that I can make jokes about anything within reason. The worst that can happen is my holiday will be extended.'

The comedian was a round little man with a pork pie hat, famous throughout Germany for his dangerous humour. His name was Weiss Ferdl and he had, indeed, had a stay in Dachau after making a joke at a theatre in Munich about seeing a big black Mercedes, commenting that it was strange because 'it had no Nazis in it'. Seb had heard all about it and was at the theatre when Ferdl was released and returned to the scene of his crime. This time he just stood on the stage in front of the audience for a full minute before saying: 'Do you know what, I think I was wrong. There *were* Nazis in that Mercedes.'

That brought the house down.

Here at the lakeside, he had a glass of beer in his hand and took a sip, then looked out across the lawn with the crowd growing by the minute. 'The good news is that official figures show the Nazis enjoy ninety-nine per cent support in Munich. I suppose I'm just unlucky – I keep meeting the one per cent.'

More laughter, still nervous.

'I see there are some Hitler Youth boys down by the lake. That's all very well, but why just boys? Where are the League of German Mattresses when they're needed?

'Talking of which, Herr Weber has promised us nipples tonight. Pagan nipples. Dozens of them. You just wait. They'll be on horses, riding bareback. Bare front, too. And look, here they come . . .'

The band gave a great drum roll and all eyes turned to the left bank of the lake where a procession of horses was trotting through the shallows. Each one ridden by a topless young woman, adorned with various accessories – swords, horned helmets, battleaxes – all designed to give an impression of Teutonic military might, but with an erotic twist.

Seb found himself laughing. 'He's really gone and done it. Uncle Christian's two great loves – beautiful naked women and horses.'

The horses turned inland from the lake and came up the centre of the lawn, the crowd parting like the Red Sea to let them pass. The orchestra had abandoned its operatic airs and the timpanist was beating his kettledrum in time with the hoofbeats.

Suddenly, Weber was standing between Seb and Hexie, an arm around each of them. 'What do you think, boy? Getting you in the mood to make babies, is it?'

Seb found himself laughing at the sheer vulgarity of it all. 'What are you up to, Uncle? What's this all about?'

'Oh, this is a practice run. I think it would work well in Munich itself, don't you? Perhaps at Nymphenburg Palace, eh? Plenty of room there. Adolf would love it. He's always been a nipple man.'

'Why didn't you invite him tonight?'

'I did, but he's in Berlin, signing off on this naval treaty with that grubby travelling salesman Ribbentrop. Evie said she'd be here, though. Probably with Henriette and Baldur. Anyway, drink up. Plenty more nipples and arses to come.'

The evening was darkening. Fireworks burst across the lake. At the water's edge, stepping from a boat, he saw a contingent including Unity Mitford, Adam Rock and various other young people of their group and from the student hostel. Frances de Pole was there, so were Clarice Goodall and Becky Waverley-Jones and half a dozen others he didn't recognise.

The same group he had seen smirking in court earlier in the day.

CHAPTER 27

'I suppose I should go and talk to the Hanfstaengls.'

'Seb, I thought this was your day off.'

'Well, just talking to someone at a party isn't work, is it?'

'Isn't it? I think I know you rather better than that.'

'I'd like to meet the famous Helene, supposedly beloved of A. H. at one time. Wouldn't you?'

'Come on then.'

At first, Putzi Hanfstaengl didn't seem to recognise him, then his hooded eyes widened. 'Ah, yes, it's you Inspector Wolff. You took me by surprise in your evening wear. Very smart, young man.'

'Thank you, sir, and may I introduce my friend Frau Schuler. Hexie Schuler.'

They shook hands. And then, seemingly flustered, Hanfstaengl turned towards his wife Helene. 'Dearest, this is the Kripo inspector who solved the dreadful murder case. Inspector Wolff and his, er, his friend Frau Schuler.'

Seb had expected someone dazzling, a movie star or a model, for this was the woman who was said to have captured Hitler's heart and persuaded him not to shoot himself after the failure of the Putsch back in '23. But Helene Hanfstaengl was rather plain and distant, like a distracted mother worried about doing the washing, preparing supper and collecting the children from school.

They exchanged introductions and awkward pleasantries and then she simply turned away and continued her conversation with Frau Regensdorf and Otto and Heidi Raspe. Seb glanced at Hexie and raised his eyebrows. His lips said, 'what do we do now?' but no sound came out.

Just then Unity Mitford and her friends arrived and mingled with the rather exclusive group. She gave Erna a hug in greeting and kissed her cheeks effusively. Of course, thought Seb, she often stays with Hanfstaengl's sister, another woman who was said to have once been the romantic interest of Hitler, long before he became Führer. Extraordinary how many women were said to have cast their spell over a man whom others swore to be a neuter.

Unity immediately turned her attention to Seb. 'Well, you seem to get everywhere, Herr Wolff. Did you enjoy the court case this morning? Always satisfying to see justice in action.'

'Indeed, true justice is sacred. That is why I became a police officer.'

'You seem to be couching your words rather carefully.'

'I've had a few drinks, Miss Mitford.'

'And who are you? I'm sure I've seen you before.'

'My name is Hexie Schuler. I work at Herr Hoffmann's studio.'

'Of course you do. I've seen you in the osteria delivering pictures to darling Heinrich. Do you have a cigarette? I'm dying for a smoke and no one seems to have any.'

'Ask a waiter,' Seb said. 'They'll fetch you a packet.'

Unity's face registered a memory. 'Now I recall, you're actually related to Christian Weber.'

'He's my uncle, my mother's younger brother.'

'Lucky you. No one better to get you out of a fix, eh? Now won't you be a darling, Inspector, and use your influence to fetch me some cigarettes. Preferably American.'

By the early hours, the party was lit by flaming torches and a waning moon. A choreographed war of naked or near-naked bodies had been waged between the glistening girls, both sides writhing in ecstasy as they fought for a flag at the centre of the lawn.

In the end, the place was littered with heaps of exhausted, panting flesh. Weber looked on with undisguised pleasure at the battlefield and had his servants walk among the combatants offering chilled champagne and choice meats, while he slumped his own vast body on a throne-like chair surrounded by his chosen naked girls. Many of the more respectable and older people – including the Hanfstaengls and Helene Bechstein – had quietly vanished into the night to drive home, perhaps worried that the party would end up as an orgy and that they would somehow be implicated in scandalous behaviour.

Seb knew he had drunk a great deal too much, but he had had no option. His body and soul cried out for oblivion, anything to stop him thinking of the doomed youth or his own missing son.

'Time for that swim,' Hexie said. 'Clear our heads.'

'Or drown.'

'I'll save you. Come on. I spotted a perfect little beach a few hundred metres to the west.' She took his hand and led him away from the party and the din of a Bavarian band and dancing troupe. In the east, the first glimmerings of the new day were scraping the edge of darkness off the hilltops.

They picked their way through the gardens and then into a patch of woodland, following a path to Hexie's chosen place. When they found it, the beach was deserted and perfect.

In a hurry now, they took off their clothes and left them in a pile by a tree, then ran side by side into the water, diving in head first.

The cold was a shock. The days might be warm in June but the meltwaters of the mountain snows that fed these lakes had not yet had a chance to heat up. As he surfaced, Seb gasped. Hexie threw herself into his arms and the warmth of their bodies – clasped together within the cold of the water – was exquisite.

Her hand went down and held him, caressing and urging. He did not need much encouragement. The chill of the water was no more. In the grey beginnings of day, all that existed in their world was each other's bodies. They were kissing and their fingers played with each other's sex. From somewhere in the distance they could hear the faint strains of an accordion and the muted chatter of voices, but here and now there was nothing and no one but Seb and Hexie, breathing in each other.

Perhaps for the first time, he had a powerful sense of love for this woman. He entered her and heard the soughing of her breath and sensed the hurried beating of her heart.

'Dear God, Sebastian.'

There were other noises, closer at hand, but he ignored them in his passion. Wild animals in the woods, perhaps. The love-making was urgent and intense. Whatever the drink had done to his cognitive powers had washed away and now he was utterly alive and sensate. He stopped, wanting the moment to never end, every nerve ending on the edge of the precipice of the little death.

And then it happened and was done and they collapsed together into cold clear water.

His feelings didn't die with the orgasm. He decided he loved her, truly, and determined that he would tell her. From now on, he would never dream of Ulrike. From now on, his nights would be full of Hexie Schuler. Or was that the drink talking?

He heard the sounds again. Animals in the woods? Quickly drying himself with his shirt, he pulled on his trousers, socks and shoes and stood there bare-chested in the dawning light.

'What is it, Seb?'

'I thought I heard something.'

'The band. We're not that far away.'

'Something else, closer, through the woods.'

She hugged her arms around herself, naked and shivering.

'Get dressed, Hexie, and wait here. I'm just going to go and take a look.'

He crept through the woods, towards the west, away from the villa and the party, not sure what he was seeking.

There was nothing. No sign of human life. Perhaps wild boar roamed these woods, snuffling and foraging through the night. Or perhaps he had imagined the noise. He knew well what the dark could do to a man's imagination. Standing guard duty through the long nights on the front line, you heard demons and saw ghosts.

Her voice came. 'Seb, Seb!' Just his name, but he could hear Hexie's distress. Without hesitating, he loped back through the woods and found her, standing there in her long skirt – the one she had chosen specially for this evening – holding up her white linen blouse.

There was little enough light still, but he could see that the article had been defaced.

'What is it? What's happened, Hex?'

'My blouse – look at it.'

He took the garment from her. In neat red writing, in what looked like lipstick, the words 'Sex Magic' had been inscribed across the reverse.

Seb was puzzled. 'Is that supposed to be some sort of compliment? Or a rather crass attempt at irony about our love-making?'

'I don't think so,' she said. She turned the blouse around to show him the front. There was another mark – a rune. It seemed to Seb to be the one mentioned by the anonymous voice on the phone. Something like an M or W on its side – ⋛. The symbol of the sun in at least one ancient Germanic language. And this was one of the summer solstice days.

What did it all mean? More importantly, who had crept here on to this secluded lakeside beach to write it on Hexie's blouse? The first thought that came to mind was the person behind the anonymous voice, but that didn't make a lot of sense. If the disembodied voice had more to say, why not just use the telephone?

Anyway, what about the words – 'sex magic'?

'It scares me, Seb.'

'I suppose he or she was watching us. But why? And what does it mean?'

'Seb, have you never heard of sex magic?'

What was she hinting at? 'They're just words. Random words.'

'No. I heard about it at school years ago. One of the girls found it in one of her father's books and showed it to us. We were all intrigued, of course. It's an occult thing, you see. I can't really remember everything because it's all a bit obscure, but the idea centres around the spiritual power of the orgasm – the most explosive of the natural forces. It's said that done correctly it can invoke the gods or the hidden masters, and make things happen.'

'What sort of things?'

'Wealth, perhaps. Death of an enemy. Make someone love you. Bring power. You know, all the things people want in life.'

Seb raised an eyebrow. 'And people believe this?'

'Apparently.' She smiled and almost laughed. 'They can certainly be quite potent things, orgasms, in case you hadn't noticed.

Anyway, if you want to know more, you'd better go to a library and find some books.'

'And then there's that rune. Is there some connection?'

'Again, Seb, you're asking the wrong person. Except that I did get the feeling that it was all somehow connected with the old *Völkisch* movement. For the moment, though, I'm more worried how I'm going to get this lipstick off my favourite, most expensive blouse.'

There was no way of cleaning it at the moment, so she just put it on as it was and, together, they found the path back through the woods to the party area. It had become much quieter since they left. Almost all the guests had gone and the host, Weber, was nowhere to be seen.

Servants were cleaning away glasses and plates, picking up cigarette ends from their master's dew-dampened lawn and generally collecting the detritus of a wild night.

'Back to Munich, then. And sleep.'

Except Seb didn't have time for sleep.

'There's just one thing I should mention, Seb, though you must never repeat it. When Evie Braun started seeing Adolf, she told me in strictest confidence that he is obsessed with a book called *Magic* by Ernst Schertel. He has a copy on one of his shelves at his Prinzregentenplatz flat and he has covered it with marks in the margins. Apparently it is like a manual for anyone interested in the occult. Evie thought it was a bit odd and wanted to know my opinion.'

'What did you say?'

'I told her he should drink more beer. That made her laugh.'

He dropped Hexie off at her lodgings and then drove home to Ainmüllerstrasse, arriving just as his mother was rising from her bed.

'Morning, Mutti.'

'You know, Sebastian, two weeks ago three people lived in this house. Now it just seems to be me.'

'I told you about Uncle Christian's party, though.'

'I knew about it anyway because he invited me, too, but I wasn't going to go to something like that. He might be my little brother, but that doesn't mean I approve of him. Night of the Pagans indeed! I'm a God-fearing Christian – unlike my brother Christian. Was ever a boy worse named?'

'It was quite entertaining. You might have liked it.'

'You know very well I'd have hated it. Anyway, look at you – you're completely dishevelled. Are you going to bed or can I get you breakfast?'

'Breakfast, please, Mutti.'

'First, though, you will shave and wash and change your clothes.'

He obeyed his mother. After breakfast, he realised he was exhausted and lay down on his bed for a five-minute rest. Two hours later, he woke up, refreshed from the brief sleep. It was almost ten o'clock.

He was at the door lacing up his shoes when his mother appeared from the kitchen. 'Jurgen telephoned while you were asleep. He told me not to wake you.'

'Is he all right? Where is he?'

'They're both fine, him and the girl, but he wouldn't say where they were. He says he'll call again in the next day or two and that he wants to speak with you.'

'Is that all? Nothing more?'

'That was all. And you, will you be home tonight?'

'Most likely.'

He drove to Ettstrasse. Being a Saturday, the Presidium was not quite as busy as normal, but the police force never took a day off. There was no sign of Sergeant Winter, which was a mercy, but there was an envelope on his desk. It had been stamped and delivered through the Reichspost rather than hand-delivered.

Before opening it, he got a coffee.

The envelope was large and brown and had a Nuremberg postmark. He slid in his letter opener to break the seal and the contents slipped out. A photograph lay on the desk in front of him. Beside it there was a note.

The photograph was similar to those taken at the Munich pathology lab. A body lay on a slab. A girl's body, with cuts in haphazard shapes – perhaps runes, though not distinguishable to Seb's untrained eye. The poor victim was slender, young and would have been very beautiful, not dissimilar in appearance to Rosie Palmer. But it was not her.

The note was unsigned and typewritten, but had an under-scored heading giving a girl's name, Hildegard Heiden, and an address.

Inspector Wolff, I thought you should see this. I would have contacted you earlier but news of the death of the English girl in Munich has just reached Nuremberg following the trial. I do not have details of your case but it seemed possible that the murder you have been investigating was perpetrated by the same person who killed our victim, Fräulein Hildegard Heiden, aged twenty. Her body was found by hikers at the top of Hesselberg three days ago (June 18th). The investigating officer is Inspector Hartmann of the Nuremberg Kripo but he is unlikely to speak to you. I think he has realised the similarities between the two cases, but is understandably nervous about drawing attention to this, given the political implications. And with that in mind, I hope you will forgive me for not revealing my own name to you.

And that was all it said. Seb looked again at the picture. It was not perfectly focused and the edges had been cut. Of course, this was not an original, but a photograph of a photograph.

CHAPTER 28

On the first morning, Jurgen and Silke simply walked north-west out of Munich, heading deep into the fields of Bavaria, avoiding the main roads – just in case Jurgen's father had alerted his police friends to look out for them and bring them back home.

Before leaving the city they had brought a loaf of spiced bread, a large chunk of cheese and had filled their flasks with water from a public drinking fountain. By early evening, they had eaten half their food and had stopped outside a small town called Markt Indersdorf, which was dominated by an ancient Augustinian abbey.

Now they were in a potato field, flat and endless. No sign of another human being.

'So where now, Jurgen? What's your plan for the night?'

'I thought you had a plan.'

They both fell about laughing and Jurgen grabbed out for her. But she was too quick and skipped away. He chased her and caught her and they both fell to the ground among the burgeoning potato leaves. The ground was soft. He tickled her and she squirmed and tried to tickle him back. Then they removed their rucksacks and lay side by side looking up into the cloudless, darkening sky.

'Perhaps we'll find a hut,' he said. 'An empty hay barn.'

'Let's just stay here. I could sleep like a potato here.'

He laughed out loud at that and she laughed too, as though neither of them had ever laughed before or heard such a childish joke.

'Do you love me, Jurgen?'

'Of course I do. What about you?'

'Yes, I love me.'

He prodded her side with his finger and she squirmed again.

'How are your wounds?'

'I think I'll live.'

'Can we have some more bread and cheese now?'

'You're the housewife. You decide.'

'You get it, Jurgen. I can't move. My legs are completely worn out and I'm stuck here for the night.'

They had left their school clothes in a friend's garden soon after leaving home and were now in their Hitler Youth and League of German Girls outfits. Much more practical for hiking and much less likely to be stopped by any officious SA man or cop. Jurgen got to his knees, fetched the bread from his rucksack and cut off two hunks with his ceremonial dagger. He handed one to Silke and she held out her hand for cheese.

She was so beautiful. He imagined his mother must have looked like that. He had never even seen a photograph of her, though he had looked all over the apartment in case his father or grandmother had hidden one away somewhere. But nothing.

Silke's eyes were closed and she was eating slowly. 'I know you're looking at me, Jurgen. Do you think I'm beautiful?'

'I think you look like a toad.'

She laughed again and began to choke. 'Don't do that!'

'A very pretty toad, though.'

'I know what you're after with your flattery, Jurgen Wolff, and you're not getting it. Not until my wedding day.'

'Not even a kiss?'

'Maybe a kiss. On the cheek.'

Wrapped in blankets, they slept in the potato field, side by side, fully dressed on canvas sheets. When the chill set in during the early hours, they turned to each other and hugged for warmth.

At dawn, they awoke, stiff and cold, and disappeared into a nearby copse and stream to perform their ablutions modestly and out of each other's sight. Cleanliness was required for every young member of the Hitler Youth or the League of German Girls, even on the hardest of hikes. And then, refreshed, they ate the last of the bread and cheese.

Having filled their flasks from the stream, they proceeded on their way north-westwards.

The day was glorious and they felt good and at peace with the world. For a while they walked hand in hand. When farmhands tilling the fields in their leather shorts spotted them in their uniforms, they saluted in the new way or doffed their hats in the old manner.

During the morning, they walked fifteen kilometres, eventually coming to a large farm village with a cafe, where they ordered hot chocolate and pastries and sat at a little table outside.

'Your father, Jurgen, he's not so bad, is he?'

'He hates the Hitler Youth. He hates Hitler.'

'You know that's just his generation.'

'You're right as always, Fräulein Stutz. As Hitler himself said, the future of Germany belongs to the youth.'

'So perhaps you should try and understand your father. Things were different for those of his age. They don't realise what good we are doing.'

'*Your* parents aren't like that.'

'Are you sure? We don't talk about politics so I have no idea what they think. But I do know that they don't want me to have babies yet – they want me to go to university. My mum does, anyway. She says she wants me to have the opportunity she never had and Papa doesn't argue with her.'

'Was he in the war?'

She nodded. 'Army Medical Service. Field hospital on the Eastern Front, then the west after Brest-Litovsk. He met my mother in the east – she was a nurse. All either of them will say is that it must never be repeated.'

'My father's the same. Won't say a word about it, so I've no idea what he did. For all I know he could have just cowered in his trench.'

'You don't believe that, Jurgen.'

'Don't I?' No, of course he didn't. He had come across the old man's Iron Cross when he was rummaging through drawers looking for pictures of his mother. The medal was hidden away beneath a pile of papers, as though he was somehow ashamed of the honour. 'Anyway, whatever he did, that doesn't excuse his thinking now. He is a disgrace, a traitor, and I disown him.'

'Jurgen, he didn't have the education we have. They weren't taught racial hygiene.'

'But I tell him, I explain everything to him and he's too stupid and ignorant to listen. The Führer promised the German people their pride back, I tell him, he promised work for all and food in everyone's belly – and he has done it all. How can he not understand these simple facts?'

'I don't know, Jurgen.'

'I wasn't surprised when they took him off to Dachau, I really wasn't. But the shame, Silke, you can't imagine how I felt. If it wasn't for Great-uncle Christian he'd probably still be there.'

She kissed him on the cheek. 'Is that better?'

He shrugged. 'I suppose so.' He took coins out of his pocket and placed them on the table. 'How much have we got left?'

'Enough to buy food. We could get some sausage and bread here probably.'

'Have we got enough to catch the bus?'

'Jurgen! You said you wanted to walk. That was the whole idea.'

'But it's a hundred and fifty kilometres. Can we really manage that in three days?'

'We won't know unless we try.'

The day wore on. They walked through flat farmland and woodland and through many little villages, some of which had banners across the roads declaring 'Jews enter here at your peril' or 'Jews not welcome here'. They finally stopped in the early evening by the River Glonn at a narrow fast-flowing gorge, to the east of Augsburg. It was a lovely spot and they decided to stay there. Both had agreed that they weren't going to make the remaining 110 kilometres in one day, so in the morning they would trek into Aichach and pick up the main road in the hope of hitching a lift.

Their mood had changed. Without discussing it, both were beginning to wonder whether this was a good idea, whether they weren't demanding a bit too much of themselves, especially as their navigational skills were dependent on a simple compass and a map that would have been out of date at the turn of the century.

They slept in woods. Jurgen stayed awake for hours, unnerved by the sounds: rustling in the undergrowth, the hoot of an owl. Eventually, he managed a couple of hours of restless sleep, but woke on the Saturday morning feeling even worse than the night before. They barely spoke over the last of their food and then set off for the town.

Lifts were easy to come by from farm vehicles, but none of them took them more than a few kilometres.

And then, in the late afternoon, they struck lucky.

A large cream-coloured car raced past their outstretched thumbs. They shrugged and watched it go, expecting it to disappear in moments, but two hundred metres along the road, it stopped and waited. Jurgen and Silke broke into a trot and caught up with it in seconds. The driver wound down the window and looked at them as though studying them for honesty.

'Where are you going?'

'Hesselberg,' Jurgen said.

'What a wonderful coincidence, so are we. You're in luck. Hop in the back.'

They settled down on the wonderfully comfortable leather bench seat and their hands found each other's for the first time that day. Suddenly the world felt good again.

The driver of the Maybach looked at his companion in the front passenger seat with raised eyebrows, then engaged gear and pulled away from the kerb. As he did so, his gaze went to the rear-view mirror and took in the beautiful young girl. He knew instantly that she would be perfect. She was the one.

CHAPTER 29

Seb found the house where Hildegard Heiden once lived a little to the south-east of Nuremberg, not far from the immense structures and paved areas where the annual rally was held.

The house was very neat, traditional Bavarian. Rather middle-class and bourgeois, not dissimilar to Baroness Laroche's house where Unity Mitford had lodged in Munich. The people who lived here must have some money and status.

Seb parked the Lancia on the street outside the front door and hesitated about knocking. He had spoken to no one in Nuremberg. The note with the photograph had mentioned that the investigating officer, Hartmann, would refuse to talk so this was not a task he could do through official channels. If he spoke to the local police, the chances were he would be instantly shut down by the higher echelons. No one in the party wanted interference in a court judgement, certainly not one concerning anything even vaguely political.

Anyway, this would be seen as a local matter, nothing to do with a Kripo inspector from another city.

At last he steeled himself and rapped his knuckles on the door and stepped back. Half a minute later the door was opened by a woman in her forties in stockinged feet. She was homely and undistinguished and he knew that she had been crying because her face was stained with tears.

'Frau Heiden?'

'Yes.'

'Heil Hitler. I am Inspector Wolff of the Munich Kripo.'

She stood glaring at him as though he had used the foulest language known to humanity. 'If you say that name again, I will slam the door in your face.'

That name? Did she mean Hitler or Wolff? It had to be Hitler, surely. He bowed his head respectfully. 'Forgive me, Frau Heiden, I know I am intruding on indescribable grief. But, please, may I come in and talk with you a while?'

'Very well. I don't suppose you have good news about my husband but yes, come inside. First, though, show me your badge and
take off your shoes.'

'This is about your daughter, not your husband. Why do you
mention him? Has something happened to him?'

'He is in Dachau, of course, for daring to tell the truth about that
man, that Lucifer. And now I am alone and my life is destroyed.'

'I am sorry. Your suffering is great, dear lady.'

'But you are here about my child, my beautiful daughter. What
does her death have to do with Munich?'

Seb was unlacing his shoes. He slid his feet into a pair of guest
slippers and followed Frau Heiden through to her parlour. The
first thing he noticed was an oil painting on the wall of a girl
in a ball gown and he knew instantly that it was Hildegard, for
having seen her picture in death he could tell that the likeness
was a good one.

'A girl was murdered in Munich and it is possible that there
are similarities to the case of your daughter. But there are political
implications, which is why I have come to you unannounced.'

She snorted. 'Political implications. I know exactly what they
are. Because my husband speaks his mind and protects the workers at his factory against the brutes, no one gives a damn about
poor Hildegard. Her death is an embarrassment to Hartmann
and the rest.'

'I believe her body was found four days ago at Hesselberg.'

She nodded. Her tears had started again. 'She was walking
home from work last Saturday, exactly a week ago. A witness said
a car stopped at her side and the driver spoke to her and then she
got in the back. That's all, that's the last time anyone saw her.'

'This car, do you know anything about it?'

'No, except that it was white or cream coloured. Nothing else.'

'Do you know anyone with such a vehicle? Could the driver
have been an acquaintance or friend?'

'I have no idea whether she knew the man – I assume it was a
man, or men. My daughter was remarkably beautiful but she lived

very quietly. She had broken up with her boyfriend just a month ago. He was a sweet boy but something happened between them. She wouldn't talk to me about it. Young people are like that.'

The tears were flowing. Seb desperately wanted to help her, to give her some comfort. But how do you help someone who has lost everything with no hope of ever getting it back?

'You mentioned she was coming home from work, Frau Heiden. What was her employment?'

'Oh, it was nothing much. She served in a cafe in the city centre, but really she was just filling in time, earning a few marks before she could train to become a teacher.'

'Perhaps you would give me details of the cafe, also the name and address of her former boyfriend. First, though, Frau Heiden, I am interested to know exactly where she was found. I am told hikers discovered her at Hesselberg, is that correct?'

She nodded helplessly. 'The sacred hill. No it wasn't hikers – Streicher's men found her. They were up there preparing the stage for the Frankentag.'

Seb had no idea what she was talking about. 'Frankentag? What is that?'

'Why, it is Streicher's big day. His gathering of the Nazis from Franconia and other parts of Germany to celebrate the pagan solstice on our holy mountain. I am told Goering will be there. Who knows, perhaps even the devil himself will pay a surprise visit.'

The devil. He assumed she was referring to Hitler, but better not to press the point. He would like to advise this woman to be careful with her tongue, but what was the use of such advice now that her husband was caged and her daughter dead?

Nor could he fail to notice that he was now in Julius Streicher territory. Her mention of the man had brought that to mind.

Nuremberg was in the Franconia region of Bavaria, and Streicher was *gauleiter* – governor – of Franconia, a region of historical rivalry with the greater Bavaria which had subsumed it. Streicher was the most fanatical of the anti-Semites. He had founded a journal called *Der Stürmer* which depicted Jews as greedy, bloodthirsty sexual fiends who were destroying the German state from within and had to be eliminated. It spoke of alleged ritual murder of innocent German girls and carried obscene cartoons of hook-nosed brutes.

One of its writers, of course, was Otto Raspe.

These facts jarred in Seb's brain. Paganism, ritual murder, sex magic, the Thule Society, Hitler's obsession with the occult, the runic symbol for the sun, the *geblōt* places of ancient Nordic sacrifices, the *Völkisch* writings of Otto Raspe. These words and concepts flashed before his inner eye like a horror film – *Nosferatu*, perhaps, or *Frankenstein*. And they were taking him nowhere except probably back to Dachau concentration camp.

He had to clear his head of this nonsense, think rationally. These mystical clues were as absurd as Streicher's accusations that Jews murdered German children as part of their blood rites.

The plain truth was this: a murderer of young women was on the loose and he had to be stopped, whatever his obscene motive, before he killed again – and before an innocent man died by guillotine to satisfy Hitler's foreign policy and his relations with Great Britain.

'I would really like to go to the place where Hildegard was found, Frau Heiden. Can you describe it to me?'

'If you have a car, we can go there.'

On the way in the Lancia, Frau Heiden told Seb about her husband. He owned a small ceramics business, making Bavarian artefacts and souvenirs for the tourist trade. He had never been a political man but when Streicher's Brownshirt thugs came around demanding that his manager be sacked for the crime of being a Jew, Albert Heiden had erupted in fury.

'He said no, he would not sack his manager. Why should he? He was a wonderful worker who had done more than anyone to build up the Heiden business. The lead Brownshirt spat on the ground and said that none of that mattered, all that mattered was the man's race. That's when Albert really exploded. He called Hitler and Streicher every name under the sun and said the Nazis were a disgrace to Germany. And then they beat him to the ground, handcuffed him and hauled him off to Dachau.'

'When was this?'

'Two months ago. I am allowed no visits and I doubt my letters are delivered to him. He doesn't even know that Hildegard is dead. And perhaps it is better that way because the news would probably kill him.'

As they approached Hesselberg, Seb was astonished by the amount of traffic building up. Not just cars and trucks, but thousands of cyclists and pedestrians, too. And everyone seemed to be in swastika-marked uniform of one sort or another. Whole troops of boys and girls marched in file – boys in their Hitler Youth uniforms and girls in their League of German Girls outfits of dark mid-length skirts, white short-sleeved blouse and loosely knotted ties.

He drove a circular route at the suggestion of Frau Heiden and approached the hill from the south, stopping at the western edge of the village of Gerolfingen to gaze upon the scene. Smoke rose from bonfires and there was a distant din of drumbeats.

'They call it the sacred mountain, the Nazis. The sacred mountain of the Franks. But does it look like a mountain to you, Herr Wolff? I would call it a hill, nothing more. Six or seven hundred metres at the most. No one who has been to the Alps could call this a mountain.'

He could understand her dismissive attitude. Why should she be impressed by this place after what had happened here?

'The detective Hartmann brought me up here at my request. I suppose it was the least he could do. I think he's actually a decent enough fellow for a coward, but he's frozen with fear because he knows that we were already a marked family and he was terrified of uncovering something that others would like to remain hidden. But he's not the worst. The worst people are certain friends who now cross the road to avoid me. They are too scared to be associated with a family of undesirables.'

There were many such people in Germany in 1935, thought Seb, men and women who simply kept their mouths shut because the consequences of speaking out were too awful to contemplate. Was he one of them? It was a shaming thought. Though he agreed with every word this woman said, he took the politik route and kept his own feelings hidden from her.

'Come, we can drive a little further and then walk.'

In the event, they had to park behind a long line of cars and trucks two kilometres from the top before embarking on the long walk up the hill. Finally, at the summit, they found an area of flat meadow crowded with what seemed like thousands of people and decorated by flagpoles, each with a swastika fluttering in the light breeze. At the very centre was a broad stage, fronted with a large white eagle design above a swastika in an oak-leaf circle. Thousands of people were gathered around, as though waiting for something.

'This area is called the Osterwiese,' Frau Heiden said. 'Our ancestors made a fortress here and this is where the Frankentag is being held today and tomorrow. Hildegard was found in woodland lower down on the northern side. Come, I'll show you.'

The milling, marching throngs of young Nazis had made their own little camps around bonfires, each with their own flag and, on each standard, a metal plate bearing the district they came from: Frankfurt, Cologne, Würzburg, Bayreuth, Essen, Stuttgart, Dresden, Bremen, Hannover, Hamburg, Leipzig, and scores of other cities and towns. They were here from all over the Reich. Many thousands and increasing by the minute as more arrived.

Seb was taken aback. He knew all about the Nuremberg rallies, of course, but this was something new to him. And with the bonfires and the setting, it was alive with excitement.

'It was not like this when I came before,' Frau Heiden said. 'It's hateful and I don't like it. Can we go, please, Inspector.'

'Can you not first show me where your daughter was found?'

'It's over there.' She nodded to the north-east. 'We can walk there, but I have to get away from these people. I feel the diabolical energy. Don't you feel it?'

In fact he did, though he did not like to admit it. 'Come then, we'll walk fast.'

It was quieter and a great deal more wooded on the eastern part of the hill, across the decline, but the smoke and the noise still drifted and swirled about them.

'This is a terrible place. They say there are many caves and tunnels beneath us, where goblins and demons live. But it is those above ground that I fear most. Do you not feel Satan's presence here?'

'I cannot answer your questions, Frau Heiden. My own feelings are immaterial. I am here to investigate a terrible murder, nothing more.'

'You are all the same. Cowards every one of you. You know the truth but you fear to speak it. My husband is ten times the man you are.'

He couldn't argue with her because she was probably right. Yes, it was true, he was taking the path of least resistance. Why? Because he had to, for who else would look after Mutti and Jurgen? Who else would investigate these murders? If he stayed free, perhaps he could do some good, perform some small service to keep the flame of justice alive in his benighted yet beloved country. For no one else was remotely interested in finding the killer of Rosie Palmer and Hildegard Heiden.

'This was where the body was found. You can still see the depression in the leaves where she lay. They said she was naked, her body exposed to the elements, though why they felt the need to tell me that I don't know.'

It was an area of dry leaves just inside the perimeter of a wooded area. Seb could imagine the scene that the workmen chanced upon. In his mind's eye, he superimposed the photograph he had been sent onto the indentation: her throat cut like Rosie's, her body covered with lesions which may or may not have been intended to represent runes. And other similar marks, perhaps drawn with lipstick, though it was difficult to tell from the monochrome image. The photograph was secreted in the Lancia; it was not something he would show the mother.

'Could I just have a few minutes to look around the area, Frau Heiden. It is always possible the killer left a clue.'

'No, Inspector, I can't bear to be here a moment longer. Come back if you must, but please take me home first.'

CHAPTER 30

Seb drove Frau Heiden home. Before he left, she gave him a copy of the local newspaper in which the murder was reported on an inside page. 'It is not much, I'm afraid. If it was any other girl it would have been a big story, but this is all there is. Ignored because her father is in Dachau KZ.'

He took the paper, thanked her and spent the remainder of the afternoon in Nuremberg, a city he did not know well. His first stop was the cafe where Hildegard had been working before her abduction. While he toyed with a cup of very weak coffee, he read and reread the newspaper story, which was very short, no more than two hundred words. It said that local waitress Hildegard Heiden had been found dead on Hesselberg, close to the site of the Frankentag, and that police suspected murder. No suspects were mentioned and the article gave no details of her parents or her personal circumstances or ambitions to be a schoolteacher. It did, however, say that she was last seen getting into a cream-coloured car, possibly a Horch or a Maybach, while on her way home.

Nothing else. The only thing Seb learnt from the piece was the possible make of the car. No description of the driver and no names for any witnesses who saw her abduction.

He approached the middle-aged woman behind the counter and showed his Munich Kripo badge.

'Such a terrible, terrible tragedy,' the woman said.

'Are you the proprietor?'

'Yes, and now I am short-staffed. I'm sorry, that sounds awful, thinking of myself at such a time. I feel so for poor Hildy and her poor mother.'

'Do you have any idea who might have abducted and killed her? Did anyone ever come in here and talk to her, or look at her strangely?'

The cafe owner shook her head. 'Not that I noticed particularly. Of course, Hildy was a gorgeous young woman and she attracted a great deal of attention. Men couldn't take their eyes off her, but that was normal. I couldn't single out any man.'

'And did you ever see a cream-coloured car, perhaps a Maybach or Horch?'

'If I did, I don't recall. But tell me, sir, why is a Munich police officer investigating? I have already spoken to Inspector Hartmann and I told him exactly the same as I have told you.'

'There has been a death in similar circumstances in Munich.'

'Do you mean the one reported in the newspaper? That is all done with surely. They have the man and he has been condemned to death.'

Seb smiled without humour. He didn't bother to confirm her supposition. 'I am told by Frau Heiden's mother that she had a boyfriend. Did he ever come in here?'

'That would be Dieter. Yes, he came here sometimes. He worked for the party, I think – dealing with memberships.'

'Did he have a car?'

'He had a bicycle. A nice boy and quite good-looking, but I don't think Hildy ever took him seriously. Just someone to accompany her to the cinema.'

'Thank you, dear lady, for your time,' he said, left two coins for his coffee and walked out. He wanted to speak with Hildegard's young boyfriend Dieter, but had only that first name and no address. The only way to make progress with this case was to talk with Inspector Hartmann, but he would leave that until he had exhausted other possible leads. And the only one that presented itself for now was examining the place where the body was found.

Jurgen and Silke arrived at Hesselberg in the evening having been dropped off in the small village of Gerolfingen and walking the last three kilometres uphill. The driver had said that he and his passenger were also attending the big event, but were staying the night in a nearby hotel. Perhaps they would see them later after they had checked in.

Up on the plateau of the hill, the Osterwiese, individual groups had set up camp over a wide area, and there was an air of expectation.

Bands were playing, songs were being sung around fires, there were boxing matches and races, marching and dancing.

The plan for Jurgen and Silke was to find their individual troops, for they would already be here, and then try to get back together later in the evening when darkness came. The problem was, they didn't really want to leave each other for five minutes, let alone a couple of hours.

Seb found nothing at the murder site, or at least the site where the victim was found. There seemed no option now but to go to Nuremberg police headquarters and try to find Hartmann. God damn it, he might not even be working on a Saturday. The thought of talking to the man filled him with gloom because he just knew that it would go nowhere and he would be packed off back to Munich.

Re-tracing his steps towards the Osterwiese where the crowds were gathering and enjoying the comradeship and anticipation of the long night to come, he saw Ernie Pope.

His first instinct was to avoid him, look the other way and carry on to his car, but then Pope spotted him and waved, so he couldn't be ignored.

The American reporter approached him with a smile.

'I have to say, Seb, whatever you or I might think of the Nazis, they know how to put on a show.'

'Don't assume you know what I think about the Nazis, Ernie.'

Pope raised an apologetic hand. 'Of course not, old man. Point taken.'

'Forgive me, I didn't mean to snap. It's just been a tough day.'

'Really? In what way?'

'Oh, nothing I can talk about. Anyway, good to meet a friendly face here. I take it you're reporting on the big event. I'll look out for your write-up.'

'It won't make a hell of a lot. The only interesting thing for my London editors is that I'm told Unity is going to get up on stage and make a speech. Spewing her anti-Semitic bile, no doubt. That'll make a paragraph or two, but not a lot more. Are you going back down the mountain? Come with me, I've got a bottle of Scotch in my motor. Got a good parking spot a few hundred yards down the hill.'

Why not? He was going in that direction anyway and a drink couldn't hurt. It was a better proposition than approaching Detective Inspector Hartmann fully sober.

After a ten-minute walk, they climbed into the back of Pope's long open-top car. He had a hamper with food and a couple of bottles, one of which he uncorked then poured two large Scotches into crystal tumblers.

'*Prost*, Seb.'

'Expenses?'

'Of course.'

'And remind me, what are we toasting?'

Pope laughed. 'Well, buddy, I know why I'm here at the Frankentag. Editor's orders because of the Unity line. But what about you? This doesn't seem like your weekend activity of choice. Should be with your girl, shouldn't you? Or solving crimes in Munich?'

On the way down from Hesselberg, he had reminded himself that it would not be healthy to discuss certain matters with the reporter. Now, out of nowhere, he changed his mind. To hell with it, questions from the foreign press might be the only way to get the execution of Karl Friedlander cancelled or delayed.

'If I tell you why I'm here, you'll want to make a story out of it.'

'Now you've really got me interested.'

'But it could cost me my job. Or worse.'

'So you want to be sure you're protected?'

He nodded.

'The question is, do you trust me?'

Seb liked to think he knew something about human beings. It was what made him a half-decent detective. He believed he knew when to trust people, just as he had trusted Max Haas and other men in the trenches. Trusted them when another friend died and he was falling apart and weeping and quivering like a baby. Trusted them with his sanity and his life.

'I do, Ernie.'

'Well, shoot. If when we've talked you change your mind and want me to steer away from the story, you have my word it'll never see the light of day.'

Seb swigged down his whisky in one, waited for a refill, then told Ernest Pope everything he knew about the death of Hildergard Heiden and the striking similarities with the murder of Rosie Palmer.

'Does this get Friedlander off the hook, though?' Pope said at last. 'Or does it mean he's a double killer. That's what my editor will ask, and so do I.'

'You mean could he have killed Hildegard too?'

'I mean exactly that. What are the timings?'

'Hildegard went missing last Saturday. I picked Friedlander up first on Sunday evening, then he was caught at Freiburg on Monday as he and his parents were trying to get to Switzerland. So yes it is possible that he killed Hildegard. But maybe he has an alibi. I just don't know because we have no record of his alleged movements on the Saturday. Wasn't something we had cause to ask him about. And then there's the question of the car. I have no reason to believe Friedlander even has a motor car, let alone a big cream one.'

'Anyone can get hold of a car. You need more, Seb. This isn't going to save Friedlander's neck. They'll just decide that the Hildegard Heiden case has been solved, too.'

'Meanwhile we have a murderer on the loose.'

'Are you really certain about this? Are you one hundred per cent that Friedlander's not our man?'

'Ninety-nine.'

'I guess that's what certain courts would call reasonable doubt. The next question is, how do I get this story printed? Who in the Munich or Nuremberg police can I quote? I need something hard – a line expressing doubt about Friedlander or something concrete linking the two cases and requiring the case to be reopened.'

'Come with me.'

Together they walked further down the hill to Seb's Lancia. He fished about under the seat and pulled out the brown envelope.

The photograph of the dead girl slid out and he handed it over to the reporter.

'Does that help?'

'God, that's grim. How similar is it to the cuts and scrawls on Rosie's corpse?'

'Very.'

'Do you have a copy of the Rosie photos?'

'They've disappeared.'

'That's inconvenient.'

'Or convenient, depending on your point of view.'

Pope reached out to take the photograph. 'Can I borrow this? They'll never print it in an English paper, but the editor would like to know that I am in possession of it. It certainly poses a question.'

'You can keep it.'

'And is it traceable to you?'

'Only via the person who sent it to me anonymously or the girl's mother. She hasn't seen it, but I referred to it.'

'Do you think she'd talk to me?'

'She might. She's heartbroken, very angry and has the courage of a cornered animal.'

'OK, give me her address. I'm going to have to work fast on this to have a cat in hell's chance of getting the story in the Sunday papers. Monday probably – but that could be too late for Friedlander, I suppose. Will you be anywhere near the Cafe Heck for a quiet coffee on Monday morning?'

'I'll make sure I am. In the meantime, how will you keep my name out of this thing? Your political police friends or Putzi Hanfstaengl are bound to press you for the source.'

'When they ask, I'll say I saw that story in the Nuremberg rag and did a bit of digging. In truth I *had* seen it because I read all the papers, but I thought nothing of it. Didn't see the connection, but no one else needs to know that.'

Seb realised he couldn't approach Hartmann now. Instead he stayed at Hesselberg. He drove around all the nearby villages looking at the cars, looking at the people. Every man he saw, he wondered, *are you the killer?*

It was a futile exercise. In the beginning, no one looked like a murderer. After a while, everyone did. And as for the cars, there were plenty of big ones and more than enough cream or white ones. Not so many Horches or Maybachs though.

He skirted the hill, looking for caves. He found an interesting one and looked inside, but there was nothing there. Returning to his car as the light faded, he was startled to see a line of black Mercedes limousines sweeping up the hill. Seb spotted the bald head of Julius Streicher in one of the cars and, beside him, the unmistakeable blonde hair of Unity Mitford.

Well, well, that might be worth following. He strode along the road in their wake. By the time he arrived at the top, the party was in full flow. No sign of Unity or Streicher, but there was fire everywhere. One huge bonfire lit the darkening sky, blazing torches sparked like a constellation of fiery stars across the hill. Great burning wagon wheels rolled dangerously downhill accompanied by whoops and shouts of primal joy.

And then Seb was brought up short. Jurgen was there, with his Hitler Youth troop.

They were sitting cross-legged around a campfire with tin plates on their laps, eating their supper.

Jurgen was laughing. His forehead had a ragged line where Dr Stutz had sewn up his wound. But then he saw his father and his face darkened and his eyes burnt.

Seb held back. His son put his plate on the ground, then said something to the boy on his right. Probably 'I'm going for a piss', thought Seb.

Jurgen didn't approach his father directly, didn't want to be seen with him. He walked around the campfire into a throng of young people, many of them in traditional costume from different parts of Germany, others in a wide variety of uniform, including priests and nuns in habits and robes, though it defied belief that they should be here in this pagan place. So many people, so many different costumes. It was like a giant party. Seb followed Jurgen. His son stood tall, taller than his father, his shoulders back like a dog at bay. Then he pushed Seb in the chest with his clenched right fist.

'What are you doing here?' His voice was enraged, almost a growl, ready for a fight.

'I'm working.'

'You followed me, God damn you. I hate you.'

'Perhaps you do, but I didn't follow you. I had no idea where you had gone and I certainly didn't know you were here. Jurgen, I didn't even know about this event until a few hours ago. I'm investigating a murder – no three murders – and one of the bodies was discovered on this very hill. That's the truth, I promise.'

'I don't believe you.'

'And yet I don't lie to you. I simply found you by chance. Anyway, how did you get here? And where is Silke?'

'We hiked – marched, if you like. Remember, you always laugh about our marching in the troop. Well, it has come in useful and saved me a bus fare.'

Seb very much wanted to take his son in his arms, but that wasn't going to happen. Not today. 'I'm sorry if I have ever laughed at your activities. It is unforgivable of me.'

'Yes, old man, it is. You think you and your generation know better than us, but what exactly did your generation do? Lost a war, created economic mayhem, kissed the feet of the French, made Germany a laughing stock in the eyes of the world. And yet you mock *my* generation for putting things right.'

Seb nodded. It was partly true, of course. But he couldn't explain the finer points here and now to his son, in the midst of this throng. Justice for all, not just the privileged. The presumption of innocence rather than flinging men into Dachau without trial or even a proper charge. Democracy, not dictatorship. Not that Jurgen was going to listen; his mind was made up.

'We are the workers' party – the Führer has made that clear. To oppose us is to oppose the workers of Germany.'

Seb could easily have retorted that if the Nazis were the workers' party, why had they banned trade unions? Why had they dispensed with workers' rights? But an argument wasn't going to get him anywhere with Jurgen in his present frame of mind.

'Tell me about Silke, you still haven't told me where she is. Her parents trust you, but they are concerned about their daughter.'

'She is with her friends in the League. We have to stay apart here but we will see each other and tomorrow we will walk back to Munich together. Not to Ainmüllerstrasse, though.'

'This will break your grandmother's heart, you know.'

'And you'd know all about that, wouldn't you. Now, I have to get back to my friends. Please don't approach me. I don't want to be seen with you – in fact I don't want any of my comrades to know you're here.'

'As you wish, but I *will* be here for a while, perhaps all night. If you change your mind and want to talk, the Lancia is down the road and you can leave a note for me. Or you'll find me up here somewhere.'

Jurgen turned on his heel without a word and went off to rejoin his comrades.

CHAPTER 31

What was he still doing here? Why had he told Jurgen he would be here all night? It was because he didn't know what to do, where to turn for clues. But deep within, there was more than that. Something, some intuition or instinct, told him that this pagan place held a secret key. If only he could find it, and then discover the secret lock.

Ernie Pope had given him the remains of the whisky bottle, along with some bread and bierwurst from his expenses-paid hamper. Seb had brought the food and drink up the hill and now found a place where he could simply watch the evening's proceedings and think. Try to find some clarity. He swigged slowly from the bottle and picked at the food. It was dark now but there were fires and flaming torches to light the evening, and airs from the Hitler Youth songbook afloat on the freshening breeze.

He wondered about Silke. How would she feel if he went and found her League of German Girls group and talked to her about Jurgen? *Get a grip, Seb. Your mind is drifting between the need to find a killer and the desire to make amends with your son. These things are not connected.*

The whisky and the lack of sleep the night before eventually took their toll. At first his mind and mood mellowed into a fantastical waking dream of swirling colours and sounds: the sounds of the thousands, the drumbeats, the voices, the accordions and the guitars.

People danced before his eyes. In uniforms and robes and gowns. The dark of the night and the fires became part of him and he closed his eyes and submitted to warm delirium.

And then he slept and the dream became darker.

He awoke slowly. That is, he was woken by being pulled and shouted at, but consciousness was far from instant. He opened his eyes and found that he was looking blearily into his son's face.

'Dad, wake up. Help me.'

Now consciousness came in a rush. He was awake and standing up. What time was it? The music wasn't stopping, nor the smoke and flames from the fires.

'Jurgen?'

'I can't find Silke. We arranged to meet but she wasn't there. I went to her troop, but they had no idea where she was and they were all laughing about something and didn't seem concerned.'

'Where were you going to meet?'

'I'll show you.'

Jurgen broke into a run and Seb followed. They zigzagged between the fires and the tents and the dancers and singers, until they came upon a tree at the eastern extremity of the Osterwiese plateau, just before it dipped down into the woods. 'Here, we were supposed to meet here.'

'Maybe she met some other friends and lost track of time, Jurgen.'

'No, not Silke. She's always punctual. She'd never do that to me.'

Seb felt cold fear. Not for himself, he'd lost that a long time ago. For the girl and for his son. 'Come, Jurgen. There's a path not far from here, away from the crowds, into the trees.'

'Why?'

'Trust me.' If she had been abducted she would have been taken away from here, away from all the people. The body of Hildegard Heiden had been found on the northern wooded slope of the hill, close to the bottom where the woodland was dense – hornbeam, ash, hazel, maple – and where he had noted tracks in the distance leading across farmland to the village of Ehingen. That was where the killer operated.

Seb led the way, moving fast down into the dip. It was darker here, a half-moon appearing and vanishing between the scudding clouds and the thick canopy of the broad-leaf trees.

He stopped, held a finger to his lips, and listened. Nothing.

'Why are we here? She can't be here.'

Seb was sure she was here. In his bones, he felt it. This sacred hill of the ancient Germans was the place of the *geblōt*, the place of sacrifice. Frau Heiden had sensed evil in these dark woods and she was right. Fully awake now, fully sober, he moved steadily deeper into the wooded area where the body of Hildegard had been discovered.

The hillside was not steep and mostly easy to negotiate. Seb led his son downwards, but still nothing.

'Dad, we've got to get back. She might be there, waiting for me.'

'You go, Jurgen. I'll continue looking here. We'll meet up.'

'You think something's happened to her, don't you?'

'I pray not.'

Dear God, this place. In the daylight it had looked so peaceful, so benign. An isolated hill in flat, pleasant farmland, surrounded by pretty villages, all with window boxes full of summer geraniums and petunias. A hill no more than six kilometres in length and two in width. A place where you could see the Alps in the distant south on a clear day. A place of abundant wildflowers and rich in wildlife. A place to walk your dog and enjoy a picnic. A place of peace, not pagan rites.

In the daylight.

At night, it felt very different.

He watched Jurgen moving away from him, up the hill back to the music and the fire and the light. Seb turned into the dark.

He was hearing every sound in the night. With his son gone, he removed his pistol from his shoulder holster and began his quest, slowly, methodically, through the thick forest, sure the key was here.

He heard a sound and stopped, his finger tightening on the trigger. A fox maybe, something scampering and snuffling in the undergrowth. But there it was again. Was that a light flickering somewhere through the woods, or a moon shadow? It was there and then it wasn't.

Seb continued forward, slower now. Again, sounds. Not a fox, not an animal grubbing through the leaves and twigs in search of food. Something else.

This time there was a light in a small clearing. A hurricane lamp on the ground, the wick turned low. He stopped and watched, first in horror and stunned disbelief, then rage.

A girl lay on the scrubby ground, naked, arms and legs stretched out, her wrists and ankles bound to stakes driven into the ground. Her mouth was gagged, her eyes blindfolded. A sacrifice.

And then there were the other two figures. Man and woman? It was difficult to tell because they both wore black robes and cowls, like Jesuit priests or giant bats.

One of the two robed figures was kneeling between the parted legs of the other, moving slowly, in a sort of ecstasy. They were within a few centimetres of the staked-out girl, almost on her, their black robes rubbing her, fingers outstretched, caressing her torso. *They* writhed in their ecstasy. *She* writhed – squirmed – in terror.

Seb assumed the one on top was a man and that the one beneath him was a woman, but there was no way of telling in the shapeless robes and faint light. The skirts were raised revealing legs and bare, clenched buttocks. Then he saw that they both had something in their outstretched hands pulsing with the rhythm of their own slow movements, scraping across the abdomen and breasts of the naked staked-out girl, the sacrifice. Pens, writing runes? Knives, cutting?

He could wait and watch no longer.

Seb pulled the trigger of the Walther PPK, aiming high above the two robed figures. He couldn't shoot them. Immoral and illegal to kill unarmed suspects but, more than that, too easy to miss and hit the girl instead. He fired across the clearing into the trees.

The robed man, the one on top, jumped up from his work, the skirts of the robe falling to once again conceal his lower body. The low light from the lamp cast his features into a sinister montage of shadowy shapes, but the cowl was too close to make him out clearly. The other one scrabbled up. Now standing, Seb was certain it was a woman but she was tall.

They both seemed to be looking at Seb, but he couldn't see their faces or their eyes, only the enveloping cowls. He moved forward, firing another shot, the gun smoking in his right hand. They moved, too. The larger of the two – the man? – kicked at the hurricane lamp and sent it flying and then they ran.

Seb fired a third speculative shot after them, but it was more of a warning than an attempt to wound or kill. He wasn't going to follow them either. For the moment, he was more concerned for the helpless young woman stretched out on the ground. Had they cut her? Was she injured? Had he got here in time?

He picked up the hurricane lamp. It was still alight and he raised the wick to intensify the light, carrying it towards the girl.

Her torso was covered in scarlet lipstick marks – strange lines, vertical, horizontal and various curls. Runes or something like runes. No cuts, thank God. And he was sure that this was Silke though he hadn't seen her in years.

He spoke reassuring words to her, told her he was Jurgen's dad, said he would free her and that she was safe now.

A long-bladed knife lay on the ground above her head, pointing downwards like the sword of Damocles. Seb picked it up and felt the edge. It was very sharp, like a dissecting tool. Quickly, he cut the ropes binding her, then removed the gag from her mouth and the blindfold from her eyes.

She was alive, her poor heart beating like a trapped bird's.

Seb found her clothes at the edge of the clearing in the woods and turned away from her while she dressed. Somehow after all this time they both recognised each other. He very much wanted to question her about the attackers, but that would have to wait. Her physical health was the first concern.

'Did they hurt you?'

She shook her head, but then nodded. He supposed she meant that she had endured no physical injury but that she had suffered.

'Come, we'll find Jurgen. You're safe now.'

She said nothing, simply shivered uncontrollably.

'Can you tell me what happened, Silke?'

She said nothing, her shivering just intensified.

'We'll talk later. Stay close at my side. I'm armed and you're safe.'

'I'll tell you. I have to tell you.'

Good, she was talking.

'I was at the meeting place, waiting for Jurgen. They just picked me up. I struggled and cried out but people nearby were just laughing as though it was some sort of game. Friends dressing up to ambush me . . .'

'Did you know them?'

'I didn't see their faces. They were in black robes. At first I thought it must have been Jurgen and one of his friends. A silly joke.'

'Do you think they were both men, or a man and a woman?'

'I don't know. One had a deeper voice.'

'What did they say?'

'Not words, not proper German words. No language I had ever heard.'

'English?'

She shook her head. 'I have learnt some English – no, not English.'

'Come on, they can't hurt you now. You're safe. If you think of anything – any little clue however insignificant that might identify them – please let me know.'

And then they walked cautiously back up the hill to the Osterwiese, not saying much. Seb carried the hurricane lamp in one hand, his pistol in the other. He had brought the dagger, too, thrust into his belt. And his eyes scanned the darkness, watching.

Jurgen was at the meeting point, pacing up and down in terror. He gasped as they arrived and he ran forward, took Silke in his arms and hugged her as though he would never let her go.

After a while, they sat down together. 'Let's try to collect our thoughts, shall we,' Seb said. 'You mentioned this jumble of words, Silke.'

'It was more like mumbling. They sounded like words, but nothing that made any sense.'

'Would you recognise their voices?'

'I'm not sure. There was something strange. Something familiar, but I didn't know them. I can't explain, I'm sorry.'

'You have nothing to be sorry about.'

'They just bundled me away, carried me as though I was weightless.'

'So they were strong?'

'Yes, the bigger one was very strong. I thought they were going to kill me.'

They were, thought Seb, *they were certainly going to kill you.* 'Could you estimate their ages?'

'No, they blindfolded me and gagged me very quickly. Before they grabbed me I hadn't noticed either of them in their robes and cowls. There are so many people here. Many of them wear our uniforms, but there are others – entertainers – who wear strange carnival costumes and religious ones in habits and robes. They just looked like monks or friars, or actors dressed as monks.'

'All right, that's enough for now. I'm sorry you've been through this ordeal, Silke. For what it's worth, we'll find them and they'll face justice. Come on, we'll talk to your troop leaders and then I'm taking you both home to Munich.'

CHAPTER 32

The journey home was a solemn, mostly silent affair. Jurgen and Silke sat in the rear of the Lancia and Seb could tell that his son was overwhelmed by a sense of unwarranted guilt over what had befallen the girl. 'If only I had been there on time to meet you, but I was only a minute or two late.'

She was silent, too wrapped up in her own horror to offer him words of comfort. Seb said nothing, merely drove in silence. He understood the boy's feelings; he was gallant and saw himself as the man who should have been taking care of the girl. Life wasn't really like that, of course, but this was something a young man of seventeen could only learn with time.

Back at the Stutz house, Silke fell weeping into her mother's arms, incoherent, while Seb tried to give a sanitised version of events. Frau Stutz wasn't really listening, just stroking her daughter's hair and whispering words of comfort, saying it was all right now. No harm done.

Jurgen stood awkwardly and watched, twisting his hands together. Seb asked if he could have a word with Dr Stutz alone and was taken through to his consulting room. He was a few years older than Seb, a serious-looking man with the attentiveness of a good doctor.

'This was very bad, Herr Doctor. It will be difficult for your daughter to get over this. She fell into the hands of extremely bad people.'

'Go on, Inspector. Please, don't hold anything back.'

Their conversation ranged over every detail of the attack at Hesselberg and the part played by Seb in rescuing the girl. 'For which I take no credit, Herr Doctor. It was pure good fortune that I found them before . . .' He left the likely conclusion hanging.

'You think they would have killed my daughter?'

Seb nodded slowly and with regret for being the bearer of such grim tidings. 'What these people – almost certainly a man and a woman – were doing was very similar to what happened in the case of two recent murders. They made marks on her body with lipstick.'

'And the marks are still there?'

'Yes, she hasn't had any chance to clean them yet.'

'Dear God, this is diabolical.'

'And I have a very difficult favour to ask you, sir. Would it be possible for you to take photographs before she washes them off.'

'Yes, her mother and I can do that.'

'Silke is an important witness.'

The doctor's eyes narrowed as though suddenly making a connection. 'Tell me, Inspector, does this involve the trial reported in yesterday's newspaper?'

'Yes.'

'And am I right in thinking the case involves high politics?'

'Why do you ask that?'

'Word gets around in Munich. It seems Hitler has taken a personal interest in the matter of the English girl's murder.' The doctor's expression turned yet more stern. He was deep in thought and Seb could almost read the way his mind was going.

'Dr Stutz, I see you have doubts, but there are killers on the loose and a man's life hangs in the balance, accused of a murder he almost certainly didn't commit.'

'But my overriding duty is to my daughter and my family.'

'I understand—'

'No, I'm not sure you do. If this was my life, I like to imagine that I would be prepared to offer it up in the name of justice. But you can't use Silke as a witness.'

'Yes, sir, I truly do understand.'

'Do you, Herr Wolff? Are you sure? Please, I beg you, don't say a word about this to anyone. And there will be no photographs.'

Seb had no option. 'I must accept your decision, Dr Stutz.'

'I know that if you asked my wife, she would say that of course we must report this incident and have Silke give you a full witness statement and present the markings on her body for examination by experts. Perhaps Silke would say the same, for she is an honourable young woman. But I am not my wife and nor am I my

daughter. For while they are idealists, I am a realist who under-
stands that no good can come to this family of being involved.
Our duty is to Silke, to treat any physical injuries and heal her
mind as well as we can.'

Seb bowed his head. There was no more to be said.

Jurgen asked his father if he could stay with the Stutz family for
the night and come home the next day. Frau Stutz was more than
happy with this and Seb agreed.

At the front door, the boy stepped forward and hugged his
father.

The drive back to Ainmüllerstrasse was unpleasant. It was two
o'clock in the morning and the streets were deserted, yet somehow threatening. Should he simply ignore Dr Stutz's decree and
call Thomas Ruff and explain all the new evidence about Silke and
Hildegard? He knew what Ruff's reaction would be: *I'll forget you
ever told me this, Inspector Wolff. Now get back to your work as
ordered and find the killer of Herr Caius Klammer.* That was certain, but without Ruff's intervention, how was Karl Friedlander to
be reprieved?

The only other people who might have influence were Putzi
Hanfstaengl, the foreign press chief, or Donald Gainer, the British
consul-general. Hanfstaengl would certainly not want the execution stopped because his own reputation and standing with the
Führer was on the line. And the diplomat? How could he be seen
to intervene in the German justice system when a man had confessed to a crime in open court?

Mutti was in bed asleep, but she had left him a note on the
kitchen table.

> *Max called. He wants you to ring him back any time, day
> or night.*

Did he mean that? Even 2 a.m? He was familiar enough with Max
Haas to know that when he said something, he meant it. Seb went

out into the corridor and called his old friend's number in Dortmund. It took a long time to get through; Max had always been a
heavy sleeper, even during British bombardments of their trench.

Finally, a croak of a voice came on the line. 'Yes.'

'Max, it's Seb.'

'God in heaven, what time do you call this? I was dreaming of
Greta Garbo.'

'And was she clothed?'

'What do you think?'

'You did say—'

'I know, I know. Ah, Seb, you woke Frau Haas, too. I'll never
hear the end of it.'

'From the message you left, I thought it might be important.'

'Well, it's certainly amusing. You decide how important it is.'

'Go on.'

'All right, I've been doing a little digging around the background of your good friend Sergeant Winter and I now know why
he was in a hurry to move from Dortmund to Munich. I think you
might enjoy this . . .'

Many people in Germany had come to fear the dawn knock on
the door in the two years since the Reichstag fire when a hundred
thousand political undesirables were dragged from their homes
and flung into jail to be tortured or killed without charge or trial.

The dawn knock now meant only one thing: an unwelcome
visit from the secret police and if your opinions, sexuality or religion diverged in any way from the dictated norm, you knew what
to expect.

Frau Angela Wolff had no such fears. Why should she? Her son
was in the police force, her grandson was a keen member of the
Hitler Youth and as far as she knew she didn't deviate from the
path decreed by Adolf Hitler.

So when she woke to a sharp, impatient rapping at the door
early on Sunday morning she climbed from her bed cursing
Sebastian for forgetting or losing his key. She liked a little lie-in
before mass and so she would give her son a piece of her mind; he

had obviously been with that Hexie again without a thought for his poor mother.

In the event, though, it was two strangers in unseasonal raincoats and hats who stood at the door. They both flashed cards identifying themselves as members of the Bavarian Political Police but gave no names.

'Frau Wolff,' the grubbier of the two said. 'We are here to talk to your son, Inspector Sebastian Wolff.'

'As far as I know, he's not here.'

'We'll make up our own mind about that.'

The two men stepped into the apartment without waiting for an invitation and quickly found Seb buried in his bed, deep in sleep.

The lead man shook him. 'Wake up, Wolff. You're coming with us.'

Seb threw himself from the bed to the floor, his hands to his ears, the way he had done a hundred times before when the shells and bombs came. And then he woke and realised that he wasn't in the trench and picked himself up. He looked at the two men standing in front of him and laughed.

'Good morning, Sergeant Winter. What is this, a personal alarm call? So thoughtful of you, but you really shouldn't have.'

Seb was naked, the way he liked to sleep in summer. His mother was behind the two secret policemen in the doorway to his room, clutching her dressing gown around her, looking on the scene with dismay. Her eyes strayed to the men's feet, clearly appalled that visitors should just come into her pristine home without removing their shoes.

'There's nothing funny about this, Wolff. You're in serious trouble. Get dressed.'

'Why?'

'You'll find out. Hurry up. And where's your gun?'

Seb nodded towards the bedside table. 'In the drawer. Shall I get it for you?'

'Don't go near it.'

CHAPTER 33

For the second time in eleven days Seb found himself in a rather nice office in Wittelsbach Palace, home of the Bavarian Political Police. Being a Sunday it was quieter than his previous visit, the one which had ended with him in a van being driven to Dachau.

The palace was a grand nineteenth-century building, once the home of royals, now headquarters of Munich's version of the Gestapo. It had crenellations like a castle and towers at the corners. And it had its own cells below ground where screams could not be heard. But Seb was not down there; he was in an upstairs office with heavy drapes and good furniture.

This time Josef Meisinger, Winter's ambitious boss, was not in attendance. Perhaps he was a religious man, thought Seb, and had gone to mass to look after his soul. A much better use of his time, though likely to be fruitless.

'Name, age, place of birth, religion.' The words rattled from Winter's lips.

'I think you know all that.'

Winter's fingers were poised over the keys of the typewriter. 'Name, age, place of birth, religion,' he repeated.

'Charlie Chaplin, ninety-eight, Timbuktu, Buddhism.'

'Damn you, Wolff. Answer the questions or pay for it.'

'One day you save my life. Two days later, you haul me from a peaceful sleep. Are you going to give me a clue as to why you have brought me here, Winter?'

'*Sergeant* Winter. I am the senior officer today, you are the felon.'

'Well, good for you.'

'And I am sure you know perfectly well why you are here.'

'Actually, I don't.'

Winter jabbed his half-smoked cigarette at Seb. 'You have been sticking your nose into police matters outside your jurisdiction, namely in Franconia. You have been talking to the foreign press when you were explicitly told not to. And there are other concerns regarding your general behaviour and dissident dealings. So you see, Wolff, I now have you exactly where I want you.'

'At your mercy, you mean?'

'Those are your words but I won't argue with them.'

Winter's BPP colleague was smirking at his side. He was rubbing his right fist with his left hand as though he had used it many times before and was looking forward to using it again. He was a great deal heavier and physically more powerful than Winter and a few years older, though almost certainly of a lower rank; his role was muscle, not thinking.

'As for talking to the foreign press, Ernest Pope is a friend of mine and a respected professional, accredited by the regime. We were just sharing a bottle of whisky, not talking about anything concerning my police work. You probably know that he also has good friends here in this building. It is his job to meet people, and he is very good at it. I like him. Perhaps you would too if you met him.'

'I doubt it. Anyway, if your conversation was so innocent, why did he go down from Hesselberg to the home of an enemy of the state named Albert Heiden, presently in Dachau for his treachery?' It was framed as a question, but it was not a question, merely an accusation.

Seb was irritated to discover that he had yet again been watched without his knowledge. Had someone actually followed him from Munich on the 150-kilometre drive to Hesselberg? If so, how had he not noticed the vehicle? Or did Winter have BPP contacts in that area? Perhaps they had been shadowing Ernie Pope and Seb simply got caught in another man's web. Either way, Seb had had enough of this. 'Sergeant Winter, do you think you and I could have a quiet word alone, just the two of us without King Kong in attendance?'

'I have nothing to say that my colleague can't hear.'

'Yes, but I have.' He leant forward, cupping his hand to Winter's ear. 'It relates to Dortmund,' he whispered.

Winter blinked rapidly. 'What did you say?'

'I'm sure you heard me loud and clear. Perhaps you'd like me to explain in a bit more detail about—' and then he simply mouthed the word *Dortmund* without speaking the name of the city. 'Your choice.'

'God damn you, Wolff, you think you're so damn smart.' He waved his arm at his underling, the smoke from his cigarette swirling. 'Go, get out. Wait outside and close the door after you.'

Seb smiled as Winter's bewildered and disappointed sidekick reluctantly trudged away and did what his master had ordered.

'So now then, Winter, do you want me to tell you what an old friend has discovered about you in Dortmund. Oh, by the way, he works for your old Gestapo team there and he has excellent contacts. So far he has spoken only to me, but I know that if ever anything untoward happened to me he would feel compelled to speak out – either in Dortmund or here in Munich. Perhaps you would like to hear what he told me?'

'No, Wolff, I want you to say nothing.' Winter's eyes were scanning the desk, the lights, the telephone as though looking for hidden microphones.

'Probably wise. Shall we call it quits then? I'd rather like to get back to my bed.'

'Are you intending to mention this to anyone else?'

'No, Sergeant, I wouldn't dream of it. And in the same spirit of friendship, I would ask you to do your utmost to keep me *out* of Dachau. A fair deal, I think. How does it sound to you?'

Instead of going straight back home to bed, he went to Hexie's apartment and woke her up. She was warm and welcoming and suggested he slip between the sheets with her, an invitation which he felt compelled to accept.

She folded herself into his arms. 'Seb, what's going on? Where have you been? I wanted to see you last night.'

'I was at Hesselberg, investigating a pair of murders and preventing another.'

'And have you come here for a day of Sunday sex magic?'

'Actually, I was wondering about going back to Hesselberg. Perhaps you'd like to come with me?' He looked at the clock on the wall. Not quite seven o'clock. It would probably take two and a half hours to drive there if he put his foot down in the Lancia. He had learnt that the big event with Streicher and Goering and Unity Mitford would be starting sometime between 10 a.m. and 11 a.m. and he very much wanted to be there. 'I think we could fit in some quick magic sex first, though.'

'You are a very smooth talker, Herr Wolff. And before we begin, let me tell you something I heard yesterday, for I know you have developed an interest in such matters. It was something about the Thule Society.'

'Now that is interesting. How would you have heard such a thing?'

'I went to work – and I hear everything in Hoffmann's studio. That's why you love me, isn't it?'

'Who mentioned Thule?'

'Herr Wandering Hands – Otto Raspe. He just happened to be there when Regensdorf turned up.'

'What time was this?'

'Oh, it must have been just before lunch because we close at one on a Saturday. I was in a bit of trouble because I was in so late after The Pig's big bash at the lake. I was actually scared I might be fired, which would be awful because I love it there. Anyway, I was told I would have to stay on for a couple of hours to do some cleaning and dusting, so that wasn't so bad. But I was warned not to be late again. But that's nothing to do with what I am trying to tell you.'

'Go on.'

'Raspe was collecting some prints – all sealed up as usual – and then Walter Regensdorf turned up with a film to develop. I think it was pure coincidence but they greeted each other like old friends and then Raspe lowered his voice and said something, but the only word I heard was "Thule". "Wouldn't miss it," Regensdorf replied. Then he clapped Raspe on the shoulder and off he went. His poor wife was waiting for him in the car outside.'

'What colour was the car?'

'Oh, black Daimler-Benz or Mercedes, I think. They're all black these cars, aren't they, these Nazi ones. And they don't come much more Nazi than Walter Regensdorf, do they?'

No, he supposed they didn't.

On the way back to Hesselberg, Seb began to wonder what this trip was about. What could he hope to learn? When this all began after his release from Dachau it had been suggested that he was Munich's finest murder detective. Well, it didn't feel like that now.

Perhaps he had got as far as convincing himself that Karl Fried-lander was not the murderer, but he had convinced no one else except an American reporter, and even he wasn't certain. But had anything come of that? Had Ernie Pope managed to get a story linking the killings of Rosie and Hildegard into one of today's London papers? They weren't available here so the only way he could find out was to speak to Ernie.

Apart from that he was getting nowhere. He hadn't even made any progress on the murder of his friend Caius Klammer.

Most of the way they drove in silence. Hexie sat back in the pas-senger seat of the Lancia Augusta with her eyes closed while Seb held the wheel and ate up the road north. It really was a superb car. They arrived as the crowd was preparing for the arrival of the big names: Goering, Streicher and various other high-ups.

'Why are we here exactly?' Hexie demanded as they trekked up the hill.

'Did you have other plans?'

'Everyone seems to be here so we could have stayed in Munich and had the English Garden to ourselves. A picnic, a bottle of cherry schnapps and a sunny day. That wouldn't have been so bad.'

They managed to weave their way to a point thirty or forty metres from the imposing eagle-fronted rostrum. Hundreds of SS men had appeared overnight and were keeping the crowds back and ensuring that the top men would be well-protected.

And then they came up the hill in their big black cars, through a tunnel of wide-eyed men, women and children. Goering and his new wife – the celebrated actress Emmy Sonnemann – were there, waving to their enthusiastic supporters. Once out of the car, Fat Hermann walked side by side with Julius Streicher. Hundreds, perhaps thousands, of flags fluttered in the stiff breeze.

Streicher, his bald bullet-head shining, his little moustache quivering like a trapped baby mouse beneath his nose, took the stage with Goering and received tumultuous cheers. Goering then stepped down to allow the Franconia *gauleiter* to introduce the session.

Julius Streicher was careful with his words as he thundered out his message to the faithful, waving his hands around as though he had studied and rehearsed newsreels of his idol, Adolf Hitler.

'We do not wish to foment hatred towards other people,' Streicher bellowed. 'We offer the hand of friendship to everyone!'

Tell that to Karl Friedlander and his parents, Seb thought.

Almost immediately Streicher was joined on stage by a black-clad Unity Mitford, and then he turned back to the audience with his punchline: 'But it is the Jew who does not want peace!'

Unity saluted the crowd with her gauntleted right arm and then delivered her own little speech denouncing international Jewry and praising the godlike qualities of Germany's wonderful leader and saying she hoped Germany and England would always be friends.

The crowd thrust out their right arms. 'Heil England!' they shouted.

Seb sensed a face close to his and turned to see Adam Rock standing at his side. 'Isn't she magnificent, Inspector?'

CHAPTER 34

Adam Rock wasn't alone, of course. He was surrounded by Unity's friends and acolytes. Frances de Pole was there and, surprisingly, Clarice Goodall, who had said that she and Unity didn't get on. The permanent shadow Fritz Mannheim was present, of course, keeping an eye on Unity, and a few others, mostly English. About ten in all.

Unity's little speech in imperfect German must have bewildered the crowd, but they seemed to enjoy it and applauded her as she left the stage with another salute, leaving it free for the enormous figure of Germany's second most powerful man, Hermann Goering.

'Damned hot today, Inspector Wolff. Why don't you join us for a drink?' Adam Rock said. 'I know that Unity admires you and speaks very highly of your cigarette-fetching skills.'

'Thank you, Mr Rock, perhaps we will seek you out later. By the way, were you and your friends here all night?'

'Oh, good Lord no, we stayed in a rather pleasant hotel not far away. A pretty little town whose name escapes me. Much more civilised than camping. Boy scouts ruined all that outdoors stuff for me.'

'Do you think we might arrange to meet up for a little talk when this is all over?'

'What a strange request.'

He shrugged. 'Nothing sinister. As I think I mentioned before, I'm still keen to talk to everyone who knew Miss Palmer.'

'Really? You have your killer. One sharp blade and that surely will be that.'

'I have reason to believe the killer was not alone, that he had an accomplice.'

'And what exactly has that got to do with me?'

'I'm being thorough, Mr Rock. That's what everyone wants from their police, isn't it? Just like your own Scotland Yard.'

'Thorough? Questioning me? That sounds more like damned impertinence. I don't know if anyone's ever mentioned it to you, but you somehow manage to make the most casual of conversations sound like an interrogation.'

'I'm sure you'd like me to find anyone who harmed your friend.'

'Is this your unsubtle way of accusing me of something?'

'I believe I was merely asking for a friendly chat at some future date. If I had cause to suspect you of a crime, I would arrest you and take you in for a proper interrogation, not arrange to meet you at your own convenience.'

'Go to hell, Wolff. I suggest you try reminding yourself who won the war and crawl back into your little hole. Now if you'll excuse us, we have to go and find Bobo. Who knows, we may run into you later.'

There again, that choice of words. On first meeting he had said, *You know what happens to 175s in the Third Reich*. Now he was saying, *We may run into you later*. Innocent enough phrases in normal conversation, perhaps, but in present circumstances, loaded.

Someone had tried to run into him on Schellingstrasse. Someone had killed Caius Klammer, ostensibly because he was a 175.

What was it about Adam Rock that made him so easy to dislike?

'I know what you're thinking, Inspector Wolff.' It was Frances de Pole, speaking in English. She had held back from the others.

'Miss de Pole.'

'Oh God, call me Frankie, won't you? Everyone does.'

'My pleasure, Frankie, and this is Frau Schuler. Hexie Schuler.' Hexie put out her hand.

'Ah, the girlfriend,' Frances de Pole said in good German. 'Very pleased to meet you, too.'

'You were saying that you knew what I was thinking,' Seb said. 'What would that be?'

'You were thinking that Adam Rock is a frightful boor. We all agree with you but he considers himself the bee's knees. Someone told me that when he was at school he considered himself a cut above everyone, including the headmaster. Anyway, we can't get rid of him.'

'Would I be right in thinking that he takes all this historical German *Völkisch* stuff rather seriously?'

'Good Lord, yes – just don't get him on the subject of runes and rituals and holy mountains.' She switched to English. 'Not so much boor with a double "o" as bore with an "o-r-e" when he lets rip on all that stuff. He thinks Adolf is the reincarnation of some Nordic god-king.'

'He may not be alone in that.'

'Dear me, Herr Wolff, do I detect a hint of scepticism in your voice? You do like to live dangerously, don't you? Anyway, must dash. We all have to tell Bobo how wonderfully she performed, or she'll sulk all day.'

The wind was getting up and Goering was droning on, striding around the stage, waving his arms even more expansively than Streicher. Hermann was in his element, a natural showman, responding with ever more enthusiasm to every cheer and round of applause. The crowd loved him.

And at the finale when Goering said, 'Adolf Hitler is everything, is Germany, is our creed, our movement, our very future!' Seb began to wonder whether the speaker and his rapt audience might not all experience one enormous simultaneous orgasm.

But then it was all over. Two hundred thousand people – all sweating in the intense midsummer heat – proved their loyalty with salutes and sieg heils and a banner went up above the stage saying, 'See You All Next Year' or words to that effect.

Some way off, among the vast mass of swastika banners and pennants, one flag caught Seb's eye: the sunwheel swastika of the Thule Society – the hooked cross with rounded edges fitting neatly within a circle, along with a short sword or dagger at its heart. So they were here mingling with the common people and Otto Raspe was certain to be amongst them. Was this what Hexie overheard them talking about in Hoffmann's studio? Was Regensdorf here, too, and perhaps even a whole group of these odd, superstitious, fanatics?

Seb began moving through the great mass of people and flags in the direction of the Thule standard, not sure why he was going there or what he hoped to find. Hexie pulled at his arm.

'Where are we going now?'

'I saw a Thule flag.'

'So?'

'I want to see who's there.'

'What exactly are you looking for, Seb? What are you hoping to find?'

'A killer . . . killers. Or a clue.'

'I wouldn't dream of doubting your skills as a detective, but don't you think you might do well to cast your net a little wider? Munich and Nuremberg are large cities with many mad and unpleasant people. Anyone could be behind this.'

'But at the moment this is all I've got. The runes . . . the *Völkisch* movement, the whole Thule thing. None of it might be solid evidence, but there are no other clues.' He looked ahead, trying to catch sight of the Thule flag. 'Come on, let's find them.'

Lines of marching bands and youth groups – Hitler Youth, SA, SS – were stamping back and forth across the open plain, tents were being dismantled and fires extinguished and cleared, and it was difficult to get through them or past them, but Seb had made a mental note of the position of the Thule standard and he forged onwards, Hexie either at his side or close behind.

Ten minutes later, Seb realised he had completely lost the flag. He had reached the eastern area of the Osterwiese where his sense of direction told him it should be, but there was no sign of the flag or Otto Raspe or anyone else he knew to be associated with the Thule Society.

'Is that it then? Can we sit down and have our picnic?' Hexie looked bored and disconsolate.

'They've just vanished.'

'Now you see me, now you don't. Must be all that *Völkisch* magic.'

Seb couldn't conceal his irritation. He looked at her hard. 'This really isn't a joke, Hexie. It wasn't a joke for Rosie Palmer, Caius Klammer and Hildegard Heiden – and it isn't a joke for Karl Friedlander.'

'I'm sorry. It all just seems so unreal.'

'Well, it's not. Jurgen's girlfriend might have died here last night. That was real enough, I promise you.'

'Forgive me.'

A flash of light to the east, across the dip known as the Druid's Valley, caught his eye. No, not light, the fluttering of a square piece of fabric in the stiff breeze. A flag perhaps. Was it possible they had made their way across there, going to ground, like a fox evading hounds.

Seb pointed in the vague direction of the flag. 'I'm going over. Why don't you stay here? Have a drink and some food. I'll meet you by the rostrum.'

'I want to come with you.'

'All right, but we're going to move with stealth now. We no longer have the protection of the crowd. Why have they left the Osterwiese, that's what I want to know? And who the hell is carrying the flag anyway?'

They strode across the gap separating the west and east uplands of the Hesselberg hill. Seb was beginning to doubt that he had seen anything, for there was no sign of the flag. Had he imagined it all from the very beginning?

He stopped near the clearing where he had found Silke the night before and looked around, his hand on his gun, half expecting to be fired on from the woods. Then moved on across the dip to the lower part of the hill, the Schlössleinbuck. In the distance he heard the sound of church bells and remembered that this was Sunday, and all was well.

Except it wasn't.

'There's nothing. I'm sorry.'

'I really don't like it here, Seb. It's eerie.'

'Hildegard Heiden's mother said much the same.'

'Let's go back. Please.'

How could a place – a gentle limestone hill of grass and trees, wildflowers, turtle doves and warblers – be so disturbing? Seb supposed it must have always been this way, which would have been why their German ancestors found themselves drawn to its strange energy and considered it sacred. Found their gods and demons here. Perhaps a better word than *sacred* might be *unholy*. Could this really have been a place of the *geblōt* – of human sacrifice?

Which brought him back to the same question that had been haunting him since discovering this place: if Hesselberg was so important to the killers, why was Rosie Palmer's body discovered 150 kilometres away in the teeming heart of Munich?

It had been an exhausting, pointless outing, leaving Seb irritable and none the wiser. Hexie was probably right; his obsession with the Thule Society and the runes and the sacred hill was taking him nowhere.

'Talk to me,' he begged her, a few kilometres along the road on the long drive home. 'Keep me awake or I might fall asleep at the wheel.' But he was wasting his breath; she was already asleep herself.

The road wasn't busy and there wasn't much to hold his attention, and as the journey dragged on he was aware that he was becoming drowsy. He stopped in a lay-by for a while, got out, stamped around and drank some water from the flask they had brought. They were on the last leg of the journey, five kilometres out of Munich, almost home. If it had been further, he might have simply slumped down and gone to sleep. But he forced himself to get back in the driver's seat and get them both home and to bed.

Setting off again the Lancia quickly gathered speed. The stop had refreshed him and he knew he'd be OK; he congratulated himself on doing it, he'd stay awake.

That was when the enormous cream-coloured Maybach appeared in his rear-view mirror. The larger, faster car swept up, then swerved in front of the Lancia. Seb jumped on the brake.

Nothing happened.

He stabbed his foot at it again, but there was no response. His reaction was immediate. He grabbed at the handbrake beneath the dashboard and wrenched it back, simultaneously trying to force the gear lever down to first, but he was too late. The Lancia was heading straight for a sharp right-hand bend and he couldn't kill the speed in time. The rear wheels were out of control from the emergency gear change; the tyres had lost their grip. Burning rubber scraped on asphalt like a streak of charcoal.

The nose of the Lancia lifted as though about to take flight, thundering onto the grassy verge, then, instantly, it came down in a nosedive with a bone-crunching impact and stopped dead.

Seb's hands were still on the wheel. His head had snapped forward and then back. In his mind, the incident had unfolded stage by stage, each one memorable like a series of scenes from a drama, from the appearance of the other car, to the failure of the brakes, his attempts at a handbrake and gear-stick stop. But in fact it had taken no more than a second or two from start to shattering finish.

Now, shaking, heart pounding, his immediate instinct was to wonder whether the whiplash had broken his neck, then all his thoughts were for Hexie. But his eyes were still on the road and the cream Maybach disappearing into the distance.

He turned towards Hexie. She was slumped forward onto the windscreen and there was blood. A lot of blood.

He could hear her breathing, see movement. She was alive, but she was unresponsive when he touched her and tried to speak to her. He realised she must be unconscious. Blood was streaming from her forehead down her face, and her body was twisted with her right shoulder forward, up against the side of her head.

'Hexie, can you hear me?'

Still no response.

He levered his door open and crawled out on to the grass and rocks. Somehow, he needed to get her to hospital. Should he try to remove her from the car? He was back in the trenches, helping injured comrades. He knew how to stem blood flow from severed limbs, knew how to bandage a head. But he was painfully aware that there had been times when moving a wounded man might have done more harm than good, resulting in permanent spinal damage and paralysis.

And yet he had to do something. There was a powerful stench of petrol. A single spark could turn the car into an inferno.

'Hexie, I'm going to try to get you out of the car.' His arms were around her, easing her gently back into the seat. She was slender and light and yet a dead weight always feels heavy and she could offer no assistance.

A van was pulling up a little way ahead. Two burly men got out and walked towards them at a fast pace. Seb moved away from Hexie and the car and his hand went to his gun, but then stopped. It was a removals van and the men were in overalls. They were trying to help.

'Are you all right, sir?' the shorter, broader of the two men said.

'Yes, but my girlfriend, she's unconscious. She's bleeding. I'm worried about moving her.'

'I was a stretcher-bearer in the war, sir,' the man said. He was grey-haired and had a reassuring smile. 'Let's take it slow and easy, check her injuries and get her to hospital. But you're sure *you're* all right, yes?'

'Don't worry about me.'

'But you're shaken up.'

'The brakes failed. I lost control.'

'Well, let's get you both to hospital, just to be sure.'

'Thank you.' The kindness of a stranger, in a time of hatred and bitter prejudice. Perhaps there was hope after all.

CHAPTER 35

Hexie regained consciousness soon after arriving at the university hospital, but she was in no state to be allowed home for there was always the fear of a skull fracture and internal bleeding. The only cause for optimism was that it was her forehead that had sustained the full force of the impact. Given the toughness of the human skull at the brow, there was optimism that all would be well.

The flow of blood had slowed to a trickle. It had come from the forehead and mouth where her tooth had cut into her lip and tongue. Those injuries were not serious but she would be bruised and they would take some time to heal.

'What happened, Seb?' she demanded as he sat at her bedside. 'I don't remember anything.'

'You were asleep. A car swerved in front of us and I braked, but nothing happened. We ended up on the verge.'

A car. Not just any car, but a big cream car that looked very much like a sleek and expensive Maybach.

Seb had been checked over himself and he stayed with Hexie for an hour, holding her hand, until the nurses told him he couldn't stay, that she would be fine but she needed sleep.

He arrived home late in the evening, exhausted and worried about Hexie and wondering what to do about the Lancia, stuck out of town on the verge of the main road. There was a chance he could get it to the garage driving slowly and using the gears to decelerate and the handbrake to stop, but his tired brain told him that it would be better to sort that out in the morning. The smell of petrol was still in his nostrils and that was a concern.

Opening the front door, he was surprised to see the light on in the kitchen. Mutti would certainly be in bed by now and she never wasted electricity by leaving lights burning. 'Hello,' he said.

A voice from within. A familiar, reedy and unwelcome voice. 'It's me, Sergeant Winter.'

Seb heard a scraping of chair legs on the floor, then there he was at the kitchen door, Hans Winter, his eyes downcast.

'Come to arrest me again and take me back to Dachau, have you?'

'Your mother let me in. I have to talk to you.'

'And has Mutti gone to bed?'

'I think so. She offered me supper and a beer, but I didn't accept. Your son's here as well, but he's gone to his room.'

'Winter, you always look a mess. Your clothes are grim and stained and you slouch like a half-starved hyena. Yet this evening you look worse than ever.'

'You look a bit rough yourself, Inspector Wolff. You've got blood on you.'

Of course he did – Hexie's blood.

'My car crashed,' he said bluntly. 'But you?' He looked him up and down. 'Well, at least you removed your shoes this time, so I suppose we should be thankful for small mercies. Mutti certainly will be.'

'Can we talk then?'

'Let's sit down and have that beer, shall we?'

'If you insist, just a small one.'

'That's all I was offering.'

They sat across the kitchen table. Winter had made sure the door was closed. 'I take it no one can overhear us?'

'Well no, unless your lot have bugged the room, Sergeant.' Seb took a large draught of his beer. He knew that neither his mother nor Jurgen would have their ear to the keyhole; it wasn't their nature. 'I take it this is about our little chat at the Wittelsbach Palace earlier today.'

'Tell me what you know? What did your friend in Dortmund say about me?'

'You must know exactly what he said.'

'I can't bring myself to say it.'

'You have Jewish blood in your veins, that's what he said, Winter. He found this out from your family who, I must tell you, are deeply ashamed of you and your reaction to this news. It seems you left Dortmund with no word of farewell and you have not been in touch with them since. Why would a man abandon his family?'

'They're ashamed of me? I'm the one who feels shame, Inspector. You can't begin to imagine my shame and disgust. I grew up a true German, a church-going Lutheran, only to discover that my grandfather was a rabbi who converted to Christianity just forty years ago.'

Seb simply listened. He might have said, 'Why would that worry you?' but that would have been cheap and disingenuous, for it was obvious why it would worry him: were it to be revealed to his seniors or anyone with a mind to denounce him, then Hans Winter would not only lose his job with the secret police but he would be persecuted in exactly the same way that he had almost certainly been persecuting other Jews as a member of the Dortmund Gestapo.

It was a bitter irony. Seb might have laughed, but he actually felt some strange pity for the man.

'My mother and father both knew but they never told me. I discovered it purely by chance while looking through an old trunk with photographs and letters. There was a picture of him – Simon Greenbaum, my mother's father – in his rabbi's shawl and cap before he converted. And there was a scroll with Hebrew script – a Jewish Bible, I think. At first I didn't make the connection, but I showed the picture to my father. "Why do you have a picture of a dirty Jew?" I said. He laughed at me. "That's your grandfather," he replied. And then he told me everything. I walked out and didn't turn back. Anyone would have done the same.'

'Drink your beer.'

'Do you have anything stronger?'

Seb got up and fetched an old bottle of Steinhäger gin from the larder, then poured them both a sizeable glass.

'And now what will you do, Inspector? Denounce me? I suppose your friend has already told everyone else at the Dortmund Gestapo office so word will be passed to Munich in no time.'

'You don't know my friend, Sergeant, and you clearly don't know me very well. My friend has told no one except me and nor will he unless you act against my interests. And nor do I have any intention of telling anyone. Unlike you, I harbour no ill will towards the Jewish race – or any other race for that matter. And despite everything, Winter, I harbour no ill will towards you.'

'Why should I trust you?'

'Do you have any option?'

Winter shook his head slowly then downed his drink in one.

He really was a miserable wretch, Seb decided, a man with no saving graces except that he had saved his life. 'This must be very difficult for you – the fear that you will be discovered. Is that why you picked on Friedlander? Overcompensating to protect yourself from suspicion of being a Jew yourself? Is that what happened?'

'Those marks looked like Jewish writing. I saw some, remember. The marks on the scroll were like writing, but nothing like our alphabet. I know what I'm talking about.'

'And that was enough to condemn a man to death? The vague belief that you could identify some scribbled lipstick marks as Hebrew script? And then you bribed the maidservant, Lena Popp, to say she saw him from her tram on the night of the murder. Perhaps I *should* denounce you, Winter.'

'You don't understand the pressure I'm under.'

'Does your family worry you? Do you fear they will tell someone?'

'What? And put their own necks in the noose? Anyway, they don't know where I am, and nor will they.' The blood drained from his gaunt face. 'God in heaven, your Dortmund friend hasn't told them I'm in Munich, has he?'

'I honestly don't know.'

Seb poured more Steinhäger. He suddenly found himself laughing, incongruously and irreverently given the circumstances. He was about to say, *So I suppose this means no more pork chops for you, Sergeant?* But that would have been vulgar and uncalled for and so, in the event, he held his counsel.

'What's so funny, Inspector? Do you take anything seriously? Can you even imagine what it is like to believe yourself a pure-blooded German one day and then to discover that you are defiled the next? I have lost so much – my sense of worth, my pride. Yet you laugh at me, the way you laugh at everything.'

'I'm sorry, Sergeant. You're right, I shouldn't laugh. By the way, are your BPP friends still trying to follow me?'

'I don't believe so.'

'The question is, what do we do now? How can we save Karl Friedlander, who we both know to be innocent?'

Winter was silent.

'Well? You're going to have to say something to the court, get it stopped.'

The secret police officer screwed up his face as though afflicted by some unknown pain, and his eyes turned away so that Seb shouldn't see them.

'We can't do anything,' he said.

'What do you mean? We have to.'

'He's dead. He was executed by guillotine in Stadelheim earlier today. I got a call to get along to the jail to be there as a witness, and I saw it.'

CHAPTER 36

'You were there? You watched him die?'

Winter nodded. 'It was terrible. Horrible.'

'And you did nothing? Said nothing to stop it?'

'What could I say?'

'You could have told the truth. You could have mentioned that the witness was bribed by you. You could have said that the allegation that the marks on Miss Palmer's body were Hebrew script was pure invention – in other words, lies.'

'But he had confessed, Wolff. If I had spoken it would have made no difference. He was already a dead man walking. Nothing could have changed the court's sentence and the executioner would have just gone ahead anyway. He would not have stopped for me. Only a call from the judge or Hitler himself would have saved Friedlander. I'm not proud of myself, but you and I both know what would have happened to my own life if I had spoken out, and still Friedlander would have died.'

Seb rose from the table, pushed it to one side and grabbed Winter by the throat with his left hand and punched his weasel-like face with his right fist, then pummelled him to the ground.

He hit him again and again and then kicked him. For a brief moment he felt for the butt of his pistol thinking to finish him off with a bullet to the head, then pulled back his hand and gave Winter a last couple of hammerings with his fist to the temples.

And all the while, Hans Winter did not scream or cry out, did not protest and did not fight back or try to defend himself. The only sound was the smack of fist on flesh, the grunts and heavy breathing of both men, the scraping of chairs and table against the floor.

The beating went on for minutes. Others in the apartment must have heard the sounds, but no one came.

Seb stood over Winter, panting, his hands still tightly balled, his knuckles bloody. Winter lay on the ground, his face and clothes streaked with blood. One eye was closed and bloody, the other open, looking up at his assailant. His arms lay limp at his side.

'God damn you, Winter. God damn your rotten soul to hell.'

'I'm sorry.'

Seb poured himself another large gin and threw it down his throat, then poured another, knelt down at Winter's side and poured it roughly between his bloody lips. Then he hauled him up and pushed him back on the chair from which he had grabbed him.

'How did he die? Did he collapse in terror? Describe it to me – every foul detail so that it is etched into both our brains forever.'

Winter wiped his sleeve across his face and blinked open his other eye.

'He died bravely. I think I was more scared than he was. Such a cold, soulless room with the guillotine. You could feel the damp on the grey, flaking walls. The executioner, Johann Reichhart, just standing there in his black funereal suit, his black bow tie and his black top hat. No colour, just black and shades of grey. Friedlander refused the black blindfold and Reichhart accepted that. Then he strapped Friedlander to the table and within seconds it was all over. Very quick and very efficient. The head fell and the blood gushed. I have never seen so much blood. The contrast of the red blood with the black . . .'

'What?'

'Nothing. I can't say it.'

'Say it.'

'It was like the colours of the swastika pennants in the streets of Munich. As though the flags themselves were bleeding into the earth.'

'Did Friedlander say any last words?'

'He looked at me as he entered the room and his mouth moved, as though whispering something. I didn't really hear but I thought it was about his mother and father.'

'And have they been freed as he was promised?'

'I don't know.'

'Do they even know their son is dead?'

'Again, I don't know.'

'Find out and go to them and make sure they are freed and try to give them comfort. Let them know their son died with courage, thinking of them to the last. Tell them he spoke only of his love for them. Can you do that?'

'I'll try.'

'It is your duty. You must do it or I will kill you. Tell them that their son's last insistent message to them was that they should get exit visas and leave this country as soon as possible. They must go wherever they have friends or relatives abroad to sponsor them so that he won't have died in vain. Tell them that, Winter.'

'Yes, I will do it.'

'And when you have done that, you will find out who in Munich owns a cream-coloured Maybach. Now get out of my sight.'

He knew that Mutti and Jurgen must have heard the fight in the night, because they both looked at him quizzically in the morning. Of course, *fight* was the wrong word, because that suggested a battle for supremacy whereas Hans Winter had put up no resistance or defence. Had merely taken his beating without a word of complaint.

Seb said good morning to his mother and son but did not mention the scuffles. Mutti certainly would not have fallen asleep; she couldn't have, not with a stranger in the house, a man who had previously arrested her son. As for Jurgen, he would have stayed awake to protect his grandmother and the house.

At breakfast, Seb asked about Silke and was told that she was quiet and withdrawn and her parents were concerned. They were worried, too, that the attacker would seek her out and find her, and they were anxious about any political ramifications after what the inspector had told them about the likely connection to other attacks.

Mutti was bustling around. Her main concern this Monday morning was that neither her son nor grandson had made it to mass the day before.

From Ainmüllerstrasse, it was a short walk to the garage where Seb found his friend Martin, who ran the place alone, as owner and mechanic. He was drinking some sort of ersatz coffee – roasted oats or acorns, probably. He offered Seb a cup but he declined.

'To what do I owe the pleasure of your company this fine morning, Herr Wolff? Oil change? Surely not yet.'

Seb told him what had happened. Martin finished off his coffee, locked up and drove them both in his van and trailer out along the road north to retrieve the Lancia.

Martin had always looked after the car since Seb bought it at the end of 1933 and was surprised by the turn of events. 'I can't believe the brakes failed,' he said as they got out of the van and walked over to inspect the crashed vehicle. 'The Lancia Augusta is a superb little motor car and those new Lockheed hydraulic brakes are the best in the business. You won't find a better system in the world.'

'They didn't work yesterday.'

'Let's have a look at her.'

Seb sat on the verge and watched while Martin gave the car a thorough going-over. Finally, the mechanic rubbed his oily hands on the rag he carried in the pocket of his overalls and gave Seb a strange look.

'You've been sabotaged, Seb. Someone wants you dead.'

'What happened?'

'One of the hoses has been punctured. Deliberately. You'd have been leaking fluid for quite a few kilometres. Perhaps you noticed the brakes becoming less and less responsive?'

Perhaps he had, now he came to think about it. The car had been slow to stop at the lay-by, the brakes sluggish. But he had put that down to his own tiredness.

'And when you tried to make an emergency stop with forceful braking nothing happened because the fluid reservoir was empty.'

'Could the puncture just have been caused by wear and tear?'

'Not in this case. This car's only two years old and I know it well. I always check the brakes when you bring her in. I can see quite clearly that a hose has been punctured with some sort of sharp instrument, probably a large needle or a bradawl or the point of a knife. Your would-be assassin could easily have done it without getting into the engine compartment. All he'd have had to do was lie down on the road and reach under the front axle. Easily done by someone who knows what they're up to.'

'Can you fix it?'

'Not here. And there's bound to be other damage anyway. We'll load her up and get her back to the garage. The bodywork will need some repairs and one of your headlights is smashed. I want to check you haven't twisted the chassis. I might need parts so it'll take me a few days – maybe a week or two – to get her roadworthy and looking like new. In the meantime, I'll find you something else to keep you on the road.'

'Thanks, Martin.'

'Don't thank me, thank Him.' He looked up to the sky. 'You're lucky to be alive.'

'By the way, who has a cream-coloured Maybach? Monster of a thing with smart running boards and spare wheels either side of the bonnet. Must be someone with some money I'd have thought.'

'No one I know. Not many of those around. I'd look around the big villas in Bogenhausen or Grünwald if I were you. Or maybe out around Starnberg. Where the rich people live. Best thing would be to talk to the nearest Maybach dealership or head office, though. They don't sell that many so they must keep a record of owners.'

'I've got someone doing that. In the meantime, keep your eyes and ears open for me, if you would.'

As arranged, Seb met Ernie Pope at the Cafe Heck by the Hofgarten. 'I suppose you heard what happened?'

'Yes, I'm afraid I did,' Pope said. 'A grisly business.'

'Especially if he was innocent.'

'I can't really comment on that. I never met the man. But I'm sorry anyway – a delay in proceeding with the sentence wouldn't have been out of order, would it? Time to reflect and consider.'

'What happened to the story, Ernie? The Nuremberg girl Hildegard Heiden?'

'I couldn't stand up a strong enough piece. No one in the Nuremberg Kripo would talk to me and the girl's home had acquired a police guard, so I couldn't even get to the mother.'

'And so here we are, an innocent man beheaded and there's still a killer preying on young women. Killers – two of them, I believe.'

The toll was mounting and Hexie was still in hospital. Seb closed his eyes and breathed in the intoxicating coffee fumes. 'Look, Ernie, I know the story can't help Friedlander now but anything you can get in the English papers will help keep the case alive.'

'Of course, but don't bank on it.'

'We simply have to find the killers before some other poor, wretched girl is slaughtered.'

Pope shrugged doubtfully. 'My problem is that news moves on. Yesterday's news is fish and chip paper. You know about fish and chips, right?'

'Yes, I had plenty of fish and chips in Tilbury and Gravesend.'

'But just because I failed to file a story for yesterday doesn't mean I've lost interest in it, because I haven't. If we can prove that the real killer of Rosie Palmer is not the man who died in Stadelheim, London will lap it up. So when you get a lead on that, let me know.'

'You'll be the first to hear.'

'Who will be the second then? I don't envy you the job of telling anyone in the Party that they decapitated the wrong man. What will the court authorities do? Thank you for your diligence, admit their mistake and say sorry? That doesn't sound much like the way things work in the Third Reich.'

'I'll work on that when the time comes.' In fact this had been his concern all along. Pope was right; there was little or no chance of this ending well for Seb. No one wanted to know that the wrong man had been executed. No one would thank him.

The reporter slid the envelope with the photograph of Hildegard Heiden's corpse across the table to him. 'You'd better keep that.'

Seb's main task this difficult morning was to go to hospital to check up on Hexie. He wanted to do that before going to the Presidium for the inevitable showdown: he knew what Ruff would say; he would say that he was neglecting his primary duty, to bring in the killer of Caius Klammer and that if he couldn't do that, then there was plenty of other work to be done.

Hexie was awake, lying back on a bank of pillows. She tried to smile at him but it looked more like a grimace. Her face was bruised, particularly around the mouth and her head was bandaged. And yet somehow, the light in her eyes burnt brighter than ever and he thought she had never been so beautiful.

'Well, you look a sight.'

She laughed and winced. 'You're very kind, Sebastian Wolff, a gentleman and a junker.'

'Here.' He handed her the bunch of red and yellow roses he had bought from the stall on the street outside the hospital. 'A nurse said she'd bring a vase. You'll be in here a day or two, I imagine.'

She nodded. 'They want to keep me in for observation. Apparently these sort of injuries can suddenly take a turn for the worse. What will Heinrich Hoffmann say when I don't turn up for work?'

'Don't worry. I've already called them and smoothed things over. They send their very best wishes for a speedy recovery.'

'Thank you. You're so thoughtful, Herr Wolff.'

'And you are very sarcastic. Anyway, I'm sure you're happier here than at work. This ward is very light and pleasant and you have lots of good company. What's the food like?'

'To hell with the food.' She cupped her mouth with her hand and glanced to the bed on her left. 'It's the people I can't stand. That old cow next to me snores like a train and someone else in the ward screams in the night.'

'Sorry to hear it. Don't worry, I'll get you out of here as soon as permissible. I've been lent a car by Martin and so I'll be able to drive you to your mother's place. She'll look after you, won't she?'

'Of course. But what about your Lancia? Are you any the wiser about what happened?'

He had a lot of news about the crash and other things, but he wasn't really sure he wanted to tell her much of it just yet. Certainly not the grim news about the execution of Karl Friedlander. As for the car, he supposed he had to give her the facts. 'Someone tried to kill us. The brakes had been tampered with.'

'I knew I should never have accepted a lift with you. You're a dangerous man to know, Seb Wolff.'

'So it seems.' He took her hand in his. 'And I suppose this isn't the best time to ask you to marry me, Hexie Schuler.'

The car Martin had lent him was a small and rickety Opel two-seater that the mechanic was intending to do up but hadn't got round to yet. On the plus side it was in working order and the brakes were sound, but it was never going to win any races. And it rattled like a dying man.

Seb drove it up to the Haus Gertrud hostel, parked it on the road outside and went indoors in search of Frances de Pole.

He found her in the dining room, sitting alone eating soup as an early lunch and reading a book.

She immediately smiled and closed the slim volume. *Death in Venice* by Thomas Mann, in the original German. Was that among the works banned and burnt by the Nazis? Perhaps not. Anyway, it wasn't his concern.

'Herr Wolff, you've come to see me. How sweet. I just knew there was some spark between us.'

'I'm afraid you're too late. I'm engaged to be married.'

'Really? Who's the lucky girl?'

'Hexie Schuler. You met her at Hesselberg. She said yes to my proposal within the past hour.'

'My congratulations to you both. But shouldn't you be with her now, making love to her on a bed of flowers rather than consorting with disreputable English girls?'

'Of course, but she is in hospital – and the nurses and other patients might not take kindly to displays of passion in a public place.'

'Hospital? Oh dear, nothing too serious, I hope.'

'A road accident yesterday on the way back from the Frankentag. The brakes in my car failed and I crashed into the verge. She was thrown forward into the windscreen. She's cut and bruised but hopefully nothing more.'

'Perhaps you should have your car serviced properly.'

'The car was fine, but the brakes were not in good order. It seems that someone of a mechanical bent did not want us to get home safely. But that's not why I'm here. The truth is I wanted to talk to you about Friday – the Night of the Pagans.'

'Gosh, wasn't it fun, Seb! May I call you Seb now that we're such good friends?'

'Inspector Wolff will do just fine, Miss de Pole.'

'Has anyone ever told you that you shouldn't take everything quite so seriously, Inspector?'

'Actually I'm often told the exact opposite – that I can be far too frivolous. But today, no frivolity. I'm here as a police officer investigating criminal offences.'

'This can't be the same case. Poor Rosie's been laid to rest and her killer's no more. All done and dusted.'

He gritted his teeth; that was a man's life she was talking about. A man's life cut short most cruelly and unjustly. Seb nodded at her bowl. 'Do you want to finish your soup and then talk?'

'No, it's disgusting. Like school food on a bad day. I don't want it.' She pushed the bowl aside.

'So as I was saying, I want to talk about the Night of the Pagans.'

'It was an absolute hoot, wasn't it? The Pig throws a wild party.'

Was she aware that Christian Weber was his uncle? He wasn't going to enlighten her. 'As you know, I was there with Hexie Schuler. Late in the evening, Hexie and I went around the lake for a cooling swim. It's something people like to do in this part of the world in summer, a little Bavarian tradition. The thing is, some-one followed us. I was wondering whether you, perhaps, might know something about that?'

She grinned and her eyes lit up. Her long, slender fingers combed her blonde bob. 'What a strange question, Inspector. Is this the serious crime you've come about?'

'It's relevant. I realise that some English people might disap-prove, but in Germany the naked body is not considered a thing of shame, so we left all our clothes on the bank close to the woods and dived in the water. When we got out, our clothing had been inter-fered with – in particular Hexie's white blouse had been defaced.'

'Really? How awful.'

'There was writing on it, in lipstick.'

'This gets more exciting by the second. What did it say?'

'I thought perhaps you might know.'

'Why, Inspector, surely you're not accusing me of committing this heinous act of vandalism?'

'You wear red lipstick, Miss de Pole.' He nodded towards her bow-shaped lips. 'Your colour is very similar – perhaps the same – as the writing. I'm afraid I notice these things.'

'But why would I do something like that? Why would you even suspect me? I'm hurt.'

'Oh, I think you know why. How many girls wear lipstick or any other makeup in Germany in 1935? Only the English and the Americans can get away with it, which is a thing I'm sure you know very well.'

'Do I?'

'How long have you been in Munich now?'

'Let me think. About eighteen months, I'd say.'

He knew from her eyes that she was the one. And he could tell from the amusement flickering about her lipstick-red lips that she didn't care that he knew, was actually rather proud of herself. The conversation didn't end there though. 'Then you most certainly understand the significance of lipstick in the Third Reich. Perhaps you wear it as an act of defiance, but that is not my concern.'

'I'm sure I wasn't the only one wearing it at the Night of the Pagans. Bobo was, too. All the English girls were. Why pick on me?'

'Because I have been a detective for a number of years, and I have a talent for reading people.'

Their eyes met and held for a few seconds, and then she laughed. 'Oh, Inspector, it was just a bit of fun. Surely even Germans enjoy a bit of fun now and then.'

'Of course. And yes, it might have been very amusing in other circumstances.'

'And I'm more than happy to pay for the cleaning, or, indeed, a new blouse if it won't come off.'

'I'm sure Hexie will manage. But I can't help wondering – who in your group of friends suggested this prank at our expense?'

'Don't you think I'm capable of coming up with a practical joke on my own?'

'Well?'

'I'm not a sneak.'

'So someone did put you up to it. I'd really like to know his or her name.'

She shrugged and grinned.

'And the lipstick itself. Do you have your lipstick on you at the moment?'

'The one I used? No.'

'Where would it be now then, Miss de Pole?'

'This is getting ridiculous. I want to read my book.'

'What do you know about the death of Rosie Palmer. Do you know how she died?'

'Yes, I was in court on Friday. The prosecution explained it all.'

'Including the marks on the body, which they said were Hebrew characters. But the prosecuting attorney didn't mention that the letters, if that's what they were, were inscribed in lipstick. Red lipstick. Very similar to the lipstick you used on Hexie's blouse.'

'Ah, so that's what this is all about. You think there's some link? This is getting silly.'

'Do you recall the words you wrote – *sex magic*? Where did those words come from?'

She shrugged. 'I don't know. The words are meaningless.'

'Oh, but they're not. Did someone suggest them to you? Perhaps the person who put you up to it? Perhaps the person who gave you the lipstick? Let me put a name to you: Adam Rock.'

'God you're ridiculous. To think I thought you were sexy. Hexie is welcome to you.'

Without another word she picked up her book, stood from the table and walked out.

CHAPTER 37

Clarice Goodall was in the main room where Seb had first met her, working on a German grammar. She smiled at his approach and welcomed him with a few stuttering words in his own language.

'Not bad, Miss Goodall,' he said in English.

'There's something about German – I love the sound of it but I find it incredibly difficult to master.'

'If you stay here long enough you'll get it eventually.'

'Well, I'm leaving at the end of the summer. Parental bloody orders. I think they've decided it's time I found a husband and settled down on a country estate somewhere with horses and dogs and children. Anyway, enough of my problems – how can I help you?'

'You were at Hesselberg when Miss Mitford made her speech. I was surprised to see you there. When we spoke before you didn't seem totally enamoured of Miss Mitford.'

'Oh God, I wouldn't have missed Bobo's pathetic little speech for the world. What an absolute buffoon she made of herself.'

'Young Mr Rock thought she was magnificent.'

'Well, that speaks volumes about *him*, doesn't it?'

'And before that I seem to recall seeing you with Miss Mitford's group at the Night of the Pagans.'

'Well, it wasn't just Bobo's group – I think we all went from the hostel.'

'Do you have any idea where Miss Mitford might be today?'

'She's in her room, sulking. Yesterday she was on top of the world and she went off with Streicher and Goering to celebrate after the big event, but today she's at the bottom – and all because the Führer was supposed to be back in Munich, but he's not. He's still in Berlin with Ribbentrop and Goebbels, so she feels her world is at an end. It's always like this when he lets her down. So utterly pathetic.'

'Perhaps I'll go upstairs and call on her. But before I do, I'm interested in Miss de Pole.'

'Frankie? Why, what has she got to do with anything?'

'Perhaps nothing. I just wondered what you thought of her.'

'Well, I think she's having lunch. Why don't you go and talk to her.'

'I just did, but she stormed off.'

'You can't be investigating Frankie de Pole, for heaven's sake. What's going on, Inspector Wolff?'

'She seems close to people who are of interest, that's all. Nothing sinister, but I have reason to suspect that the murder of Miss Palmer was committed by more than one person. And so I am still interested in everyone who knew her. People such as Adam Rock and Fritz Mannheim and Otto Raspe. That doesn't mean I suspect these people – just that they might be able to provide me with clues.'

'And Bobo. You didn't mention her.'

'Yes, indeed, and Miss Mitford herself. She says she was closer than anyone to Rosie Palmer. But please, don't get me wrong – I say again I am not accusing any of these people of anything. It's just that in a case of murder, the inquiry always begins with those who knew the deceased.'

'Message received and understood. Well, so Frankie de Pole – where do I start? She's unusual, to say the least. Studies hard and then goes wild. Don't tell her I said so, but I believe her ambition is to work her way through every presentable man in Munich, particularly those in SS uniforms.' Clarice grinned, then grimaced. 'Ah, I really shouldn't have said that, should I?'

'Don't worry. I won't say a word. But tell me, is she close to Adam Rock?'

'Well, they're in the same circle, with Bobo and Fritz and one or two others.'

'Thank you.'

'Is that all?'

'For the moment. But if you think of anything else that might help, perhaps you'd let me know.'

'How do I get in touch with you? The Police Presidium switch-board, I suppose.'

'Not always.' He took out a pen and wrote a number on a corner of her exercise book. 'That's my home number. You can always get a message to me there. Probably better than the Presidium.'

He left her and made his way up the staircase to the room he knew to be Unity Mitford's. He knocked at the door, but there was no reply. He knocked again and heard a quiet voice from within, that seemed to say, 'Go away, leave me alone.'

Seb turned the handle and opened the door. She was on her bed, flat out, her fair hair splayed on the pillow and her right arm in the air in the Hitler salute. She turned her head to look at him.

'Oh God, it's you. What are you doing here?'

'I want to talk to you.'

'Well, I don't want to talk to you, so get out.'

'You must be feeling very pleased with yourself, Miss Mitford. I'm sure you've heard that Karl Friedlander died yesterday morning, thanks in large part to your efforts.'

'He got everything he deserved.'

She still hadn't moved, was still prostrate on the bed, right arm rigid and her sausage fingers pointing at a little over ninety degrees from horizontal.

'My assistant, Sergeant Winter, was there. He tells me that Karl died very bravely, refusing the blindfold and sending his love to his mother and father. He did not cry or quake, but went to his death with courage.'

Suddenly she sat up and swung her legs off the bed. She stared at him. 'Why are you telling me this?'

'Oh, I just thought you might like to know. You took such an interest in him and did more than anyone to bring him to justice. I wouldn't have even heard of the man had it not been for you. So on behalf of the people of Munich, I wanted to thank you.'

'You don't sound remotely sincere.'

'Really? I'm sorry about that.'

'Yes, I helped Friedlander to his deserved fate, and I can do the same for you, Inspector Wolff. I have friends in the Party, high-up friends. The very highest. Perhaps you would like a similar destiny to the worm Friedlander. I'm sure I could arrange it for you.'

'Indeed, I'm sure you could, Miss Mitford.'

He smiled at her, though inside he was raging. There was nothing more to be said.

There was, of course, a message awaiting him at the Presidium. A demand from Deputy Police President Thomas Ruff to make contact urgently.

Seb put a call through to his secretary, then made his way up to the fifth floor. Before the door was fully open, Ruff began shouting. 'God in heaven, Wolff, what in the whole of damnation do you think you are up to? This case is finished, done, resolved.'

'I had always thought it my place to solve crimes and seek justice.'

'You go out of your jurisdiction. You talk to the international press. I have had Nuremberg on to me all morning demanding to know what is going on. They have an investigation of their own and you think it fit and proper to intrude – interrogating their witnesses, trampling over their crime scene. All this without once consulting me or even making contact with Nuremberg Kripo. What is the matter with you, Wolff? Have you lost your mind?'

Seb had had enough of this. 'Herr Ruff, there is a killer on the loose in Bavaria – almost certainly two killers. They have struck in Munich and at Hesselberg in Franconia. There have been two attempts on my own life. And it is entirely likely that an innocent man has been executed.' He was not going to mention the assault on Silke, out of respect for her father's wishes. 'Do you want these killers to remain at large, to kill more young women? Is that what you want?'

'How dare you talk to me like that, Wolff? Consider yourself dismissed from the service with immediate effect.'

So that was it. No more a cop. It was both a relief and an irritation. He would have preferred to have quit of his own accord. Let Ruff know what he thought of him. Thrown his badge at the man.

Back in his office, he saw Sergeant Winter.

'Well?'

'I've been fired.'

'Are you serious?'

'Deadly.'

'But that's ridiculous.'

'Don't worry, it saved me the bother of quitting. Anyway, what about you, Winter? Have you done what I ordered you to do?'

He nodded. 'The parents have been freed and are home. I spoke to them. They are heartbroken. I'm worried they might do something stupid.'

'You mean like kill themselves? Perhaps that wouldn't be such a bad idea these days. And you told them he died bravely?'

Winter's face was pale and gaunt. 'Yes, I told them that. It wasn't much comfort. He was their only child. Their whole life revolved around him.'

Seb almost wanted to put an arm around Hans Winter to give *him* comfort. He looked utterly broken. All his beliefs shattered. Was he part of his beloved Germany now, or was he a despised alien?

'Well, see if you can help them. It must be best for them to leave the country. They are not too old, they could start a new life. Maybe they have relatives abroad who could sponsor them. Actually, I could look into it myself as I should have plenty of spare time on my hands now.'

'No, I'll do it. Easier to organise such things at the Wittelsbach Palace.'

'The thing is, how do you seek truth and justice in a system that is content to go along with convenient lies? Better to be out of such a world altogether.' Seb grabbed a couple of things off his desk – pens, a notebook. 'So I'll see you around.'

'Where are you going now?'

'To the beer hall, where else.'

'Can I come with you?'

Seb laughed. 'Wouldn't you be embarrassed to be seen with me?'

'I'll risk it, Inspector.'

'Not Inspector, just Herr Wolff to you now. Or Seb if you prefer.'

The Tirolkeller reeked of smoke and alcohol, but at least the house zither player didn't have to compete with the raucous farm boys this time.

'Gudrun,' Seb said as the waitress brought their order of beer, 'meet Sergeant Hans Winter of the Bavarian Political Police.'

'Pleased to meet you, Sergeant,' she said with her usual smile, plonking two full-to-the-brim half-litre steins down on the table. She was too polite to mention the bruises on his face. 'Very good to see the secret police working with the regular cops.'

They watched her traipsing to her next customer, her dirndl swirling around her ample figure. 'You should ask her out, Sergeant Winter. Take her dancing. She's single, believe it or not. Lord knows why no one's snapped her up yet.'

'She's twice my size. And sweaty.'

'Well you'd be sweaty if you did any actual physical labour. Apart from which, have you looked at yourself in the mirror lately, Sergeant?'

'I have standards.'

'Not very high ones. Anyway, you should consider her physical attributes a bonus. A big, generous girl with breasts to get lost in and the aroma of the earth. Many men would pay good money for such a woman, but with Gudrun it's all free, because she's not a whore. She'd make you a fine wife and give you many wonderful children.'

Seb took a hefty draught of the beer and gasped. 'Anyway, talking of wives, how am I to support a wife without a job, Hans? Tell me that.'

'You don't have a wife.'

'But I will have soon. I proposed to Hexie and she said yes. A rather cool, suspicious yes, but a yes all the same. She'll want children and I'll have to support them. The Lancia will have to go, I suppose. God, who will employ me now? Maybe Uncle Christian will give me a job, but do I really want to work for the most corrupt man in Munich?'

'Ruff will have you back. You just need to apologise and beg.'

'Hah.'

'Have you handed in your badge and gun?'

'What do you think?'

'I don't think you have. I can see the bulge under your jacket.'

'They'll make a detective of you yet, Sergeant Winter. And have you done what I asked you? Found who owns a cream-coloured Maybach in Munich?'

'I was about to put my mind to it when you dragged me here.'

Seb put an arm around the secret policeman's shoulders. 'The strange thing is, Hans, I have you in my power now, and I don't really give a damn. Your race or religion mean nothing to me. If I suspected you of murder or theft or any other crime, I would do my duty as a citizen and turn you in or denounce you without a moment's hesitation. But that Dortmund stuff? Never. I would keep your family's ridiculous secret to my dying day. Tell me one thing, though . . .'

'Yes?'

'When you arrested me that day outside the Osteria Bavaria and despatched me to Dachau, were you under orders? I know I have enemies in this town.'

'No, no one ordered it. I was there on other business and was shocked by your lack of respect for the Führer, nothing more. Maybe I was overcompensating, as you have suggested. I had to be more rigorous than the others to protect myself.'

'But this surveillance? Watching my every move?'

'That's different. That came after you were assigned to the murder case. That order came from on high.'

Those words again. *On high.* The governor of Stadelheim had said those words or something similar to Seb when explaining why he could not see the prisoner Karl Friedlander.

On high. That could be any senior party member, any of their friends or anyone with influence in this decadent city. The city he loved but was beginning to hate.

'Who, specifically, gave you the order to have me followed?'

'Josef Meisinger, my immediate boss. He just said that this was from on high.'

'Heydrich? Himmler?'

'I don't think so. Meisinger would have no reason not to mention those names.'

There was silence for a few moments. The zither player had plucked his last note and the black cat was sidling up to Gudrun, hoping for a scrap of food. And then Winter spoke again.

'There was something else. I heard something.'

His voice was so soft that Seb barely caught it.

'What did you say?'

'Can we go for a walk, Inspector? I can't speak here. There are too many people around.'

'If you wish. But drink up first. This is good beer, Hans, not to be wasted.'

They walked through Marienplatz and Tal, eastwards towards the river. Everywhere they looked they saw a uniform, SS or SA or ordinary police. And what of the others, the men in plain clothes? How many were secret policemen or spies? Every now and then they passed someone Seb knew and he nodded at them and smiled.

At the water's edge, near the bridge, they stopped. No one was about. They could not be overheard. The Isar flowed shallow and wide here. A raft of logs drifted by with a single poler aboard, guiding it downstream towards its eventual destination at some distant timber mill.

'I heard something,' Winter repeated. 'If I tell you what I heard and if it ever comes out, then my life will be over.'

'Then perhaps you shouldn't tell me.'

'No I shouldn't. I have kept it to myself for several days now and it would be politic never to refer to it, to anyone. But after watching Friedlander die . . . well, I think I have to atone somehow.'

Seb waited. There were times in any interrogation or inquiry when silence was better than posing a question. This was one such occasion. Hans Winter had been building himself up to this revelation, whatever it was, and he must be allowed time. As much time as he needed.

'It was at Wittelsbach Palace.'

Secret police headquarters. *Yes, go on.*

'Two of my colleagues, two BPP officers, were in the locker room. They were talking quietly, but not that quietly, and they were laughing. Smirking and sniggering like mischievous schoolboys who had set a cat's tail on fire. Proud of themselves. Defiant. It was last Tuesday, June the eighteenth. That date's important. One of them said, "Did you see the way his head split open? Like a melon. I never laughed so much. Dirty 175."'

'The day after Caius Klammer's murder.'

Winter nodded.

'And you have no doubt those were the words you heard?' That was important, because with a slight change of wording or inflection it might seem that the two men had been the investigating officers looking at the body. But the way Winter told it, they were the killers.

'Those were the exact words. And though they spoke them quietly, I know that they meant me to hear them. They were boasting about what they had done, laughing at me, knowing that I could never do or say anything about it.'

CHAPTER 38

'This is difficult, Hans. No proof, no evidence except your word. And as you obviously realise, any word from you will simply put a target on your back.'

'I know that.'

One thing that was immediately obvious to Seb was that the two BPP men had almost certainly been working for someone else. Why would two BPP men want to kill a harmless academic? Only because they had been paid to; they were hired killers, getting rid of a witness. In which case, perhaps there was some trail to be followed. Would they be making contact again with the person who hired them? Demanding more money, perhaps?

'You haven't told me their names, Hans.'

'Do I have to?'

'I can't force you to do anything.' Another thought was occurring to him: were these two men behind the attempts on his own life – the car in the street in Schellingstrasse, the tampering with the Lancia's brakes?

'Matthäus and Fuchs. Lukas Matthäus and Rudi Fuchs.'

'I know them,' Seb said. And nor was he surprised. They had both been Kripo men who moved across to the political police. They had been corrupt and brutal when they worked at the Presidium. They were on the take and they beat the hell out of anyone who got in their way; old-time Brownshirt bruisers for the Nazis, protecting the beer halls where Hitler spoke, beating up Reds.

Seb and everyone else had been glad to see them go from the criminal police. It was a shame they hadn't gone even further, somewhere in the Arctic Circle perhaps, where they could try their strong-arm tactics with the polar bears.

At least he now knew who had pulled the trigger that killed his friend. And he knew what sort of men he was up against. They were dangerous, all right. But what of the faceless ones behind them? Perhaps, at last, he had a link.

'I suppose they were the ones who tried to run me down on Schellingstrasse.'

Winter hesitated momentarily, then nodded.

'Good God, Winter, you saw them – you knew what they were about to do – that's how you had the time push me out of the way.'

Winter smiled bleakly. 'What will you do now, Inspector?' The secret policeman's unprepossessing figure was rigid. There was sweat on his brow, and not just from the warmth of the day. He was immersed in a terror that Seb had seen in the new recruits arriving at the front and experiencing their first bombardment. The terror in which men cried for their mothers or soiled themselves like infants.

Of course he was scared – because Seb's next move was a matter of life and death for him.

'You mean am I going to approach them? Tell them what I know? No, I'm not going to do that.' He knew exactly what Matthäus and Fuchs would do if the roles were reversed; they would take him to a cellar, shackle him against the wall and torture him until they had the name they wanted. And then, when they were satisfied that they had all the information they needed, they would club him to death or, if they were in a generous mood, finish him off with a bullet in the head.

But Seb was not Matthäus and nor was he Fuchs.

'However,' he said. 'That doesn't mean I'm done with you, Hans. You might not yet be the best detective in the world, but you have skills. You managed to shadow me for quite a while without discovery. So now put that skill to good use. Watch Matthäus and Fuchs. Find out who they talk to and why. Can you do that?'

He hesitated.

'Can you? Will you?'

'It will be dangerous.'

'Oh yes, that's true enough. But there's hope for you yet, Sergeant Winter. And don't forget the damned Maybach.'

Seb drove the old Opel up to Schellingstrasse and marched into the entrance hall of the *Völkischer Beobachter*.

'Can I help you, sir?' the girl on the reception desk said.

'Is Colonel Raspe in?'

'I'll just check for you.'

'Don't worry, I'll go up.'

Otto Raspe was on the phone when Seb pushed open his door. Their eyes met, then Raspe said, 'I'll call you back,' and put down the receiver. He stood up and smiled. 'Well, Inspector Wolff, what brings you here this fine morning.'

'I was hoping to talk to you about runes again, Colonel.' He removed the picture of Hildegard Heiden from the envelope he was carrying and handed it over to Raspe.

The sight of the photograph had an immediate effect, a stiffening of the shoulders and a tightening of the mouth. 'What is this?'

'A dead girl with marks on her body. I told you I would show the picture to you to determine whether the marks are runes?'

'This isn't Rosie Palmer. You said you had a picture of Miss Palmer to show me. Who is this girl?'

'Her name is Hildegard Heiden. I thought you might know her.'

'Why would I know this poor girl? From the picture it is clear she has been murdered. What are you implying, Wolff? Is this a damned accusation?'

Seb ignored the question. 'Hildegard's body was found at Hesselberg. I couldn't help noticing that the marks are very similar to those on Rosie Palmer. Any detective would immediately deduce that both girls were murdered by the same killer or killers. And so, in the absence of photographs of Miss Palmer – which have been mislaid – it occurred to me to show you this picture. I ask you again – as an expert not a suspect – are the markings runes?'

Raspe glared at Seb, then lowered his eyes once more to the photograph. Then he sat down at his desk, switched on his lamp and studied the picture closely. Finally, he looked up and met Seb's eyes. 'It is possible,' he said.

'Could you say what the runes might be? What they might communicate?'

'No. And I doubt whether anyone else could either. There is no sense or form to the markings. Not that I can divine, anyway. A child with a crayon could have done this.'

'Thank you, Colonel.'

Otto Raspe's glare softened. 'Sit down, Inspector Wolff.'

'*Herr* Wolff will do. I was fired this morning.'

'Really? I thought your star was in the ascendant.'

'It was, but I'm like a dog with a bone and that is not popular in Munich these days. Such dogs tend to get put down. You see I have been asking too many uncomfortable questions. In particular I have been asking whether the wrong man was executed yesterday.'

'He confessed.'

'Under duress. It was made clear to him that he would be convicted and executed even if he pleaded not guilty and that his parents would be incarcerated as accessories for giving him a false alibi. His lawyer negotiated a deal whereby if he pleaded guilty they would be released. He did the decent thing as he saw it. He was a brave young man.'

Raspe was nodding, deep in thought, his eyes once more on the picture. He sighed. 'Well, these markings, whatever else they are, are certainly not Hebrew script.'

Seb pointed his finger at the lipstick mark on the corpse's belly – the ⚡. 'I believe that is called sowilo and refers to the sun. Is it possible that there is some connection to the solstice?'

'Yes, that could be the sowilo, but as to the solstice I have no idea.'

'What do you know of Hesselberg. Might it have been a place of sacrifice for the ancient Germans?'

'Herr Wolff, you are now entering the realms of demented fantasy.'

'It is the killers who are demented, sir.'

'I take your point.'

'You drive a large black Mercedes, I believe, Colonel.'

'I do, but it belongs to the *Beobachter*. Anyway, what has that to do with anything? You certainly come up with some strange lines of questioning, Wolff.'

'And the young Englishman who is lodging with you in Altbogenhausen, what does he drive?'

'A Maybach, the spoilt brat. Rather nice creamy white motor. Ridiculous thing. One seventy kph top speed apparently. The devil knows what his parents were thinking in giving him such a large allowance.'

'What do you know about him, sir?'

'Oh, I know that his father is a wealthy lawyer. I believe they have some German ancestry and they have a great love for our country, which was why he was so keen for the boy to come here to study.'

'Do you know the family?'

'No, I don't. Funnily enough, they sought me out. I think they had read some of my works and knew of my interest in the *Völkisch* movement. I received a letter out of the blue expressing their admiration and asking if they could send their son to me to lodge. They offered a very high price for board and lodging. Money that was too good to refuse. Having been a professional soldier and now working as a professional writer I have always earnt a decent enough living, but I am not wealthy like Walter Regensdorf or your esteemed uncle, Christian Weber. The money Adam Rock's family pays me is very useful.'

'And his character?'

'Do you think he's a killer? Is that where this is going?'

Seb shrugged. 'He knew Rosie.'

'So did many people. You'd need more than that to convince me, let alone a court of law.'

'Karl Friedlander was convicted on little more.'

'He pleaded guilty. If a man says he has committed a crime, why should a court doubt him? Look, to get back to Adam Rock, I must confess I don't much like the young man. He is arrogant and unpleasant. But I work long hours and so it is quite easy for me to avoid him. Why don't you talk to my wife for she is very much the mistress of the house, and obviously sees more of him.'

'Will she talk to me? She seemed rather shy and disinclined to talk when I called at your house.'

'I'll telephone her now. Go and see her. I doubt you'll get very much – because I doubt whether Mr Rock is the man you seek – but at least you can clear the air.'

'Thank you, Colonel.'

'Well, good luck. And let's hope you sort out your own problems, too. By the way, last time you were here we talked about the Thule Society. Why don't you come along to our meeting this evening? You're a patriotic German, fought for your country with valour. You should fit in well.'

'What happens at your meetings?'

'Nothing mysterious. No human sacrifices.'

'I do believe you're laughing at me, Colonel.'

'The Vier Jahreszeiten Hotel at nine. I'll make sure you have entry as my guest.'

'Very well. I might just do that.' He was interested to see who else turned up.

'I realise you are a sceptic, but you could be pleasantly surprised.'

CHAPTER 39

Heidi Raspe opened the door and stood aside to let him in. As before, she was makeup-free and dressed in a traditional dirndl in the Bavarian colours of blue and white. She cast her eyes down demurely. Seb guessed her age at twenty-three or twenty-four, but she could easily have been younger: clear-skinned, perfectly braided hair.

She looked for all the world like a sweeter-smelling, slimmer and more innocent version of Gudrun the beer hall waitress.

'Please, come through to the kitchen, Herr Wolff. I'm afraid Adam Rock is not home at present.'

'Actually, it was you I wished to talk to.'

'Ah yes, of course.'

'I believe the colonel telephoned and asked you to talk to me.'

'That is so. Perhaps I can make you coffee? My husband said that would be a good idea.'

'Coffee would be a fine thing, Frau Raspe.'

Seb took a seat at the kitchen table while his hostess bustled about preparing the percolator. It occurred to him that even the use of the kitchen as the room for the interview had been pre-approved by the hausfrau's overbearing husband.

'Did you ever meet Rosie Palmer, Frau Raspe?'

Her brow knitted. 'I was told you wanted to ask me about Adam.'

'In relation to Miss Palmer. Although one man has confessed and been executed, there are grounds to believe there may have been an accomplice, and so the inquiry continues. I wish to discover all I can about those who knew her.'

'I see,' she said, though it was clear to Seb that she didn't.

'I believe Miss Palmer and Master Rock were friends. It occurred to me that perhaps she had been here and you had met her.'

'Yes, that is so. Her German was not as good as Adam's so our conversation was not very easy. But I would say she was a nice girl, except for—' She stopped in mid-sentence.

'Except for what, Frau Raspe?'

'Well, I do not like to speak ill of her, but she was not modest. I could tell from the smell of her hair and clothes that she had been smoking cigarettes. Also, she wore makeup.'

'But apart from that, she was nice?'

'I would say so. Yes, I would not like to say a word against her without having known her better.'

'And was she close to Adam Rock?'

'Well, they must have been friends or she would not have come here with him. But beyond that I don't really know.' She paused, cups in hand. 'Please, Herr Wolff, where exactly is this conversation going?'

Seb was beginning to wonder how any woman could be quite as submissive as Heidi Raspe. In his mind, he found himself thinking of some of the more puritanical sects of the past three or four hundred years: women meekly baking bread and feeding babies while their menfolk tilled the fields and made the rules both at home and in church. Was this what Herr Raspe demanded of her, or was it the way she had been brought up?

He knew what Hexie would say about the woman: she would dismiss her as plain stupid, a disgrace to her sex and probably deserving of all she got.

'Forgive me,' he continued. 'Perhaps I am straying from my original purpose. Yes, I came to talk about young Adam Rock. Is he easy to get on with?'

'He is always very correct with me.'

'Describe his life here if you would.'

She hesitated. 'I am not sure what you mean, but he has a room at the top of the house. He rises late – about nine – and has fruit, bread, cheeses and sliced meats for his breakfast. Just like Colonel Raspe and me. Also coffee, always two cups, with milk and sugar. And then he might read during the morning or go out to his lessons – German language with Frau Baum and also some classes at the university. I think German history and European politics. Like my husband, he has a great interest in the history of the German race. He also participates in various sports. Is that the kind of thing you wanted, Herr Wolff?'

'What about his evenings, his social life? I believe he is friends with Miss Unity Mitford – have you met her?'

'Indeed I have. Like Miss Palmer, she has her English vices but no one is perfect and I know that she is a strong National Socialist and a good friend of the Führer, so I certainly would not criticise her.'

'Is Adam a Party member?'

'Of course.'

Why *of course*, wondered Seb? He doubted whether the majority of English students were paid-up Nazis, however dazzled they might be by the SS uniforms.

'Has Adam had any romantic attachments since he has been staying here with you?'

She seemed to gasp. Her pale skin reddened as though shocked that anyone could pose such a question.

'Frau Raspe?'

'How would I know such a thing? You would have to ask him that yourself. Such matters must surely be private.'

The truth hit him like a bullet and he smiled. She would know such a thing, of course, if she had been the object of his affections. She was a good-looking young woman, much closer in age to Adam Rock than to her husband who was perhaps thirty years her senior. And from appearances, Adam appeared to be the prescribed Nordic ideal of Aryan manhood. Oh yes, he could see this romantic attachment clearly enough.

The perfect hausfrau Heidi Raspe wasn't quite so pure after all.

Before he could pursue his questioning, he heard a key turning in the front door lock.

'I think you have a visitor.'

Now she was really flustered. 'That will be Adam. He is the only one with a key other than Herr Raspe and myself. I can't let him know we were talking about him. You must ask no more questions.'

'Just tell him that I arrived hoping to find him here and you invited me in for coffee while I waited.'

'Yes, yes, I will do that.'

*

Rock swept in like a film star. He had a silk scarf around his neck and his hair was tousled by the summer breeze. He smiled at Heidi Raspe and then spotted Seb.

'Oh, it's you,' he said. 'I wondered who owned that rather dilapidated Opel.'

'It's not mine. My own car was driven off the road when the brakes failed.'

'Really? How careless of you. Anyway, to what do we owe the pleasure?'

'As I mentioned at Hesselberg, I was hoping to have a few words with you.'

'There's an English expression you may or may not have heard: turning up like a bad penny.'

'Yes, I know it. And I apologise if it was my fault that we got off on the wrong foot. And talking of cars and faulty brakes, what do you drive, Mr Rock?'

'A gorgeous Maybach. My pride and joy.'

'What a coincidence – it was a Maybach that drove me of the road. Cream coloured.'

'Now that is a remarkable coincidence – same colour as mine. And I have to say, you couldn't have been cut up by a better car. As for your apology, I'll accept it. So, what shall we talk about? And whose language?'

'German is fine. I know you have become fluent – Frau Baum speaks very highly of your progress. And perhaps Frau Raspe would like to join the conversation.'

'Splendid. Fire away with your questions.'

Adam Rock was still standing up. He had his arms folded across his chest and was leaning back, looking down at Seb with haughty disdain. Perhaps this young man *was* destined to lead his country as suggested by Rosie's brother, because he undoubtedly thought himself superior to those around him. Seb glanced sideways at Heidi Raspe and saw that she was looking at her lodger with adoring eyes. So it was true, his suspicions about their relationship.

'I just wanted to know about your recollections of Rosie Palmer. When did you meet her? Who was in your group of friends and what did you all do together?'

'That's easy enough. We must have arrived in Munich about the same time and we first met at Gretchen Baum's place, where we were both booked in for German lessons. Bobo – Unity Mitford – was there too, as well as the other girls from the student hostel and various young men. It was natural that we would all get together in the evenings. Drinking, dancing, opera, picnics on the lakes. Also we had mutual friends back in England, so it was obvious that we would socialise.'

'And a few SS men?'

'Indeed. Bobo and Rosie both attracted them like magnets and there always seemed to be a few about, particularly Fritz Mannheim, the spy.'

'The spy?'

'He's one of Hitler's junior adjutants, I believe. When Bobo became chums with the big boss, we assumed Fritz was deputed to keep an eye on her. It was a bit of a joke among us. We tease him about it, and he has always taken it in good part. A fine chap.'

Seb nodded. Of course he was a spy.

'In the winter, we all went skiing together at GP,' Rock continued. 'Garmisch-Partenkirchen.'

'Heaven on earth. My favourite place in the world. One day I shall buy a chalet and spend all my winters skiing up on the Zugspitze.' His eyes strayed to Heidi. 'You've been there, haven't you, Frau Raspe?'

'Many times, Herr Rock.'

Frau Raspe, Herr Rock. How wonderfully formal for two young lovers.

'Anyway, we have all been having a riot of a time, autumn, winter, spring and summer. Day and night.'

'Tell me about Rosie.'

'What do you want to know? She was beautiful, charming, we all loved her.'

'Somebody didn't.'

'The Jew, you mean. Karl whatever his name was. He was a nasty little housefly and now he's been swatted. Good riddance to him.'

'And yet other evidence suggests that Karl Friedlander also loved Rosie. And that she loved him.'

'If you believe that, Inspector Wolff, you will believe anything. Rosie was a properly brought-up young Englishwoman from an impeccable family. She wouldn't have let the likes of that dreadful oik near her – unless of course the swine forced himself on her.'

'Who else might have disliked her?'

'I can't imagine. There was nothing to dislike.'

'What about her own feelings? Did she ever confide in you any antipathy towards anyone? Did she like Unity Mitford as much as one is led to believe?'

'Of course she did. They got on famously, went almost everywhere together. Mind you, Bobo has had less time for us in recent weeks since she became friends with the great Adolf. Best day of my life when she introduced me to him at the Sterneckerbrau. I envy you Germans for having such a remarkable leader.'

'And how did Miss Palmer get on with Frances de Pole and Clarice Goodall? No ill feeling?'

'None that I noticed.'

'What about the boys?'

'They'd have all given their lives for her. And she liked them all back, though not in a romantic way.'

'Well, thank you for your time, Mr Rock. You have been a great help.'

'Of course the only person she couldn't get on with was Huber.'

Seb frowned. 'Huber?'

'Irmgard Huber – Walter Regensdorf's secretary or general factotum or whatever she is at the Villa Saphir. Where Rosie lodged. They couldn't abide each other. Rosie said the ghastly woman was always poking around in her business.'

'Did something cause a rift between them?'

The Englishman shrugged. 'I suppose it must have, but the devil knows what it was. Rosie wouldn't go into details. I just recall her seething with fury one day and when we asked her what the problem was she said something about that bloody cold bitch Huber causing her some grief. Which was strange language for Rosie, because though she wasn't a prude she never spoke like a damned navvy. Never used a swear word and never spoke ill of anyone.'

'Do you recall what the "grief" was?'

'No, Rosie simply wouldn't go there, but she was clearly very upset.'

'And did she ever bring up the subject of Frau Huber again?'

'Once or twice. To complain about her going through her things. She was also convinced that she steamed open her letters.'

'And what might she have found if she went through Miss Palmer's things?'

'Who knows? That's not the point. It's simply not done, especially not by a damned serving wench.'

Seb looked at his watch, then rose to his feet and turned to his hostess. He had learnt more than he hoped, but not what he expected. He had come to this place distracted by his loathing for the entitled Adam Rock. But that initial hostility was evaporating. First lesson for all detectives – keep your personal feelings out of it. Listen to instinct, trust intuition, ignore emotion.

'Forgive me, Frau Raspe, but I have another urgent appointment and I am running out of time. And you, Mr Rock, you have been most informative and helpful. Perhaps we might catch up another day. Please get in touch with me if you have any other thoughts.'

'You really are tediously persistent, aren't you, Inspector.'

'I do my best to protect the people of Munich.'

'Good for you, old man, good for you.'

The truth was, there was nothing more for him here in the charged environment of this suburban kitchen. Leave Adam and Heidi to their own adulterous devices.

As he drove away, back across the river, he wondered about the strange dynamic of the Raspe household. Perhaps the colonel knew about his wife and their lodger. Perhaps that was why he didn't like Adam Rock and considered him arrogant and unpleasant. Perhaps the truth was that not all was as well as it might be with Otto Raspe's finances and he needed the money that Adam Rock's family was paying him.

And what was he supposed to make of Adam Rock anyway? What else could he have asked? Have you killed two girls? Did you try to kill Silke Stutz two nights ago in the woods at Hesselberg? And if so, who was your accomplice?

He needed to stand back from this and think more clearly. He now knew the names of the men who had killed Caius Klammer. How could he make the connection between them and their paymaster? How could a young man like Adam Rock have found his way to such men? That didn't seem to make sense.

Only someone at the very heart of this city, particularly its noxious underbelly, could know of men like Matthäus and Fuchs. So that ruled out Adam Rock – didn't it? What about the car, though? The cream-coloured Maybach owned by Adam Rock? That was the only possible link.

For the moment, he wished to know more about Frau Huber. He recalled her crow-like presence as he and Sergeant Winter looked around Rosie Palmer's room at the Regensdorfs' immense mansion at Karolinenplatz.

She had dressed in black and white and had the austere aspect of a nun. He remembered that she had intimated her disapproval of Miss Palmer's lifestyle and morals. He could understand why a vibrant girl and such a stern woman might have clashed. But was that all there was to it?

CHAPTER 40

He went back to the hospital. He needed a voice of sanity to calm him down and try to make sense of what he knew and didn't know – and how to proceed. No one better than Hexie for that.

Before he entered, a car's horn caught his attention. He turned and saw a black Mercedes and instantly recognised Uncle Christian's driver.

'Are you here for me?'

'Councillor Weber wants you.'

'Well, he can wait. I'm here to visit someone. Tell him I'll come and see him later today.'

'He wants you now.' The driver pulled out a pistol.

Seb laughed. 'I don't think he'd be very happy if you shot his beloved nephew.' He turned his back on the driver and strode into the hospital. Then he turned again and retraced his steps. Let Hexie sleep, he might just get more out of The Pig. 'All right,' he said, 'put your toy pistol away, I'll see him now. Is he at the Residenz?'

'Yes.'

'I'll follow you in my car. I don't like your driving.'

Fifteen minutes later he found himself once more in the Black Hall of the royal palace. Christian Weber had a face of rolling dark clouds. He had a toothpick and was trying to pull something – probably a stringy bit of pork – from between his incisors. He didn't bother with small talk.

'You are making enemies, boy, and you are embarrassing me. What in the name of your sainted mother are you up to?'

'I'm not sure what you mean.'

'I mean that with my assistance you were given an important case, a *very* important case with international implications. One that meant a great deal to the Führer himself and by extension to me. You solved it, there was a guilty plea, sentence was passed and executed. I had even brought in Munich's finest lawyer on the defendant's behalf at your request so that there could be no question of a mistrial, no doubt about the result. Yet for some reason known only to yourself you won't let it go. And now, to cap it all, you have been dismissed from the police force.'

'The case needs to be reopened. I have new evidence. The killer is still at large and no young woman is safe.'

'And what will you do when you find this killer? Tell the court that they executed the wrong man? Tell the British government that the German police are utter incompetents? Do you think your Führer would thank you for that?'

'I don't have any option.'

'Really? You're not even a police officer any longer. This is not your responsibility. Or perhaps you want to go back to Dachau? Well, if that's the case, you're going the right way about it and I won't be getting you out this time.'

'This isn't easy for me, Uncle. There have been two attempts on my life. You know about one of them because your driver was at the hospital and so you must have heard about my so-called accident. I also have the names of two BPP men who killed a witness who just happened to be helping me with my inquiries, but I am powerless to do anything about it. Does no one care about the murder of a decent man in this godforsaken city just because he is of a different sexual orientation? Does no one care that an innocent man has been guillotined just because he is of a different religion or race? Does no one care that girls are having their throats cut?'

Weber's voice softened. 'You're rambling, boy. This is getting you nowhere, and it's not helping me. I can only dig you out of so much shit, you know, and then you're on your own. Anyway, who are these two BPP assassins?'

'What would you do with the names if I told you?'

'I could make life difficult for them.'

'I can't tell you, Uncle. I wish I could, but I can't. I've made a promise. Anyway, they're pretty well untouchable with their contacts at Wittelsbach Palace.'

'Let me guess then. Matthäus and Fuchs.'

Seb couldn't reply.

'Your silence confirms it, boy. Those two holy cunts would kill their own mothers for a litre of beer and a plate of grilled sausages.'

'Even if it was them – and I'm not confirming or denying it – there's nothing to be done. Your friends Heydrich and Himmler aren't going to admit that they employ murderers.'

'There are always ways and means.'

'You mustn't front them up for they would know my source and do for him.'

'Front them up? Why would I do that? Sometimes I wonder about you.'

'I need to know who hired them.'

'I could extract that from them.'

'No. Leave it to me.' He could only imagine what methods Uncle Christian might bring to bear.

Weber shrugged. 'Anyway, let's get you back on the force.'

'I doubt it will happen.'

His uncle grinned and his vast belly wobbled. 'Now that's something you *can* leave to me. In the meantime, how's that girl of yours? Bashed her head, I hear.'

'The doctors think she'll be all right.'

'And have you asked her to marry you yet?'

Seb couldn't help smiling. 'Funnily enough, I have. And the yet more remarkable thing is, she said yes.'

Weber's little eyes widened. He tossed away the toothpick and threw his arms wide.

'Well done, boy, well done.' He moved forward and enveloped Seb in a sweat-and-cologne embrace. 'My heartiest wishes to you both. She'll make a man of you yet.'

'Thank you.'

'It'll be the Munich wedding of the year. I'll get Adolf along as guest of honour. That will see you right for a long and fruitful union and do your career no harm either.'

'I'll have to talk to Hexie about that, Uncle.'

'Nonsense. Leave this all to me. Money will be no object. We'll get you promotion and a good pay rise. You'll need to keep the copper pfennigs coming in to raise a healthy brood of children. Your mother will be so proud – and what of young Jurgen? He'll be happy for you, won't he?'

'Perhaps. I'm not sure.'

'It'll be a tremendous day. If you live long enough to see it, of course.'

Seb turned up at the Vier Jahreszeiten Hotel with no real idea what might lie in store. He had wondered whether to go home and change into a smarter suit, but thought better of it. Why in damnation should he kowtow to this strange, credulous bunch of people? Otto Raspe, who had extended the invitation, knew what sort of man he was; if he or the rest didn't like his appearance, that was their business and none of his.

A valet in the smart entrance lobby directed him to a lift and told the liveried operator to take him up to the fourth floor. The man somehow doffed his peaked cap and did a Heil Hitler simultaneously, and then set the elevator on its way.

'This is my first Thule meeting,' Seb said.

'Indeed, sir.'

'Does the society meet here often.'

'Every month. It has always been associated with the Vier Jahreszeiten, of course, but it hasn't been so well attended recently. I believe it is not well thought of by some of the senior men in the movement these days.'

Seb nodded. That was the way he understood it. Though an outright ban had not been imposed, the Thule Society did not have Hitler's approval, not since its founder Rudolf von Sebbotendorf wrote a book titled *Before Hitler Came*, which seemed to suggest that the Führer learnt all his politics from the society. Sebbotendorf had since scarpered abroad somewhere, leaving only the diehards like Raspe and a few others, almost always among the more wealthy and influential members of Munich and the other cities with branches.

It was true that in 1919 two of the original members, Karl Harrer and Anton Drexler, had founded the German Workers Party, which

Hitler would soon transform into the National Socialist German Workers Party, otherwise known as the Nazis. It was also true that Sebottendorf had acquired the *Münchener Beobachter* newspaper on behalf of Thule, changing its title to *Völkischer Beobachter* before it was sold to Hitler.

So there were links. But such truths did nothing to endear Sebottendorf or the Thule Society to Hitler. He was his own man, his politics were his own and no one else's. That was the way he saw it, and no one was going to take an iota of credit for what he had devised and built. The Nazi movement was his achievement and his alone.

Despite this, the links were strong. Hadn't Alfred Rosenberg – Hitler's ideological chief man – been a member of the Thule Society well before the Nazis came into existence? And didn't he still write at great length about Teutonic mythology and the mystical destiny of the Germanic peoples? And what of that other early member of Thule, Rudolf Hess; he was now the Führer's official deputy.

And those other names, what had become of them? Well, Sebottendorf had disappeared, Harrer was dead and Drexler was still around and well thought of, though had no power within the Party. Perhaps he would be here tonight.

Meanwhile, Germany's love affair with the occult continued unabated. And if the state came down hard on frauds and charlatans, they still allowed room for those – like the Thule Society – who laid claim to a scientific basis for their risible beliefs of mythical northern islands and Norse gods.

'Ah, you've actually come, Herr Wolff. Welcome, welcome.'

It was Otto Raspe.

'Thank you,' Seb said.

'And Heil Hitler, of course.' They exchanged salutes. 'And was Frau Raspe of assistance?'

'Perhaps. It's difficult to tell. I hadn't been at your house long before Adam Rock turned up. He was actually more forthcoming than I expected, so I learnt a few things about Rosie Palmer and her friends. Time will tell whether I can make any progress.'

'Well, for the moment, you can simply think of Germany and the German race for the evening. This is all very gentle, I promise you. We'll have a talk, a conversation. There will be a break for drinks and I hope you find it all as engrossing as I do.'

'Thank you.'

'And if you like us, perhaps you'll consider applying for membership. The main qualification, of course, is proof of pure Aryan blood.'

Raspe led Seb through to a room with a smart lectern at one end and several rows of straight-backed wooden chairs arranged in a semicircle around it. The room wasn't large. There was easily room for the thirty of forty chairs, but a hundred would have been a squeeze. Two rifles dating back to pre-war days hung on a wall opposite the window that looked out onto Maximilianstrasse. Above them was a pennant bearing the curved swastika of the Thule Society, much like the one Seb was certain he had seen fluttering in the distance at Hesselberg.

'Looking at the guns, eh, Wolff?' Raspe said. 'Mementoes of 1919 when we resisted the Bolshevik Jews who imposed their dirty politics on Munich for four mad weeks. We used this room even back then, but our arsenal was considerably bigger, as was our membership – in the region of sixteen hundred for the whole of Bavaria. It didn't take us long to clean up the Bolshevik pigsty.'

'I believe you came under attack.'

'The Reds raided us here on April twenty-sixth of that year. Some of our finest were dragged away, but I shot my way out. If I had been captured I would doubtless have been murdered in cold blood by those Russian Jews like my good friends Countess Haila von Westarp and the Prince Gustav von Thurn und Taxis. Two of the most delightful and upstanding people you could hope to meet. Haila was simply beautiful and a glorious spirit. That was the Thule Society's darkest day, and yet also its proudest. One must always admire someone prepared to die for their country and their race.' He sighed, seemingly lost in his memories.

Seb decided it was wiser not to mention that the version of events he had heard involved a great deal of bloodshed on *both* sides.

'But that is a story for another time,' Raspe continued. 'Come, Herr Wolff, it is a great deal more peaceful now. Sit with me at the front, won't you? And I hope you won't mind if I introduce you to my co-members.'

A gramophone record was playing softly, background music, very German befitting the nature of the meeting; Seb was pretty sure it was Wagner, but could not have identified which of his works it was.

The room was filling up: the wealthy and titled of Munich. Helene Bechstein, Hugo and Elsa Bruckmann, Erna Hanfstaengl. He spotted Walter Regensdorf, who nodded his glistening bald head in the direction of Raspe, but not to Seb; clearly a Kripo officer – even a defenestrated one – was far too lowly to be recognised by the great magnate. Nor was he alone, but accompanied by his drab but expensively dressed wife Maria and his severe secretary Frau Huber, who took seats either side of him. Suddenly, Seb found himself having yet more sympathy for the poor deceased English girl. It can't have been much fun for Rosie Palmer lodging with the overbearing Regensdorf clan.

There was a fourth member of the party, too. The Mitford girl, Bobo. That was a surprise. How close was she to the Regensdorfs?

Seb wondered whether he might have a chance to talk to Irmgard Huber before the end of the evening. He would like to hear her own version of her difficult relationship with Miss Palmer; not that it was likely to amount to much. Certain people – men and women – could be scarily judgemental in their stern morals. That had always been the way in the old Germany and the new Third Reich only sharpened the pursed lips and disapproving looks. Hence the rising numbers of homosexual men in Dachau and the absence of rouge on young girls' cheeks.

At last there was silence and a man Seb did not recognise took the lectern and introduced the talk. The subject was to be 'Versailles: the Jews' greatest crime'. Seb groaned inwardly, unable to believe that they were still going over this absurd ground, arguing that surrender and humiliation in the war was a Jewish conspiracy rather than the blindingly obvious truth that with America pouring men and weapons into the Western Front, Germany was hopelessly outgunned.

And then the speaker rose to the lectern to loud applause. It was Anton Drexler himself. The man who helped found the German

Workers Party which Hitler took over and turned into the Nazi Party. The man whom some said had discovered Hitler.

He was a glum-looking man – thick face behind thick spectacles with a small untidy moustache. He wore an old suit that had seen better days and spoke in flat tones with a slurred working-class Munich accent. The next hour passed in a haze of invectives against Judaism, the perfidious French and the bloodthirsty Reds, and Seb had trouble staying awake.

The applause this time was more muted, probably because everyone else in the room was as bored as Seb was. Perhaps they had disapproved of the large glass of aqua vitae at the speaker's side, which he continually imbibed. Seb found himself looking at his watch as the assembled members and guests rose from their chairs to mingle and drink.

'Got to be somewhere, Wolff?' Raspe said.

'My girlfriend – fiancée – is in hospital. I'm worried about her.'

'Then you must go to her without delay. And I want to apologise for Herr Drexler. He is not the most inspiring speaker. In fact he has been rather a hollow man since his role in the party waned. Next time I will seek out Germany's finest expert on runes. Now that should be a great deal more interesting.'

'Well thank you anyway, Colonel. It has been enlightening.'

'Which sounds like a polite way of saying deathly dull.'

Seb smiled and shook Raspe's hand. He hadn't known what to expect when he accepted the invitation to come here, but it hadn't been this. Where was the mysticism of ancient Germany, the mythology of the runes and the pagan gods? Despicable though Drexler's views might be, the whole tenor of the evening was closer to a drunken chat in a beer hall than a journey into the occult. There was no clue here to the violent deaths of Rosie Palmer and Hildegard Heiden.

'By the way, sir, did the Thule Society have representation at the Hesselberg day this weekend? I was there and thought I saw one of your flags.'

'Well, not me, but perhaps others went. I couldn't say.'

'No matter.' Seb thanked his host, said goodbye and moved towards the door. A face appeared before his eyes, out of nowhere: Maria Regensdorf.

'Inspector Wolff, yes?'

He found himself bowing and clicking his heels. Old military habits die hard when a private soldier meets the officer class. 'Frau Regensdorf.'

'I thought it was you.'

'I was just about to go.'

'Yes, yes, go.'

'You were going to say something?'

'No. I'm sorry, I'm holding you up.'

'Can I assist you in any way?'

She shook her head and moved away. Seb watched her go, confused. She had moved over to him deliberately as though she wanted to talk about something, but had changed her mind.

The elevator took him down to the ground floor and he made his way out through the lobby onto Maximilianstrasse. Darkness had fallen but a couple of street lights illuminated the road. He crossed the street towards the dilapidated Opel, but stumbled and juddered forward as though hit by an electric current.

The barrel of a gun was pressing hard against his spine. He turned and came face to brutish face with Lukas Matthäus and Rudi Fuchs. They both held Walther PPKs and they were both grinning.

Seb's hand went inside his jacket for the butt of his own gun, but Fuchs, the smaller of the two secret police officers, was quicker, shoved the muzzle of his own pistol into Seb's face and removed the pistol from his grasp with his left hand. 'We'll take that, I think.'

Matthäus smacked his own pistol into the side of Seb's head. Hard enough to draw blood and stun him, but not hard enough to kill or render him unconscious.

'Time for a little ride, Wolff.'

CHAPTER 41

Matthäus drove while Fuchs sat in the back of the car with Seb. They travelled eastwards through the darkened streets of Munich and the fact that they didn't blindfold him told him they had no intention of letting him survive the night.

Nor had they bothered to bind him because in their minds there was no need. They had the guns and Seb had no way out.

'You should have stayed in Dachau, Wolff. Much safer.'

The voice came from the front of the car, from Lukas Matthäus. Seb knew a fair bit about the man. He was a few years older than Seb, thickset with slaughterman's hands – rough, heavy and strong. He had fought in the war and had been a street fighter in the early twenties before joining the criminal police, continuing his taste for violence without a pause. His nose had been broken more than once and he bore plenty of other scars on his face; though not as many as the ones he had inflicted on others.

'Can't you open the window?'

'So you can jump out?'

'For some air. Your car stinks.'

Fuchs, sitting beside him in the rear, laughed. 'He says we smell, Lukas. And here's us kindly giving the fellow a lift. You do people a favour and that's what you get. It's not right.'

'Well, tell him not to worry, he won't have to put up with it much longer.'

Seb was finding it hard not to gag. The car reeked of beer and smoke and piss and shit. He wondered how many others had come this way with these two killers. Some, the more timid, would have soiled themselves in this vehicle. Such was the nature of fear, a thing Seb had lost many years ago.

'That girl of yours,' Fuchs said. 'With you out the way, she'll be wanting another man. I think I'll give that one a go. Not a bad looker.'

Fuchs might have been smaller than Matthäus but Seb was under no illusion about him. He had been in plenty of fights of his own and had invariably come off best thanks to his training as a boxer back in his early years. If anything, he had a reputation for being smarter and more cold-blooded than his partner. The thought of the swine going after Hexie made him feel sick.

Seb was close to vomiting. The stuffy, noxious air in this vehicle. Did they not notice the stench? Why would they not clean it and disinfect it?

'You won't be doing yourselves any favours if you kill me, you know.'

'Big Uncle Christian come after us, will he?' Fuchs laughed again. 'You really think he gives a whore's fuck about you?'

Matthäus grunted. 'Farm boy, I was. Sliced up a few pigs in my time. Wouldn't mind spending an hour or two with Weber and a filleting knife. See if there's any meat beneath those hectares of fat.'

That made Fuchs laugh even louder.

'Who's paying you for this?'

Fuchs was pressed up against Wolff, shoulder to shoulder, arm to arm so that Seb could not avoid his sickening heat. He was smoking some kind of cigarillo and occasionally tipped the ash from the end, always and deliberately into Seb's lap. In his other hand he held his Walther PPK, his service pistol, constantly trained on Seb.

'Paying us, Wolff? We don't need pay for this. It's our hobby. We do it for pleasure.'

'Yes, of course you do. I remember you from Kripo. You were both crooked and depraved then. Nothing's changed.'

'Ah, but it has. Now we're untouchable.'

'So tell me, who's the paymaster? You've nothing to lose by telling me now. Satisfy my curiosity.'

Fuchs blew smoke into Seb's face. 'We could tell you, but then we would have to kill you.'

'That's funny. Very funny. I could die laughing.'

'No chance of that, Wolff. You'll die screaming and begging for your mother. We know our work, you see.'

Once outside the city, past the suburbs and towns and into the trees, they drove down a foresters' path into the dark woodland which Seb recognised as the vast Ebersberger Forest. So this was it, this was where he would spend eternity. Not much different from the Western Front, and a bullet from a German secret policeman's pistol was unlikely to feel any different to a bullet from a British gun. At least he was close to home here, deep in the heart of his beloved Bavaria.

Ten minutes later, the car stopped. Matthäus got out from the driver's seat and removed his pistol and an electric torch, which he switched on. Then he pulled open the rear door on Seb's side, blinding him with the beam. 'Slowly now, Wolff, slide out slowly. Don't want any nasty accidents.'

This was thick forest, not a clearing, but Seb understood that his captors knew the place well; they had been here before. He had no option but to comply with Matthäus's command. They were capable of inflicting horror and he saw no point in making death more painful than necessary.

'Now get yourself down on your belly and stay there, nice and quiet and still.'

Again, he did as he was told. He was brought up a Catholic, but he hadn't said any prayers under shellfire and enemy assault in 1918 and he wasn't going to say one now. Just close his eyes and then the bullet in the back of the head and he wouldn't even know about it. Death was the great mystery. Except it wasn't. He had seen so much of it and there was nothing mysterious about it. There one moment, gone the next. Instant oblivion. Nothingness.

Fuchs was out of the car. He was doing something around the rear of the vehicle.

Seb felt a tug on his left ankle. A length of rope was being knotted to it.

After a few moments, he heard Matthäus saying something to Fuchs but couldn't hear what.

'Get up, Wolff.' It was Fuchs speaking.

Slowly, he raised himself onto his hands and knees, then pushed himself to his feet. He saw now that his left ankle was attached to the car door handle by the length of rope. He could walk just so far, but he couldn't make a dash for the cover of the trees, couldn't escape.

Matthäus and Fuchs were lounging against the car. Both held their pistols. Matthäus still had the torch and Fuchs had something else. Difficult to tell what in this light, but then he threw it at Seb's feet and he recognised it straightaway. An entrenching tool from the war: shovel one side, pick the other.

'Now dig your fucking grave. Make it good. Two metres long, one metre wide, two metres deep. We don't want the foxes chewing you. We don't want you found.'

'I'm not going to dig. Just shoot me now.'

Fuchs flicked a lighter and a flame shone in the dark woods. 'If you prefer to be cremated alive, we can accommodate that, too. We have a litre or two of petrol to start you off. Your choice, Wolff.'

Which was no choice. No one would choose to die by fire. Seb picked up the tool and began digging, through the carpet of leaves, into the tough, mulchy soil. Slowly and methodically.

'God in heaven, how did you survive the fucking war? Put some muscle into it. We haven't got all night.' Matthäus was drinking from a bottle. He passed it to Fuchs.

'At least you'll have company,' Fuchs said. 'How many we put down here, Lukas?'

'I lose count, Rudi. Arithmetic was never my strong point.'

'Get digging, Wolff. Satan's getting impatient for your soul.' Fuchs drank deeply from the bottle. 'Nice weapon an entrenching tool, I always said. Often preferred it to the bayonet in the heat of battle. Split open many a French head with an entrenching tool. You can stab with a bayonet, but you can swing with either end of the tool. A more nimble weapon once you're in the narrow confines of an enemy trench, and a blow to the head will often stop someone quicker and surer than a stab to the chest or belly. I just mention this in case you might think I was unaware of its potential in the wrong hands. Yours.'

Seb stopped for a moment. 'At least give me a swig of that schnapps. I haven't done this sort of work in a while.'

'Fuck you. Dig. If you're a good lad, we'll give you a last smoke before the bullet.'

Even for a professional, it's not quick and it's not easy digging a grave, and it was many years since Seb had handled an
entrenching tool. The ground wasn't rock hard, but nor was it
easily broken. There were stones to contend with and roots. He
thrust downwards and scooped up dirt, all the while aware of the
eyes of the men who would take his life.

He heard their laughing, saw the bottle become empty and then
Matthäus fetched another from the car. He smelt the smoke of
their cigarillos.

The minutes wore on. It was a cool night, but he was drenched in
sweat and earth. He could taste mud and salt in his mouth. His nostrils were clogged and gritty. How long had he been digging? Half
an hour? No, an hour at least, maybe more. He was never going to
get to two metres down. Surely, they'd give up before then and just
shoot him and kick him into a shallow grave. How long left?

Without warning, Matthäus strode over to the edge of the
hole and looked in. It was still less than a metre deep. He swore,
stepped down into the recess, then took a swing at Seb, crunching
his ribcage with his gnarled fist, pushing the breath from his lungs.
Seb lurched backwards and gasped. Matthäus hit him again, this
time with his pistol, sharp metal smashing into his shoulder blade
from the side. 'You fucking useless cunt, Wolff. A fucking nun
could dig a better fucking hole.'

The blow knocked Seb to the ground, inside the half-formed
hole. He found himself scrabbling in the dirt and stones and felt a
hard kick to the hip. This time from Fuchs who had been watching but now moved over to join in.

They were both kicking him, both grunting and swearing. This
was always going to happen, of course. They weren't going to let
him die without a beating. It was what they did, what they had
always done: inflict pain.

His instinct might have been to curl up like a foetus to protect
himself, but he had discovered long ago that things didn't work
that way with him. Even as a young boy in school he had discovered that when he was scared and when he was attacked, his fear
dissolved like snow in warm rain.

He recalled the first time. He was part of a gang facing another gang from a nearby school, fighting over something insignificant, probably the bullying of the juniors. Seb hung around at the back of his group, scared and small, avoiding the confrontation but unable to just slip away for fear of being seen as a coward.

Unseen, one of the other gang had come around to the back. The first Seb knew of it was a flash of light. Something had been thrown at him, some sort of incendiary device – weedkiller or benzine or gunpowder from a firework. Something home-made, but it hit his jacket and caught fire.

Seb had turned away from the light at the last moment and the fire missed his face. He beat at the flames and extinguished them but he knew his precious school jacket was ruined. In his hand he had a leather belt, knotted. They all had weapons – clubs, knives – but no one thought they were really going to use them.

But Seb's fear had evaporated. Still in his scorched jacket, he strode through the ranks of his own gang straight into the ranks of the enemy, straight for the boy who had attacked him. He beat him about the head with his leather belt, beat him to the ground.

Now, once again, more than twenty years later, he was under attack. Somehow he had managed to retain his grip on the entrenching tool and he swung it, lashing out in rage, not sure what he was trying to hit, simply responding to violence with violence. It was his nature, his animal nature, like his near namesake the wolf when cornered. Don't cower, attack.

One of the two men let out a cry of agony. From the pitch of the scream, on the high side, he thought it had to be Fuchs he had hit rather than the brawnier, deeper-voiced Matthäus. The sharp-edged tool must have caught his legs.

Seb expended no time or energy wondering what he had done; he was still flailing, hitting out in all directions, trying to cause the men injury. At least die fighting, not begging. The torch had been knocked out of Fuchs's grip in the confusion and it now lay on the ground outside the hole, its beam slicing through the accumulated earth and leaves, casting a dim glow on the car. A stark, mechanical outline in the lee of the towering trees.

Matthäus and Fuchs were moving shadows. He couldn't make them out, but nor could they see him clearly. One of them lurched away towards the torch. Seb threw himself at his retreating back. From his bulk, he knew it was Matthäus, wolf against bear. The sharp, angry crack of a gunshot split the air. It came from behind him, from Fuchs, but no bullet hit him.

He was wrestling Matthäus. The force of his tackle had smacked the bigger man's face into the ground as he lost his footing. Seb grabbed his hair, pulled his head back and smashed it forward once more. There was a satisfying crack of bone and gristle on hard ground, mingled with a grunt of pain and confusion. Seb fell away to the right and he saw Fuchs coming at him. The dark profile of the pistol against the darker background of the forest.

A second gunshot rent the night. A muzzle flash of light.

Seb realised he still had the entrenching tool in his right hand. He wanted to run, but the rope was still bound tight around his ankle. The entrenching tool wouldn't cut it, not quickly enough. He twisted away then flung the tool at the shadow he assumed to be Fuchs. A dull thud and a curse told him he had hit the man with some force. In the same movement, Seb thrust forward and grabbed the torch.

He swept the light in an arc and in less than a second saw all he wanted to see. Saw Fuchs regaining his balance, gun still in hand, saw Matthäus scraping his fingers at the earth, trying to gain purchase, saw his pistol on the ground, close to his head.

Seb instantly flicked the switch to off; light was not his friend.

His mind was beginning to function now, not just acting on instinct. He knew that Matthäus and Fuchs had drunk a great deal of spirits. He knew, too, that they had done this work many times before and had always been totally in control, even in drink, because their victims were incapacitated by fear and resigned to their fate. No one fought back, they took their beating and accepted the bullet in the head with grim fatalism.

But now these two *weren't* in total control and with things getting rough and unpredictable, their thought processes were slowed by alcohol. This was a situation they hadn't expected and, in drink, weren't sure how to counter.

That didn't mean they didn't have the advantage, though, because they did. Matthäus might be groggy, but he wasn't out and could quickly regain his senses. One of them might have suffered an injured leg from his attack with the entrenching tool, but which one? And what did the injury amount to?

Seb was still at a grave disadvantage. The only difference was, he had a sliver of a chance now. But there was no escape while he was still tethered to the car by several metres of tough cord. He needed one of the pistols.

There were still guns out there – at least three including his own. But he knew where one of them was – the one by Matthäus's head – and he hurled himself at it. Matthäus had seen it too and his hand touched it at the same time as Seb's.

Seb's grip was better. His right hand held the butt of the pistol. Matthäus was holding the barrel. Seb grasped at earth and found what he wanted: a rock the size of a tennis ball. In one swift movement, he brought it down onto Matthäus's knuckles. The man roared with pain.

Another crack of gunfire from Fuchs's pistol behind him and Seb was certain he felt the whistle of a bullet passing his temple. Now, though, he had a gun himself.

He fired in the vague direction of Fuchs. Once, twice.

Then he had a thought. He switched to a kneeling position. Took a grip of the rope near his ankle, held the muzzle of the gun onto the rope and fired. The gun recoiled, throwing back his arm as the bullet cut through fibres and dug into the earth.

It wasn't enough to sever the rope, so he tried again. This time the remaining fibres parted. He was free.

Except his two assailants were still alive and still armed. Seb could see nothing. Here, beneath the dark canopy, the darkness was absolute. A flame struck up. The lighter Fuchs had flicked before. Seb saw him and loosed off a shot in his direction. He heard another cry and assumed he had hit the man, but he wasn't going to wait to find out.

Seb just ran, into the dark.

CHAPTER 42

He was feeling his way through the trees, unaware of his direction or where he was. Somewhere, perhaps three or four hundred metres behind him, he saw the beam of the torch, scanning across a wide arc. It was supposed to pick out Seb as a target, but in fact it gave him a coordinate, something to work on. He moved to the left, at right angles to the path his pursuers seemed to be following.

Two minutes later he realised he had to stop. Their best hope of finding him was the sound he was making. They were following his footfalls. The more he moved, the more noise he would make.

He slid behind a tree, tried desperately to calm his pounding heart and his rasping breath. He mustn't make a sound. He needed silence, absolute silence.

The air was cool, almost cold, but his body was boiling with a fever. He rested his arms on his thighs, breathed deeply and slowly, listened to the night. He heard voices, now a little closer, now further away. Occasionally he saw a distant spot of light.

How long did he stay here, perfectly still, perfectly silent? An hour? Two hours. It was the depths of the night in the heart of the forest and other sounds came to him. Animal sounds. Boar, deer, night owls.

Finally he heard the sound he had been waiting for. The car engine turning over and coming to life. He heard it driving away, back along the path towards the west of the forest, in the direction of Munich. Still he didn't move.

He awoke with the dawn, his body now cold. God in heaven, had he really fallen asleep here? Had Fuchs and Matthäus really gone, or were they waiting for him, ready to ambush him as soon as he made a move?

He couldn't go westwards, because they could be parked along the path. From the sun and the blue sky above the high green canopy, he worked out which way was north and began to walk slowly in that direction.

He arrived at a small and very beautiful farm village just after eight thirty. The sun was up now and it was a glorious day. He realised he must look a mess, his clothes, hair and face covered with dirt and dust, but he approached an old woman and asked her if there was anywhere he could make a telephone call.

She looked him up and down suspiciously until he showed her his Kripo badge, then she nodded and said, 'I have a telephone, you can use that.'

Her house was nearby and she invited him in, then left him with the phone while she made ersatz coffee and buttered a slice of black bread for him.

Seb got through to Sergeant Winter at the Presidium and told him where he was without going into too much detail of what had befallen him.

'I'll be with you in half an hour, Inspector.'

The coffee and bread had tasted wonderful and Seb had given profuse thanks to the old woman who helped him. She had naturally been curious about the circumstances surrounding his arrival in the village, but he had merely said that it was a confidential police matter and he couldn't say more.

Now he was being driven back towards Munich by Hans Winter, past the endless suburban streets and the factories, their chimneys belching out smoke into the blue sky.

'Well, Inspector?'

'Your friends, Matthäus and Fuchs, took me for a ride into the Ebersberger Forest. It was supposed to be a one-way ticket.'

'Then it is a miracle you're here. Are they still with us?'

'Somewhere. But they'll have hangovers and bruises. Maybe a bullet hole and a broken bone, but that might be too much to ask. Anyway, you had a task to perform for me, remember. Any results?'

'Through talking to the dealers, I have found four cream-coloured Maybachs in Munich, but of course there could be more purchased elsewhere. One of them is particularly interesting. A Maybach Zeppelin.'

'The one belonging to the young Englishman Adam Rock.'

'No, I have no information on that one. I was thinking of the one belonging to Walter Regensdorf.'

Winter dropped Seb off at the Vier Jahreszeiten Hotel, where his borrowed car was still parked. He thanked Winter and they agreed to meet later, then he drove home to Ainmüllerstrasse.

His mother was all over him, hugged him and offered him food and coffee. Surprisingly, Jurgen was at home, too.

'Shouldn't you be at school?'

'Shouldn't you be at work, catching murderers?'

'I see you have regained your healthy disrespect for your father, Jurgen.'

'You saved Silke, but that doesn't mean we see eye to eye on other matters.'

'Indeed not, and perhaps we never will.'

'You have a short memory, old man. Do you not recall the failed economy just five years ago when almost every German subsisted on porridge and cabbage soup and veterans of the war starved in the street? Look at the food we eat now – pork, cheese, veal. And who do we have to thank for that? Who has stood up to the French and the Jews and the Bolsheviks and given us back our pride. You know the answer.'

'Please, Jurgen, no politics today.'

'You just want to avoid the truth, won't admit you're wrong.'

'I'm not going to argue with you. Just tell me about Silke, how is she?'

'I think she is very shaken up. Her parents won't let her out of their sight. I don't feel very welcome there at the moment. Perhaps they blame me for what happened, I don't know.'

'You have nothing to blame yourself for, Jurgen. You are both the same age – you didn't force her to go on your adventure. It was the choice of both of you.'

'Yet I was the man – I must take responsibility.'

Seb nodded. He understood the boy. He had felt responsibility for Ulrike all those years ago, even though in post-war Germany women had been given the vote equal with men. Even though it was Ulrike who made the first move in their love affair. It was simply the way he was brought up: the world belonged to man, the home to woman.

Not that he agreed with the idea of man's superiority, simply that it was deeply ingrained in the culture and in the church and in his upbringing. Such presumptions were difficult to cast off, even though Hexie had done her best to disabuse him of his out-dated attitudes and re-educate him.

He washed and shaved and changed and felt a great deal better. Mutti looked at the bruises to his head where Matthäus had hit him and sighed in resignation.

'Don't worry,' he said. 'The other man came off worse.'

'Why don't you get an office job, Seb? I'm sure Christian would be happy to find you something in one of his concerns. You have a good brain – you could learn accounting, perhaps.'

'Maybe I will.' Maybe he would have no option. He didn't bother telling her that he had been dismissed from the police force. There was time enough for that when things became calmer.

He settled down at the kitchen table with his pen and a blank sheet of paper and began writing down words and names, joining them with lines when he saw a connection: *Rosie Palmer, Anglo-German Naval Agreement, Karl Friedlander, Otto Raspe, Heidi Raspe, Adam Rock, Thule, Hesselberg, Herzogpark, rune, lipstick, Persian rug, Unity Mitford, Walter Regensdorf, Maria Regensdorf, Irmgard Huber, Caius Klammer, 175, Walther PPK, Hildegard Heiden, geblöt, cream-coloured Maybach, brake fluid, Fritz Mann-heim, Frances de Pole, Silke Stutz, sex magic, Clarice Goodall, Lukas Matthäus, Rudi Fuchs, the BPP, Ernst Hanfstaengl . . .*

Outside the front door, on the landing, the telephone was ring-ing, then stopped. There was a knock at the door. Seb put down his pen and opened it to their neighbour, Frau Miedler.

'There is a telephone call for you, Herr Wolff.'

'Thank you.'

It was Winter on the line. 'Ruff demands your presence.'

'I'm not sure he has the power to demand anything of me any-more.'

'I'm just the messenger, Inspector. He told me to get you here sharpish.'

'I'll be there in twenty minutes.'

What, he wondered as he drove southwards towards the Police Presidium, was he to do with the new information that Walter Regensdorf was in possession of a cream-coloured Maybach Zeppelin? What did it amount to?

Such a car had been used to pick up Hildegard Heiden in Nuremberg, almost certainly driven by her killer. Such a car had cut him up on the road home to Munich when the brakes failed.

That evidence was merely circumstantial. But there was some-thing else: the similarities between the deaths of Hildegard Heiden – who had been last seen accepting a lift from a cream-coloured Maybach – and Rosie Palmer, whose hosts, the Regensdorfs, owned such a car.

'If it was up to me, you would never be allowed in the Munich police again,' Thomas Ruff said. 'But it appears that it is not up to me, so you are to have your badge back, Wolff.'

'Thank you, sir, but I am not certain that I want it.'

'What you want and what I want are beside the point. This is an order from the Brown House. And not just that. It seems you are to accept promotion to Captain of Detectives. Should I now congratulate you, or commiserate with you?'

'Is there a pay rise?'

'Of course.'

'Well, I suppose as I am about to get married and will need the money I have no option but to accept the post, and also your congratulations, sir.'

'Have you ever heard of an American escape artist named Harry Houdini, Wolff?'

'Of course.'

'I think you must be related to him in some way, because I have no other explanation for your ability to wriggle out of impossible situations.'

Seb smiled. This was nothing to do with Houdini, and everything to do with Uncle Christian and his influence with the very highest level of Nazidom. Perhaps with a little extra help from Putzi Hanfstaengl who wanted nothing to reflect badly on his publicity coup in finding the right cop to clear up the Rosie Palmer case and keep both the English government and the Führer happy.

'However,' Ruff said, 'I suggest that you bear in mind that Houdini's final trick did not end well. So collect your badge and gun and get back to work. Solve the murder of that 175 to start with.'

'I think I know who killed him, but you might not like to hear it, sir.'

Ruff began to twitch nervously. 'Go on.'

'Two members of the Bavarian Political Police.'

'Ah. And you're certain of this?'

'Yes, sir.'

'And do you have names and evidence?'

'Names but no evidence.'

'Well then nothing can be done. Time for you to move on to another case, perhaps.'

'Don't you want to know the names, Herr Ruff?'

'Not without solid evidence, no. Consider the case closed.'

Seb bowed obediently. He had known exactly what Ruff would say.

'And for a short while you will remain with the rank of inspector,' Ruff continued, 'pending the retirement of Captain of Detectives Erler, who will leave his post at the end of July.'

'Heil Hitler, sir.'

'Heil Hitler, Wolff, you lucky bastard.'

CHAPTER 43

Seb realised that the gun he was carrying wasn't his but Matthäus's, so he would have to ditch it. He collected a new pistol from stores, explaining that his weapon had gone missing during a secret operation. He offered no further explanation and none was demanded of him. Word had moved fast around the building that he was to be the new Captain of Detectives and Erler was to take retirement. Erler had been off sick for several weeks anyway, so it was no surprise that his days in post were numbered. Which meant that Seb had new respect in the Presidium and wasn't to be questioned or gainsaid.

He collected Winter and they made the short walk to Karolinen-platz together.

A uniformed police officer was standing on the pavement outside the front gate of the Villa Saphir. Seb approached him and flashed his badge.

'What's going on, Officer?'

'Haven't you heard, sir? Frau Regensdorf is dead.'

'Are you serious?'

'Very much so, sir. Fell down the stairs and broke her neck by all accounts. The ambulance has just taken her away but a hearse might have been more appropriate.'

Maria Regensdorf dead? Last night at the Thule Society meeting she had been trying to say something to him until she clammed up.

'Who's inside?'

'One of my colleagues and some members of the Regensdorf staff. That's all I know.'

'All right, Officer, just stay where you are. We'll take over here.'

Seb and Winter entered the enormous villa. Frau Huber was standing in the hallway in her severe black and white outfit. She was talking to a policeman but when she turned and caught sight of Seb and Winter, she immediately brushed aside the uniformed officer and approached them.

'This has been an appalling tragedy, Inspector Wolff.'

'What happened?'

'Frau Regensdorf is dead. It happened a little over half an hour ago. Her body was at the bottom of the stairs, lifeless. No pulse, no sign of breathing. She must have tripped and fallen. From the position of her body I would imagine she broke her neck. It is awful, simply awful.'

'Who found her?'

'I did, Inspector. I was working with Herr Regensdorf in his study and heard a noise. I came out and there she was. I did what I could, but it was clear straightaway that she was dead. I have always thought this staircase to be dangerous and I make it my business to advise everyone to hold on to the banister when they ascend or descend.'

'And where is Herr Regensdorf now? I want to speak with him.'

'He is in his study, overcome with grief.'

'Did anyone see the fall? Any member of staff?'

'No.'

'So no one was with her when it happened. You're certain of that?'

'Yes, Inspector. I am certain.'

'Let's go and talk to Herr Regensdorf.'

'He is in deep shock. Perhaps give him a little time . . .'

'You can leave such decisions to me, Frau Huber. Will you lead the way?' He turned to Winter. 'Sergeant, go through the rest of the house and talk to all members of staff to see what they know.' He indicated the staircase to the uniformed officer. 'Stay here. No one is to use this staircase or touch anything, either upstairs or down here in the hall.'

'Yes, sir.'

Seb followed Irmgard Huber to the study and she knocked at the door. When there was no answer, he stepped past her, turned the handle and walked in.

Walter Regensdorf was standing at the window looking out. He turned around slowly and Seb saw that he had an even more impressive physique than he had noted at their first meeting. His head was large and the forehead shone. His eyes were blue and his goatee beard was flecked with various shades of grey. He did not look shrunken by events.

'I am sorry to walk in at this time, sir. May I offer my condolences.'

'Yes?' His eyes were blank but seemed to conceal some pent-up fury. Was he angry with fate for taking his wife, or angry with Seb for standing there at a time when he wished only solitude?

'I am Inspector Wolff. Perhaps you might remember me.'

'Yes?'

'I was hoping to have a few words, sir.'

'About what exactly? Have you not heard that tragedy has just befallen this house?'

'So I have learnt.'

'The most dreadful accident. My wife is dead, and it is absolutely no concern of the police. I insist you leave. This is a time of mourning and I must somehow find the strength to spend the day calling my beloved wife's relatives. Do you not understand such protocols?'

'Actually, sir, my initial reason for being here was to ask you about your car.'

Regensdorf recoiled as though struck. 'My car?'

'Indeed, sir.'

'Have you lost your power of reason? A man's wife has died within the hour, her body not yet cold, and you ask him about a damned car? You are a disgrace to your badge, Wolff. Get out.'

Seb ignored his bluster. 'I believe you have a Maybach motor, a cream-coloured Maybach. The Zeppelin model.'

'I have several cars but what of it? No, don't answer that because I really don't care. I won't listen to this.'

'It is a matter of grave importance, Herr Regensdorf.'

'Importance? If my chauffeur has been speeding, then to hell with it. I allow him the use of my vehicles. Anyway, in the scheme of life and death, speeding is a small meaningless thing.'

'Do you ever drive the car yourself?'

'What is this? Are you insane? Get out, man! Go! Shall I call Himmler?' He jutted his chin towards his secretary, standing stiffly by door. 'Take this man away and deposit him on the street, Frau Huber. And put a report through to Deputy Police President Thomas Ruff.'

'Yes, sir.'

Seb didn't move. 'Have you perhaps driven the Maybach to Nuremberg in the past week or two?'

Regensdorf took two steps towards Seb, his fist raised. As it came forward at his face, Seb caught it in the palm of his hand and pushed back. 'I understand your anger and grief, Herr Regensdorf, but assaulting a police officer will do you no favours.'

He released the man's hand and clicked his heels together sharply. 'We will talk soon.' Without another word, he turned and left the room.

Why had Seb subjected Regensdorf to such intrusive questioning at this of all moments? It was because he was now certain: the clue to the deaths of two young women lay here within this house.

He stood in the hallway looking up at the stairs, then he climbed them, seeking out loose or slippery steps. They were all made of hardwood and they all seemed absolutely sound and secure. There were no visible marks. The banister was polished but afforded a firm grip.

At the foot of the stairs, a small patch of blood and a few strands of hair were the only evidence that someone had just fallen to their death in this place. Standing at the top, on the first floor landing with the steps falling straight beneath him, he looked down. Did Maria Regensdorf stand here looking down before she fell? Before she was pushed?

She had not just 'clammed up' last night. She had approached him because she was scared and had something of importance to say. But then she had moved away because she was even more fearful of being seen talking to him. But scared of what? And why?

He felt it now. The darkness in this house. This was not only the place where the English girl Rosie Palmer lived during her months in Germany. It was where she died. No one saw her outside this house on the night she died, because she never left this house alive.

What happened here though? He thought of the Persian rug in which her body was wrapped; that was an extremely expensive item and so it must have come from a wealthy household. Was there somewhere in this building a patch of floorboards less bleached by the sun?

Irmgard Huber appeared from the corridor. 'You're still here, Inspector. My master told you to go. You are trespassing on private property.'

'I told the uniformed officer to wait here. Do you know what happened to him?'

'Like you, he was told to go. This is nothing to do with the police.'

'Where is your chauffeur? What is his name? I want to talk to him.'

'I am not at liberty to say anything to you.'

'Then I am not leaving this house. By the way, Frau Huber, I am told that you and Miss Palmer did not get on well. What was the cause of your antipathy?'

'You are talking nonsense, Herr Wolff. I have summoned assistance. Now please go or you will be removed without ceremony.'

'You didn't like each other. What was that about? Did you disapprove of her English ways? Her lipstick and powder?'

The front door opened. Two large SS men filled the space, blocking out the light. They looked around, caught Frau Huber's eye and she indicated Seb with her right index finger. Without a word, the SS men marched up to him, took told of his arms and carried him out of the house, down the steps, along the path and dropped him outside the gate. They turned and strode back up to the front door, where they stayed, like guard dogs.

He stood there fuming, powerless. In the pecking order of the Third Reich the criminal police ranked well below the SS. Even the political police would find it hard to argue with the Schutzstaffel. He felt a tap on his shoulder. 'What's going on, Seb?'

It was the American reporter, Ernie Pope.

Seb shook his head. 'I wish I knew, Ernie. What have *you* heard?'

'A whisper from a pal at the hospital that Maria Regensdorf has departed this life. Fell downstairs.'

'Yes, she's dead. How she came to fall down the stairs is another matter. But it seems I am not welcome in the house. They say it was an accident, no one else involved. Nothing to report and no concern of the police. I doubt you will be very welcome either.'

'I have to try. It's my job.'

'Well, good luck.'

Seb watched him try to enter the house. He got no further than the front door, his way barred by the silent SS men.

The reporter shrugged. 'I thought the SS was set up to protect Adolf. Seems Regensdorf uses them as a private army. Well, Seb, it's pointless hanging around here. Do you want to go and find a drink somewhere?'

'I'm waiting for my sergeant. He's still in there, though God knows how.'

'That political guy? Isn't he a worm?'

'Actually, he's not so bad.'

'I thought he was the one who had you consigned to Dachau.'

'An error of judgement. Anyway, he's grown on me.'

'You're a very forgiving man, Detective.'

Two minutes later, Winter was hurled out of the house. As he appeared at the door, the two SS men grabbed him and tossed him down the stairs like a sack of coal. Seb picked him up and tried to dust down his clothes, which was a hopeless task given the plethora of stains that had already accumulated on his jacket, trousers and tie.

'Are you all right, Sergeant? Nothing broken?'

'I've had worse.'

'They don't like us in there.'

'Oh, I got on all right in the kitchens, sir. Talkative bunch, they were.'

'And what did they say?'

'They don't believe for a moment that it was an accident.'

'Let's walk. You can tell me as we go.'

CHAPTER 44

They walked away slowly. The pneumatic hammering from the building work at Königsplatz receding as they went. Seb told Winter to give him every detail about the domestic staff he had met.

'They get paid well, the job is secure, but no one actually likes working for Walter Regensdorf.'

'His secretary Frau Huber doesn't seem to mind.'

'She's part of the problem. She's not just a secretary, she runs the whole household. Even the wife, Maria, didn't seem to be able to overrule her.'

'And they told you all this? Not a very discreet lot.'

'They've kept their mouths shut until now, but I think they've all had enough and will be handing in their notice at the end of the week. En masse.'

'Very wise. It's not a healthy house. How many staff did you talk to?'

'The cook, her assistant, two maids, the gardener. They were all clustered in the kitchen, horrified and bewildered. There were five of them in all. I've made a note of their names.'

'Don't worry about that for the moment. What about the chauffeur – was he there?'

'I was about to come to him. He wasn't there, but they talked about him. Surprise, surprise, Herr Wolff, his name is Huber. Stefan Huber.'

'Now that *is* interesting. Related to Frau Huber by any chance?'

'Her husband. They both live in so they can be on hand at a moment's notice, but they also have a property of their own in Schleissheimerstrasse, an apartment which they use on their days off and where they will one day retire.'

'And where was Herr Huber if he wasn't in the kitchen with the others? Did they say where he was?'

'They didn't know. Apparently they don't have a lot to do with him. But I got his address off them, so maybe he's there now.'

'Sergeant Winter, you really do have the makings of a detective.'

'Thank you, Inspector. That means a great deal to me.'

'But you still have plenty more to learn. And get someone to launder your clothes. You're a disgrace to the service. Now, let's go and see if we can find Herr Huber.'

The Hubers' apartment was in a pleasant street a little way to the east of the Dachau Road, but still very central.

He answered the door in his underpants and vest, scratched his belly and looked at them blankly.

'Herr Huber?'

'Yes, who are you?'

'My name is Inspector Wolff, Kripo. This is Sergeant Winter. We would like a few words with you.'

'Better come in then, I suppose.'

Stefan Huber had a toothbrush moustache not dissimilar to the Führer's, but there the similarity ended. He had a heavy build and protruding stomach that spoke of a liking for beer and fried food. It was difficult for Seb to understand the attraction between this rather slovenly man and the brisk, austere Frau Irmgard Huber.

'Do you want something to drink? A bottle of Augustiner?'

'No thank you.'

He took them through to their front parlour with a view from the window onto the street. It was a well-furnished though rather unwelcoming room. The wood surfaces were polished and cold.

'So what's this all about, gentlemen?'

'You drive for Walter Regensdorf?'

'Of course, but it's my day off.'

'Then perhaps you won't have heard . . .'

'Heard what?'

'About the death of Frau Regensdorf.'

His brow knitted. 'What do you mean? Why would she have died?'

'Fell down the stairs. Probably broke her neck.'

'Well, I don't know what to say, Inspector. That's awful. Dreadful. When did this happen?'

'Within the past couple of hours. Your wife found her body. No one saw it happen.'

'Irmgard found her? Dear God.'

Seb was not surprised by Stefan Huber's Hitler moustache, but he was surprised by the rest of him; he had expected someone small and mouse-like and timid, under the thumb of the frosty mother superior Irmgard. This man looked anything but timid, he looked as though he could hold his own in a brawl.

'That isn't the main reason we're here,' Seb said. 'Actually, we're very interested in your work as Regensdorf's chauffeur and the cars you drive. There are several cars, I believe.'

'Three fine ones, four workhorses. The nice ones are very nice. Mercedes-Benz 770 supercharged, Rolls-Royce Phantom and a lovely Maybach Zeppelin, my favourite. The king of cars – three tonnes of pure German artistry and precision engineering. Twelve cylinders, eight gears. Goes like a dream on a good road but will pull your arms out on difficult corners.' He flexed his upper arms. 'Still got my weightlifter's muscles, even if the rest of me has gone to sausage and beer.'

'Are you always the driver?'

'Of course. Also the mechanic and polisher. I love those cars like mothers love babies.'

'So no one else drives them?'

'Wouldn't let anyone else near them. Save the boss, of course. Couldn't really stop him now, could I? Anyway, he's got some muscle, too.'

'So you drove your master to Hesselberg at the weekend?'

'Hesselberg? What's that?'

'Oh come on, Herr Huber. You know what Hesselberg is – the site of the Frankentag.'

'You've lost me. I don't know what Hesselberg is and I don't know what the Frankentag is, though from the name it's obviously something to do with Franconia – up Nuremberg way.'

'Are you serious about this? You didn't go there?'

'I didn't go there. Why would I lie about something like that?'

'One more question. Excuse me if I seem rude, but you're a shambling wreck, Herr Huber, and yet your home is clean and tidy and polished.'

Huber laughed. 'That's my wife's doing. She sends one of the maids over three times a week.'

Seb turned to Winter. 'Sergeant, what do you think? Any more questions?'

'Yes, where are the cars kept?'

'We have a garage behind the house in Karolinenplatz. Big workshop place with its own pit and fuel storage. As good as any commercial set-up.'

'Just you?'

'Just me. I know cars inside and out. I used to work at Mercedes in Stuttgart.'

'And were you at your workshop at the weekend?'

'No, I was here. I've had a touch of flu. Had a few days off.'

'Did anyone see you over the weekend?'

'What do you mean?'

'I mean, could anyone vouch for the fact that you were here, at home.'

'Like who?'

'Neighbours, friends, relatives.'

'I didn't see anyone.'

'Not even your wife?'

'Irmgard? No. We don't see a lot of each other at the best of times. She's kept busy, usually stays at the Villa Saphir – he likes her to be on call twenty-four hours a day.'

'So you have no evidence that you were here, not at Hesselberg?'

'What is this? What's this all about. I don't much like these questions.'

'Are you stupid, Herr Huber? I think you would have to be stupid not to have any idea what this is about. Perhaps the influenza has damaged your brain.'

'Now you are insulting me again. First you call me a shambling wreck, now you call me stupid. Do I have to put up with this?'

'You know very well what this is about. This is about the death of Miss Rosie Palmer, the English girl who lodged at the Villa Saphir.'

Seb simply listened to Winter's questions and the driver's answers. As a detective and interrogator of several years standing he might not himself have used the second insult, but he knew that sometimes it could be effective to incense a suspect or witness. Their reaction when angry could be revealing. In this case, he wasn't sure. He couldn't quite work out Stefan Huber.

'The murdered girl? What has that to do with me?'

Seb and Winter remained silent. Simply stood and looked at him. Waited.

Huber let out a sigh of exasperation. 'Come on fellers, this is all finished. The killer's already been for the chop.'

'What if he had an accomplice?' Seb said. 'Or what if he was innocent after all? What if Frau Regensdorf knew something and paid the ultimate price for that knowledge?'

'This is ridiculous. I don't know why you've come to me.'

'Because of the car, Herr Huber. The cream-coloured Maybach. If you didn't drive it to Nuremberg or Hesselberg, who did?'

'I didn't know anyone had.'

Seb looked at Winter. 'Should we take him in, Sergeant? I don't believe he's being entirely honest with us.'

'I think you're right, Inspector.'

Seb saw panic in the chauffeur's eyes. 'Take me in where? I've done nothing.'

'Perhaps a few nights in Dachau.'

'No, this is madness.'

'Easiest thing in the world to put you in protective custody, Herr Huber. If necessary, you could stay there six months. Free board and lodging, a little light physical work to keep you fit and healthy.' Winter took out his BPP badge. 'No hearing needed. My word alone will give you all that. But if you want to start giving us some interesting answers here and now, that might be avoidable.'

'What do you want to know, for God's sake? Don't send me to Dachau, please. It would kill me.'

'We'll see. Well for a start, why don't you tell us why the other domestic staff – your wife excluded – believe Maria Regensdorf's death might not have been an accident.'

'They hate Regensdorf and they don't much like my wife.'

'Why?'

'Well, you've met them, haven't you?'

'Is there something between them – your wife and her master?'

'Of course. It's obvious, isn't it? The cold bitch. He's welcome to her.'

Seb and Winter stopped at a cafe on the way back to the Presidium. 'I think we have our killer or killers, Sergeant. But what we don't have is hard evidence or clear motive – and we certainly do not have proof.'

'And if we did have proof, sir, what then?'

'That's an even better point.' Seb lowered his voice. 'When a murderer has the protection of his very good friends Heinrich Himmler and Adolf Hitler we are stuck, and the only heads likely to roll are our own. This is the world you and your political police friends have been working for, Herr Winter. A world in which the rich and powerful and the Party members are beyond the reach of the law. Congratulations.'

'Perhaps I have made mistakes, but I still maintain that the movement has been correct in bringing back employment and pride to the nation. The enemies of the state are many.'

'You mean the Jews, the Reds and the 175s?'

'Do we need this conversation now, Inspector Wolff?'

'No. And certainly not here in a public place.'

Seb needed some sanity and time to think. He was sealed in an airless box with no way out. He believed now that Walter Regensdorf and Frau Irmgard Huber were directly involved in the murder of two young women and Frau Regensdorf and complicit in the killing of Caius Klammer. Also the attempted murders of

Silke Stutz and himself. Their motive was obscure, but that did not mean they weren't guilty.

What now? How to proceed?

The day had gone, he had barely eaten and he was still aching from his night in the woods with Matthäus and Fuchs. His instinct was to go and see Hexie, but he was pretty sure he had missed the strict visiting times, so he went home instead.

Mutti immediately offered him a bowl of soup and went off to the kitchen. He followed her and found Jurgen there at the table, studying his schoolbooks, still dressed in his Hitler Youth outfit having been out on some sort of manoeuvres with his troop.

'Don't say anything.'

Seb groaned. 'I wouldn't dare.'

'And why have you been writing about a cream-coloured Maybach?'

'I'm sorry, what are you talking about?'

'Here, this.' He picked up a sheet of paper. 'You left this. Loads of names and weird stuff – words like lipstick and runes and rugs. It says "cream-coloured Maybach". Why?'

Seb took the paper off him. 'It's the way I work when I'm trying to solve a case. I write down the names of witnesses and suspects and everything even vaguely relevant to the investigation and try to make connections between them. It's an effective method.'

'But the Maybach, that's what I want to know about.'

'All right. Well a girl in Nuremberg, name of Hildegard Heiden, was last seen getting into a cream-coloured car, probably a Maybach. Her body was found at Hesselberg at the same place where Silke was taken. I didn't want to mention it – I thought you were both distraught enough as it was, without mentioning it.'

'My God, so you thought Silke was abducted by the killers of this other girl?'

'I did think that, yes. I still do.'

'So they were going to kill Silke, too! You should have told me!'

'But, Jurgen, I was trying to protect you both. I saw how distressed you both were. I didn't want to add fuel to the fire.'

'You should have said something.'

Seb threw up his hands. What could he say?

Jurgen seemed wound up like a clock. Finally he came out with it. 'There's something I have to tell you. Silke and I were given a lift to Hesselberg in such a car.'

'I thought you walked there.'

'Well, of course, I wanted you to think that. Thumbing a lift seemed like cheating.'

CHAPTER 45

Seb sat down opposite his son. 'Tell me more, Jurgen.'

'I realised we couldn't make it in time for the Frankentag. We had told my Hitler Youth troop and Silke's League of German Girls group that we would meet them there and it all seemed like a bit of an adventure. Silke and I just needed to get away on our own. It all went fine but we were getting behind and we realised we'd miss all the fun, so we decided to hitch a lift. This big Maybach came along, whizzed past us, but then braked and waited for us. It was too good to be true. Who wouldn't want a ride in a Maybach?'

'Carry on.'

'Well, I'm not a fool, I knew it was the sight of Silke that made them stop. They weren't going to stop for me, were they?'

'They? So there was more than one person in the car?'

'Yes, a man driving and a woman in the front passenger seat.'

'Can you describe them?'

'He was a big strong guy, older than you, maybe fifty, I don't know. A big face, small beard.'

Walter Regensdorf. It had to be him. 'And the woman?'

'Stiff, quite tall and slim. Not so talkative.'

Mutti always kept newspapers, often for weeks on end. She twisted them up and used them as firelighters in the wood-burning stove that warmed the kitchen. Seb was sure he had seen a picture of the Regensdorfs in one of the papers in the past few weeks; they frequently adorned the culture pages. The old papers lay in a tidy pile in a deep wooden box by the window. Seb quickly worked his way through them and came across the one he was thinking of, from late April. He smoothed it down on the table in front of Jurgen. The Regensdorfs were on the front page, pictured outside the theatre, both smiling for the camera.

'Was it these people?'

He didn't need to look closely. 'The man definitely, not the woman. Who is he? Why's he in the paper?'

As Seb thought, the woman must have been Irmgard Huber. 'His name is Walter Regensdorf. He's extremely wealthy.'

'And you think it might have been them – in the hoods and robes?'

'It's possible,' he said, all the while thinking it was certain. 'But think back, Jurgen – was there anything about them that troubled you when you met them?'

'Not at the time, but seeing those words there on your sheet of paper, it suddenly seemed sinister. Now I come to think of it, the man did keep looking at Silke in the rear-view mirror, so much so that she slid over towards me. But she just laughs about things like that; she's used to men looking at her. Everyone in my troop fancies her.'

'Did she say anything after the attack, anything to suggest she thought her assailants were the people from the car?'

'No. She won't talk to me about it. She won't even talk to her parents. I wanted to comfort her but I couldn't get close. That's why I couldn't stay at the Stutz house any longer.'

'In the car, did either of you reveal anything about yourself?'

'Well, they did ask her a few things. She just mentioned that her dad was a doctor and they asked his name, nothing more than that.'

'And she gave them his name?'

'Just Dr Stutz, that's all. Didn't give her address or where he worked.'

So they knew her father was Dr Stutz of Munich. That was plenty. With Regensdorf's contacts, that was more than enough to track someone down.

Dr Helmut Stutz answered the telephone and Seb quickly explained to him what had happened and what he had learnt.

'And you think they might come for Silke again?'

'Hopefully not, but it has to be a fear. There was obviously something about her that caught their eye.'

'But I can protect my house against this man and woman. I have an old pistol from the war – I'm sure my family is safe with me here.'

'It's not just them we have to worry about. This man has some unpleasant friends. Professional killers. They believe they are beyond the law, that they could break down your door in full sight of the police and nothing would happen to them. And they are probably right because they have BPP badges. Is there anywhere you could take Silke for a day or two? Somewhere secure and known only to you?'

'My mother-in-law, I suppose. She lives in a village near Rosenheim. But I need to stay here – I have my patients to look after. How long would this be for?'

'I don't know, Dr Stutz. But I promise I am not going to rest until it's sorted out.'

Putzi Hanfstaengl wasn't at the Brown House, but the night officer there told Seb that he *was* in Munich, probably at his home address, which they could not give out. They could put a call through to him, however.

'Don't worry, I know it. It's just over the river – I'll drive there.'

Fifteen minutes later, he pulled up outside Hanfstaengl's luxuriously appointed new-build in Pienzenauerstrasse, not far from the place where Rosie Palmer's body was discovered.

Hanfstaengl was at home. He didn't seem pleased to see Seb.

'Inspector Wolff, have you any idea what the time is? I have just finished my dinner and was enjoying a glass of bourbon and a few gramophone recordings with my wife. It is a rare treat for us to have some time together away from the cares of state.'

'Forgive me, sir. I would not have come unless I believed you were the only person who might help me.'

'Come in, man, come in.'

They settled in Hanfstaengl's book-lined study. A pile of the world's newspapers had been thrown on the floor. A benefit of his work overseeing the foreign press was that he was able to read what other countries thought of the Third Reich, not a privilege afforded the common man.

Hanfstaengl poured himself another tumbler of American whiskey, and one for Seb.

'Well, Inspector? This better be good.'

'I take it you heard what happened to Maria Regensdorf today, sir?'

'A great tragedy. She was one of my dearest friends.'

'Indeed, she said the same about you when I met her at the start of the Rosie Palmer investigation. But, sir, please tell me, do your feelings of affection for Frau Regensdorf extend to her husband?'

'That's a very direct and strange question, Inspector. But also, as it happens, a very astute one. No, is my answer. I never warmed to Walter. In truth, I think Maria made the worst error of her life when she wed the man. I saw a hardness and cruelty in him. Forged in him, perhaps, by his years at an English boarding school. I have met other upper-class Englishmen with the same haughty disregard for their fellow man. What do you know about him, Inspector?'

'I know that he is extremely rich and powerful, that he has funded the Party since the early twenties, that he is a Thulist and that he has published many tracts for both the party and the *Völkisch* movement.'

'Ah yes, Thule and the *Völkisch* movement. He was into all that ridiculous shit. Fancied himself a Viking god, perhaps. In fact he is an insignificant, arrogant and odious man. Born into great wealth, he managed to avoid risking his neck in the war and came out of it even wealthier than he went in, having secured wartime contracts. There was always something sinister about him. Before the war, his first wife drowned in the Mediterranean when they were on his yacht. It was unexplained and no body was found. I don't believe I am the only person who wondered . . .'

Seb took a good draught of the Bourbon. He understood what Hanfstaengl was saying and it gave him the impetus to have his own say, whatever the consequences. 'I didn't know he had a first wife, but I think he has now killed his second wife, Herr Hanfstaengl. I also believe he killed Rosie Palmer and another girl named Hilde-gard Heiden. In this he was aided and abetted by his secretary, Frau Irmgard Huber, and they have been protected by powerful forces within the political police and the SS.'

The words had tumbled out in a rush and had been precise, for these were his firm beliefs. There was no point in trying to soften the blow. If Hanfstaengl didn't believe him or did not take his part, then his career, his freedom and probably his life would be over. It was a risk he had to take because there was no other way to proceed.

'Carry on.'

'That's it, sir.'

'You have some sort of evidence?'

'Yes. Slender, perhaps, but it's there, and I believe in it unreservedly.'

'Are you going to share it with me?'

'Of course.' For the next ten minutes he went through the whole investigation. The car involved in the abduction of Hildegard Heiden, the similarity of her wounds and the marks on her body to those on Rosie Palmer, the attack on Silke Stutz and the car she travelled in to Hesselberg, his own abduction by Matthäus and Fuchs and their involvement in the murder of Caius Klammer, the hostility between Frau Huber and Rosie Palmer, the belief that Maria Regensdorf feared for her life.

'And that's it?'

'Yes, that's it.'

'Well, I can see why you have come to your conclusion, Detective, but it's all very circumstantial. My enthusiasm as a student was always for music and Goethe – the classics – but I know enough law to see the holes in your case.'

'But do you believe me?'

'If there is any suggestion my wonderful friend Maria was murdered, a price will be paid. But for the moment, let me sleep on it.'

'I fear I cannot wait another night.'

'If you want my help, then you have to.'

That wasn't enough for Seb. 'I'm sure you see my problem, sir. Given Herr Regensdorf's standing with the most powerful figures in Munich and wider Germany, how can he be brought to book? He has an iron ring around him and I am on the outside, powerless. Even my boss, Thomas Ruff, is powerless, added to which he has no stomach for the fight. But if we do nothing the killer will continue his depraved, murderous ways and young girls will die at his hands. What can I do? Please tell me.'

'As I said, I will give you my answer in due course. I have listened to you and you have given me much to consider, but I need time to work out the best course of action. You can see for yourself that this is not straightforward – it involves diplomacy and politics and has international implications.'

'What would you advise me to do while you sleep?'

'Don't take that tone with me, Wolff. Simply wait. And keep yourself safe.'

Easier said than done, thought Seb. A great deal easier said than done when the outlaws were in charge of the city. Perhaps he should go and find Ernie Pope and give him the full story. But then again, perhaps not. That way could lie death and destruction, not just for Seb but Mutti and Jurgen, too. The Nazi hierarchy was not to be goaded. One did not poke a sleeping bear with a stick and hope to survive.

'And find me another piece of evidence,' Hanfstaengl said, his dark, glowering eyes piercing into Seb's. 'Something solid and conclusive. Something I might show to the Führer.'

CHAPTER 46

He parked outside the Haus Gertrud hostel. All the lights were on inside, which caught his attention but perhaps wasn't unusual in a group of young students. He was here because he had had a thought. It was a long shot, but better than nothing perhaps. He recalled when he first met Frances de Pole that she mentioned her mother being an old friend of Maria Regensdorf. Was it possible – just possible – that the person who put Frances up to writing in lipstick on Hexie's shirt when they went swimming was that very same friend? Maria Regensdorf was certainly there that night.

And if so, were the words – *sex magic* – supposed to be some sort of message that the tragic woman was trying to get to Seb, as a police officer? Less a warning, more a clue.

So he needed to talk to Frances de Pole, try to prise more information out of her. Now that Maria was dead, perhaps the young woman might realise the potential gravity involved in an action she had considered no more than a playful prank.

The main room of the hostel was bustling with activity. He spotted Clarice Goodall and approached her.

'Something up, Miss Goodall? I was looking for Frances de Pole.'

'She's gone missing. We aren't sure what to do.'

The evening was warm, but Seb went cold. 'You'd better explain.'

'Well, we were all supposed to be going out, but there's no sign of her. She's not in her room and she hasn't left a message. It's most unlike her.'

'Could she be with a boyfriend?'

'That's possible, but unlikely given that she was here this afternoon when we were arranging it. In fact it was all her idea. We were going to go off to the Sterneckerbrau, then a club or two. Probably one of those SS places – they always let us in. It's just rather strange, Inspector.'

'And no one here knows anything?'

'No. I suppose we'll just have to go without her and leave a note in case she can catch us up.'

'Has she said anything else to you about recent events?'

'What do you mean?'

'Well, the murder of Rosie Palmer, of course, but also you might have heard today's news of the death of Frau Regensdorf, where Rosie was lodging.'

'I did hear something about that. Didn't she fall down the stairs?'

'That's what the police are trying to establish. I just know that Frances had a family connection to Maria Regensdorf. Did she say anything to you? Did she have any theories?'

'I don't think so.'

'Who is close to Frances here?'

'Bobo is closest, I suppose.'

'And is she here now?'

'In her room moping. Adolf won't be back in Munich until Saturday or Sunday for the House of German Art topping out ceremony. By then, Bobo will have worked herself into a fever of excitement but for now she won't leave her room. She really is a sad creature.'

Seb found Unity Mitford in her room. Her pet rat was running down her left arm, then up her right arm. She turned to Seb with an insincere smile.

'Would you like a go? Ratular is very friendly.'

'Perhaps not just now. The other students are worried that Frances de Pole seems to be missing. I wondered if you had any idea where she might be.'

'Not a clue. None of my business.'

'There was something else I wanted to ask you, something that has been nagging at me for a few days now.'

Unity bent down and replaced Ratular in his cage with great care, then stood to her full impressive height, which was not far off Seb's. 'Go on.'

'What is your relationship to the Regensdorf household?'

Unity's curiously bland face contorted momentarily, as though trying to make sense of the question. 'You had better explain, Inspector.'

For the first time, Seb noticed how poor her teeth were; yellow and uneven. 'You are friendly with them, yes? With Walter Regensdorf and his family?'

'What makes you say that?'

'Well, you know everyone who's anyone in Munich, don't you?'

'Yes, of course I know them. Walter is a good National Socialist, an important member of the movement. I admire him greatly. Where is this going?'

'You were very quick to come to me with your suspicions about Karl Friedlander after the murder of Rosie Palmer.'

'I knew he was guilty.'

'Did Herr Regensdorf discuss the matter with you?'

'Why would he have done something like that?'

'He must have wanted the case solved. Miss Palmer was under his care. He was a friend of her late father, I believe. Did he perhaps suggest to you that it would be your duty to bring Karl Friedlander to my attention?'

Unity didn't pause in her reply. 'No,' she said. 'I am quite capable of thinking things through for myself.'

'But perhaps you discussed your suspicions with him. Perhaps he suggested that Sergeant Winter and I were the people to contact?'

Seb smiled but she didn't reply and he realised that he was going to get no more out of her. She was telling the truth, however: Walter Regensdorf had not made the suggestion that Friedlander was the guilty party, but that did not mean that someone else in his household was not responsible. Very convenient to have a ready-made suspect for the police to investigate, thus shifting their attention away from the true killer.

'Heil Hitler, Miss Mitford,' he said, snapping a salute. 'My compliments to your rat.'

He was desperately worried about the disappearance of Frances de Pole. He was sure that in some way she was a witness to what had happened inside the Villa Saphir, just as Maria Regensdorf had been. Had Maria said something to her? Or did they merely fear that she might have done, given the closeness of Maria to Frances's family. The killers were covering their traces.

Putzi Hanfstaengl wanted to sleep on it. But this was happening now. The morning would be too late.

The warmth of the day had given way to a light summer shower. To the south in the far distance, lightning broke over the Alps. Seb had parked the car in a side street and was waiting at the corner of Brienner Strasse and Maximilianplatz.

'Good evening, Inspector.'

Seb nodded at Sergeant Winter. 'We have a decision to make. I believe they have taken another of the English girls. Her name is Frances de Pole. It's possible she's alive, but where is she and what are they planning?'

'Do you think they've gone to Hesselberg?'

'That was my first thought, in which case we are certainly too late. It's close to a three-hour drive in a fast, reliable car, and my borrowed Opel is neither of those.'

'What then?'

'That's what I'm asking you.'

'Could she be at the Villa Saphir?'

'Yes, she could. But knocking on the door and asking about her isn't going to get us very far.'

'No. I see that.'

'So we need to find another way in.'

'What about the cars? They must have a garage somewhere.'

'Good thought. It's behind the villa. Huber told us about it.'

Momentarily, a spurt of lightning cast electric shadows all down the street. Across the road, a group of SS men were laughing and talking as they made their way eastwards in the direction of the city centre. Seb and Winter clicked their heels and saluted them, a greeting which was returned in kind.

'I don't like lightning,' Winter said.

'How many people do you know have been struck?'

'None.'

'There you go then. By the way, there will be dogs. Guard dogs.'

'I like dogs even less than I like lightning. What do we do, kill them?'

'The dogs or Regensdorf?'

'Once again, Inspector, you cannot resist making light of a matter that might be the death of us.'

'Are you breathing? Can you feel the tips of your fingers?'

'Yes, of course.'

'Then you're not dead, so stop complaining. In fact, just maintain utter silence from here on in.' He put his hands into his jacket pockets and handed something to Winter, something he had collected at home on the way to his meeting with the sergeant, who now recoiled in horror.

'My God, what is it?'

'Pork belly. I have some, too. If a dog approaches, throw it in their direction. Much too good for them, but hopefully they'll find it more appetising than our balls.'

'Were you a burglar before you joined the police, Inspector?'

'I have had one or two jobs, but not that.'

They walked along Brienner Strasse, watching all the while for anyone connected with Regensdorf, but the evening was quiet and the road deserted, save for the two sentries on guard outside the Brown House, neither of whom responded to their salutes.

Ahead of them, the obelisk on the circular open space of Karolinenplatz stood dark and sharp in the rain. Further beyond, the ghostly outlines of builders' machines and vehicles blocked their view of Königsplatz and the Propyläen city gate.

Seb led the way, skirting the Villa Saphir looking for the path out of which cars must proceed. It was easily found and, beyond it, along a short roadway, the large garage was obvious. Two cars were parked outside, neither of them among the three that Stefan Huber had mentioned; they must be locked away being the most expensive and sought after.

'You stay just by the gatepost. I'll go to the garage. Keep still in the shade of the trees and you are unlikely to be seen. Don't use your gun unless your life is in imminent danger. If we kill anyone in here, we're unlikely to avoid the guillotine. Did you bring the torches?'

Winter handed him one from his pocket.

'New batteries?'

'Yes.'

Seb flicked the switch on and off. It had a good, bright beam.

The gate was padlocked, but it wasn't high and Seb climbed over it with ease. The garage was a hundred metres from the house, the two buildings hidden from each other by tall hedging at the bottom of a long garden, which Seb knew to be planted very much in the English style with flower beds and lawns and a mature spreading cedar. He had seen it from the windows when examining Rosie Palmer's room.

It occurred to him that Walter Regensdorf must have spent weekends and holidays at his friends' houses while at public school in England to have developed a taste for such gardens.

Large barn-style doors enclosed the garage; there was a single smaller postern to the side. He pulled the handle down and it opened. He closed it behind him and switched on the torch.

The place was much as Stefan Huber, the chauffeur-cum-mechanic, had described it, having all the amenities of a professionally run garage. All three cars that he had mentioned were there: the Rolls-Royce Phantom, the Mercedes 770 – both black – and the massive cream-coloured Maybach Zeppelin. Seb put his hand on the engine compartment of each car; none seemed to have been driven particularly recently, though there was a little warmth under the bonnet of the eight-litre Maybach.

Which almost certainly meant that no one from the Villa Saphir had gone to Hesselberg. They were here, but was Frances here too?

Back at the gate, he signalled Winter to follow him. 'The cars are accounted for and none of their engines are hot. Also, no dogs – so far,' he whispered. 'But we're going into the back garden of the house itself. There will be dogs there.'

They found a gap in the hedge and slipped cautiously into the garden. Seb could sense Winter's fear.

The back of the house was partially lit. The main downstairs room had a large window, curtained but still exuding a little light at the edges. Upstairs, two rooms had lights on, and Seb reckoned that one of them had been Rosie's.

Winter stayed Seb with a hand to his elbow. 'That door on the ground floor, on the right-hand side, goes into the kitchen. I made a note of it this morning when I spoke to the servants.'

The door was dark, as was the small window set into the wall next to it. It was late and the kitchen staff must surely have gone home or to their rooms if they had quarters in the villa itself.

'We'll split up. You go first, I'll move to the side and follow.' Seb pointed at the door. 'Go.'

He was expecting the soft thud of paws on grass, the ferocious barking, the bared teeth and growls. The sheer power of a mastiff? The speed and ferocity of a Dobermann pinscher? The indomitable aggression of a Rottweiler? He was expecting this – and it came. From the far side of the house.

They were Rottweilers. Two of them. It was a breed he had always loved and knew well. Calm and placid at best, deadly at worst. These two were in full attack mode. This was their territory and they would defend it to the death.

But as they bounded forward, they weren't barking. And both came towards *him*, not Winter.

Seb tossed the meat down for them when they were three metres away. He didn't back off a centimetre. Their reaction to the meat was instant – they went for the food, as if that was what they had been hunting down all along.

Rottweilers were natural guards, but these ones hadn't been trained further. Hadn't been trained to ignore gifts of food or to attack an incomer who did not shy away.

His eyes turned towards Winter. He was now only an outline in the shadow of the house but Seb gave two short flashes of his torch as the sign that all was well. He then leant down and patted the two dogs, letting them know that he was the master and no threat to them. They were too busy tearing the meat apart to take any notice of him and, within seconds, he was at the kitchen door with Winter.

The door was unlocked and they stepped inside. Seb took out his pistol. He had no intention of using it, but one never knew.

CHAPTER 47

Frances de Pole couldn't move, couldn't see, couldn't make a sound. She was bound tightly, both arms and legs, and blindfolded and gagged, lying on her side on the wooden floor. The evening was warm enough, but she was bitterly cold and shivering. Her shoulder was in agony but she couldn't even turn over.

The pain was bad, but the terror was far worse.

She was going to be killed.

The thought that she had climbed into the car of her own volition was tearing her sanity to shreds. There had been a moment of hesitation, hadn't there? But she had cast her doubts aside, for she knew the man and why wouldn't she trust him? Nothing could happen to Frankie. She was the life and soul of every party, the girl who never said no to a good time. She was half English, half German and spoke both languages fluently. She could go anywhere in this town and a friend was always at hand.

And then . . . what had happened then in the car? There must have been someone in the seat behind, crouching low, thrusting a hood over her head, injecting her with something. She recalled panic and then a curious blur before unconsciousness.

Now she was awake and she was about to die. She tried to calm her breathing, but the gag was tight in her mouth and she could scarcely get enough air into her nostrils. She couldn't even cry, let alone cry out.

She thought of Rosie. Was this the way it had been for her? This hopeless terror?

She thought of home in the Oxfordshire countryside. Her mama, so German in many ways – her precision, her taste in food, her Bavarian Catholicism – but also so desperate to be English. She had married her father in 1910, and even when Europe exploded into war four years later she had never had any doubts that her place was in England with her new family rather than with her family of birth in Germany. Frankie understood that she had suffered greatly for it in those war years.

She spoke good English, but her southern German accent was strong and she was shunned in the village in the beautiful Vale of the White Horse. The butcher and the baker simply ignored her, wouldn't take her orders, until she gave up going into their shops and had food sent from Fortnum's in London instead. At least her best friends stood by her, but even that must have been strained at times, especially when they lost sons at the Somme and Passchendaele.

Daddy was away fighting, of course, and so Mama was alone with Frankie and her younger brother. The fact that her husband had a distinguished war as an artillery officer and was mentioned in dispatches, helped a bit, but it was never going to be easy. And when peace was declared, he rejoined the Foreign Office and rose to great heights.

If only he were here now to help her. Daddy. Her beloved father. *Please*, she begged God, *please let him come and save me from the horror.*

The house was quiet. Seb wondered who was here. Walter Regens-dorf, of course. And his secretary/housekeeper Irmgard Huber. Had they retired to bed, worn out by the events of the day? Had they, perhaps, retired to the same bed?

Had they finished their filthy work and disposed of another corpse?

Seb closed the garden door softly, then removed his shoes and indicated Winter to do the same. They both switched on their torches and proceeded through the entrails of the great villa, first the work rooms – kitchen, pantry, boot room, laundry, scullery. All were in darkness and no sound emanated from elsewhere in the house.

Slowly, with great caution, they went through all the rooms on the ground floor – an immense reception room clearly designed for important events and, next to it, an exquisite dining room with a table that would seat twenty or more guests with ease, the master's study, a smaller writing room and an administrative office that would have served as Frau Huber's place of work when she wasn't taking dictation or whatever it was she did. And, of course, the library where they had first been asked to wait by Maria Regensdorf all those days ago.

The books hadn't meant much to him then, but now they did: Guido von List, Helena Blavatsky, Aleister Crowley, all those *Völkisch* tracts that served to tell a tale of what sort of man lived here. By your friends you shall be known, but perhaps even truer, *by your books you shall be known*. List and Blavatsky, Crowley and others – purveyors of mad occult, sexual, mystic, sadistic nonsense. Seb saw now what he hadn't seen then.

Back in the front hallway, he pointed his torch at the staircase then down at the floor. The blood and hair had gone now.

Seb and Winter began to climb the stairs. Seb feared the wood might creak but in fact it was so solidly built that it made not a sound and their sock-clad feet were as quiet as cat paws.

As they reached the top, the landing was suddenly flooded with light.

Walter Regensdorf was standing there, fully dressed. His hand was at the wall where he had just flicked the switch.

'You could have knocked at the front door, you know. And you can put your guns away.'

'Herr Regensdorf,' Seb said, for want of something better to say. He did not accept the invitation to lower his pistol.

'Were you expecting someone else, perhaps?'

'We are looking for a girl. Frances de Pole.'

'Ah yes, my dear departed wife knew her mother. Well, I don't believe I've seen her. In fact, I can think of no circumstances under which she might be here. There are maids, of course, and manservants, kitchen staff, my secretary – all now in their rooms and probably sleeping soundly – but no one named Frances de Pole. You have had a wasted trip, and a highly illegal one. I hope you haven't harmed my dogs.'

'Your dogs are fine but I can tell you they are not well trained. Guard dogs should not be diverted by a slab of meat.' He eyed up his jacket and tie. 'Were you going somewhere?'

'To bed. As all honest men should at this time of night. So what do we do now, gentlemen? I'm not going to call Adolf for he has the cares of the world on his shoulders and he needs his sleep. But I could have ten heavily armed SS men here within five minutes, and that would be the end of you both.'

'No, you won't do that. We are going to look in every room in this house. I think we should start with your bedroom. Is that it?' Seb indicated the open door beside the light switch.

'Do come in.' His voice was urbane, almost that of an English gentlemen, but beneath the skin, there was murderous fury. It seemed impossible to Seb that both he and Walter Regensdorf should come out of this encounter alive.

They searched his room, the wardrobes, his en suite bathroom, under the bed, in a linen chest and found nothing.

'Stay here with him, Sergeant. I'll search alone.'

'Yes, sir.'

'Don't take your gun off him for a moment.'

'Your time's up, Wolff – your uncle won't be able to save you this time.' Regensdorf was wound like a coil, his voice no longer cultivated but seething with bile. He turned towards Winter, whose right hand was gripped like iron on the butt of his Walther. 'And you, what manner of creature are you? You bring shame on your service and your people.'

His people, thought Seb. Thankfully, this man had no knowledge of Winter's people.

'If he tries anything, Sergeant, shoot him in the leg. If that doesn't stop him, go for his chest.'

Seb left the room and, for the next hour went up through the five storeys of the villa. He explored the bedrooms and the bath-rooms, woke servants – male and female – from their slumbers and questioned them. He looked in the attics and the corridors and returned downstairs to search for cellars or basements, but found none.

This was bad, very bad. There was no way out of this. Once he left this building, he and Winter would be arrested within a short time. Dachau would likely follow, or trial and execution if some capital offence could be framed against them. He felt a surge of guilt for bringing Hans Winter into this scheme.

Returning to the bedroom, he found Regensdorf smirking as though he knew exactly what Seb would discover.

'No sign of your secretary Frau Huber.'

'That's hardly my business, Wolff. People come and go – they have lives of their own.'

Seb walked across to the telephone and ripped it from the wall. 'Come, Sergeant, let's get out of this hellhole.'

'You won't get very far.'

'Don't worry about us, Herr Regensdorf. You're not getting out of this a free man.'

'You know, Wolff, I saw you at the Thule meeting and I wondered what you were doing there as you clearly understand nothing. You do not understand the old ways of our race, the blood honour, duty and sacrifice of Germany and German people. There are mysteries that are so far beyond your comprehension that you are nothing but a naive child.'

'Sex magic?'

'What do you know of that? What do you know of the gods?'

'More than I want to.' He nodded to Winter. 'This place gives me the creeps.' Still carrying the telephone, Seb took the key from the inside of the door and closed it and locked it as they left. 'That'll give us a bit of time. And we need it, badly. Let's get our shoes.'

'What do we do then, Inspector?'

'I was sure we would find her here. Maybe we didn't look everywhere.'

'Perhaps there are outhouses.'

'We can't look again now. His SS friends will be here any minute.'

Either they didn't know she was fluent in German or they didn't care. Perhaps they said these things out of cruelty, to intensify her terror, if that was possible.

How many voices were there? Definitely one woman and at least one man. They were talking about murdering her, slitting her throat at Hesselberg. Saying these things casually, as though they might discuss when to slaughter the Christmas pig.

She heard the words 'sex magic' and thought of the message Maria had begged her to write in lipstick on the blouse of Inspector Wolff's girlfriend. What had she become involved in? Why hadn't she spoken more openly to Wolff? Perhaps he would have understood what was really happening. Perhaps he could have protected her.

Frances was still bound, still on the floor, still unable to see or speak, but she could hear perfectly and she knew that her fate was imminent and that she was powerless to stop it.

She felt hands. Damp, clammy hands on her skin and through the thin fabric of her summer dress and tried in vain to wriggle away. The hands were lifting her from the floor as though she weighed nothing. A man's hands and arms. She knew it was a man from the smell of beer and smoke and armpit sweat and from the strength of his arms. He slung her onto his back like a coalman with a sack.

'This will be the best,' the woman said. 'We will have all the time in the world, no hurry, no interruption.'

'If you say so,' the man grunted, his lack of interest evident. 'To be honest, Irmgard, I don't give a monkey's fuck so long as I get my money.'

The woman's voice? Was that the stern-looking secretary from the Villa Saphir? Was her name Irmgard? She had only met her once and seemed to recall she was called Huber, but that was a surname. Beyond that, voices were difficult when not spoken in your first tongue. Frankie was fluent in German, but English was the language of home.

CHAPTER 48

The servants had all gathered in the front hall, mostly in their nightclothes. In silence, they gazed wide-eyed at the two officers and their handguns and they drew apart to let them pass to the front door.

Outside, the air was fresh. Seb stopped suddenly at the bottom of the steps as though a light had come on in his brain. 'Of course,' he said.

'Inspector?'

'Why didn't I see it before? God in heaven, perhaps I'm losing my touch. Come on – time is against us.'

'What is it?'

'The brakes on my Lancia, of course. They were tampered with when I was at Hesselberg. Who could have done that?'

'Someone who knows about cars.'

'Precisely. Most people wouldn't have any idea how to do such a thing. I had thought it must be your BPP friends, but there's a far more likely candidate: the chauffeur Stefan Huber. He seemed a harmless, lazy slob, married to an unfaithful woman he despised and had nothing to do with all this. But by his own words, no one in Munich knows more about cars.'

'You think he did it?'

'I think I made a mistake about him. I think he's up to his thick, bovine neck in it. Let's move, Sergeant.'

They collected the old Opel and Seb drove at speed through the damp streets. In the distance, he heard an occasional clap of thunder, but nothing over Munich itself, no more lightning, and the rain was little more than a soft, summer drizzle.

A few minutes later, he pulled up with a juddering of brakes at the Hubers' apartment. A small black car parked just in front of them was departing as they climbed out of the Opel, entered the building and hurried upstairs to the first floor.

There was no answer. The door was unlocked and they went in. 'Hello?' Seb called but there was no reply. The apartment was empty, save for the heat and stench of sweat and beer and smoke. Someone had been here very recently. They must have left within the last minute or two.

'That car, Inspector – just as you were pulling up at the kerb it was pulling away.'

It had to be Irmgard Huber and her husband. But what of Frances de Pole? Was she with them? Was she being held by them? Was she alive? Where were they going? To pick up Regens-dorf, perhaps, and the Maybach. A trip to Hesselberg, the sacred site. The place of sacrifice. That would explain why he was fully dressed at a time when most people were heading for bed. Seb shook his head; his imagination was running away with him.

And yet . . . and yet, there was a twisted logic to the thought.

'It's our best hope,' Seb said.

They ran from the room, down the dark steps, back to the Opel. Seb took the wheel, skidded away into a sharp U-turn, then ham-mered through the gears, using every ounce of muscle to contort more speed out of the machine. The tyres were almost slick and slid like skates on the rain-wet roads, but they saw the black car ahead. At least, they hoped it was the car.

They caught it at Theresienstrasse, just as it was manoeuvring to turn right into Barer Strasse – heading towards Karolinenplatz and the Villa Saphir. But the driver spotted them in his mirror and, without hesitation, threw the vehicle in the opposite direction, swerving away left with a screeching of tyres, cutting up an oncom-ing car and hurtling onto the wrong side of the road heading north.

Seb did the same, the Opel's offside tyres leaving the road and almost turning the car over. But he used his own weight and pushed Winter sideways until the offside wheels thudded down on the wet road and the car veered away, barely in control.

Up ahead, the black car was gaining speed and seemed about to turn left into Hess-strasse. It would be too quick for the old Opel, but a heavy lorry came out of the dark, trundling south, blocking its path. The black car braked and its rear wheels spun. The car slid and wobbled and crunched into the rear corner of the long vehicle.

The lorry driver carried on, blissfully unaware that he had even been hit; his vehicle was so large and heavy that the collision must have felt like little more than a brush of the kerb. But it had taken all impetus from the black car and Seb had no hesitation, he was on it in a moment and simply drove into the side of the spinning vehicle, crushing it sideways – up onto the pavement and into a shop window. In a screech of metal and shattering glass, both cars juddered to a halt.

Seb and Winter leapt out, both with pistols in their hands. There were two people in the front seats of the black car, a man and a woman, clearly stunned. Seb dragged open the driver's door. Stefan Huber sat there, dazed, his bulk filling the space, his hands still on the wheel, blood trickling from his nose.

'Out,' Seb said, his pistol aimed directly at the man's head. 'With your hands up.'

'Jesus Christus, what is this?'

Seb grabbed the man's collar and pulled him out of the car, pushing him down flat onto the stone paving. He put his foot on the man's broad back. 'Don't move or I'll blow your brains out.'

On the other side of the car, Winter was rather more gentle in removing Frau Huber.

Too gentle. She ducked to the side, wrenched herself free from his grasp and ran.

'Winter, here!' Seb shouted. 'Keep this man down. If he moves, shoot him.'

Seb saw Irmgard Huber disappearing into the darkness behind the New Pinakothek, one of the great art museums that graced the city. He ran and he knew he would probably outstrip her so long as he didn't lose her, for he had always been a runner.

But where in the name of God was she? One moment he saw her, the next she was gone. He stopped and listened to the night. At first, he heard nothing, then the soft soughing of rapid breathing. He turned his gaze in the direction of the sound, straining his eyes into the dark. There she was, a still, almost invisible shadow silhouetted flat against the museum wall.

He moved towards her and she moved too, breaking into a run. But she wasn't quick enough and within moments he was on her, grabbing at her arm, pulling her back. He put the gun to her head.

'Where is she?'

'You're not going to shoot me.'

'No?'

'Shoot an unarmed woman in cold blood?'

'Try me.' He started pulling her back in the direction of the road. 'Come on.'

A small crowd was gathering around the wreckage of the two cars. Irmgard Huber's husband was still flat on the ground. Winter had cuffed his wrists behind his back. 'No one else? No sign of the girl?'

Winter shook his head.

'Have you looked in the car?'

'No.'

Seb pushed Frau Huber into Winter's orbit and handed him his own handcuffs. 'Don't let her go this time.'

The doors of the black car were wide open but there was no sign of life. He peered into the back. No sign of life. He was about to turn away, but then he noticed a tightly bound parcel in the footwell. Except it wasn't a parcel, it was a human being. With a blonde bob.

He turned to Winter. 'It's her.' He was thinking, *please let her be alive*. 'Keep your gun on those murderous dogs. If they make a move, shoot them dead. No hesitation.' He climbed into the cramped rear of the car and gently moved the bound figure of Frances de Pole. He knew instantly from her warmth and her racing heartbeat that she was alive. He spoke soothingly to her in English. 'You're safe now, Frankie. It's Seb Wolff. I just need to untie you.'

She was bound so tightly that releasing her took five minutes – untying her arms and legs and removing the blindfold and the gag. He lifted her shaking body out of the car and helped her to her feet.

'You're safe now,' he repeated, 'I promise you. Just stand there and get your breath back.'

The small crowd was becoming larger, watching the scene unfold with astonishment. Women in nightdresses with their arms folded, men with their hands in their pockets or smoking cigarettes, all gawping.

Seb enlisted one of the men, a large fellow with an SA cap, and showed him his badge. 'Help my sergeant get these two felons to Ettstrasse. They are to be held for kidnap and conspiracy to commit murder. I have to get medical help for this young woman.'

'Yes, Officer.' The man seemed thrilled to be included in the drama.

Seb turned to the rest of the crowd. 'Does anyone have a vehicle – car or van? We need to get to hospital.'

Frances shook her head. 'I don't want to go to hospital.'

'I'm sorry, but that's where you're going.'

'No. Please no. I just want to stay with you.'

'I'll be there. Don't worry.'

'They were going to kill me.'

'They can't harm you now.'

Rolling thunder echoed across the city street.

Seb stayed in the hospital all night. Frances was sedated and put in a room by herself. Seb sat on a chair at the side of her bed, watching her, protecting her.

He wanted to get to the Presidium to interrogate Irmgard and Stefan Huber. He had much to ask them, but his overriding duty for the moment was to be here for this poor girl. She was alone in a strange country and when she woke from her sedation it was important that she see a face she could trust.

He would also have liked to go to the ward a few doors down to visit Hexie, but that would have to wait and, anyway, she was almost certainly asleep. Hexie was made of strong stuff; she could look after herself.

There was one other thing that needed doing as a matter of urgency: the arrest of Walter Regensdorf. It was a prospect that filled him with apprehension. Did they truthfully have a strong enough case against him? Much depended on whether either of the Hubers were willing to speak against the man, implicate him in their foul designs.

Perhaps a suggestion that denouncing their boss might save them from the executioner's blade might reap some reward.

Soon after dawn, Donald Gainer the British consul-general arrived at the hospital. Seb had asked the duty doctor to put through a call to him a couple of hours earlier. Frances was still asleep so the two men met outside her room so as not to disturb her.

'All I know is what the doctor told me on the telephone, Inspector Wolff – that an English girl was in trouble and you wanted me to come here urgently.'

Seb told him a short version of what had happened. 'Hopefully when she wakes up and is ready to talk, we will get a full version from Miss de Pole. I haven't been able to question her.'

'Good man, thank you for summoning me so promptly.'

'You will have to care for her, sir. She has had a dreadful experience and will not feel safe until she is home with her family in England. Just being bound the way she was, unable to move or see or speak, yet knowing all the time that she would be killed. I would not wish such a thing on my worst enemy.'

'Quite.'

From inside the room, they heard a sound, like a groan and they went back in. Frances was struggling to sit up against her pillows. Her eyes were half open and she was evidently tearful and in some pain.

Seb smiled at her. 'I believe you know Mr Gainer, the British consul-general.'

She nodded bleakly.

'He will be looking after you when the doctors release you from hospital.'

Gainer touched the back of her hand gently. 'You will be staying at my residence and you will be completely safe. No harm can come to you now.'

'Before I leave you in Mr Gainer's hands, Miss de Pole, I must beg you to answer one question: how did you come to be abducted?'

'I feel such a fool. I was offered a lift by a man I knew and even though I hesitated, I accepted it. Then I was attacked from behind. After that . . . nothing.'

'You're not a fool.'

'But after what happened to Rosie . . .'

'You say it was a man you knew?'

She nodded. 'Walter Regensdorf.'

'Thank you,' Seb said.

At last he had the link. Not just the evidence that Putzi Hanf-staengl was demanding, but proof positive, the testimony of a reliable witness. Seb looked at Donald Gainer and saw sheer astonishment in his eyes.

'There was one other thing I should have told you, Herr Wolff. It was Maria who begged me to write those words on your girl-friend's blouse. She asked me to write "sex magic murder", but I couldn't bring myself to write that third word.'

CHAPTER 49

Seb arrived at the Presidium late in the morning after a quick visit to Hexie, who was out of bed and about to be taken home. He hugged her, told her he would come and see her at her mother's in the evening and then he went for a short sleep, wash, shave and food before the trip to police headquarters.

Sergeant Winter was bleary-eyed and almost asleep at his desk. He shook him by the hand. 'We have him, Hans, we have the bastard. The English girl confirmed it was Regensdorf and Mr Gainer heard her say it. I can't wait to see his arrogant, depraved face when I arrive on his doorstep and arrest the swine. We have him, God damn it.'

'Except we don't, Inspector. He's vanished.'

'What do you mean?'

'We've already tried to pick him up, but he wasn't there. When the Hubers didn't call for him with the girl, he must have panicked. Knew he was done for. Probably taken off in one of his fancy cars, probably has his own aeroplane, too. Likely already sunning himself on the Riviera.'

'Who went to the house?'

'Ruff sent men to bring him in for questioning a couple of hours ago. He wasn't there, and the servants knew nothing.'

'No, I won't believe it. We had him, Sergeant, we had him. He can't have slipped through our fingers.'

Winter shrugged. 'Anyway, the boss wants you. Can I go and get some sleep now? I can't think straight.'

'Be back here at six.'

Seb made his way up to the fifth floor. Deputy President of Police Thomas Ruff was not smiling, nor did he seem angry. But he was pacing, his default mode.

'I suppose I have to congratulate you, Wolff.'

'Thank you, sir.'

'You saved a girl's life.'

Seb nodded. There was a 'but' coming.

'But you left the Munich Criminal Police up to its neck in foul-smelling sewage. How will this all be explained in a court of law? Who will not see the link to the death of Miss Palmer, damn it? Do you imagine the Führer will wish the world to think our justice system executes the innocent?'

'That is a matter for better minds than mine to deal with, sir. Herr Hanfstaengl, for instance.'

'Have they picked up Herr Regensdorf yet? I wanted to question him myself after Sergeant Winter told me what had happened.'

'Still no sign of him, sir.'

Ruff stopped pacing and stood looking out of the window, scratching his chin, then turned to Seb. 'Perhaps it were better if he is never found.'

Seb had Frau Huber brought to him from her cell. Her eyes were cold, bright and defiant. She sat across the table from him, in handcuffs.

He questioned her for half an hour and she said not a word. Not a single answer. She just sat on the high-backed wooden chair, her face a mask of stone, and looked through her interrogator into some unknown distance.

'Well,' Seb said at last. 'It makes no difference whether you talk or not. We have all the evidence we need and you will be sentenced to death.' He nodded to the constable who stood behind her at the door. 'Return Frau Huber to her cell. She is to remain in handcuffs and shackles. I don't want her taking her own life.'

'Yes, sir.'

'And bring Herr Huber to me.'

Seb got a coffee and returned to the interview rooms. Ten minutes later, the constable appeared.

'You had better come quickly, sir. The suspect Stefan Huber has been found hanging from the bars of his cell window.'

'Is he alive or dead?'

'I think dead, sir. But the doctor has been called anyway.'

'Damn it. Double the guard on the woman.'

In the afternoon, he called Martin at the garage. 'Any progress on my beautiful Lancia?'

'I've worked my magic already, Detective. Perfectly fine to drive, but could still do with a bit of bodywork to make her like new. How's the little Opel been?'

'It's had a bit of a crash. Probably removed to the police pound. I'll get it to you in due course. Just let me know how much the repairs will be.'

'May not be worth the effort, but I'll take a look. You haven't been having much luck with your motors, have you?'

Or various other things, Seb thought. But there was good news: Hexie was out of hospital, Frances de Pole was alive and Regensdorf was, hopefully, no longer a danger to the women of Bavaria. But he'd only believe that for certain when the man was under lock and key.

'Any chance I could have the Lancia this afternoon? The bodywork can wait.'

'I'll get her to you within the hour. Ettstrasse or Ainmüller-strasse?'

'Ettstrasse. Thanks, Martin.' He replaced the phone and it rang again immediately.

'Wolff, murder team.'

'Hanfstaengl here. I believe you saved the English girl. What's the story?'

'The whole story, sir? We may never know. Regensdorf has fled, his secretary won't say a word and her husband, the chauffeur, has topped himself.'

'Keep it like that, Inspector.'

'What do you mean, Herr Hanfstaengl?'

'Exactly what I said.' The line went dead.

He held the phone for a few moments. He had a bad feeling, a knot in his stomach that he couldn't adequately explain.

Two faces he had no wish to see were drifting past his office. They both turned to him and smirked. One of them, Rudi Fuchs, was limping. The other one, Lukas Matthäus, had bruises on his forehead and a sticking plaster across his nose. Slowly, he drew a finger across his throat.

'Where are we going, inspector?'

'Patience, Sergeant. Be patient.'

Seb had his beloved Lancia back. She still looked a little forlorn about the front end, but she drove just fine. They were heading eastwards out of Munich. The damp and chill of the previous night had gone and this early evening was a proper late June day in Bavaria.

The Ebersberger Forest, an expanse of woodland the size of a city, looked lush and inviting, very unlike the last time he had been here when it was dark and foreboding. Seb drove along the same track that Fuchs and Matthäus had brought him.

They went deep and straight until the path was divided and he took the left fork.

'We can't be that far from that village where I picked you up.'

'Not too far. Two or three kilometres' walk, but we're not going there. I trust you don't believe in ghosts, because legend suggests there are quite a few in these woods, especially the White Lady.'

Winter laughed, an edge of nervousness all too evident.

It was still full daylight, so no need for torches or even headlights this early in the evening. Seb stopped. This was the place. Ahead of him he could see the piled earth where he had dug with the entrenching tool. Last time it had seemed eerie and full of ghosts here. Now it might be a restful place for a couple of dog-walkers to stop and enjoy the quiet.

'They brought me here to kill me and bury me,' Seb said, half to himself, half to his sergeant. 'They made me dig my own grave. They told me there were other bodies buried here, and I believed them.'

'*They?*'

'Your BPP friends Matthäus and Fuchs. I've brought a couple of spades and some bottles of beer. We can do a little digging, see what we can find.'

They didn't need to dig.

The body of Walter Regensdorf lay stretched out and uncovered in the shallow grave that Seb had prepared for himself. The head had been cleanly removed and lay half a metre from the rest of the corpse.

'Not quite the Riviera, is it?' Seb said.

CHAPTER 50

It was hardly worth investigating the death of Walter Regensdorf because nothing was going to come of it. Someone high up had decided he was an embarrassment and had deployed Matthäus and Fuchs to dispose of him in the way prescribed by law for the execution of murderers. The way that Karl Friedlander had also met his end.

Someone high up.

Had Putzi Hanfstaengl put that call through to the boss, or had he enlisted the help of Himmler or Heydrich? Or someone closer to home perhaps – Uncle Christian? The richest, most powerful man in Munich? Seb could guess but he would never know. All he knew was that the deed had been ordered and carried out.

'I think we'll pass this inquiry on to someone else in the department, Sergeant.'

Hans Winter nodded. 'Probably for the best.'

They left the body where it was and returned to Munich in silence.

Back at the Presidium, he ordered that Irmgard Huber be brought to him again. She entered the room without a word and sat down when ordered to.

He did not have a constable with him, nor Winter. He wanted to do this alone.

'Would you like a cup of coffee or a cigarette, Frau Huber?'

She gazed through him and did not reply.

'I must tell you that you are protecting no one. Your husband has taken his own life and your master's body has been found in the woods, decapitated.'

That changed her expression. She blinked and suddenly her eyes were focused on Seb rather than beyond him.

'Killed by the men he hired to kill me. No sense of loyalty, these murderers. Work for the highest bidder. But you're loyal, aren't you, Frau Huber? You're loyal to your headless master and whatever else he was. Lover, was he? Partner in sex magic and murder?'

'You disgust me.'

'Ah, so you have not lost the power of speech.'

'You defile his name by speaking of him, yet he was among the greatest of men. A true German of pure blood. A man worthy to stand alongside the Führer himself.'

'Do you want to tell me what this was all about. There is no one left to incriminate – only yourself, and you have no defence to offer anyway.'

'Yes, I want to tell you. I want you to know, I want the world to know.'

Seb did not reply. He had no need to, because it all spilt from her in a rush, as though the valves had opened and the sewage poured forth.

'I caught her in bed with that Jew. She was naked and shameless. I saw them. I saw their vile bodies moving like venomous snakes, like demons squirming and crawling. A Jew in my master's house, in one of his beds. Can you imagine it? A Jew corrupting the very place my master called home? What was I to do? What would any true German do?'

She paused, almost breathless. Seb could have asked a question, but he gave her space.

'I watched them, but they didn't see me. And then he crept out like a serpent through our front door. I wanted to kill them both. Overnight, my anger did not abate but became more powerful. I had to do something. And then the next evening she was going out to meet her disgusting friends. I called her to my office and confronted her. The words she used! The corruption at her heart! The lipstick on her blood-red mouth! The mouth that had kissed the lips and body of the heathen. I had a filleting knife from the kitchen. I suppose I had taken it because I knew what I would do, and then it was in my hand and I slashed at her. My first stroke caught her throat and she fell to the ground, clutching at herself as the blood gushed through her fingers. I stood there at a loss. What could I do? And then . . .'

She stopped again. This time Seb intervened with just one word. 'Regensdorf.'

'He was there. He had seen what I did and he took the knife from my hand, then he closed the door and locked it and lay me down on the wooden floor and raised my skirts and entered me. And the ecstasy. Oh the ecstasy of death and life together in the defiler's blood. I touched the god of gods that night. We both did.'

'And then?'

Her eyes met Seb's. 'When you are halfway to Valhalla, you do not just stop and return whence you came. You must carry on, you must go the whole way, wherever the path takes you.'

'And so you carried on. Hildegard Heiden, Silke Stutz, Frances de Pole.'

'Their names meant nothing, but they were fit and proper subjects, given up to us by the gods.'

'The runes, the symbols – what were they for?'

'That is for the gods to know.'

'And Hesselberg? Why there?'

'Because it is a sacred temple to the gods.'

'A place of *geblōt*, perhaps?'

'My master used that word.'

'It is a form of sacrifice.'

'Then yes, a *geblōt*.'

'And Frau Regensdorf?'

'She was a danger to us. She suspected. I think the master had read a great deal about sex magic – the deep well of power that it gives us – but she was an unbeliever and held him off. She had the brains of a milk cow and she worked against us.'

'You killed her?'

'Do you care? Do you really care?'

Yes, he cared very much, but he did not wish to engage in philosophical or moral debate with this murderess. 'Did you see the god of gods again?'

She closed her eyes as though searching for something beyond human vision. 'We would have done. We felt its presence and were so close to touching it. We came so close, so very close.'

Seb had nothing more to ask. And there was nothing more to say; from what little he knew of psychiatry, it seemed likely that Huber and Regensdorf had been bound together by some strange and depraved *folie à deux*, and that he controlled her and used her, and that she was a more than willing partner. As for her seeing the gods, he couldn't help wondering whether what she actually experienced was her first ever orgasm.

'But I will be dead soon,' she said. 'They have killed my master and my husband, they will never let me see the inside of a courtroom.'

And Seb knew that she was probably right. That was the way the Third Reich dealt with its sewage problems.

He sent her back to her cell and to her fate and went to his office, where Winter was still waiting for him. 'I have one last task for you, Sergeant. And then you can have the rest of the week off and sleep to your heart's content. Am I right in thinking you still have friends in the Bavarian Political Police and in Dachau?'

'Friends no, contacts yes.'

'People who owe you a favour?'

'There is one such.'

'There is a man presently held in Dachau for insulting the Führer. His name is Albert Heiden and he is the father of Hildegard, the girl killed at Hesselberg. He has suffered more than any man deserves and I want him freed, not just for his sake but for his wife's too. If you can fix that for me, I will consider my own spell in that hellish place forgiven and it will never be mentioned again.'

'I will do my best.'

'Call me at home. I want to take him back to Nuremberg myself.'

'I was about to throw your supper away, Sebastian,' his mother said. 'Do you really live here anymore? You come and go like a stranger at a hotel.' She removed a frying pan from the oven: rösti. 'I'll fry two eggs with it – you look thin and wan. You need food.'

'Thank you, Mutti, and please forgive me. Things should be quieter now.'

'Here.' She handed him a bottle of beer.

RORY CLEMENTS | 379

He thanked her again and poured it. 'By the way, is Jurgen here? He should be home surely.'

'He's gone to see that girl.'

'Silke?'

'Yes, that one.'

'I'd better make a phone call.'

He went out into the corridor and called the Stutz family. Silke's mother answered the phone.

'Good evening, Inspector Wolff.'

'Good evening, Frau Stutz. I'm told Jurgen is there.'

'This is a very late call, you know. Nothing that I am not used to as a doctor's wife, of course, but still, a little impolite. And yes, Jurgen is here. Silke asked if he could come round. I think she needed the company of another young person. They are both fine. The storm is passed and the worst is over.'

'But did you not take her to your mother's home near Rosenheim as I suggested?'

'My husband decided it was unnecessary. He can protect us.'

'Well, I'm glad that all is well, and I can tell you that the danger is now indeed passed. Please accept my best regards for you, your husband and daughter – and my apologies for the late call.'

'And our regards in equal measure to you, Inspector.'

As he settled down to eat his long-delayed supper, one thought kept spinning through his consciousness: how on earth was he going to tell Mutti that he had asked Hexie to marry him? And what was he going to say to her brother, Uncle Christian?

Councillor Weber had called him just before he left the Presidium and immediately he heard The Pig's sultry tones he wished he hadn't picked up the phone.

'Everything all right with you now, Captain of Detectives?'

'All is well, Uncle, but my new title isn't official yet.'

'It will be, boy, it will be. Now then, I want to talk about the wedding. Where shall we hold the reception? The Vier Jahreszeiten Hotel, perhaps? The Residenz? Or my villa by the lake. That would be perfect for a summer wedding. And don't forget, we have to fit in with Adolf's movements because I want him to be guest of honour. I suppose we'll have to have that swine Hoffmann as photographer.'

'Can we talk about this another day?'

'As you wish, but we'll need to finalise everything sooner rather than later. Make an appointment to come and see me, yes?'

'I'll do that.'

'Oh and talking of weddings, I advise you very strongly never to have anything more to do with that big blonde English valkyrie again.'

'Mitford?'

'That's the one. Fancies she'll wed Adolf, which she won't, of course. She may seem a rather bone-headed and ineffectual girl, but I tell you this: she is the most dangerous woman in Munich and she can do you much harm. Steer clear of her.'

CHAPTER 51

It was among the hardest things he would ever have to do. How do you tell a man his daughter has been murdered?

He collected Albert Heiden at nine thirty the next morning from the front office at Dachau concentration camp. At first the man looked bewildered by the offer of a lift.

'Who are you? What is going on?'

'I am Inspector Wolff of Munich criminal police. You are a free man, Herr Heiden.'

'I was always free in my mind.'

Seb felt a surge of relief: this man had not been broken by his incarceration. But the relief did not last more than a few moments.

'Well, why are you here? I don't know you. Are you taking me somewhere quiet to shoot me?'

This was it. He had to tell him.

'No, I am taking you home to your wife, who needs you badly. Very badly, sir, for there has been a dreadful occurrence.' *Don't wait, Seb, you have to say the words. Now.* 'I must tell you, Herr Heiden, that your daughter Hildegard is dead.'

Albert Heiden had walked with pride and strength from his unwarranted imprisonment. He had survived and maintained his manhood. Now he looked Seb in the eye and saw within moments that he was telling the truth and that of all the terrible things he had suffered these past weeks, this was the worst.

He simply slumped, and Seb had to catch him and hold him.

The breeze was gloriously cooling. The sun was hot, hotter than it had been all summer. The waters of the lakes were warming up, shimmering in the light. It was late afternoon and Seb and Hexie were on their way to the exquisite lake of Starnbergersee and that little beach on the far side where they had planned to spend his birthday two weeks earlier.

'And unlike our last swim, no one will be creeping through the undergrowth spying on us,' he said.

'You hope. Personally I don't give a fig.'

They had a picnic with them in a basket. Sausage, cheese, bread, Austrian wine, fruit. Even cutlery, plates, glasses and a cloth to lay out their little banquet. This was the way it should have been all those days ago.

Hexie didn't hesitate. She slipped out of her clothes and stood in front of him, bold and unashamed as he feasted his eyes on her.

'It all belongs to you now, Seb. I have a Reserved sticker on me.'

'You're more beautiful than ever.'

'And you meant it – what you said in hospital?'

'What was that? What did I say?'

She hit him and laughed.

'Don't forget, Hexie, you were delirious. The knock on your head. You probably imagined some conversation that didn't happen.'

'You're an easy man to hate sometimes, Sebastian Wolff.'

'Then you won't want to marry me, will you?'

'Come on, get your clothes off and I'll see whether you're up to the task. I'm a hard girl to please.'

Acknowledgements

Munich Wolf is a thriller, but it is also a book about a place in time: Munich in the 1930s. Not only was it the spiritual home of the Nazi movement, but it was also a sort of finishing school for thousands of upper class young British men and women. So I am delighted to give heartfelt thanks to the historian Dr David Hall, who probably knows more about the subject than anyone else and who gave me invaluable help. His book *Hitler's Munich* (published by Pen & Sword) is a superb portrait of the city from the early days of the Nazi movement to the end of the Second World War. It stands out from the many histories I have read for its depth of scholarship and readability. A Research Fellow with King's College London and a Fellow of The Royal Historical Society, Dr Hall showed great kindness and generosity in granting me long conversations, putting me right when I was wrong and suggesting places I should visit on my trips to Bavaria.

I would also like to thank Nick Adams, who helped me with technical details of the Lancia Augusta which features in the book. He describes himself as 'a lucky engineer who realised his boyhood dream of working with Lotus cars for thirty years and ended up proud to be part of the core design and development team behind the marque's most successful cars'. And, as ever, I owe a huge amount to my brother Brian, who assisted me with important firearms information. As always, my wife Naomi's assistance and perseverance were crucial. Last but not least, thanks go to my agent Teresa Chris and my editor Ben Willis and the rest of the fabulous team at Bonnier Zaffre for their fantastic efforts on my behalf.

If you enjoyed *Munich Wolf,*
why not join the
RORY CLEMENTS READERS' CLUB

When you sign up you'll receive a free copy of
an exclusive short story, plus news about upcoming books,
sneak previews, and exclusive behind-the-scenes material.
To join, simply visit:
bit.ly/RoryClementsClub

Keep reading for a letter from the author . . .

Hello!

I'd like to explain a couple of things about *Munich Wolf* and its background. Much has been written about Berlin in the pre-war years, far less about Munich.

And yet Munich, the capital of the southern German state of Bavaria, was the spiritual home and playground of Hitler and the Nazi movement. This is where they had their headquarters, the Brown House, and this is where they built the Führerbau – Hitler's own base. He had an apartment in the city at 16 Prinzregentenplatz and a mountain house nearby at Berchtesgaden.

Munich is the city where he fomented revolution in the beer halls and where he led a failed putsch in 1923. It is the city where the love of his life, his niece Geli Raubal, died mysteriously from a bullet wound before he came to power and where he met his future wife, Eva Braun, when she worked in the photographic shop of his friend Heinrich Hoffmann.

Most of it exists to this day. You can still eat in Hitler's favourite restaurant the Osteria Bavaria (though it is called the Osteria Italiana now), you can drink and carouse in the same vast beer halls and cafes that he frequented. The Führerbau is still there, used as a music college, his apartment is used as offices.

But there was more to Munich in the 1930s: there were also the many hundreds of upper-class young men and women from Britain and other countries, who stayed in the homes of impoverished aristocrats and treated Bavaria as a rather nice finishing school, with skiing, drinking, music and love.

Among them was one particular English girl - Unity Mitford, the fourth of the six celebrated Mitford sisters. She was a rabid anti-semite devoted to Hitler. He took her under his wing and they met frequently - perhaps 150 times in four years. Her sister Diana married the British fascist leader Oswald Mosley and there is no doubt that Unity harboured hopes of exchanging vows with Hitler. Some people loved her, many loathed her.

Munich was both a fun party city and the corrupt heart of the most evil movement devised by man. This is the febrile atmosphere in which I have put my main character Sebastian Wolff, a detective who hates the Nazis but is hemmed in by them on all sides - even in his own home.

And for anyone new to the period it is worth remembering that most Germans were not Nazis and did not vote for Hitler. They were trapped.

If you would like to hear more about my books, you can visit my website www.roryclements.co.uk where you can join the Rory Clements Readers' Club (www.bit.ly/RoryClementsClub). It only takes a few moments to sign up, there are no catches or costs.

Bonnier Zaffre will keep your data private and confidential, and it will never be passed on to a third party. We won't spam you with loads of emails, just get in touch now and again with news about my books, and you can unsubscribe any time you want.

And if you would like to get involved in a wider conversation about my books, please do review *Munich Wolf* on Amazon, on Goodreads, on any other e-store, on your own blog and social media accounts, or talk about it with friends, family or reader groups! Sharing your thoughts helps other readers, and I always enjoy hearing about what people experience from my writing.

Thank you again for reading *Munich Wolf*. With best wishes,
Rory Clements